Always be ... ou had to marry a so ... A handsome young Harvard lawyer. A society wedding. A promising future. Then came the house in the suburbs. The children. The model life of the model wife of an ambitious man. And the boredom. And the secrets. And the burning question: What if . . . ?

Kate

Thought otherwise, that life could be as wide as the world—and as exciting—if she lived only for herself. So she built a future on ambition. Rose to the top of the advertising game. Wore the best clothes, went to the best parties and bedded down with the best lovers all over the world . . . and tried hard not to wonder what was missing . . .

Options

The provocative novel for every woman who ever made a choice—and wondered . . . What if . . . ?

OPTIONS

A novel by

Freda Bright

PUBLISHED BY POCKET BOOKS NEW YORK

Another *Original* publication of POCKET BOOKS

POCKET BOOKS, a Simon & Schuster division of
GULF & WESTERN CORPORATION
1230 Avenue of the Americas, New York, N.Y. 10020

ISBN: 0-671-41270-1

First Pocket Books printing February, 1982

10 9 8 7 6 5 4 3 2 1

POCKET and colophon are trademarks of Simon & Schuster.

Printed in the U.S.A.

To A. A. for what was.
To V. R. for what will be.

He found all things came back to the question of what he personally might have been, how he might have led his life and "turned out," if he had not so, at the outset, given it up.

Henry James—*The Jolly Corner*

OPTIONS

CATHERINE

"MEN."

Oh, God, Catherine thought and braced herself for the verbal onslaught.

Men.

It was the word that opened each chapter in her roommate's not-so-private life.

Men.

It was just a word, not even a four-letter word, for that matter, but in Phyllis's mouth it was capable of infinite interpretation.

There was "Men"—uttered with the wonder of an Einstein facing the universe. There was "Aaaahh . . . men"—worshipfully, an early Christian martyr invoking God. And there was "Men . . . fuck 'em!"—the Delphic sybil, prophesying doom unto a hundred generations.

It was the opening gun. The grand finale. The endless topic alongside which all other life matters were reduced to their just and trivial proportions.

The H-Bomb . . . Nietzsche . . . the meaning of determinism . . . the recent and thoroughly disgraceful performance of the Boston Red Sox: they were ephemera—mere ephemera—compared to the one truly boggling subject that

1

would be served up, savored, chewed and rechewed. But never, never fully digested.

Watching Phyllis scrunch down in the tattered easy chair—as soft and rosy as the chintz that enveloped her—Catherine marvelled for the hundredth time at the playful fate that had paired her off with the campus nymphomaniac. It was ironic, really.

Actually, Phyllis's sex life was the least of it. No, her nymphomania was not the problem, and it did give Catherine the advantage of having the room to herself most nights and every weekend. It was the *mono*mania she found so wearying. The endless talk about men men men.

For two years Catherine had listened politely (for she had been raised to listen politely) while her roommate spewed out the latest installment of *Phyllis Faces Life*. Which was remarkably like the previous installment of *Phyllis Faces Life*, given minor variations of name, hair coloring and subtle points of sexual performance.

There had been Phyllis and Dick. Phyllis and Andrew. Phyllis and Bob. Phyllis and Professor Morton. Phyllis and—if her word were to be credited—the entire brass section of the Boston Symphony.

Only the names were changed to protect the guilty.

In a remarkably short time, it seemed to Catherine, Phyllis had gone through the male population of Boston the way Dracula went through London.

At first, Catherine had been fascinated. Had listened, clucked, felt vicarious indignation, offered sympathetic "there there's." But by the end of their freshman year, she had already lost count of Phyllis's catalogue. Shock had trailed off into boredom. And though Phyllis wasn't the only girl Catherine knew to have "gone all the way," she was unquestionably the only one to have done it with such frequency. Such gusto. Such singleness of purpose.

Not today, Catherine pleaded inwardly. *It's a new semester, a new year.* She burrowed into her book with feigned diligence, pretending not to have heard the magic word. And for once, mercifully, Phyllis seemed more absorbed in the scrutiny of her perfect fingernails than in pursuing the eternal topic.

The two girls could not have been more different.

On those rare occasions when they ventured forth together,

they were known as Mutt and Jeff. The designation was apt, with Catherine the Jeff to Phyllis's short bouncy Mutt.

Indecently tall by her own reckoning, although her mother preferred the word "stately," with strong clear features and a great tangle of coppery hair that went in every direction but that which fashion dictated, Catherine Chapman was distinctly self-conscious. Connoisseurs of a grander generation would have deemed her "handsome." But that was not how she saw herself in an age that thrust up such feminine ideals as Debbie Reynolds and Marilyn Monroe. An age when girls were considered desirable for being cute or bosomy or both. And Catherine Chapman was neither.

Conceivably, she might have glided through the pages of a Henry James novel—cool, discerning and faintly tragic. Or inspired a Bronte romance—all anger and high intelligence. A heroine for a proper hero. But there were, sadly, no Heathcliffs, no Mr. Rochesters in the Boston of 1956. Only horny, hot-handed boys with monosyllabic names—Chuck, Don, Rock, Skeets—who made her feel awkward.

"You just don't do enough for yourself, honey," Phyllis reprimanded her on one occasion. "Just look at your underwear."

"What's wrong with my underwear?" Catherine had been incensed. As underwear went, it was best quality white cotton and certainly clean, which was more, she suspected, than could be said about Phyllis's.

"The point is it's *underwear*—boring underwear. You shouldn't be wearing underwear. You should be wearing *lingerie*."

Phyllis herself had drawers full of lingerie. Fragile silky bras that crumpled into nothing, lacy garter belts trimmed with rosettes, embroidered French panties in black satin, in beige, in shimmering blues and greens.

At first, Catherine was puzzled at the richness of this collection, for she knew that Phyllis's clothes allowance was nowhere near as extensive as her own. But the mystery was solved halfway through their freshman year when Phyllis returned triumphant from an expedition to Tremont Street. She divested herself of three embroidered half-slips, one on top of the other, while Catherine stared in disbelief.

"You mean you *stole* them?"

Phyllis giggled. "I wouldn't put it like that. Let's just say

Crawford Hollidge is investing in my future. That's such a terrific store!"

"Investing indeed," Catherine snorted.

"Look at it this way," Phyllis explained. "When I marry my Mr. Rich, I'll go back as a regular customer. Why, they'd make it all back on just one mink coat. In a way, you could say they're subsidizing me."

Catherine, whose sense of probity was such that she couldn't take free matchbooks from a restaurant, was repelled by Phyllis's tales of shoplifting.

And while she certainly would have condoned the socially "useful" theft of bread by the poor or a stolen joyride by an unemployed teenager, Catherine could find no justification for snitching bits of lace and satin from Boston's best stores. That Phyllis could bring herself to *wear* things that were not bought and paid for was reprehensible in the extreme.

In the casual swap shop of the girls' dormitory, Catherine would not borrow as much as a dime-store earring from her light-fingered roommate. To her, even those items which Phyllis had honestly acquired reeked of mortal taint by association.

That Phyllis stole was upsetting. That she slept around, rather less so. For, in a grudging way, Catherine secretly admired Phyllis's utter lack of hypocrisy in sexual affairs.

Perhaps even envied her a bit. At nineteen, Catherine was still a virgin, not so much out of moral scruples as from fear of pregnancy—a fear not to be scoffed at in the Massachusetts of those days, where all forms of birth control were illegal. She was not quite convinced that virginity was a virtue. And to be honest with herself—something Catherine was with unsparing frequency—she had not been truly tempted. Not yet, at any rate. Nor had she been pursued that hotly by the opposite sex, although she did her fair share of dating.

Her height put some boys off, she knew, as did her penchant for snappy retorts. Well, if a boy was going to take flight at the first sign of a wisecrack, then let him. Whoever the beneficiary of Catherine's carefully stored virtue might be, it would have to be more than a boy.

A man. Yes. A man who was strong, capable, loving, mature. A man who would sweep her off her feet. A man worth risking her affections for, to say nothing of those other more palpable risks. And if not now, no matter. She had all the time in the world.

"You're going to be an old maid," Phyllis forecast once when Catherine had turned down the offer of a double date. "I mean, here you are in the most fantastic hunting ground in America. Count 'em"—she ticked off her fingers one by one—"There's Harvard, MIT, Boston College, Tufts . . . and that's just the *men's* schools. Wow! By the time you've added B.U., Northeastern, Suffolk Law and the rest, you've probably got the greatest concentration of male undergraduates anywhere in the world. It's like shooting fish in a barrel."

Catherine hadn't cared for the metaphor—the fish were mostly sardines—yet she knew that many coeds had chosen Boston schools for precisely the same reason as Phyllis: the sheer number of undergraduate men. It was a paradise for husband-hunters; for less virtuous girls, a playground of infinite diversity.

Was Catherine the only young woman who had come to the "Athens of America" simply to learn, to study, to grow? Sometimes it felt that way. It felt that way now as she returned to her book while Phyllis examined her nail polish.

"But one man loved the pilgrim soul in you
And loved the sorrows of your changing face."

God, Yeats was wonderful!

"Do you mind if I interrupt for a moment? I want your opinion about something important."

Catherine put down her book. *I'll give her one half-hour and no more.* "Yes?"

"It's about my nails," Phyllis said, splaying ten perfect fingers, shaped and polished to the specifications of last month's *Vogue*. "Do you think they're too long?"

"Depends what you want to use them for."

"I've broken up with Dick, and it was over my nails. He claims I scratched him up so badly, he doesn't dare show his face at his mother's."

"His *face?*" Catherine arched her eyebrows.

"Well, OK, not his face. His back, his sides, but he made such an issue of it. We had this big scene and he said . . . well, what it came down to was either the nails go or he goes."

"So . . ."

"So I told him he could go; in fact, I specified where. Fouls up my weekend, but it's no great loss. He was only a Five on the scale."

Only a Five? Was this the same Dick Phyllis had been crowing about for the past couple of weeks as a man truly worthy of his nickname?

For Phyllis employed a graduating scale ranging from One to Ten, based entirely on sexual performance. There were no Tens, she had explained to Catherine; that was the impossible ideal, the Grail one eternally quested for. Most men were Fives, an acceptable rating. If you were lucky, you might hit an occasional Seven or Eight. She had known but two Nines and they'd been hard to hang on to—men who had ascertained their own value and had graced many beds. There was a distressing percentage of Ones and Twos and—quite off the scale—some unspeakable Zeros. A Zero, in Phyllis's report card, was incapable of even the simplest mechanical functions. "A true horizontal . . . and there are more of them around than you think."

Catherine found it curious that for all of her roommate's application, she had yet to find a man who passed muster. Some, Phyllis claimed, were the love of her life, some just a lay for the night. But in one way or another, they were all imperfect. They had wives or fiancées or homosexual tendencies or, as in Dick's case, mothers; they suffered from clap or bad breath or undescended testicles. Every lover, sooner or later, joined the swelling list of rejects.

"You know, I think the real trouble with Dick is that he's subconsciously Oedipal."

"Edible?" Catherine asked blandly.

"Oedipal. You know, the Oedipus complex, when you've got the hots for your mother." Catherine laughed. "Really, Cath, you know perfectly well what I mean. Ah, what the hell," she sighed. "Screw him."

"I thought you already had."

Phyllis scrutinized her with the same objectivity with which she had earlier studied her manicure.

"You know, Cath, you don't do yourself a whole lot of good with all these smart-ass answers."

She went to the dressing table and began applying makeup with the cool, practiced hand of the artist. "Far be it from me to give advice"—smoothing in great dollops of Ultima—"but you are making a big mistake going through life like it's some kind of quiz show. Whoever gives the brightest answer gets a medal . . . the great brain race and winner takes all. Men don't give a damn about that sort of thing. Or this sort of thing either."

She indicated Catherine's book lying on the desk. *"Selected poems of William Butler Yeats.* Keats and Yeats," she snorted, rhyming the two.

"It's pronounced Yates," Catherine said mildly.

"It's pronounced old maid," Phyllis retorted. "Believe me, men don't go to the Dean's List when they're looking for wives."

"Well, believe me," Catherine said, irritated, "I didn't go to college to get a husband."

"Yeah, yeah, I know. You're going to set the world on fire and write the Great American Novel. Or is it going to be Catherine Chapman, Girl Reporter? When it comes right down to it, what's your degree going to get you . . . a job as a teller in a bank? Or, if you're lucky, you can do research at Time-Life for what . . . a lousy fifty bucks a week? Who wants educated women anyhow? Men don't. That's for sure. And if you think businessmen are any different, you're crazy. Ask a man to choose between a girl with a Ph.D. and one with forty-inch knockers, and which do you think he's going to hire?"

It was, of course, the old argument, but leave it to Phyllis to put it so crassly. And while getting a Ph.D. was within the realms of possibility, growing a forty-inch bosom was science fiction. At least for Catherine, who bristled at the implication.

"You're full of bull," she said. It was her strongest expletive.

"Oh, am I!" Phyllis stopped in mid-mascara. "OK, then, you name me ten . . . no, on second thought make it five. You name me five women in America today who really have clout. No sopranos, no actresses either. Just five women who've made it in a man's world."

"Oh, come on, Phyllis, where have you been? Women gave up the bustle fifty years ago. They can even vote now . . . remember?"

"Yeah, I remember. So go ahead and name me . . ."

"Right."

Catherine paused, and suddenly her mental horizon was teeming with names: names and images of *men*. There were presidents and scientists and generals and Hollywood directors and not a pair of nylon stockings among them. It was an intellectual stag line. In desperation, she rifled through a stack of women's first names: Mary, Joan, Elizabeth, Anna . . .

"OK," she smiled, "let's start with Eleanor . . ,"

"Don't say Eleanor Roosevelt," Phyllis broke in. "You never would have heard of her if not for Franklin."

"I protest!"

"Aw, be honest, Cath. She was just another society woman until her husband went into politics. No, I'm talking about women who've made it on their lonesome."

"Well, how about Clare Boothe Luce?"

"No good . . . married to Henry."

Phyllis's rules certainly narrowed the field. Catherine mentally skimmed the Cabinet, the Senate.

"Ah!" she snapped her fingers. "What's-her-name . . . the woman senator from Maine."

"What's-her-name," Phyllis nodded sagely. "Now there's a description that will ring through the ages. No good."

"Margaret Mead!" Catherine posited. *Got you that time.*

"OK, Mead. That's one."

"Margaret Bourke-White." She was off and running now.

"Margaret *who?*" Phyllis looked skeptical.

"Bourke-White, the famous photographer: I think she's with *Life* magazine."

"I never heard of her, so she can't be that famous. I'll only give you half a point on that. So who else?"

Who else? Catherine's mind went blank. There must be more, hundreds more—in business, the arts, politics, everywhere. Everywhere but on the tip of her tongue. Phyllis jumped into the pause and claimed victory.

"See? So all you can name in what—three minutes?—is Margaret Mead and this photographer dame. One and a half points in all. In other words, out of a population of two hundred million Americans—and say a hundred million of them are women—you come up with a grand total of one and a half. To which small select company, I presume, you will one day add the name of Catherine Chapman."

"I'm not saying the system is perfect," Catherine conceded. "I'm just saying that it's changing."

"Yeah, changing," Phyllis snorted. "It'll change when women grow peckers. Come back and talk to me some other time when a woman's chairman of the board at General

Motors. Or a publisher of the *Times*. Or president of the stock exchange. There isn't even one lousy lady in the whole of the stock exchange. It's easier to get into the men's room at the Ritz. Because the competition isn't between men and women. It's between women and women, with men as the prize. Take my word, duckie. If you really want to *be* a somebody, *marry* a somebody."

"If that's such hot advice, why don't you follow it?"

"Oh, I will, Catherine, believe me, I will. Don't think, just because I screw around a lot, I don't have my eye on the main event. The way I figure, this is my fun time. When it's over I'm going to latch on to some guy who's nice and solid and"—she gave a smutty laugh—"thoroughly pretested."

She returned to the mirror with renewed concentration, and Catherine—with less success—to her Yeats.

"I'm going out now." Phyllis rose in a cloud of Sortilege. "Going to have a couple of beers at the Barn. Wanna come?"

"No, thanks."

"Lots of guys down there. Who knows, you might even meet someone. Or are you saving it all for Adlai? Madly for Adlai—isn't that what they say?"

She indicated the wall above Catherine's bed, where a photo of the Presidential candidate was Scotch-taped in the place of honor.

The smile in the picture was warm, the eyes baggy but humorous. And the weary stance expressive of campaign fatigue. You couldn't miss the gaping hole in the sole of his shoe.

"Funny you should mention it," Catherine laughed. "I've got a date with the Governor tonight."

The headquarters of Concerned Students for Stevenson was less grand than its name implied. Like many other organizations devoted to high ideals, the best it could afford was a flyblown shop front in a low-rent district, with a pizzeria on one side, a defunct dry-cleaning establishment on the other. Inside, too, the premises reeked of failure, from the grime of the windows to the battered, stacked chairs to the listless pile of campaign literature that rested untouched—like aging virgins who had given up all hope of being ravished.

The club had sprung up spontaneously the month before, a sounding board for those young but politically-minded mavericks who *didn't* like Ike in '56.

The membership consisted of serious, bookish girls and hot-eyed boys in shabby sweaters. Many of them were Jewish and almost all of them—like Catherine—still too young to vote. But not too young to talk the night away happily in passionate indictments of John Foster Dulles and the H-Bomb. Catherine always enjoyed the exuberance of their discussions despite the gnawing suspicion that these evenings, stimulating though they were, contributed little to Stevenson's progress toward the White House. True, they had written letters to editors (alas! rarely published) and mimeo'd tracts for campus distribution. But for the most part they talked and dreamed and reasoned and argued in an atmosphere of pleasant chaos. But what did they actually accomplish? It was, Catherine feared, an exercise in futility.

By the time Catherine got there, the meeting was well under way. The moment she opened the door, she knew something was up. The place even looked different, the chairs lined neatly in rows, the several dozen members sitting quietly.

She looked around for Harry Rubin, who traditionally ran things—or, more precisely, let them run wild. But tonight even Harry was sedately seated, listening intently to the man who stood before the group. And for once it *was* a man, not a boy.

That was different too.

The speaker caught her eye and nodded brusquely, indicating she should take a seat quickly and quietly. He waited, fingers drumming, while Catherine dragged a chair across the noisy floorboards and opened it with a sharp metallic screech.

"As I was saying," he continued when silence finally reigned, "we are not running a discussion group here. We are running a political campaign. So if you've come to gossip or get fixed up for Saturday night, I suggest you try somewhere else. We are here for one purpose only—the election of Adlai Stevenson. First of all, I'd like to know . . . how many of you are old enough to vote. Hands please?"

A half-dozen of the thirty-odd present raised hands.

"OK, most of you are under twenty-one, but that's all right. You're all old enough to get out and ring doorbells. So let's get down to the realities. Number one," he raised his index finger, "the question of voter registration . . ."

He was remarkably handsome, Catherine thought—like James Dean, only taller and manlier. But it took more than that to account for the electricity. His voice, his manner, his crisp no-nonsense comments were light years beyond the burbling fuzziness that had characterized the club thus far. He was *focused*. That's it. He was focused.

"Now this club has been assigned to cover three specific areas—the North End, Roxbury and Dorchester. And we are going to ring the doorbell of every registered Democrat in those wards between now and election eve. I expect you all know that outside the Deep South, Boston is one of the party's greatest strongholds. The voters are here and victory on election day will depend on exactly how many of them we can get to the polls. *It will not depend upon issues.* I won't kid you that it's anything but grueling legwork. Unfortunately, that's how elections get won. It's an imperfect world, I'm afraid. First of all, if there are people here who feel they can't devote three hours a night, three nights a week between now and the first Tuesday in November, I suggest they find a social group more to their liking."

No one stirred, and for the first time that evening the speaker smiled, a beautiful smile that embraced them all. Blessed them all. He was even handsomer when he smiled.

"Splendid. Now let's get organized. I'm going to break you up into boy-girl teams. We find that's a most effective unit for canvassing, particularly in some of the rougher areas. I don't mind you looking like college kids; in fact, I think it can be an advantage. But I want you to look like *clean-cut* college kids. Boys will wear shirts and ties"—somebody groaned, but he continued, unperturbed. "Girls will wear skirts or dresses, not slacks. And I strongly advise sensible shoes. Each team will be given a list of voters to be contacted and it will be broken down block by block."

"What do we say once we've got our foot in the door?" Harry asked.

"Don't worry, I'll teach you the spiel. But first," he said, beckoning them out of their seats, "let me get you set up into teams."

They lined up neatly, like schoolchildren being readied for an outing. His choices were based on some inner criteria. Was it height? Was it coloring? Catherine could not discern; he clearly bypassed the students' own preferences.

"You," picking a girl from here—and "you," selecting a boy from there; then he'd size up the two together. "Yes, that's fine."

Choose me. Choose me. Catherine pleaded inwardly. It would be thrilling to work with him. But as the unassigned dwindled, so did her chances, for there were distinctly more girls than boys. At last, there was only himself and four unaffiliated girls.

Choose me, Catherine willed him silently.

"We seem to have an overage of girls," he said smiling.

"That's the story of my life," wailed Susan Glantz. Everybody giggled except him. "Don't worry, there's plenty of work for everyone." He turned to Catherine. "Do you like climbing stairs?"

"I love it." Her eyes shone with relief.

"OK, then, it's you and I."

His name was Michael Matheson, he was in his last year at Harvard Law and he would meet her tomorrow at the Copley Square subway station. "Six o'clock sharp, and wear comfortable shoes."

She decided to say nothing of him to Phyllis when she got home, but Phyllis, back early from the Barn, where the quarry had been thin, possessed a sixth sense where men were concerned.

"Looks like you scored better than I did," she said, divining something sexual in Catherine's glow. "Maybe I should give up beer and go into politics. So tell me, who is he?"

"It was just a meeting." Catherine protested and reddened even further. "We don't play spin-the-bottle, you know. Tonight, for instance, we set up teams to go out canvassing."

"Teams!" Anything that suggested pairing off commanded Phyllis's immediate interest. "Well, from the looks of it they must have teamed you up with a stand-in for Gregory Peck."

"No such luck," Catherine lied. "He's just another guy."

"Yeah, yeah." Phyllis made her disbelief clear. "Well, if you want him to be something *more* than just another guy, take my advice for once. Keep your mouth shut tight and your legs wide open."

"Thank you, Phyllis Asgard," Catherine snapped back. "My own mother couldn't have put it more nicely."

In fact, Emily Sayre Chapman wouldn't have put it any way at all. A pale, vague woman much given to chiffon scarves and collecting wooden jigsaw puzzles (the collection was insured for $6000), she limited the instruction of her only child to discreet guidelines as to what was "nice" and "not nice."

Boston, where Emily had been born, was "nice." Athol, the Massachusetts manufacturing town where they lived, was, she would say with a sigh, "not very nice." "Nice" was the highest approbation in her lexicon; "not nice" her profoundest criticism.

Ergo. White gloves in summer were *nice*. Chicken with broccoli was nice, as were Seth Thomas clocks, the *Ladies Home Journal* and Governor Leverett Saltonstall, to whom she was related. The Brewster family that lived down the street was nice, although the youngest boy had acne, which was not nice. Marriage was nice. Babies were nice. Novel reading was nice, provided you stuck to the nineteenth century.

Certain things were not nice. Putting your elbows on the table at mealtime. Wearing lipstick before your sixteenth birthday. Hitler.

Hitler was decidedly not nice.

But beneath the surface of the "not nice," there were certain areas so horrendous that they eluded the conversational net entirely. Always, lurking in the depths like killer sharks, were what Catherine had come to think of as The Great Unmentionables. Worse even than "not nice." Rape. Rioting. Poverty. Perversion. Topics so awesome they must be silenced into nonexistence.

So, in a descending scale of values, English cardigans were nice. Tight pullovers were not nice. Breasts were unmentionable.

As a child, Catherine could never comprehend how so much of the world beyond their home, so many events and actions and, indeed, people, should wither into invisibility once the front door was closed.

Their house was large and comfortable and in one of the few "good neighborhoods." Beyond it, monsters lurked.

And when Bob Sylvester, who manned the soda fountain at Logan's drugstore, took to wearing mascara and dousing himself in great lashings of Bourjois' Evening in Paris (a peculiarity that fascinated the ten-year-old Catherine), her mother received the news with the blankest of stares.

"Oh?" said Emily, and returned to her puzzle, a thousand-piece reproduction of Gainsborough's "Blue Boy."

"But what a funny thing to do, Mom." Catherine pranced across the sun room in crude imitation. "He even walks like a girl." Emily continued with her puzzle, fitting male knobs into female apertures. Still Catherine persisted in her mincing charade, till the poor woman, able to tolerate no more, was cornered into some kind of explanation.

"Sit down, dear," she said, mustering her best impersonation of mother-daughter intimacy, and Catherine felt a delicious chill. Truths were to be told. Abysses plumbed. Here at last was the end of innocence. The sharks from the lower depths.

With an air of great solemnity, Emily put down the puzzle pieces and folded her hands on the table's polished surface. "There are certain things in life . . ." For a moment she faltered, while Catherine waited expectantly. And then, in what was the closest Emily had ever come to a statement of philosophy: "If I'm walking down the street and I come across . . ." She struggled for the word, but maternal duty drove her on. . . . "I come across some 'dog do' . . . there's no reason for me to step in it. No," she concluded significantly, "I simply turn my head aside and *walk around it*. You see?"

Catherine did not see. This was hardly the revelation she had thirsted for, and, puzzle though she might, she could find no connection between Bob Sylvester's mascaraed lashes and her mother's "dog do."

She waited until it was plain there would be no more to come, then rose to leave the room.

"Catherine dear," her mother called after her, and Catherine wheeled around. Perhaps now . . . ? But all Emily said was "Don't tell your father we've had this little talk." And she returned to her puzzle pieces, fitting males into females, males into females, with unruffled innocence.

The likelihood of Catherine telling her father anything was remote at best, for Spencer Chapman was not a man who invited confidences.

New York-born and Princeton-educated, he viewed the two hundred miles that lay between his native city and Boston as a cultural desert. And what was worse, an ethnic cesspool. And Athol the very dregs of the cesspool.

He hated everything about his adopted town: its vulgarity, its occasional vitality, its smokestacks, its residents.

Above all he hated the rank-and-file workers at Saginaw Paper and Pulp, the company of which he was president.

He viewed them, quite simply, as peasants. And mongrel peasants at that.

Even Mrs. Antonelli, who'd kept house for the Chapmans from the days before Catherine was born, who had cooked his dinners and starched his shirts and ironed his underpants— even Mrs. Antonelli, born and bred in Athol, was, in Spencer's phrase, "that Italian woman." He rarely addressed her directly.

"Tell the Italian woman the roast beef was overcooked," he would instruct Emily after an unsatisfactory meal, and then retire to his study with the *Wall Street Journal*.

To Catherine he was always "the absent presence." He preferred the company of gentlemen to that of his family or any of the local society. He thought nothing of driving the sullen black Packard to Boston of a Sunday (a round trip of over one hundred miles) for the sole purpose of playing golf with those whom he considered his peers.

Whether it was his involvement with Sag Pap & Pulp (as the firm was known locally) that was the cause of his wife's vagaries or whether it was Emily's formless dithering that induced him to spend ever longer hours at the mill was something Catherine never ascertained.

He was an excessively tall man with good aquiline features and liked to refer to himself as a "rock-ribbed Republican." Catherine could not remember ever having seen him in his shirt sleeves. He disliked Negroes, Jews and Catholics with democratic impartiality, and as for unions—they were a communist conspiracy. It was a point of view that little endeared him to the toilers of Sag Pap & Pulp.

Although politics were of no interest to the passive Emily ("I always vote as Spencer tells me"), she took great care to treat her formidable husband with a judicious mixture of sympathy and respect. It may have fooled Spencer. It didn't fool Catherine, who had early discerned her mother's profound apathy in all matters Spencerian.

True, Emily made worried noises when he was late in getting home from work; honored his preference for Pale Ale over beer ("Gentlemen don't drink beer"); helped him on with his coat in the morning (it was the only act of physical

contact Catherine could ever recall her parents engaging in);
but otherwise, Emily ignored him totally.

And even lip service stopped short of kissing.

Emily was docile. Had she always been so, Catherine
would later wonder, or was it the price she paid for living in domestic peace with a humorless and inflexible husband?

Docility was not a characteristic commonly associated with
the Sayre family of Boston. Neither as rich as the Lodges nor
as stuffy as the Cabots, the Sayres of Back Bay had prided
themselves for generations on moral fervor and intellectual
diversity.

There had been Sayre poets and judges and hymn-writers
and antivivisectionists, with more than a sprinkling of cranks.
Sayre women, too, had risen to the occasions time demanded
by hiding runaway slaves and chaining themselves to lamp-
posts. But by the time Emily was born, the family fortunes,
founded sensibly on clipper ships, had been largely squan-
dered in good causes and bad investments. And the hot
reforming blood that had coursed through Sayre veins had, in
Emily's case at least, dissipated into the merest blue.

Emily was, if nothing else—and perhaps nothing else—a
lady. A docile lady.

Docile even with her daughter, who had, as daughters will,
come home over the years with scraped knees, stray dogs
and, latterly, visions of remaking society. Emily had ban-
daged the knees, found homes for the dogs and answered
Catherine's impassioned pleas for the redistribution of
wealth with an abstracted "Yes, dear . . . that would be
nice. Should I ask Mrs. Antonelli to make salmon for dinner?"

In that large house in Athol, distances were great and
intimacies few.

At eleven, Catherine was sent to boarding school.

"You're a very special girl," Spencer told her with unaccustomed warmth, "and you deserve a special education. After
all, we're not raising you to be a factory hand. Or," he added
sourly, "to *marry* one."

And Catherine glowed at the feeling that she was somehow
"set apart," the only girl in her class to be thus distinguished.

A few months later, with her first watch, her first bras and a
wardrobe from Peck & Peck, she arrived at Miss Ellery's

Academy for Young Ladies, in the leafy Boston suburb of Chestnut Hill.

> *We are not a finishing school,* the brochure stated. *We are a starting school, dedicated to preparing young women intellectually, culturally and morally for a life of achievement and social service.*

The school had been founded in 1867 by Miss Harriet Ellery, a Boston abolitionist of unimpeachable family. When Lee's surrender at Appomattox robbed her of her vocation, she turned her considerable energies from the liberation of slaves to the liberation of women.

Over the years, the Academy had produced suffragettes, prohibitionists and an astonishing number of senators' wives. Set on thirty rolling acres and comprising half a dozen handsome buildings, it was neither an insular establishment nor a stuffy one. It did, however, set a high moral tone.

Within five years, the school fulfilled virtually all of the Chapmans' expectations. Catherine's Athol twang mellowed into a cultivated Boston accent. She learned passable Latin and excellent French.

And of course, the school served its unspoken function by initiating Catherine into those mysteries of life Emily had been so reluctant to impart. It happened the very first week, after lights-out, when a snuffle-nosed girl named Anne Sowerby astonished Catherine by informing her that "he puts what he goes to the bathroom with into what you go to the bathroom with and then you have babies."

Two years later, the biology mistress put it in rather more clinical terms, beginning with frogs and winding up with what she discreetly called "primates." All things told, it seemed to Catherine, it came down to pretty much the same thing.

One bonus that Spencer had not foreseen was his daughter's introduction to liberal politics. In no way did the school promote "radicalism" as part of the curriculum, but certain of the mistresses encouraged a free and often irreverent exchange of ideas.

"History does not stop happening simply because the text books have gone to press," Miss Evers would announce. "And today our text will be the *New York Times.*"

They might then launch into discussions ranging from the Korean War to the desirability of loyalty oaths to an item reporting that *Robin Hood* had been blacklisted from a library in Indiana. For those were the McCarthy years.

And it often happened that ideas implanted in the classroom would be argued well into the night by the girls. For Catherine this assault of new concepts was breathtaking. The girls at Miss Ellery's were a curious lot, and it was not a school for academic slouches. For the most part rich, many of the girls were either secure enough—or arrogant enough—to poke about mercilessly for holes and snags in the social blanket that had swathed them since birth.

Little by little, then faster and faster, Catherine divested herself of her father's long-held prejudices and her mother's unquestioning docility. And it was here, in this quiet enclave of New England elite, that she awoke to the injustices of the world.

She yearned, yearned passionately, to have a Negro in the school. Spencer Chapman's daughter learned to flush with shame for the unemployed of Appalachia. Like many of her classmates, she turned her back on the prospect of "coming out" in Boston.

Catherine's concern for injustice might have remained theoretical were it not for the sudden arrival of Jan Littlemarch. The girl arrived in midterm (an unprecedented event) of Catherine's senior year. "You must all be understanding," the headmistress told the older girls in advance. "She has been through a terrible ordeal." And then—in an even greater departure from precedent—had gone on to say that the sins of the fathers *should not* be visited upon ensuing generations. "Even the Bible is sometimes wrong."

For Jan was the daughter of the notorious Franklin Littlemarch—"The Man Who Sold Out America," as one of the tabloids put it. A senior member of the State Department's China Desk, a former adviser to President Roosevelt, Littlemarch had become overnight one of the most spectacular—or tragic, depending on one's point of view—victims of the Washington witch hunt. He had been summarily dismissed and deprived of his pension amidst talk of prosecution for crimes and high treason. Two months after his abrupt dismissal his wife drowned herself in the Delaware River.

"The exact spot," Jan later told Catherine, "where Washington crossed in the American Revolution."

Jan was tall, almost as tall as Catherine, with lank dark hair and the haunted eyes of a shipwreck survivor.

To her less imaginative classmates, Jan Littlemarch was a freak; to the rest, a celebrity. But to Catherine she was a heroine. And a martyr. And a challenge.

Here at last, close to hand, was the long-awaited victim of American injustice. More than the Rosenberg Defense Fund, to which Catherine earmarked part of her allowance; more than the mythical black classmate she had so yearned to welcome; more than anything else in her comfortable life, Jan Littlemarch represented a unique opportunity for good works. Here, indeed, was life. Torment. Wrongs to be righted. Here was tragedy.

Neither friendly nor hostile, Jan greeted the overtures of other girls with the minimum of polite answer possible. "No, thank you" to suggested outings or invitations of shared study. "Yes, please" to second helpings of rice pudding. In class her responses were usually correct, often brilliant and original, but always characterized by the absence of passion. No one had ever seen her smile. And once the novelty of her arrival had worn off, most of the girls, in the face of her continued rebuffs, left Jan to her somber isolation.

Not so Catherine.

"I will make her smile," Catherine pledged, the blood of Sayre generations pulsing through her veins. "I will make her smile before graduation day."

She invited Jan home for Christmas vacation. Jan declined politely. She offered her smuggled-in goodies from S.S. Pierce—chocolate truffles, English marmalade. Jan would sometimes accept, sometimes refuse. But in neither circumstance did it lead to further conversation.

Catherine would have liked to discuss the events of the day—fallout shelters, the peace talks at Panmunjon—in the hope that she would hit upon the cue that would ultimately lead to greater confidences. But Jan confined her replies to the monosyllabic and Catherine was too much of a lady to pursue.

At the first sign of assault, Jan would withdraw into herself, a battle-blasted soldier retreating into the fortress of pride. The more she withdrew, the more Catherine grieved, and the more determined she was to prevail.

Almost every day after class, Jan would disappear, only to reemerge at dinner time.

Where did she vanish, Catherine wondered. She must have a secret hideaway. She soon concluded it was someplace outside, for when the weather was totally unspeakable, Jan spent the afternoons in the library.

But the grounds were large and varied. Part were maintained, part permitted to run to seed. For two weeks, Catherine stalked the area: the tennis courts, the ornamental ponds, the gardens, the hockey field, the abandoned summer house. Nothing. Nowhere.

And then, one raw February afternoon, her luck turned.

At the farthest end of the campus, behind a neglected stand of ancient oaks, was an archery court. It had long ago fallen into disuse, as, indeed, had archery with modern Ellery generations, the Dianas of the '50s preferring to flaunt their prowess on the tennis courts and Ping-Pong tables. It was no longer even mentioned in the brochure.

Yet there it stood, with its rotting shack for stored equipment; in summer a jungle of grass and weeds, in winter a depressing muddy flat.

But today the shack was open, the target set in place. From her vantage point behind a rotting stump, Catherine silently watched Jan Littlemarch flex her bow, straighten her back and unloose the arrows with a sharp eye and savagery of purpose. She rarely missed.

Very well, Catherine said to herself. It will be archery.

She decided to work it so that next time Jan went to the court, she would find Catherine already there. No matter that Catherine had never once in her life held a bow. All the better. Ignorance can sometimes be useful.

It rained the next day and the one after that, but Thursday finally dawned clear and cold. Catherine had been struggling with the bow for at least a half hour when she felt, rather than heard, Jan's approach. For a moment she was swept with misgivings. Would her presence in the court drive Jan away? Deprive the poor girl of her refuge? Cursing herself for being all kinds of a fool, she pulled back and unleashed the arrow. It missed the target by a good ten feet.

A long silence, and then, "You're not holding it correctly." Catherine turned quickly and smiled.

"Oh." How easy it was to feign surprise. "I didn't know you were interested in archery."

"Moderately."

"Well, I don't know a thing about it, but I'm absolutely determined to learn. Would you mind helping me out a bit?"

Jan hesitated for a long, painful moment, then went into the shed to fetch a bow.

And so it began.

The two girls became inseparable. They studied together. They played together. They traded sweaters and books and confidences. Within weeks, at Jan's request, there was a reshuffling of roommates, and the headmistress was only too happy to move Jan in with Catherine.

And in the private darkness of their room, Jan was at last able to laugh, to cry, to relive her torment and, finally, to mourn.

She could never, Catherine knew, totally obliterate Jan's pain; but she could relieve it. Share it. Take that slender, fine-boned, nail-bitten hand in her own and by a touch, a gentle stroke, feel Jan's anguish dissipate, like poison being drained from a wound.

What marvels one could work with only a touch.

And only Catherine could make her smile. Years later, she could recall that smile, even to the little wayward chip in Jan's front tooth. It was a flaw that gave that long pale face humanity, if not beauty.

It was the first time Catherine had ever felt so close to anyone.

"You've done wonders with Jan," the headmistress told Catherine privately. "Have you ever considered a career in social work?"

Catherine was graduated third in her class. She won the English Gold Medal, the Endicott History Prize and made the valedictory speech. June came. School was over. A few months later, the Ellery girls had dispersed to a dozen different colleges. Jan went to UCLA to study political science. Catherine opted for Boston University.

"Why B.U., of all places?" her mother had asked. "Why not someplace nice like Radcliffe or Vassar? Not that B.U. isn't nice, dear. I just thought you'd prefer one of the women's schools."

But by then, Catherine had had her fill of the genteel feminine world, of girls in housecoats sharing cups of cocoa. She welcomed the idea of a bustling city university, welcomed the chance to join the mainstream. At seventeen, she wanted a world where there were streetcars and police sirens and movie houses and coffee shops. Above all, she wanted a world where there were men.

Surely, even Emily could understand that.

And so one crisp September morning on the train platform at Athol, Mrs. Chapman completed her motherly duties. As the train pulled in that would deliver Catherine to Boston—and to men—Emily gave her daughter her complete store of knowledge. It only took one sentence.

"Don't ever let them see how smart you are, dear."

It was a piece of advice that Catherine would remember, though not always heed, for years to come.

"Mulcahey, Apartment 6D. That's the last." He folded up the checklist and handed it to Catherine.

"6D." Catherine gave a weary sigh. "Does that mean it's on the sixth floor?"

She scanned the narrow greasy staircase with wry disgust.

"Afraid it does." Michael grinned and viewed the prospect. "I think this is what the pollsters had in mind when they said we were in for an uphill battle."

It was the last of the several dozen evenings she and Michael had spent together, exhorting Boston Democrats to go to the polls next Tuesday and vote for Adlai Stevenson. The Dev Dems was Michael's name for them. The Devoted Democrats. That great mass of party faithfuls whose presence or absence on election day would determine the fate of a nation.

Yet for all the bull-session fervor she had so frequently expended on the Appalachian miners, the southern Negroes, Catherine found it difficult to identify with Boston's poor and near-poor. They were aliens, and she a visitor from a distant planet.

On her own, she never would have known what to say; the prospect of small talk tied her tongue. But fortunately Michael handled the "spiel" with a fluency and charm that filled her with admiration. With unflappable good nature, he'd muster scraps of Italian, rag-bag bits of Yiddish, whatever came to hand; and if his attempts at dialect were ungrammatical and mispronounced, the Dev Dems were nonetheless flattered by his efforts. Catherine wished she could have trotted out her French, which was really awfully good, but there was a lack of Gallic ethnics in the Boston melting pot. Instead, she stroked dogs and held babies and smiled her clean New England smile while Michael held forth and cajoled.

The night before, they'd worked the Italian North End. Tonight it was the classic Irish stronghold of Dorchester.

"Well, at least they speak English." Michael rang the 6D doorbell. "Mr. and Mrs. Francis X. Mulcahey."

The woman who answered was in her sixties, short and moon-faced with little blueberry eyes. Michael instantly flashed his party ID.

"Ah," she beamed, "from the party, are ye?" Her voice was rich with the echoes of Erin. "Come in, come in." She ushered them into the little living room, all knick-knacked and tidy, as if she'd been awaiting their arrival. Which perhaps she had. A lonely old woman eager for a chat, Catherine thought, seating herself on the horsehair sofa. Party visits were probably the highlight of her life. There was no evidence of a Mr. Mulcahey.

"We should have been here sooner," Michael said, "but we like to save the best for last." It was the opening line of his pitch.

Catherine looked about her while Michael went on; it was like hundreds of other places she had seen. There was the patterned carpet, the crocheted antimacassars, one or two good pieces of Belleek. And there on the wall, of course, the mandatory crucifixion scene, this one more florid than most. The Christ was replete with purple rays; the blood dripped in geometrical precision. She dropped her eyes to the mantel below. Now there was something she hadn't seen before.

Her first impression was of a religious shrine, but looking at it more closely, she saw it was a photograph—a photograph of a scraggy-necked bespectacled man hand-tinted in garish colors. The photo was set in an elaborate silver frame and nestled in a bed of wax flowers. At its base there was a neatly tied bow of blackest silk entwined with a tiny gold rosary.

The *late* Mr. Mulcahey, Catherine guessed. She turned her attention to Michael, who was now in full sail.

"Now, I know you'll vote for Jim Donovan for City Council." An acquiescent hum from Mrs. Mulcahey. In this ward, Michael had informed her, so entrenched was the Democratic party that the Republicans didn't even bother fielding candidates for local office.

"And now," he continued, "I'm asking you to cast a vote for Mr. Adlai Stevenson too."

Catherine's ears pricked up. Had she imagined it, or was there a faint Irish lilt in Michael's voice?

"Well, ye know," Mrs. Mulcahey said, shaking her head, "he's a divorced man, your Mr. Stevenson. I've never voted for a divorced man in all me life. I'd have to discuss it with the Father."

"Ach, Mrs. Mulcahey." Yes, there was definitely an Irish lilt in Michael's voice, and it was getting broader with every word. "Sure an' it's true the poor man's divorced—a terrible, terrible tragedy. Married to a shrew he was, and then she up and left him to go live in sin. Aaach, if you knew the whole story, Mrs. Mulcahey, you'd say the man was a saint."

OK, Michael, you've had your little joke. Catherine tried to catch his eye and signal him to stop. But Michael's fine gray eyes were focussed solely on the widow, and for all his joking, Catherine had never seen him look so earnest. He gave a weary sigh, and in that sigh one could hear despair over the woman's infidelity. Compassion for the abandoned Mr. Stevenson.

"Well, it's a blessing herself is dead. Adlai's mother, that is. It would have broken her Irish heart."

"And was she Irish?" The bluebell eyes widened in wonder.

"Was she Irish! Why, Mrs. Mulcahey, sure ye know Adlai is an old Celtic name? Of course, the Republicans don't let you in on the secret, but Adlai's mother was as Irish as you are. Came from County Mayo, she did."

"I'm from County Cork."

Michael beamed. "Are ye now? A beautiful place." He turned to Catherine. "Isn't it, Kathleen?"

Kathleen! Catherine was too stunned to do anything but gape open-mouthed.

"And now, Mrs. Mulcahey, we've got to be going." Catherine rose with relief. "And I know you'll be voting for Adlai. By the way,"—with a barely perceptible nod to the photograph on the mantle—"be sure and have Mr. Mulcahey cast his vote, too."

My God, Catherine thought. *How stupid. How cruel.* But to her astonishment, Mrs. Mulcahey smiled—and her smile was as broad as wink.

"I'll do that," she said, displaying a mouthful of gold.

"God bless you," Michael returned. "Don't trouble, we'll see ourselves out."

Michael said nothing until they were halfway down the

stairs, and when he spoke, there was no lilt of Old Ireland in his voice.

"Let's eat Chinese, sweetheart. We've earned it."

"Well, Michael, what was that all about?"

They were settled in a booth at the Canton Palace, the table a panorama of platters. Subgum chow mein. Fried rice. Spareribs. Egg rolls. Noodles and mustard and plum sauce.

"What was *what* all about?" He was engrossed in dipping noodles into mustard, Dorchester far from his mind.

"Why, that Irish opera I just sat through." She put down her chopsticks and mimicked his tone. 'God bless ye, mavourneen, and suren Adlai is an Oirish name.' I half expected you to burst into a few choruses of *Danny Boy*. How could you do that to her!"

"But what did I do, Catherine?" He was clearly amused. "What did I do, if you cut away the blarney, except give her a good reason to vote? All she needed was a little push, some sort of alibi, and now she'll be voting for the best man since Roosevelt. So what's the crime?"

"You lied to her," Catherine said flatly.

"All right, so I lied to her and she'll be voting for all the wrong reasons. The point is, she'll be voting for the right candidate. Believe me, Catherine. . . ."

"Oh, I thought my name was Kathleen!"

"Catherine, Kathleen . . ." he laughed. "In the North End, I've called you Caterina. You know, life isn't quite the way it looks from the college dorms, and people aren't what you think they are. The great mass of 'em, anyhow. Oh, I know those university bull sessions—I've been through them myself. The H-Bomb, civil rights, all the worthy causes. They don't amount to a hill of beans when you're out on the streets looking for votes. Ideals are a luxury. Maybe they're a luxury you can afford, in which case you're a lucky girl. I don't imagine you've ever had to worry about meeting the rent or bringing some cousin over from the Old Country. Or maybe getting your husband a job in the civil service, where he won't be fired next time the wind blows cold."

No, those were not her problems, Catherine admitted.

"Then you're fortunate. You can worry about larger issues. But most people can't. Take my father, for instance. He sells farm equipment up in Caribou, Maine—that's all potato country, you know. Well, do you think he's worrying about World War III or integration? Hell, they don't even have Negroes up there. No . . . what my father wants to know is whether Stevenson is going to support the price of potatoes. That's the burning issue up there. It's the same everywhere. Your Boston Irish, for example . . . they'll vote for the candidate who says he's going to get them public aid for parochial schools. The Jews . . . with them it's Zionism."

"In other words," she said, shocked by his cynicism, "the only interest is self-interest. Is that what you're saying?"

"Yup. Pretty much. In fact, I'd say the only group that votes consistently against its own self-interest . . . is *women!* Not all of them, of course—I'm sure you wouldn't—just most of 'em. They'll vote for the good-looking face and the romantic figure every damn time. Let's face it," he said amiably. "Lincoln wouldn't stand to get elected dogcatcher if he were running today."

But you would, she thought. Five weeks of close association had not dulled her sense of his handsomeness.

"And the older women, as far as I can see . . . why, they're even worse. They vote whichever way their husbands tell them. When you think of it, Catherine, it's really rather sad, after women worked so hard to get the vote. I bet those great old suffragettes must be turning over in the grave seeing what women have done with the vote. Susan B. Anthony . . . Annabel Sayre . . ."

"Annabel Sayre isn't turning in her grave," Catherine was quick to interrupt. "At least she wasn't last Wednesday when I had tea with her."

"When you *what?*" He was incredulous.

"Had tea with her." Suddenly Catherine was enjoying herself hugely. He'd been so busy proving her wrong in everything thus far; it was splendid being in the right for once. She smiled at the recollection of that tiny basement flat off Beacon Hill, reeking with the smell of cats and ancient flesh.

"You had tea with Annabel Sayre." Michael pushed away his plate and stared at her. "And tell me, how did that come to be?"

"She's my great-aunt, my grandfather's sister."

"Then your grandfather was Winthrop Sayre."

She nodded.

He seemed oddly impressed by this information. Was it

because she was a Sayre? That was silly. No, it simply must have been the shock of discovering that the legendary Annabel could still be numbered among the living. And speaking of the living and the dead . . .

"I'd like to ask you something else, Michael."

"Ask away." He sounded distracted. Still pondering old Annabel, no doubt.

"About tonight at Mrs. Mulcahey's . . . all that business of having her husband vote. It was so obvious the woman is a widow."

Michael leaned back and laughed, as though she'd said something witty.

"You mean you never heard of voting the dead?"

Catherine shook her head in confusion.

"Why, it's an old Boston custom, especially in the Irish wards. I thought you knew. Someone dies . . . your Mr. Mulcahey, for instance. Which means that all of a sudden Mrs. Mulcahey's political clout is cut down by fifty percent. Right? Wrong! Because until the Election Board's notified that the old boy is dead and buried, his name stays on the rolls. Even if the registrar attended the dead man's funeral, officially the Board doesn't know. And who's going to tell 'em? Mrs. Mulcahey? Not on your life! No . . . she'll get some local yokel to go down to the polls and sign the old man's name in on election day. Roll up another vote for Big Jim Donovan—and then someday, when maybe Mrs. Mulcahey wants a favor from the ward boss . . . well, she knows she's still got friends where it counts. Don't look so shocked. Just think of it this way: you can die in Boston and still be immortal, at least on the election rolls."

Catherine was appalled. Practicality was one thing; this kind of flippancy was another.

"Tell me, Michael," she said, her voice rich in sarcasm, "is everyone at Harvard Law as idealistic as you?"

He sat up as if stung, and she knew she'd hit a chord, for suddenly the laughter fled from his eyes.

"Don't misunderstand me, Catherine. I'm more idealistic than you think. I don't like things the way they are. I don't approve of getting votes in this way. If it were up to me, I'd change the system, but meanwhile I have to work within it." He must have felt the need for self-defense, for he continued. "It may interest you to know that I'm one of the very few in my class who's going into the practice of criminal law. And everyone says I should have my head examined. It would be the easiest thing in the world for me to line up with all the others and grab some nice corporation job in Wall Street. And I could do it. You know, come next spring the recruiters from all the big law firms will be popping up in Harvard Yard just like crocuses. All I'd have to do is give the word and I'd have my pick of offers. After that, it would all be laid out. My whole life. A junior partnership by thirty, say. Senior partner by forty, forty-five. A house in the country. Membership in the yacht club. And a list of blue-chip clients that would read like a column in the New York Stock Exchange. And believe me, that's very tempting indeed when you've spent your entire youth counting pennies. But I'm not going to do it, it's not what I want because—believe it or not—I'm committed. Committed to whatever you want to call it—fair play, social justice—committed enough to see that the losers of this world get their day in court. You don't like what I did tonight and I'm sorry. But I've been around long enough and I'm realistic enough to know there are ways of getting things done. Like I've said, it's an imperfect world and you have to use the instruments at hand."

"Like Mrs. Mulcahey?" She was mollified now.

"Like Mrs. Mulcahey." He relaxed and signaled the waiter. "Now, what do you say we get some fortune cookies and see what the future has in store?"

But, unlike Michael, the fortune cookies proved to be disappointingly noncommittal.

Michael took the Eisenhower landslide with alarming good grace. "You win some, you lose some," he told her. He had called her up a few days after the election to thank her for her efforts and they chatted for a while about this and that. Catherine kept hoping the conversation would take a more personal turn, but it did not. It was, she suspected, a routine post-election "Thank you"; he'd probably called every other club member as well.

When she hung up the phone, she felt mildly depressed, for he was the first man she might conceivably have cared for. Oh, well, chances were he had a girl. A terrific girl. Those Harvard Law students were the catch of the town. And what would a man like that see in Catherine? Naive, gawky Catherine. She must have put her foot in her mouth a dozen times with him. "And are all you Harvard men so idealistic?"

She writhed, remembering the bitchiness in her tone. Whatever possessed her to be so nasty? Phyllis was right. Next time she'd know better, she'd keep her mouth shut. If there was a next time.

For a few weeks, she hung around the dorm on the off chance he might call again. But he didn't. And by spring, she no longer really thought about him, except to remember how very, very handsome he was.

Oh, well. You win some, you lose some.

As usual, she spent the summer with her mother on Cape Cod and, in September, began her final year. She came back to Boston with a beautiful tan, a larger dress allowance and the inner certainty that she would graduate with honors.

"I don't know if you remember me," said the voice on the other end of the line. "Michael Matheson. We did some canvassing together last October."

Remember him! The mere sound of his name conjured up an instant image—an image that had danced just beneath the surface of her consciousness a thousand times in the long year past. *Remember* him! How do you forget the handsomest man you've ever met?

"Yes." Catherine wrestled down her voice into blandness. "Of course I remember you."

He sounded pleasant and cheerful, as if the lapse of a year had been but a day or two. And when he asked her to dinner the next Saturday night, Catherine was elated. This time, she wasn't going to muff it.

Michael called for her at six in a dusty old Dodge that made him look even more glowing by contrast.

She had dressed for the occasion—if occasion it was—in an agony of choice. She had wanted to look beautiful and glamorous (although those were terms she hardly ever dared to apply to herself) without giving the appearance of having fussed. Of expecting something grander, more expensive than a young and impecunious lawyer might afford. *After all,* she chided herself, *it's only a dinner date.*

But if she had doubts about the little black dress and pearl earrings, the dab of eye shadow, the double-dab of Arpege, it was clear that he had none, for the moment she came into the lobby he welcomed her with a broad grin of appreciation.

"You look," he said, "beautiful." And in that moment, she felt so.

An occasion. Yes, in his eyes, too, she recognized that it was to be an occasion. He had planned their evening meticulously—dinner at a famous country steakhouse topped off by dancing at the Kenmore Roof. From the moment he handed Catherine into the car to the moment he delivered her home to her door, he was charming. Charming—treating her as a desirable and intelligent woman, not a gawky college kid. He asked her opinions and listened intently to her replies, as though each word were of considerable value.

"Do you really prefer Tolstoy to Dostoievski? Guess I'll have to read *War and Peace* again."

Or, "I'm wondering if I should break down and get a TV set. What do you think?"

Or, noticing her untouched steak—and how could she concentrate on both food and him simultaneously?—he asked, "Is the steak too well done? I'll send it back."

"Oh, no, it's fine." She flushed, momentarily disconcerted by this evidence that she had found him far more interesting than his high-priced dinner.

"At any rate, it must be cold by now. Waiter!"—he had but to raise a finger and the waiter came scurrying. "Take the young lady's steak back to the kitchen and have them warm it up."

"Of course, sir."

He was so commanding, so confident, so manly. And on the steps of her dorm, Catherine—who didn't believe in first-night kissing as a matter of principle—raised her face to his in unconscious expectation. He cupped her face in his hands for one long moment, studied her with smiling eyes, then kissed her lovingly, lightly. Just this and no more.

Just right, thought Catherine, inhaling the fresh smell of his skin, feeling the strong, cool fingers on her cheeks.

"Next Saturday?" he asked.

"Next Saturday." And she floated up the stairs, drunk on the memory of his touch.

From then on she saw him every weekend, and often once or twice during the week. He was a lawyer now, having passed the bar, and was working as a voluntary defender in Boston. Catherine never asked him why he took so long to call; she presumed it was the pressure of bar exams. But once he did call, he didn't stop—and that was all that really mattered.

Just what it was he saw in her she couldn't imagine, but it was clear that he saw a great deal. Her height didn't put him off (he was six foot two to her five foot nine) nor her comparative youth (she was twenty to his mature twenty-seven).

And after three years of fraternity dances and student socials, three years of fumbling with hot-handed undergraduates, it was a pleasure to be treated as a lady instead of just another piece of meat.

Not that he wasn't affectionate, for he was. And considerate. He treated her with a deference she found touching, a protectiveness that was infinitely reassuring.

At first, she had agonized about what she would do when he made that sequential progression that always followed good-night kisses. The clumsy clutching of brassiere straps, the hesitant stroke of the thigh, the probing and gropings and grabbings and jabbings that had hitherto signified the start of a cold war between Catherine and all her other dates.

Would she or wouldn't she, if Michael put it on the line? She admitted to herself she didn't know. She would simply have to wait for the moment.

But the moment never came, for Michael was in both action and words every six-foot-two inch a gentleman. She knew he found her attractive. It was apparent in his every look, in the pride with which he introduced her to his friends and colleagues. His reticence derived, she was certain, neither from lack of desire nor lack of experience. It welled from some deep inner seriousness that separated his feelings for her from the lunge and thrust of college dating patterns.

They talked.

And talked and talked and talked and talked. About books and movies and politics and education. But most of all they talked about themselves.

Michael took a genuine interest in her boring old family: her crazy aunts, her New York relatives, the legions of Sayre cousins who populated the hills of Milton and the country clubs of Brookline. Catherine herself had always found them tiresome and, as much as possible, limited her contacts with them to weddings and funerals. Still, it was terribly nice of Michael to take an interest.

His own life and family seemed far more rugged. He was

descended from generations of farmers who had scratched for their livings in the hardscrabble country of northern Maine.

"We grow them lean and mean up there," Michael said.

"The potatoes?"

"No, the Mathesons. Lean and mean."

His father was the first to break the farming mold, managing somehow or other to scrape up enough cash to buy an agricultural equipment business. But the business had not prospered and after years of hard work he was only marginally better off than the farmers he served. The cost of raising seven children saw to that. Michael's mother taught Sunday school and sometimes helped in the business, as the children were expected to do.

Catherine, who as a child had yearned for brothers and sisters, envied him this wealth of siblings. "Don't," said Michael, assuring her that a large family did not necessarily mean a close family. "It's easy to get lost in the shuffle."

It troubled her that he spoke of them with so little affection, but it was easy enough to understand why.

"My parents did not wish big for me," he once said bitterly.

Even as a child, he had dreamt of the law, of going to Harvard, of a great career as a jurist. But his parents' aspirations had not matched his own. They told him grudgingly that they would see him through four years at the University of Maine (naturally, he would work weekends and summers), and after that he was on his own. There would be no further concessions. "In their eyes, the greatest achievement I could hope for would be teaching school in Caribou. Or maybe, just maybe, hit the big time as a certified public accountant in Portland. As for Boston . . ." He rolled his eyes. "To them it was always Sin City."

He did four years of work in three at the University of Maine and was only twenty when he graduated. He could, he believed, have got into Harvard then, but there was no conceivable way he could finance it.

Anyhow, it became a moot question, for by then the Korean War had broken out. Michael didn't wait to be drafted. He joined the Air Force instead, and when he was discharged some two years later it was with the rank of Second Lieutenant and twenty four months of back pay in his pocket. "I didn't realize you could actually make any money in the service," Catherine commented.

"Ah, but you can if you live like a monk." So with his

service savings and the GI Bill, he achieved his dream of Harvard Law. "And the rest you know."

Catherine was thrilled and she was proud of him. Of his tenacity, his energy, his zest for new ideas, his fervor for struggle and change. She had long ago forgiven him Mrs. Mulcahey. She loved his quick compassion for those whom he affectionately dubbed "life's losers." In fact loved him. Loved him—it was not too strong a word—for his humanity, for the ease and ready sympathy with which he met every social situation.

All during that long busy winter, she and Michael compared tastes about everything. From sports (Michael was a Red Sox fan with the full fury of the convert) to music (he loved opera, she couldn't abide it) to movies (they both agreed that in a perfect world, Bergman's *Wild Strawberries* would have won that year's Academy Award). They swapped stories and records and books and jokes.

For Christmas he gave her a beautiful diary of hand-tooled Florentine leather. As she riffled delightedly through the gold-tipped pages, she noticed he had written in it. He had written in his name for every Saturday throughout the year, for every foreseeable event from Harvard Alumni dances to Fourth of July fireworks to the anniversary of their very first date.

As winter turned to spring, they played chess in the Boston Gardens and tennis out at Longwood, courtesy of the Brookline branch of the Sayres.

She monitored her conversation less and less, for there was less and less she wanted to keep from him. Only Phyllis. She never spoke to him of Phyllis except to say she had a roommate. And never never spoke to Phyllis of *him*. Not that she didn't trust her, not quite that. It was that she really didn't trust herself. She worried constantly that compared to Phyllis, Michael might find Catherine bland and sexless.

She invited Michael to Athol over Easter weekend and was delighted when he accepted with pleasure.

"Now don't talk politics with my father," Catherine warned as they were driving down in Michael's battered Dodge. "He's so far to the right, he defies all the pigeonholes; he even thinks Eisenhower's a Communist stooge."

But she had nothing to worry about, for Michael toed the line scrupulously and always called Spencer "Sir." After he left, Spencer unbent so far as to pronounce him "a sound young fellow." As for Emily, she could scarcely mask her delight. "He's so nice, and so good-looking too."

"It appears you're going to graduate with honors." Professor Robson smiled as she closed Catherine's file with a snap.

"I hope so." But Catherine knew so. Still the words were always welcome. Especially from Professor Robson, who combined the teaching of poetry with the more informal function of student counselor.

It was unseasonably hot, even for early May, and the small basement office was stuffy. It was nice of Professor Robson to spare her the time, especially with graduation only a few weeks away.

"So you've definitely decided against graduate work."

"Yes, I have," Catherine nodded vigorously. "I can't see myself as a perennial scholar. I want to see if I can get some kind of writing job, if that doesn't sound too ambitious."

"No, not too ambitious at all," Robson smiled. "I'm frankly delighted you're not going to throw it all away. It wearies me, it really does, to see so many top girls getting married as soon as they graduate. Not that I have anything against marriage. I'm married myself. My oldest son is older than you. Still," she said, running a hand over her crisp gray hair, "I always feel it's deplorable when girls with good academic records run off to the suburbs like lemmings. Such a waste. A waste of money, a waste of university facilities, a waste of talent. I like to think of this college as something more than a high-priced marriage brokerage. You're not getting married, are you, Catherine?"

Catherine raised her bare ring finger by way of answer. "And in any case, no one has asked me," she laughed. "No. My plan is to go to New York and try to land something in journalism there. I know you're going to tell me it's a tough nut to crack . . ."

"Oh, it's a very tough nut indeed," came the answer, "especially for girls without experience. But that doesn't mean it can't be cracked. If you're really serious about working as a reporter, however, I'd suggest you try for a job on a small-town newspaper first."

They talked about possibilities for a while.

Catherine rose to go and Professor Robson rose with her. "I envy you, you know," the older woman said, "being young and bright in 1958. When I got my degree there wasn't much one could do. A girl could teach or type or get married. Period. But now a girl like you can be anything you want professionally." She spread her hands and offered Catherine the world. "Yes, a bright girl like you can be anything."

Catherine was walking on air when she got back to the dorm.

Anything. A bright girl like you can be anything.

Sure, college had been great. Michael had been great. But a bright girl like her could be anything!

"Who's Michael?" Phyllis demanded when she opened the door.

"Who's Michael who?" Catherine countered.

"Who's Michael who phoned about twenty times this afternoon to remind you that you're to meet him at"—she checked the scribbled message—"at the Canton Palace. Seven o'clock sharp and don't be late. He says he has something important to tell you. By the way, he sounded absolutely gorgeous."

"Oh, he's just a guy I date now and then." She could feel the blood rushing to her cheeks.

"Jes a li'l ole guy, Ah do declayah." Phyllis loved to play the teasing Mammy to Catherine's Scarlett O'Hara. "Ah do declayah, honey chile, y'all are blushing."

Which made Catherine turn all the redder.

The beige or not the beige, that is the question. After long deliberation and careful study, Catherine took the dress out of the closet and cautiously removed the price tag. It was a silk pongee shirtwaist the color of sand and had cost her a whole semester's dress allowance. She'd been saving it for graduation-week parties.

"Not too dressy, not too tailored," the girl at Bonwit's had told her. "You could wear it anywhere." And once Catherine tried it on, she was hooked. Everything about it was perfect— the tiny rows of cloth-covered buttons, the ease and flow of the skirt, the romantic fullness of the sleeves tapering down to thin and elegant wrists. Even in the glare of Bonwit's dressing room, the dress had endowed her with grace. And when she wrote out the check, she rationalized the price. *I can always wear it for job-hunting in New York.*

She would wear it tonight with pearly button earrings and the dangling silver charm bracelet her mother had given her.

It was quarter to seven when she pulled it all together, relieved that Phyllis wasn't around to make remarks. With a self-conscious admission that she looked rather nice, Catherine headed for Commonwealth Avenue. Michael always hated waiting, so she'd better flag a cab. She looked up and down the length of the avenue.

KIT

IT WAS TWENTY PAST SEVEN WHEN SHE GOT THERE AND THE Canton Palace was absolutely jammed. Everything in Boston was jampacked that night; there'd been a double-header at Fenway Park. Stupid, really stupid of her to have forgotten. The fans had taken over the town.

Needless to say, you couldn't get a cab for love or money and Catherine had wound up running all the way to China-town. She was breathless when she got there and knew Michael would be furious. He had such a thing about time. Perhaps he'd got impatient and left.

But no, there he was in their usual corner booth, smiling and waving over the heads of the waiters. No, he wasn't angry—dear Michael—just handsome. So handsome it made her heart skip.

"Sorry I'm late," she was still panting from her trek. "Stupid me, I forgot all about the ballgame. Wow! I've never seen the place so packed. It looks like the whole of Boston is here tonight."

"It is *now*." He smiled and stood up to greet her. She squeezed herself into the booth.

"Sorry again. Did you order already?"

"Yes, I did. In fact, I ordered something special. I thought we'd start off with some lobster rolls and spareribs and then that *char shue ding* dish you like so much. Meanwhile, how about some tea?"

When she poured the tea, she noticed the pot was getting cool. He must have been waiting for ages. He could really be very nice.

"Now tell me your news. Phyllis said it was important. Have you been nominated for governor or something?"

"My news can wait." His eyes were sparkling. "First tell me how you spent *your* day."

She told him. About the interview with Professor Robson. About the glowing words, the atmosphere of promise. About her plans—firm now—for going to New York. Plans that she and Michael had discussed and probed and picked over a dozen times during the winter.

Until today, they had been more dreams than plans, to be sure; vague unfocused visions of a glamorous future. But the interview with Robson had revved her up, made her eager to plunge in, even though it meant starting at the bottom of the ladder.

"Of course, I told her I don't expect to land a job on the *Times*. At least not right away. Meanwhile, I'll take anything that comes along."

Her enthusiasm must have been striking, for Michael furrowed his brow, as if hearing it all for the first time.

"Just how serious are you, Catherine?" he asked, his voice suddenly solemn. It was not what she had expected him to say. Without warning, her stomach began to churn in apprehension.

Why, he's going to propose. He's actually going to propose!

"Pretty serious."

"And is pretty serious more serious than very serious?"

He reached across the table and put his hand on her arm at the very moment the waiter arrived with the ribs.

"We'd better make room for Harry," she said, smiling a smile of relief and moving the teapot to make room for the platter.

Yes, she was sure he was going to propose, *but please, God, not this very moment.*

During the course of the winter, she had occasionally wondered if Michael might propose one day. *Might.* It was all very iffy, and she certainly wasn't going to count on it. And when the thought did arise, she tried to banish it. The likelihood seemed so remote.

Her youth, her gawkiness—real or imagined—the fact that Michael had never made a serious sexual overture: in Catherine's mind these were all clear indications that he never thought of her "that way."

Let other girls build rose-covered cottages in the air only to see them crumble to earth with a plop. Well, they were fools . . . but not Catherine. No. She was too wary, too frightened and, above all, too reserved to reveal the depths of her feelings for this man who, most likely, saw her simply as a friend and companion. She could envision no greater humiliation than to offer her love only to have it refused.

As for marriage . . . well, for once, perhaps her mother was right.

"There's all the time in the world, dear. All the time in the world."

And now, time was all Catherine asked for. Not all the time in the world, of course, simply enough time to pull her emotions together. Thinking time. A stay of execution. And meanwhile . . . *let's change the subject.*

"Now tell me about your day, Michael," she said, wishing he hadn't ordered spareribs. They made such a mess of your lipstick. "Anything exciting?"

"I'll say." His face glowed with joy. "I've quit as a voluntary defender and joined a new law firm."

Catherine was flabbergasted. So! His joy was not for her. Not for her but for some job or other. For a moment her emotions wavered between the high of relief and the unsuspected depths of disappointment. Disappointment prevailed, much to her surprise, and now the food seemed flat and tasteless.

"Well, not really a new firm. An old firm, in fact, but they're determined to get young blood. The long and short of it is, they've promised me work up to here . . ."

Catherine picked at her ribs, listening with only half an ear as Michael waxed enthusiastic about his future.

You dolt, she reprimanded herself. *You were so convinced that you were his news.*

She watched, rather than heard, him talk. For the hundredth time, she took in the finely modeled mouth. The clean curves of his cheekbones. The gray eyes now bright with excitement.

How beautiful he was! The most beautiful man she had

ever met. *Would* ever meet, most likely. And what an idiot she'd been even to think . . .

Surely, Michael could marry any girl in Boston he had a mind to. Prettier girls, pleasanter girls, richer girls. For the hundredth time, she felt bony and awkward. Even the Bonwit dress seemed out of place.

She felt a sudden impulse to take his hand, the hand that only a few minutes past had been touching her. The hand now busily punctuating the highlights of his conversation.

She wanted to take that hand, that cool elegant hand, and press it to her burning cheek. But that, of course, seemed a forward thing to do. So she did not.

Yet if he were to ask her at that moment to go to bed with him, perhaps she would. She *definitely* would. Yes, she would risk everything for him. But it was painfully clear the thought had never entered his mind, that he saw her as nothing more than a friend. A pal—that dreadful word—with whom he would share the odd joke and confidence while reserving the very deepest part of his life for somebody else. She was sure now that there was somebody else. How ironic it was that she could have so misread him, so misinterpreted the happiness with which he had greeted her. No, he was not going to propose. Not tonight. Not ever.

"So I figure it should be worth an extra two thousand a year plus first-class courtroom experience. Well, Catherine, what do you think?"

"I think . . ." she collected her thoughts quickly and bundled them out of view. She even managed a smile. "I think it all sounds very exciting. I'm terribly happy for you, Michael."

"Me, too," he grinned and snapped a finger for the waiter. "Now let's have some dessert. I've ordered something very special tonight."

The "something special" proved to be an elaborate dish of lychee nuts and kumquats, garnished with half a dozen fortune cookies.

"I'm afraid I'm not awfully hungry, Michael. I hope I won't hurt Harry Chow's feelings." The dish was complicated and it was clear that the chef had gone to some trouble to prepare it.

"Oh, well." Michael was only mildly disappointed. "At least have a fortune cookie. Go ahead. I insist on it. May as well learn what the future has in store."

They each took a cookie.

"What's yours?" she asked.

"Oh, no," he said. "Ladies first."

She crumbled the biscuit, found the little paper ribbon and smoothed it out on the soy-stained tablecloth.

It read: *YOU ARE GOING TO MARRY MICHAEL MATHESON.*

She blinked, then read it again. When she looked up, his eyes were radiant. But this time they were radiant only for her.

"Do they all have the same message?" Her voice was shaking.

"All of them. Every last one."

"Oh, Michael." A tear coursed down her cheek. "That's the most fantastic proposal anyone's ever had. I just . . . I just don't know what to say."

"Say yes."

"Oh, Michael . . ." She reached for the hand that only moments ago had been forbidden her. "Yes."

Yes yes yes yes yes.

He brought her hand to his lips and kissed her fingers one by one. He stopped when he came to the ring finger.

"Mrs. Catherine Matheson. How does that sound?"

"Wonderful. Strange but wonderful." He was stroking her hand now, the way one strokes a cat, the rhythm soft and gentle.

"Actually, it's really quite a mouthful. Cath-e-rine Math-e-son. Practically a tongue twister. From now on I'm going to call you Kit. My Kit. My own darling kitten."

And the newly christened kitten purred.

It was a lovely wedding.

Emily said so. The *Boston Herald* said so. The *Globe* said so. Even *The New York Times* said so. ("*I* should say so," Spencer grumbled the morning after, "considering what the damn thing cost.")

Kit herself would have preferred something simpler—a quiet ceremony at Christ Church in Athol followed by a reception in the Chapmans' rose garden. But—and not for the last time—she found herself overruled.

"After all, dear," Emily pointed out, "you only get married once." And when Kit had appealed to Michael for a second opinion, he came down quickly and firmly on Mrs. Chapman's side.

"But Michael," she protested, "it seems a criminal waste to spend that kind of money on a wedding. Why, you could probably feed a family of sharecroppers for a year on just what the reception will cost."

"I know, darling, and believe me, I don't want it for myself. But think of your mother. You are her only daughter, so she'll never have another chance. Why deprive her of her one big moment?"

Spencer appeared totally indifferent. "Just tell me when and where," he said grimly when Kit handed him the guest list.

So . . . the "when" was her twenty-first birthday. The "where," Boston's Trinity Church, with a bishop presiding, followed by a splendid reception at the Ritz-Carlton.

The New York Chapmans turned out in force, as did the Boston Sayres. There was a rather smaller contingent of "lean and mean" Mathesons who, despite Michael's warning, proved a harmless lot. Kit found them amusing in a Grant Woods sort of way.

There were Michael's friends from Harvard, Kit's from B.U. and Miss Ellery's . . . those who hadn't already scattered by September.

Phyllis couldn't come. ("You mean I'm never going to meet her?" Michael had teased.) The week before graduation, when she learned she was flunking out, Phyllis had taken herself off to Arizona, where—according to the sole postcard she sent her former roommate—"the pickings are absolutely fantastic."

At the reception, everyone agreed that Kit made a beautiful bride (she glowed) and that Michael was the luckiest of men (he agreed).

Even Spencer seemed to so far lose his usual reserve that he challenged Michael's mother to a cha-cha. Emily was amused and Kit amazed.

Kit gave her new husband a magnificent set of gold cufflinks from Shreve, Crump and Low. Michael gave her a silver cigarette lighter. It was inscribed *To my matchless Kit*. At the time she thought it very clever.

And Spencer gave them a handsome check.

KATE

SHE GOT THERE TWENTY MINUTES LATE AND THE CANTON
Palace was packed. Baseball fans. That explained it. Explained why she couldn't get a cab for love or money. She'd
run practically all the way to Chinatown. Michael would
probably be annoyed, he had such a thing about promptness,
but no—when she got there he was smiling. Good God, he
was handsome. It made her heart skip.

She apologized for her tardiness and squeezed into the
booth. And when he smiled, she knew all was forgiven.

He'd ordered something special, he told her, so she poured
some tea while they waited. She noticed the tea was getting
cold.

He was full of some news that had clearly made him happy,
but when she asked him what, he said it could wait. Asked her
instead what she'd done that day.

She described her interview with Professor Robson, how
well it had gone. She spoke of her hopes and her dreams and
her plans. He listened as though for the first time.

"Just how serious are you, Catherine?" Her stomach
churned with apprehension and then she knew he was going
to propose.

"Pretty serious."

"And is pretty serious more serious than very serious?" He reached across the table and put his hand on her sleeve at the precise moment the waiter arrived with the ribs.

"We'd better make room." She drew her hand away abruptly to make way for the food and as she did, her bracelet caught on the button of Michael's sleeve. The more she tried to wriggle free, the more entangled she became. It was embarrassing, really. With a swift sudden jerk, she pulled her arm back with such force that the button pulled free. Her elbow hit the teapot with the impact of a bomb. And then there was tea . . . tea everywhere.

"You clu . . ." The words froze on his lips as they both jumped to sheer away from the deluge.

Tea. Gallons of it. Oceans of it. Tea, seeping through the tablecloth, draining onto the seat, staining the sand of her dress a muddy brown. Tea, running down her legs, dripping into her pumps, forming angry pools at her feet. Who would have believed one little pot could hold so much, create such havoc? Everyone turned around to stare.

"I'm sorry, Harry." This to poor Harry Chow, who, still hanging on to the spareribs, was trying to stem the flow of tea with rapid, futile gestures.

"I'm sorry." This to Michael, who was now on his feet, his face a model of compassion. Had she imagined the white lips, the quick flash of anger, the words suddenly swallowed? But he was all sympathy now.

"Did you burn yourself, Catherine?" The anguish was genuine.

"No, I'm OK. Thank God the tea was cold." She looked down at her dress, her sodden shoes. "Oh, Christ, what a mess I've made."

And somewhere inside her, a tiny voice giggled: *Hey! that was some romantic moment!*

"You're sure you're all right?" He was so thoughtful, so concerned.

Catherine bobbed her head and managed a smile. "Let me just go to the ladies' room and get cleaned up. As they say, *après moi le deluge.*"

Harry had given her a heap of linen towels and she'd done the best she could. Still, no question about it—the dress was ruined. So much for her big splurge at Bonwit's.

She sat down on the little plastic stool before the mirror

and fished a damp cigarette out of her bag. The pungent smell of tobacco couldn't quite mask the cloying sweetness of that abominable stuff they used to disinfect the toilets.

Wow! Freud says there are no accidents. Well, for once, Sigmund was wrong.

She reconsidered.

On second thought, maybe he wasn't.

Any way you looked at it, Catherine had certainly managed to muck up the one moment in her life that had been rich in romantic promise. She had always pooh-poohed, as a matter of routine, the power of the unconscious, but now she wondered if she hadn't engineered the "accident." Had done it to give herself thinking time. Because her gut reaction to his impending proposal had been fear. Unadulterated fear.

A flood of panic followed by a flood of tea.

Yes, she knew now he had been going to propose. And still might, if he hadn't been too disgusted with her clumsiness.

"You clu . . ."

She suddenly recalled his face, the quick flash of almost irrepressible anger.

"You clu . . ."

You clumsy fool. You clumsy idiot. You cluck. You klutz. She didn't know exactly what *klutz* actually meant. One thing she was sure of: it wasn't complimentary.

She had never before seen Michael off his guard. My God, he had been angry.

Be reasonable, Catherine, she told herself. After all, he had every right to be angry. The poor man had set the scene with care and precision. Their favorite booth. Their favorite restaurant. He'd even ordered some special dish or other. And there was silly, clumsy Catherine turning this Garbo-Gable moment into a scene from a Marx Brothers movie.

Oh, well, no point crying about spilt tea. If he's going to propose he'll propose. She had been long aware that Michael Matheson was not a man easily deflected. The point was—did she want to marry him or didn't she? For that matter, did she want to marry anyone at all?

She was not even twenty-one, younger than most of her classmates. All the time in the world, her mother liked to say. Curious how Emily had never pushed marriage to Catherine, other than to say it was "nice." Nor had Spencer, for that matter. Surely a comment on their own married life.

On the other hand, twenty wasn't all that young. A lot of

her girl friends were engaged. Some were already married—
and to men nowhere near as attractive as Michael.

No question—Michael was decidedly a "catch."

Another five minutes. She looked at her watch, which had
been miraculously spared The Great Flood. *I'll sit here
another five minutes.*

It was quiet in the Ladies' Room. Quiet and restful. A port
against the emotional storm that was waiting on the other side
of the green baize door.

"You OK, honey?"

She was big and brash with hair as dark as Dragon Lady's, a
black that appeared nowhere in nature. Two businesslike
torpedoes masquerading as breasts struggled against the pink
of her sequin-flocked cardigan. Rather much for the poor old
Canton Palace.

"Yes, I'm fine, thank you. Just an accident."

"Mummy, Mummy"—the screech jarred like a fingernail
on a blackboard. Its source was a pudgy boy in a Red Sox tee
shirt, four, maybe five years old. He pulled up behind Dragon
Lady like a dory bobbing in the wake of a battleship.

"Mummy, look. She wet her pants." He pointed to Catherine's spattered dress and squealed.

"Shaddap, Kenny," Dragon Lady screamed back, "and get
in there and do what you hafta." She grabbed the offender by
the neck of his shirt and propelled him into the nearest toilet.

"Friggin' kids," she muttered. *"And don't lock the door!"*

She turned to Catherine with a heavy sigh. "Jesus, honey,
those spots look terrible. What is it . . . tea stains?"

Catherine nodded and Dragon Lady shook her head
gravely.

"Ya might try white vinegar . . ." She took a pinch of
Catherine's skirt and rubbed the material thoughtfully.
"Naa . . . silk. Naa . . . it's never gonna come out."

All woman-to-woman compassion, then suddenly Dragon
Lady, shouting "Kenny! Are you making?"

"I can't." Defiance from behind the closed door.

"Whaddya mean ya *can't?*"

The two women waited in silent expectation for the dribble
of piss, the plop of a turd. More silence.

Catherine gathered her things and squeezed into her shoes.
They must have shrunk a size or two.

And still only silence from the besieged toilet.

"Maybe he'd feel more at ease if someone took him to the Men's Room," she suggested.

"The Men's Room! Don't make me laugh. What—my husband should innarupt his dinner to take his son to the friggin' Men's Room? That'll be the day."

She was extricating lint from the sequins of her sweater, then moved in toward the mirror for closer study.

"Toilet training," she confided. "It's all in the toilet training. I made a mistake with this one." A wayward spit curl now caught her attention. She wet her fingers and put it to right. "I mean, I had him on the potty from when he was six months old, and it's been nothin' but trouble ever since. Now you take my younger one, Sondra. With her, I figured ta hell with it, she'll do it when she's ready . . . ya know what I mean? I mean, what's the diff if you do diapers for another few months? Shit is shit. Ya know what I mean?"

Catherine managed her other shoe and began edging to the door, but Dragon Lady had not yet had her say. She turned to Catherine and shook her head sagely.

"Believe me, honey, once the kids start coming, your life isn't your own any more. Ya know what I mean?"

"Yes," said Catherine, "I think I know what you mean." She closed the door behind her and from the other side, she could hear Dragon Lady's agonized wail.

"Kenny . . . are you making?"

Michael was drumming his fingers on the fresh white tablecloth with the air of an actor before the curtain goes up.

"Sorry," she said the moment she sat down, then wondered why she felt obliged to apologize. The ribs looked cold and gelatinous.

"Well, no harm done, and that's what matters. How about some fresh tea, Cath"—he smiled indulgently—"and this time *I'll* pour."

"I'll pour," she said coolly, "I'm perfectly capable. Now, what were we talking about? Oh, yes . . . my interview with Robson . . ."

From the corner of her eye, she could see Dragon Lady maneuvering the dread Kenny past their booth. Did Kenny make? she wondered. Inadvertently, she caught the boy's eye.

"Ooooh," Kenny screamed, "There's the lady who wet her

pants." Dragon Lady smacked him lightly across his buttocks. It was clearly a reproof administered more for form's sake than out of any real sense of outrage.

"If people can't bring up children, they shouldn't be allowed to have them," Michael snapped loud enough for Dragon Lady to hear and then, turning to Catherine— "Goddam brat. My turn to say I'm sorry, I suppose, but those kind of people turn me off."

"Surely, she's one of the Dev Dems, wouldn't you say?" Michael shrugged.

"Just because I work with them doesn't mean I have to love them. Anyhow, you were saying about your talk with Robson."

"Robson. Yes." Catherine was thoughtful. "The long and short of it is, I've definitely decided to go to New York."

"When?"

"Right after graduation."

"As soon as that?" He looked anxious. "Oh, Catherine." She could see he was struggling to recreate the earlier mood, but that had vanished with the tea. He reached for her hand, this time cautiously across the barricade of Chinese dishes. Catherine dropped her hands to her lap.

"I think it only fair to tell you, I've reached several decisions today. I'm not going to marry you, Michael."

He recoiled as if slapped.

"Where I come from, women wait to be asked before they go ahead and turn down proposals."

"Then don't ask me and I won't have to turn you down."

"Catherine darling, please." He had turned quite pale. "You read my mind, but I can't read yours. Yes, I was going to propose to you tonight, and I will if you'll only hear me out. I don't understand why you find it so distasteful. OK, you're nervous . . . that business with the teapot. But I'm nervous too . . . nervous as hell. I've never proposed to anyone before." He averted his eyes, uncharacteristically flustered. "Even though I've been thinking of it all winter long. It's like when I was in law school and we'd have moot court trials . . . all the brilliant things we used to say. Eloquent! Then all of a sudden you're in a real courtroom for the first time in your life and you can't string two words together. That's how I feel now. Maybe I should have said something long before this, but all those months we were going together . . . I was thinking about it, Catherine, all the time.

Thinking about our future—*our* future, yours and mine biding my time till the right job came along."

"You never said anything—not a single word."

"I thought you understood. You seemed to. When you asked me down for Easter to meet your parents, I naturally assumed it was a trial run. That you wanted to see if they approved of me. Didn't they? Is *that* it?" he asked sharply.

"Oh, they approved. They like you fine. My father thought you were a sound young fellow. And my mother . . . what did she say? Oh, yes, that you were 'absolutely nifty.' "

She smiled. Emily's penchant for dated slang had always amused her.

"Then it's you," Michael persisted. "It's you who don't like me. Although that's not what you led me to believe."

The phrase struck Catherine as one out of a Victorian novel, but on balance she thought it a fair complaint.

"I like you fine, Michael. I always have. You are far and away the most attractive man I've ever met." She swallowed hard twice to hold back the tears and twisted her hands in her lap. Why did it have to be so awful, this end of a dream? Why did it have to be either/or? She didn't want to hurt Michael, loathed the thought of hurting anyone. But she wouldn't, *couldn't* consign her future into his hands. Surely there had to be something between the nothingness of "no" and the total commitment of saying "yes." She dropped her eyes, not daring to see his face.

"If you want," she whispered in a small pained voice, "I will go to bed with you. Yes, I'm perfectly willing if that will make you happy. I don't want to hurt you, Michael, but that's as much as I can give."

"Thanks for nothing," he burst out. He was trembling with anger. "But if all I want is a roll in the hay, I can go down to Scollay Square and get myself a whore. You surprise me, Catherine, you really do. I make an honest offer and you treat me like dirt. Tell me, would you have liked me any better if I were always pawing you, sticking my hand under your skirt like some horny kid? That's the thanks I get for acting like a gentleman. You're amazing!"

His anger was contagious and Catherine got up to go, mustering as much dignity as her bedraggled dress and squeaking shoes allowed. From out of nowhere, Harry Chow whipped across the floor, distress written large on his face.

"Missy, Missy, wait for your dessert. Very special dessert,

very special." Poor Harry! He was far more distraught than even she was. She slid past him and headed towards the door.

"Forget the dessert," Michael said, pushing the waiter away, "and just give me the bill. We already know our fortunes."

Walking north on Madison Avenue from the Roosevelt Hotel, one might easily miss the Marsden-Baker Building. A modest affair of a mere eight stories, it presented a sedate contrast to the glass and steel towers that were burgeoning all about it like tropical vegetation after a rainstorm. A discreet gray shrub in the architectural jungle.

In a business dominated by modernity and flash, Marsden-Baker maintained a dignified aura. For over forty years, the company had prided itself as the doyen of New York's advertising agencies. And dollar for dollar, one of the most successful.

For while Marsden-Baker believed implicitly in the virtue of shouting loud and clear on behalf of its clients, for itself it proclaimed a superior stance, above the more vulgar forms of self-promotion.

Dignity was all, and the lobby's sole admission of company purpose was a discreet panel next to the elevator. There the ignorant might read, in fine Spencerian script, that this was indeed an advertising agency and that its clients—listed in strict alphabetical order—included a dozen of America's greatest corporations.

American Light and Power
The Bakersfield Corporation
Consolidated Motors Inc.

And so on. It was a lineup to warm a stockbroker's heart.

But if the lobby was a grim girdled dowager, the fifth floor was an unbuttoned wanton.

"Hi! I'm Sharon." The girl who met her at the elevator slid her chewing gum from one cheek to the other. "Come with me." The floor was a rabbit warren of aisles and desks and cubbyholes, where young men and the occasional woman babbled and shouted and answered phones. A few were slunk in deep despair.

Being creative, no doubt.

The gum-slinger ushered Catherine into a modest corner office, with LEN J. SAPERSTEIN neatly lettered on the glass of the door.

The lettering was the neatest thing on view, for inside chaos reigned supreme. There were layouts everywhere—tacked to the walls, strewn on the floor, piled high on chairs. *Good Lord, if it looks like this at ten in the morning, what's it like by going-home time?* As for the desk, it was barely visible beneath a battlefield of pencils, books, memos, Ektachromes, overflowing ashtrays, paper cups bearing the dregs of yesterday's coffee. But perhaps its most conspicuous adornment was a pair of crossed legs resting casually on a copy of *Standard Rate & Data.* Legs presumably belonging to Mr. Len J. Saperstein.

The man on the phone was a perfect complement to the disorder that raged around him. Shirt-sleeved, tie loosened and askew, black tousled hair that seemed a stranger to the barber's art.

With a wave of his hand he motioned her to a chair—the only chair unencumbered by layouts—then continued his conversation without a break.

Catherine tried strenuously to avoid giving the impression that she was listening in on his talk. For all she knew it might be confidential stuff—trade secrets, privy information.

But there was no shutting out the voice on the phone.

"Naaaah . . . not De Luca's." The man in the swivel chair leaned back. "I was there last week and the trout was lousy. How about that new Korean joint over on Lex and 40th?"

My first big advertising secret, Catherine thought. *The trout is lousy at De Luca's.*

"Yeah, yeah . . . that's the place." He winked at Catherine. "OK, Max, I'll see you at one."

He hung up and turned around to Catherine, taking her in for a long silent moment.

"Mr. Saperstein?"

"Yeah . . . but no one calls me that except my wife. The name is Len. And you are . . . ?"

"Catherine Chapman?" For a moment she doubted it herself. There was no corresponding flash of recognition. "Personnel told me to report to you?"

"Oh, yeah," he nodded, "the new copy trainee. They told me you were coming up. Now wait a minute, honey, I've got it all here."

He took his feet down from the desk top and began riffling through the litter.

Aaaah, thought Catherine. She knew exactly what was

going to happen. She'd seen it in an old W. C. Fields movie. He would dive into the wreckage and in two seconds flat emerge with exactly the right piece of paper.

But in this instance life did not follow art, and the object of Len's search remained elusive.

"Ah, shit!" Papers were sliding off the edge of the desk, layouts tumbling to the floor while Catherine did her best to retrieve them unobtrusively. It was three or four minutes before he finally unearthed a copy of the green form she'd submitted to personnel.

"OK, Catherine . . . what do they call you—Kate?"

She could see he didn't care for formality.

"OK, Kate, let's see what we've got here." He scanned the form with the swiftness of a speed reader, then looked at it again more carefully.

"It says here you're"—he calculated mentally—"twenty-one. Twenty-one as of today, is that right? Mazeltov." And when she furrowed her brow, he explained. "Mazeltov . . . that's the local dialect for happy birthday, congratulations and 'Look, Ma, no Cossacks.' You know what they say around here—look British, think Yiddish." He returned to the form.

"Well, you were quite the college hotshot, I see. *Summa cum* and all that jazz. What makes you want to join the great world of advertising?"

"Frankly, it was the only job I could find."

"Jesus Christ," he let out a whoop of laughter. "You're honest! We'll have to change all that."

Well, at least he hadn't taken offense, and she had the feeling they were going to get along.

"I suppose I should give you the standard company spiel—Marsden-Baker, The Most Respected Name in Advertising—but I imagine they did that number down in personnel. In the meantime, is there anything particular you want to know?"

"Is there a Marsden or a Baker anywhere?"

"Is there a Santa Claus?"

"I like to think so."

"Don't we all, Kate, but for your information there hasn't been a Marsden in thirty years. They're just too cheap to change the letterheads. There is a Baker in the woodwork someplace; they trot him out once a year for the stockholders' meeting. Rumor has it that he's actually dead and stuffed, but you couldn't prove it by me. I never laid eyes on the man. Anything else?"

"Well, I've always heard that advertising was such a rat race . . ."

"Marsden-Baker a rat race? I wouldn't say that." He gave an affectionate smile. "I'd say it was more of a snake pit."

For all his talk, it was clear he loved the place. She wondered if she would too. He told her about the accounts she'd be working on. Not the glamor end, he took pains to inform her, but all the odd bits and pieces, the scruffy little jobs that were too time-consuming for the better-paid copywriters.

"Trade ads. Catalogues. There's a lot of routine crap. But if you've got the stuff you'll find a way to make it sparkle. Remember, it's the client's money you'll be spending, so don't write any assignment off as too trivial. Now, come on and I'll show you round the office and Sharon will steal you a typewriter from somewhere."

As Kate unfurled herself in all her height, he looked up with mock respect.

"Hey, *bubbele*, you're a big one. The Large Economy Size."

KIT

LOOKING OUT FROM THE BEDROOM OF HER AUNT'S HOUSE IN Hyannis, you could almost believe you were sea-borne.

Michael had suggested the Caribbean, Emily had proffered Paris, but it was Kit who had chosen Hyannis. To lie with her husband on the sands where she had spent so many summers, to share with him the sun that had warmed her childhood—this, Kit felt, would give her life a continuity. A seamless join between childhood and womanhood.

"Should we unpack first?" Michael placed the suitcases inside the door.

First. Kit shivered in delicious anticipation of Michael's *next.* At last, it was going to be something more than kisses. Yet now that the moment was almost upon her she felt flustered, frightened—like an actress insufficiently rehearsed for opening night.

"Yes, let's unpack." She wondered if perhaps Michael were a little nervous, too. But of course he wouldn't be—this veteran, this Harvard lawyer, this man of the world.

They went to their separate suitcases, Kit drawing from hers the delicate confection—all white silk and *broderie anglaise*—that her mother had deemed an essential part of her trousseau.

"I guess this is the moment," Kit giggled, "when I say excuse me while I slip into something more comfortable."

"I guess it is," Michael smiled.

She went into the bathroom and put it on. A far cry from balbriggan pyjamas, she thought, smoothing out the folds. Now wash your face, brush your teeth.

She washed. She brushed. Then brushed her teeth again.

Kit, you're dawdling, the inner voice reproved. She had a swift vision of Michael beyond the door—all love and impatience and masculine desire—while she stood there brushing her teeth like a robot and wondering what in God's name she was so afraid of. At least it wouldn't be a blood-stained wedding night. A fall from a horse at Miss Ellery's had seen to that long ago. And yet . . .

"Darling, are you all right?" She heard his soft rap on the bathroom door.

"Just brushing my teeth. I'll be out in a minute."

"I thought you'd fallen asleep in there."

She brushed her teeth a third and final time, then resolutely stepped back into the bedroom. He was lying in bed, his face pale in the moonlight, his nakedness covered only by a sheet.

"Do you like it?" She came and sat beside him on the bed.

"Like it!" he exclaimed.

"I mean my nightgown."

His answer was to slip his hand beneath one silken strap and slide it down across her body. "Best of all," he said, as his hand touched her breast. She felt her nipple go suddenly, startlingly rigid. "Best of all, I love what's beneath it. Now take it off and come into bed."

She stood up and peeled the silk from her shoulders. It fell to the floor in a gentle whoosh, leaving her exposed, defenseless, vulnerable as she had never felt before. Gingerly she climbed into bed beside him, gingerly placed her fingers on his cheek.

"Well, here we are, Michael."

He kissed her fingers; then, taking her hand in his, he drew it down the length of his body—over the firm chin, along the tensely muscled throat, past his smooth, nearly hairless, chest, over that lean, taut stomach, splaying her fingers out and suddenly wrapping them around . . . this object. This large, thick, heaving bundle of muscle that seemed to lead a life of its own.

"Hold me," he said.

Involuntarily she recoiled, her fingers paralyzed.

"Don't be frightened, Kit. It's not going to bite you."

Oh, God, Kit thought, trembling, I've hurt his feelings. Then, steeling herself to his desire, she reformed her hand around that strange and throbbing spear of flesh, while her mouth sought his for more familiar reassurance.

He returned her kiss with an intensity that left her breathless. Then, suddenly, he was on top of her, heaving, sweating —Michael, who never sweated!—crushing her tentative hand between their bodies. Should she hold onto him still? Let him go?

"Put me in you. Put me in you quick."

If only she could breathe! If only she could rescue her hand from this weight that was pinioning her into immobility. She was hanging on to "the object" like a shipwreck survivor hanging on to the corner of a raft. Groping. Moving it. Trying to place it into that space between her legs that had been there all her life yet now seemed to have vanished. Yet it had to be there. It *had* to.

"You're breaking my hand, Michael."

"Put me in you," he was gasping. "For God's sake!"

He suddenly raised himself to his knees and with one great heaving thrust found his way into her body.

It was all over in a minute. In one vast sticky shudder. It hadn't hurt. Hadn't horrified. Had been, in its way, almost exciting.

"I'm sorry, darling." Michael slowly pulled out and rolled away. But why was he sorry? She could tell from his stickiness that he had "come," as Phyllis used to say. And wasn't that what it was all about?

"You were fine, Michael," she said guiltily. "You made me very happy." And her reward was to be taken in his arms, to be kissed with a tenderness that was indeed consummation. That's what she loved best, she thought. His tenderness. Five minutes later he was asleep on her breast.

Lying there, listening to his breathing—not stertorous now, but as gentle as the lapping of the waves beyond, Kit thought: So this is love. Not the horror of the Victorian moralists. Not the mind-rending rapture of sensational fiction. But something in between.

She had been stiff. Frightened. She would be better next time. But when all was said and done, perhaps the very best part was knowing that this handsome man—never more handsome than now—this sensitive man ("I'm sorry, darling") was hers forever.

Marriage didn't live up to Kit's expectations. It surpassed them.

It was more absorbing than any English lit class, more fun than drinking cocoa in the dorms. Gone forever was the tyranny of Saturday nights—boring dates or, even worse, being dateless. Never again would she have to submit to the scrutiny of the fraternity stag lines—a duty she had found more painful than pleasurable. *For this relief, much thanks.*

Wisely, Michael had decided to postpone buying their own home, though this had undeniably been the purpose of Spencer's wedding present, and even though Kit had spent the summer of their engagement combing the real estate ads.

But Michael had been right, of course. He always was. After all, there were only the two of them, and it made a lot more sense to bank the check and let it earn interest against the day when they would own their own home. A *nice* one. He had promised her *that*.

In the meantime, he had found them an apartment that combined ample room with a moderate rent and was only a twenty-minute ride to his office.

It was in a district Kit remembered from their canvassing days as a stronghold of Michael's Dev Dems. Not a slum exactly—that might have proved exciting—but a drab working-class area devoid equally of elegance and vigor. Long treeless avenues down which streetcars rumbled; faded yellow-brick buildings with hideous fire escapes; shops that specialized in outsized dresses and discount children's wear. There was nothing within to tempt the browser.

Kit, whose idea of apartment living was something small but fashionable in the Beacon Hill area, found it hard to mask her disappointment. *Anyhow, it's only for a year or two.* And as Michael pointed out, once you climbed the four flights, you were in your own private realm. That was all that mattered, wasn't it?

Like the blue-plate special at the Canton Palace, it was big and it was cheap.

The living room was spacious and caught the morning sun. The bedroom, though dark, was rich in closets.

(When Kit opened the closet door, the sight of her old familiar wardrobe nuzzling up against his jackets filled her with a delicious sense of intimacy. It was almost like lovemaking.) And there were two extra rooms besides.

They painted everything white from floorboards to ceilings. Brightened the walls with cheap Indian mirrors and a print of Rousseau's "Sleeping Gypsy," a strange picture of a dreaming woman and a lion. Something in that picture haunted her.

Furniture, of course, was the problem, and after much hesitation they agreed to splurge on a few good pieces. They bought two Herman Miller chairs, as advertised in the *New Yorker,* and one of Michael's clients got them a discount on a bedroom set.

For the rest, they fell back on the Salvation Army. Like their dreamhouse, the furniture could wait.

Then, of course, there were the wedding presents, which Michael had pronounced "quite a haul."

Waterford crystal, Derbyshire tea sets, silver candlesticks and chicken shears and pickle forks.

They used a few of the more practical gifts and packed the rest of them back into tissue. *Against the day.*

Like any old apartment, the place had its fair share of quirks, and some took a deal of getting used to.

There were cracks in the ceiling and a number of broken window sashes which excluded fresh air though not city grime. The toilet flushed with a roar that could waken the dead and the tank took a full five minutes to refill. But the worst offender was the kitchen linoleum.

"My God, I've never seen anything so hideous," Kit had cried on first view, and even the usually imperturbable Michael had paled. It writhed beneath your feet like a sea of snakes, a nightmare from a paranoiac brain. Ostensibly, the pattern was one of cabbage roses. Giant cabbage roses in colors nature never conceived—vomitous mauves and pinks and wounded purples.

Kit talked and talked about replacing it; she had seen some handsome vinyl tile in *House and Garden.* But Michael was adamant. It was throwing money out the window, he said.

"I hate it as much as you do, puss, but look at it this way. Any tile we put in becomes the property of the landlord; it's like giving him a hundred-dollar present. Learn to live with it, just for awhile. It's not as if we'll stay here forever."

Kit did better than learn to live with it. She learned to laugh at it. It reminded her of a story she'd read in boarding school by a writer named Charlotte Gilman. "The Yellow Wallpaper" was the story's title, and it chronicled the breakdown of a woman who envisioned monsters lurking in the patterns of her bedroom wall. It was a horror story. Kit managed to track it down in the local library and brought it home for Michael to read.

They'd both wound up rolling with laughter.

After that, the linoleum became a private joke. They would consult it, like oracles divining entrails, in search of insights buried in the scuff marks, fantastic likenesses amid the wealth of cabbage roses.

There was one giant rose with bits of backing showing through that Michael swore looked just like Spencer frowning. And so it did, if you squinted at it crosswise. There were extinct brontosauri, demons out of Hieronymous Bosch and even Caribbean sunsets waiting to be discovered by imaginative eyes.

Still, what did linoleum matter? Or noisy toilets? Or Woolworth curtains? Being poor was almost fun provided it was temporary, and most of their friends lived in no grander style.

What *did* matter was that the place was theirs. *Hers.* And that she herself was now somebody else.

It struck her like a revelation, the day she put her name on the lease. "Sign here please, Mrs. Matheson."

Mrs. Matheson!

How extraordinary it was—writing down *Catherine Matheson* on an official legal document. For a moment, she had felt like a forger. Or an actress signing a stage name in an autograph book.

Yet she was . . . she was indeed Mrs. Michael Matheson.

Her notepaper proclaimed it. The man in Sam's deli confirmed it. The white-on-black stencil on their mailbox proved it conclusively.

Nonetheless it took her several months to get used to her new identity, and when she did, she had the distinct sensation of coming to grips with real life. Finally.

She would see young women on the street—secretaries scurrying to work, schoolgirls rushing to classes as she herself had done only last spring. She would see them and she would think: *I am Mrs. Michael Matheson. The former Catherine*

Chapman. I am a married woman. A respectable married woman, knowledgeable and mature. Truth to tell, she felt mildly patronizing toward those young women she now considered her juniors. As though a handful of words muttered in Trinity Church had in some wondrous way endowed her with all the ancient wisdom of her sex.

It was a new feeling.

Also new was the sense of unbounded freedom.

"So much for those girls who look on marriage as enslavement," Kit snapped her fingers mentally. It was nonsense. Sour grapes. Marriage was nothing of the sort. In fact, it was total liberation.

For the first time in twenty-one years, she was free. Free of parents and classrooms and curfews and exams. Free to shop in the morning, nap in the afternoon, or to reverse the order should she choose. She could cut up her day and slice it any way she wanted, provided she was home in time for Michael's dinner.

At first, she kept up with a handful of classmates, the girls who'd stayed on in Boston to do their graduate work.

She spent some long afternoons with her friend Helen Ince, who had chosen for her thesis an analysis of Methodist symbolism in the works of George Eliot. It was interesting enough, but only to a point, and one day when Helen had gone on interminably about the deeper significance of *Silas Marner,* Kit blurted out "Oh, Helen, what on earth does it matter?"

The two parted in chill formality, each privately convinced *hers* was the superior course.

All the way home on the subway, Kit could think of nothing except how tactless she'd been. Still! Who needs it! Who needs those fruitless and interminable discussions? The dualism of Dostoievski . . . the Methodism of Eliot . . . was Nietzsche a good guy or a bad guy? *And how many angels can dance on the head of a pin, please?* It was all so . . . so sophomoric!

Yet later that night she cried in Michael's arms. "I feel awful, darling. I behaved like such a philistine."

Michael's answer was to wind himself around her. "I think, pure and simple, your little bluestocking friend is just jealous."

Jealous. Michael was probably right. For though Kit was now a marriage veteran of almost two months standing, she could still hardly conceal her pride of going out on Michael's arm, that irrepressible glow of ownership. A few nights previous at a party for some local Dev Dems where Michael was making a brief address, the woman sitting next to Kit nudged her and whispered "Who is that gorgeous guy up there?" and Kit had to bite back a smile.

"That's my husband."

"Oohh," her neighbor sighed in disappointment. "Aren't *you* the lucky one."

It was flattering to be an object of envy, to know she had effortlessly won a prize that other women hungered for. And even more flattering was the pride he took in her.

Michael loved it when she'd meet him at the office, or come down to watch him in court. "This is my wife," he'd beam, introducing her to everyone as though she were a visiting celebrity. Or when a client called with some nocturnal crisis and Michael would say: "I can't take care of it tonight. You'll have to wait until morning. After all, I'm a married man now."

With every week that passed, his lovemaking had become less urgent, more tender; the initial panic of her wedding night was slipping into ancient history. And if it wasn't quite the transport she had read about in D. H. Lawrence, it was *nice*. Quite nice enough for her.

Now and then she regretted her diminishing relations with the more academic of her friends, but their lives had diverged and, on the whole, she preferred the company of other married women.

Not that Kit intended to be your dumb bunny housewife. Absolutely not! There was nothing in the marriage vows that said you have to love, honor and become a vegetable. Besides, that would be so boring for Michael.

No, ma'am! She was going to utilize her leisure to the full, broaden her horizons in meaningful ways. She'd read Balzac in the French and keep abreast of the Boston galleries, and it wouldn't hurt to learn a thing or two about the law.

That certainly was all Michael talked about.

He usually got home about seven in the evening, sometimes happy and excited, occasionally a trifle depressed, but always eager to relive with her the triumphs and indignities of his day.

His practice was confined exclusively to criminal law. A few of his cases were court referrals, but increasingly he was winning a private clientele. In those parts of Boston where crime bred and flourished, Michael was gradually becoming known as a good man to have on your side. Most of his clients were poor—who else robs candy stores?—but even the poor have families. There was often a sister somewhere with savings in the bank or a mother willing to take out a second mortgage. Surprising how many would scrounge and scrape to provide a "private attorney" for a kinsman. A "private attorney." In certain parts of Boston, it was as much a status symbol as a Cadillac.

Night after night, Michael would bring his cases home, usually accompanied by paperwork. He had a way of making his clients come alive to Kit: their sufferings, the grimness of their environment, their troubles with everything from wives to narcotics. There was no question in Kit's mind but that Michael's people were far more dramatic than George Eliot's.

His stories ranged from the trivial to the violent, from the ludicrously comic to the cosmically lurid.

There were outrageous accounts of private vendettas: "So when the landlady cut off his heat, he decided to poison her dog."

Tales from the pathetic roster of petty crime: "She claimed she had no idea how this three-pound sirloin got weighed in with her bag of potatoes. Naturally, she's willing to pay, but that's after the fact, and Ace Market is dead set on prosecuting."

And sometimes stories so horrendous that Kit could barely credit their existence outside the pages of Greek mythology: "So he went out and had a few. More than a few would be my guess. 'Cause when he got back he grabbed this carving knife and stabbed her eighteen times. Heart. Liver. Kidneys. The works. And then, in case she wasn't quite dead enough, he strangled her with a stocking. Claims he doesn't remember a thing."

His clients were inevitably poor and often black. Rather oftener than Kit in her harried liberalism wished to believe. And they almost always were "guilty as hell."

That their troubles brewed and festered in Boston— Boston, the hub of the universe, the Athens of America, the city that had been the center of her world for nearly ten years—that there existed a Boston so different from her own never failed to astonish her. She was fascinated by the glimpses Michael afforded her into this savage and alien city—a city where people robbed and raped and even murdered with the regularity of the Friday afternoon concerts at Symphony Hall. Sometimes she felt like a cork bobbling on top of a cesspool.

"But doesn't it bother you when you know your clients are guilty?" she asked one night over takeout pizzas.

"First of all," he said, raising his index finger, "my clients are always innocent. Innocent," he repeated "until the judge or the jury deem otherwise. I mean, if this guy tells me he was standing on the corner of Essex and Washington thinking up new ways to help crippled children and—whoosh—suddenly this five-ounce packet of heroin falls out of a passing airplane and by some freak of fate lands in his inside vest pocket . . . well, who am I to call him a liar?"

"In the second place"—up popped another finger—"even admitting my client isn't Little Lord Fauntleroy, he has every right to a good defense. Let's face it, most of the people I deal with have been losers from the day they were born. Everybody's lined up against them. The courts, the cops, the juries, even the school system. So if I don't at least make a pretense of believing what these poor slobs tell me, then who in God's name will? Yeah, I stretch my credulity every now and then. I wouldn't be able to live with myself otherwise."

"And in the third place"—he raised another finger to form the Boy Scout high sign—"in the third place, they usually cop a plea."

It was Michael's greatest grievance that there was so little courtroom work, for he relished it and prepared for it meticulously. But only a tiny handful of cases ever came to trial. Most were settled by plea-bargaining.

Michael would sit in a room with his opposite number, an equally young assistant district attorney, and the two men would haggle like Arabs in a bazaar. Only the merchandise was not rugs but prison sentences.

"Will you take five years?" the ADA might ask, and Michael would try to get it down to two. Then, perhaps, after a few minutes of bargaining, they'd settle on maybe three. Three years—minus waiting time already served—for stabbing a wife or shooting up a liquor store.

Thus murderers pled guilty to manslaughter, muggers to simple assault, heroin dealers to possession of narcotics, prostitutes to vagrancy and loitering.

It was like a discount store, Michael explained, with items marked down from $5 to $2.98.

Most clients were urged to plea guilty.

"But what if they're innocent?" Kit had asked, although she gathered very few of them were.

"Well, if I'm convinced that we really have a case, then maybe I'll hold out for trial."

"Maybe?"

Maybe. Michael explained. There was a shortage of judges, a shortage of courts, a shortage of jails, a shortage of everything but criminals.

"For instance. Say I have a client who's up for a crime that might get him two to five on conviction. For the sake of argument, say my client is innocent, a case of mistaken identity. I may be able to prove it in court, I may not. I won't know until trial. Now let's suppose my client can't make bond. He's going to have to wait in jail until his case comes up on the calendar. He could easily spend six months in jail, maybe more, maybe even a year. In which case, he'd probably be better off pleading guilty to a lesser charge where he could be out on the street in a couple of months."

"But that's so unjust!"

"We're talking about law, Kit, not about justice."

"In other words . . ." Kit chewed the idea, and the more she chewed it, the more she found it indigestible. "In other words, your client would be better off pleading guilty to something he didn't do than taking his chances in court."

"That's about it."

"And what would you advise in that situation?"

"Aah," he sighed, "that's the sixty-four-dollar question. We live in an imperfect world."

Only later did she remember he hadn't really answered her question.

Kit made the transition easily, almost seamlessly, from the campus to the noisier milieu of ambitious young lawyers and their often equally ambitious wives.

The law, she discovered, was a gregarious profession, and weekend evenings were spent with Michael's colleagues and counterparts in an informal round of cheap meals.

Whatever the setting, the talk was always shop. Not abstract obeisance to ethics and justice (that didn't go down well with Italian food), but practical, good-natured banter about fees and the problems of collecting them. About which of the local judges were "pussycats," which were sons of bitches. About who was going to work where for how much. And, ultimately, about their own careers careers careers.

Kit didn't mind; in fact, she drank it all up, for the men were amusing and the wives, too, as a rule, bright and well-educated. And if the chatter wasn't exactly elevating, at least it was lively and unpretentious.

Of the dozen or so couples who formed the basis of their social life, Kit was most drawn to Tim and Marian Keegan. It was Tim who'd brought Michael into the firm. They shared an office and swapped cases back and forth. And Tim alone—of all the lawyers she'd met—seemed to share Michael's sense of commitment. He could use the word "justice" without a laugh or a snicker and unlike the others—Michael included—rarely talked about personal ambition and never, she noticed, about money.

"He doesn't have to," Michael commented when she pointed this out. "His father's a Federal judge. Yup, Old Man Keegan's connections go all the way down to Washington. And as for money, Marian's got a bundle. Believe me, honey, all Tim has to say is 'I want' and Tim's going to get."

But even Michael's barely concealed envy detracted not one whit from her admiration of Tim's distinctive blend of urban toughness coupled with an almost romantic idealism.

And her husband agreed with her that Tim represented the Boston Irish at their best. In some ways he reminded her of Senator John F. Kennedy, and indeed there was a link, since the Kennedy and Keegan families knew each other from way back when. There were resemblances, too, in energy, in tension, in speech patterns (Boston-cum-Harvard) between the Senator and the brisk young lawyer. The resemblance stopped short of the physical, however, for Tim was slim and small-boned, with hair as dark as Li'l Abner's.

They dined together at least once a week, either at the Keegans's place in Brookline or at the Mathesons'. And it was over dinner at the Keegans' one evening that Tim confided his earliest ambition had been the priesthood. The moment he said it, Kit could picture him, dog-collared and cassock skirts swinging, making the rounds in a Dorchester parish, playing basketball with neighborhood kids. He would have been that kind of priest.

He gave up the idea before he turned twelve when he

realized "I couldn't bring myself to believe in original sin. And anyhow, so little sin is really original."

"Don't you believe a word of it," Marian interjected.

"About my wanting to be a priest?" Tim feigned indignation.

"About why he gave it up. The real reason is that Tim couldn't face a lifetime of celibacy. Father Timothy Keegan," she put her hand on her heart, "the scourge of the Radcliffe virgins."

"There are no virgins at Radcliffe," Tim countered, and they all had a modest laugh.

Virgin scourge or not, he was delightful company. And so, in her own arch way, was Marian. Four years older than Kit and with an M.A. in history, she was neither Irish nor Catholic. Simply Boston, with her own wry twist. Kit had vague memories of seeing her during her own first year at Miss Ellery's, when Marian had been the star of the Senior Debating Society. She'd spoken softly, Kit recalled, and carried a big vocabulary.

She was tall, mousey-haired and painfully thin—at first glance the most unprepossessing of women. Michael often wondered what Tim had seen in her, pronouncing her "plain as a sack of Maine potatoes." Kit disagreed. For the eyes that peered out behind the owlish glasses missed nothing of import; the drawling "society voice" talked a great deal of sense. Plain she may have been, but Marian was shrewd and kind, a rare combination. She took an immediate liking to Kit and the two women spent many afternoons together.

And so the first months of marriage passed, full of pleasant days and sociable evenings. The only cloud that speckled the marital horizon was the question of Kit's housekeeping. Or lack of it, as Michael sometimes implied.

No doubt about it. Emily had set a poor example with her jigsaw puzzles, her twice-weekly bridge parties and her reliance on the skills of Mrs. Antonelli. Kit could recall no situation that required her mother to do anything more strenuous than tick off the laundry list or help with the hors d'oeuvres.

Nor had Miss Ellery's rushed into the breach to fill the gaps that Emily had left. The domestic arts were a low priority item; and beneath this neglect lay the unspoken premise that while Ellery girls would eventually marry, they would also have kitchen help. Somewhere along the line, Kit had learned to make a passable white sauce, but to what end she could never determine.

Michael was not a gourmet. He always ordered the same dishes at restaurants, downing them quickly with more interest in the talk than the food. Nonetheless, within a couple of months he had tired of Kit's slapdash dinners. The takeout Chinese, the frozen pizzas, the cold cuts and salads from the deli downstairs.

"We must be the only family in Massachusetts," he grumbled one night, "to eat store-bought potato salad with antique silver." There was no note of whimsy in his voice.

"Which do you object to," Kit asked mildly, "the potato salad or the antique silver?"

"Both, as a matter of fact. In the first place," he said picking up the massive rattail fork and examining it closely for scratches, "this is very handsome stuff—I suppose you'd call it heirloom—but it's not for everyday use. I'm sure your mother doesn't bring out the best silver every night in the week for ordinary family meals."

Kit was not so sure, but she said nothing. And Emily always had candles on the table.

"I mean," Michael pursued, "this is the sort of thing you truck out for guests, and someday, when we have our own home and do proper entertaining, it'll impress the hell out of them. But you don't have to impress *me*. So why don't you go down to the five and ten tomorrow and buy a few bucks' worth of stainless. Let's save this for best from now on."

Kit assented. That was the first place. She hoped he'd forget about the second—the potato salad—but of course he didn't. Even before they were married, she had noted his passion for putting things in order, making lists, organizing arguments one-two-three, so they proceeded with the relentlessness of red-ant armies on the march.

"In the second place, I can't believe you're so busy these days you don't have time to shop for and cook a proper meal. I'm curious . . . what do you do with yourself all day? What did you do today, for instance?"

"Today . . . well!" She had the uneasy feeling he was cross-examining her, and she didn't care for it one little bit. Still, he *did* put in such long hours; she perceived the justice of his argument.

"Well, today I went to the Fine Arts with Marian; they had

a lecture on Whistler . . . very interesting. Then we walked over to Brigham's and had some ice cream and . . . I don't know, the afternoon just disappeared. I'm sorry, Michael." She came and put her arms around his shoulders. "You're absolutely right, of course, and I *will* make an effort, I promise. It's just all . . . so new to me."

"I know it is, honey." He took her hand and squeezed it. "But you can learn. Good God, if you can conjugate French subjunctives, you can learn to make an occasional pot roast, too."

The next morning she went down to Liggett's and ravaged the shelves for paperback cookbooks. *A Hundred Ways to Make Hamburger. Casseroles for Two.* Peg Bracken. Fanny Farmer. Even a book on Chinese food.

For the next few months she tried her hand at all sorts of odd combinations. Quick 'n easy chili. Tuna with cashews. Meatloaf surprise. When Michael liked one, she'd mark it with a little red tick, to remind herself to make it again. Some were fair, a few surprisingly good, and she managed to avoid complete disaster.

After a while she found it almost enjoyable, although if you had told her that in another ten years she'd be considered one of the best cooks on the North Shore, she would have laughed in your face.

Cleaning was another matter. She didn't like it and knew she could never bring herself to like it. In her heart of hearts, she considered herself a cut above it.

Had she not done French, Greek, read Cicero in Latin? Did this not excuse her from scrubbing toilet bowls?

Even less onerous chores—bedmaking, dishwashing, vacuuming—filled her with resentment. She would rather paint the whole place again from top to bottom than recommence the tiresome round of daily housework. Washing. Dusting. They were useless jobs that left her with no sense of accomplishment. She placed it on a par with the Supreme Court's definition of pornography: work of no redeeming social or artistic value.

Still there was no question; it had to be done. Michael was . . . well, a bit of a stickler. He was always straightening, sorting, lining things up. Always emptying ashtrays with a great show of conspicuousness, for she smoked and he did not.

And there was no conceivable fit of passion that would get him into bed before he had hung up his jacket, folded his trousers and put his dirty clothes in the hamper.

"You have to expect to put up with personal idiosyncracies," Emily had warned her daughter a week before the wedding. It was the closest Mrs. Chapman ever came to the transmission of mother-daughter lore the occasion traditionally demanded.

And while other women might alert their daughters to such potential hazards as wife-beating or in-laws or anal sex, Emily had limited her remarks to personal idiosyncracies. "All men have them, dear—even your father. It's simply a question of making the adjustment."

Well, "personal idiosyncracies" covered the spectrum and Kit, forewarned, had come to recognize Michael's.

A passion for order. Certainly. It was at once his strength and his weakness. And while she acknowledged the nuisance value to her own life—this endless fussing over ashtrays—she suspected it formed the basis of such success as would come her husband's way.

On balance, she wasn't sure if this was "personal idiosyncracy" at all. Perhaps the idiosyncracy was on her part. A decided inaptitude for domestic work; a self-indulgence, a sloppiness towards those daily routines that millions of other women took in their stride.

His concern about fitness.

That, Kit conceded, might be a wee bit idiosyncratic. The first morning of their honeymoon she had been astonished to see him leap out of bed, don his shorts and begin an exacting regimen of push-ups and knee-bends. She had been uncouth enough to laugh—more out of surprise than any sense of ridicule—and he had taken her laughter with good nature.

"Go ahead, laugh. I don't mind," he twitted her, "although it wouldn't be a half-bad idea if you joined me." And afterward, panting slightly, he came back to bed. "Put your hand on my stomach," he urged her. She did. It was flat and hard as an athlete's. "You know, I weigh exactly the same as I did when I was in Korea. Not a pound more. When we get back home, you take a look around at all the lawyers and businessmen. Just look at 'em, all piling on the pounds. Lining up to see who'll be the first in the heart-attack sweepstakes. Heart. Yup, it's the number one killer among men with sedentary jobs." Then, thinking he might have alarmed her—"Anyhow, you wouldn't like it if I went all flabby."

She couldn't picture Michael flabby, and if he took great pride in his body, well, why not? It was justified. It was a beautiful body. Lean, firm, slim-hipped, long-legged; and though she still suppressed the occasional smile when he embarked on this morning ritual, she enjoyed lying in bed watching him, too. He moved with an athlete's grace, an artist's economy. There was a satisfaction in watching the rhythmic interplay of muscle, feeling the elasticity of healthy flesh.

Then there was his shaving routine.

He disavowed electric razors, even safety razors. Wrote them off as gadgets. When he was sixteen, his father had given him a pair of old-fashioned straight razors, bone-handled and sharp as surgical knives. Michael used them still. That, too, was a ritual. The thick bristle shaving brush, the white china soap mug (not for Michael the aerosol can), followed with a brisk splash of witch hazel.

If that was an idiosyncracy, it was a tolerable one, and Kit soon came to love the smell of witch hazel.

As for the rest, he was singularly free of those minor habits which she presumed could drive the most adoring wife to distraction. He didn't snore or snuffle or pick his teeth or crack his knuckles; and the assiduous use of mouthwash made his breath as sweet as a field of cloves. Tot it all up—the pros and cons—and he was decidedly a husband one might be proud of. And Kit was proud.

Her sole anxiety was in herself, for Michael was determined that they live on his income. Was she pulling her own weight? Was she goofing off? Was she fiddling while Michael burned and achieved?

"Maybe I should go back to school," she said, their first married New Year's Eve. "Maybe I should go back and get my Masters."

"In what?"

"Oh, English, I suppose. Or maybe Romance languages. What do you think, darling?"

He looked at her quizzically. "I think it's a waste. What's the matter, have you been talking to Marian?"

"Oh, no. It's just, here I am almost twenty-two, and I bet I couldn't even get work as a salesgirl."

"And getting a Master's in Romance languages is going to equip you for a job as a salesgirl? Assuming, of course, that that's the kind of career you really have in mind."

"But I feel so useless."

"Not useless to me. If you're really serious about a job, that's OK with me. But not selling girdles in Filene's basement. If you want to do something practical, go to secretarial school. Learn some typing, shorthand, maybe bookkeeping."

She must have pulled a face, for he continued—"And don't feel you're coming down in the world. My bet is that if you went to Katherine Gibbs, you'd find half your graduating class there doing just that. The more I think of it, the more it makes sense. Suppose something happened to me . . ."

"Oh, Michael!"

"Well, suppose it did; at least you'd have something to fall back on."

She promised she would think about it and did all that January. Thought about it quite positively, in fact. But when the time came for spring registration, things had changed. It seemed pointless, for Kit had learned she was pregnant.

KATE

WITHIN TWO WEEKS OF SETTLING IN AT MARSDEN, SHE MADE HER first office friend. His name was Barry Warden, and she suspected he was a homosexual. But thus far, anyway, he was the only one of her colleagues to seek her out.

"Man does not live by cottage cheese alone," he said when he caught her lunching at her desk. "Or woman either, for that matter." He invited her to join him at the Champlain the following day. They soon fell into the habit of lunching weekly and after the first time always went Dutch.

Barry was, as he delighted in putting it, the sole "WASP" in an art department so loaded with Italians that it was known as the Marsden Mafia. Very early on, he made it clear to Kate that he was an inveterate and unrepentant homosexual. That bothered her briefly, but she then brushed it aside, for she enjoyed the affability of their lunches. Indeed, she sometimes wondered if his sexual preference didn't make their friendship easier, for she could relax in his company, drop her guard. There would be no wandering hand, no kneesies under the table. Just talk, at which Barry excelled.

He was amusing, pleasant and delightfully acerbic.

He was also extremely useful.

For to Barry, the eight floors of Marsden Baker represented the world in microcosm. He was fascinated by the play of office politics, observing it with the eye of a scientist who has discovered strange life forms in his microscope. Sometimes he had the cunning of a general sounding out the disposition of the enemy.

He showed Kate the ropes, steered her away from the pitfalls. Became her friend, her confidante, her guide.

"It's a pyramid," he explained on their first lunch together as she sipped her first genuine dry martini. "Just a great big beautiful pyramid."

"And I'm at the bottom, I suppose."

"Well, you know," he said chewing his olive thoughtfully, "the bottom's not a bad place to be. It could be worse—you could be outside the pyramid completely. Like the secretaries, the kids in traffic. Completely out of it. Nobodies going nowhere. By the way," he added, "don't ever let on that you take shorthand."

"I don't, but I was thinking of learning, maybe taking a course at Katherine Gibbs . . ."

"Well, forget it!" He was emphatic. "Don't give 'em any excuse to dump you out into the typing pool. If you do, you'll never be heard from again. And for Chrissakes, don't socialize with the typists, not even if they're earning more than you."

Kate was confused. She couldn't see the harm in sharing an occasional gossip session with Sharon.

"Like the other day." It was an accusation. "I saw you getting coffee for Len. *Don't do it.* Because the moment you start running and fetching, you've labeled yourself as just another 'girl.' Let Sharon do it. Let the girl get his coffee. You stay where you are in the pyramid."

"OK," Kate acknowledged, "point taken. It's better at the bottom of the pyramid than it is being out in the cold. Where do you figure in the scale of things? Are you on the bottom with me?"

"Just one step up, say level number two, along with most of the other art directors. The general wisdom is that if a man can draw, he's functionally incapable of reading and writing. At least in this place. On the next step up—level three—are guys like Len Saperstein, Mark Pritchard. The group heads, the senior art directors, most of the account executives. The twenty, thirty-grand-a-year bracket. After that the field really narrows."

"Level four?"

"Level four: the heavy money. Account supervisors, associate creative directors. At that level nearly everyone's a vice president. And beyond that, you're on the summit with the Gods. Just two of 'em. Don Farebrother and Gully."

"Gully?" She'd heard of Farebrother, naturally; he was the company president, but the other name was news to her.

"My God," Barry shook his head in dismay. "You mean you've been here two whole weeks and haven't learned to tremble at the name of F.P. Gulliver? 'Look upon my works, ye mighty, and despair.'"

Now the name was vaguely familiar. "Mr. Gulliver is the creative director . . . isn't he? What does the F.P. stand for?"

"Fucking Prick, that's my guess."

Kate winced at the language, although everyone at the agency seemed to use it. Not her. Not ever. Not if she worked there a thousand years.

But if Barry had observed her discomfort, it didn't seem to bother him, for he repeated the epithet with gusto.

"Fucking Prick . . . as you'll probably one day learn to your grief. In the meantime, should you have the misfortune to meet him, call him Gully. Honest Hully Gully—that's his office persona. You know," he added thoughtfully, "that he's the guy who fixed the *Get Rich Quick Show*."

No! Kate was stunned. Barry had just referred to the greatest scandal that had ever hit television. For over four years, the *Get Rich Quick* show had been the hottest program on network television. The audience ratings ran into multiple millions. Half the nation stayed home on Saturday night, forgoing movies and dances and bridge parties for the greatest human drama on the box.

The show operated on the simplest of premises: double or nothing. The jackpots ran into hundred of thousands.

But it was more than the money—it was the agony, the sheer agony of the contestants that riveted all those millions of viewers.

Would the little tailor from the Lower East Side take the $50,000 and run? It was more than he'd earned in his lifetime. Or would he risk all—every last penny—on his knowledge of Greek mythology?

For it was the contrast between the contestants and their chosen subjects that gave the show its ultimate crunch. There had been a farmer from Idaho whose hobby was nuclear physics. A grandmother from El Paso with a knowledge of boxing statistics that verged on the encyclopedic.

It was almost too good to be true.

Then last winter, the dam had burst. A kindergarten teacher from Lowell, in a paroxysm of New England guilt, confessed all to a *New York Times* reporter. Admitted that she had been fed correct answers days in advance. Had been coached in every lip-biting, handkerchief-twisting gesture that had wrung the hearts of the millions. Ironically, her subject had been gangster movies.

And now here was Barry telling Kate that the man in the eighth floor office had engineered the nation's biggest swindle.

"Well, if it were true—and no one has proved it—he couldn't be holding down such a big job. What respectable agency would want to hire him? Why, the man would be a leper on Madison Avenue."

"A leper!" Barry laughed. "You must be kidding. The son of a bitch is the biggest hero since Rin Tin Tin. Just think of it, Kate, to have the vision—the *genius*—to fix the biggest goddamn show on television. Even I have to hand it to him. That's class. Oh, sure, he quit the agency until it simmered down, but that was just for form's sake. And once it blew over, Marsden couldn't hire him back fast enough."

Kate threw up her hands in disgust. "And they say politics is bad. Wow! A couple of years ago I did some canvassing in Boston, and I thought that what went on *there* was pretty slimy."

Barry's ears pricked up.

"Canvassing for whom? For Stevenson? Well, don't drop that little bombshell at the office. You know Marsden isn't exactly the vanguard of progress. In fact, there are a lot of subjects it's wise to steer clear of if they ever come up for general discussion."

"Such as . . . ?"

"Such as Stevenson . . . advertising ethics . . . civil rights. You get the picture."

She did. And remarked now that he'd mentioned it, she had never seen a Negro at Marsden. "Not even in the mailroom."

"No, and you never will," Barry confirmed. "You know, according to Gully, the niggers are coming out of the woodwork and planning to take over Madison Avenue. He

figures Marsden will be the last white stronghold, even if he
has to personally machine-gun them down."

"Oh, Barry, it can't be that bad. Look . . . there are so
many Italians at the agency and . . . um, Jewish people too.
Len, Jack Silverman, lots of 'em. So how can you say they
discriminate?"

"Ah, but you see," he explained, "they're just toilers in
the vineyard. Peasants. Believe you me, when it gets to
the top—vice presidents and all that jazz—the sign is out.
WASPS only."

Kate pondered that a bit.

"And men only?"

"So far, yes," Barry conceded, "but that could change. On
the whole, I'd say a woman has a better chance than a Jew.
And as for Negroes—forget it. Lincoln never lived."

"Wow," came the rejoinder. "You make it sound like a
police state."

And in its way, Marsden-Baker was a police state.

A benign police state, to be sure, peopled with well-paid
and largely happy prisoners. Yet even granted the peculiar
nature of the advertising business, Marsden-Baker had cultivated some eccentricities all its own.

What kind of advertising agency would we be, President
Don Farebrother liked to say, if we asked all America to buy
our clients' products while our own employees are driving the
competition's cars or smoking the competition's cigarettes?

In line with this stated philosophy, Marsdenites were
constantly being exhorted, via interoffice memo, to eat,
drink, drive, smoke and even menstruate exclusively with
products from the agency's client list.

When Marsden secured an office equipment account, Kate
marvelled at the way the agency swung into action. Overnight
the old typewriters were rooted out as if contaminated and
replaced by models manufactured by the new client.

But the worst offender was the cigarette machine.

There was one to every floor, placed at the entrance to the
restrooms, a standard model designed to stock a dozen
different brands. It stocked only one: Norfolks. You put in
your 40¢ and pulled out a lever, but whichever lever you
pulled out, you got Norfolks. Norfolk Tobacco was a valued
Marsden client.

In her own mind, Kate dubbed the machine "The Russian voting booth" and for a while considered giving up smoking.

Within a month at Marsden, she had settled in and set the pattern she would follow for years to come.

New York rush hours, she quickly discovered, were even worse than the Boston variety. Besides which, the subway stank. Kate preferred to set out early in the morning and walk the thirty odd blocks from her room on the Upper West Side. It was pleasant to amble across Central Park, then stroll down Fifth Avenue with just enough time to sneak a look into Bergdorf's windows. If the weather was foul or the thermometer fell below freezing, she would treat herself to a cab.

Either way, she arrived at the office about eight o'clock, an hour earlier than anyone else. But that was all right. She enjoyed the early morning quiet, found it the most productive time of the day. For by 9:30, the phones would start ringing, Len would start shouting, the daily havoc would switch into high gear.

Work finished, she'd come home the same way.

"Home" was a tatty furnished room with a bath and a so-called Hollywood kitchen—really a hot plate and a pint-sized refrigerator.

Not fancy, certainly, but not any worse than the dormitory room in Boston. In fact, the two places shared a certain sameness of decor. Tired chintz slipcovers, scatter rugs verging on the threadbare, the same insidious layer of grime that worked its way through closed doors and windows. Kate's sole contribution to the weary decor was a print of Rousseau's "Sleeping Gypsy"—a dream portrait of a woman and a lion. Something in that picture haunted her.

And unlike the dorm, there was mercifully no Phyllis to burst in upon her privacy. There was sufficient crockery and nonmatching silver to serve four people exactly, three more than Kate had any call for.

For Kate was singularly free of the "nesting instinct" that overtakes most girls in their twenties. She almost never entertained there, preferring to meet her dates on some more neutral territory—a restaurant or a hotel lobby. And on those evenings she stayed home, dinner consisted of sandwiches from the deli or cottage cheese and fruit, washed down with a mug of instant coffee.

She was neither proud nor apologetic of the way she lived.
It suited her. Her only extravagances were taxis, a once-a-
week cleaning woman (Kate couldn't picture herself scrubbing out toilet bowls) and—as time went on—an increasing
interest in clothes.

It was Barry who weaned her away from the Peck & Peck
sweater sets that had marked her college years.

"This is New York, kiddo, where the dudes are." He was
always splendidly turned out. "So why don't you give that
stuff to some deserving charity and do justice to those great
American legs?"

When she cried poverty, he laughed her off.

"You don't have to be rich," Barry was fond of saying.
"Just be bold."

At Christmas sale time, he dragged her bodily off to Lord
& Taylor's, having extracted a promise that she'd let *him* pick
out something. He clearly enjoyed playing Pygmalion to
Kate's unformed Galatea.

Within five minutes, he'd taken a dress off the rack.

"Oh, Barry, it's so skimpy." It was a fine silk jersey that
couldn't have weighed more than a couple of ounces.

"You'll love it."

"And the color! With *my* hair?" It was Tyrian purple with a
pattern of pink and black abstracts.

"You'll love it."

"There's no point in my even trying it on," she protested as
he steered her toward the dressing room.

"You'll love it."

She loved it. After half a dozen eye-blinking moments,
she loved it. It was by a young Italian designer, a somebody Pucci, whom Kate had never heard of, though Barry
had.

Once the dam was broken, the rest followed swiftly.
Dangling earrings and a pair of strappy sandals with three-
inch heels.

"I feel like a freak," Kate said, peering down from her new
height.

"You look like a million," Barry answered.

She wore it to the office a few days later, as self-conscious
as a showgirl at a Baptist convention. Even Len—the eternally weary Len—dropped his jaw in open-mouthed appreciation.

"Why, Miss Jones," he said in a mock-Clark Gable accent. "You're beautiful without your glasses."

From the very start she enjoyed her job.

Looking at it from the outside, it had all seemed so simple. You just thought up some clever little slogan. *There's a Ford in Your Future. Promise Her Anything But Give Her Arpege. I Dreamt I Took the Staten Island Ferry in My Maidenform Bra. Diamonds Are Forever.*

And so are the payments, she snorted. Really, how long could it take to write that stuff. What was it . . . a few words of headline? A paragraph or two of text? You couldn't compare it to writing a term paper or an article for The *New York Times.* Certainly not to writing a novel, filling hundreds of blank pages with thousands upon thousands of words.

When she took the job, she thought she'd give it a year at most. Just until something turned up in journalism.

But from the inside, it all looked different.

The writing part was enjoyable, and anyhow, she'd always had a flair for words. That only took a couple of hours a day. It was the thinking part that came as a surprise, that engaged the largest portion of her time.

Thinking.

About the most effective way of convincing Midwest automotive dealers to stock a different brand of antifreeze. Do you try to bribe them? Or reason with them? Or seduce them with the picture of a girl in a bikini?

Thinking.

About how to alert the bad-breath brigade to the benefits inherent in mouthwash. Do you promise them health? Do you promise them romance? Or do you tell them frankly that they stink?

Thinking.

Trying to figure out why it was that the poorer women would spend themselves silly on nationally advertised brands. Why their better-heeled sisters with money to burn often picked the cheaper brand of soap-flakes.

The work was absorbing. Far more absorbing than any of the men who called for dates. On the whole, she decided, she'd rather wrestle with an ad campaign than with an overeager male.

And after her experience with Michael, she was wary of becoming too involved.

Len spotted her capacity for sheer hard work, her tenacity in thinking problems through. "Odd jobs," he'd shout, and Kate would come scampering down the corridor to be laden with everybody else's leftover assignments. She didn't complain. And with raises coming in thick and fast, she'd soon be outearning many a seasoned reporter. But above all, it was the work itself that absorbed her.

Once she was into it, she could utterly forget who and where she was. She was no longer Kate Chapman of Athol and Miss Ellery's and Boston. She could obliterate that identity and transform herself—however momentarily—into an elderly widow with denture problems. A used-car dealer hungry for a buck. A young bride picking out linoleum patterns.

She fell just a little bit in love with each product she worked on, crediting its claims, succumbing to its promises. True, once the job was done, she could sit back and laugh. But while she was doing it, she believed. Believed every word she wrote.

KIT

NEVER BELIEVE A WORD OF WHAT YOU READ.

That was Kit's conclusion five months into pregnancy.

She had waited expectantly—surely the proper term—for any or all the symptoms described in the pamphlet Dr. Gordon had given her on her first visit.

So You're Going to Have a Baby, it was entitled—rather coyly, she thought. After a few banal paragraphs about the impending joys of motherhood, it launched into graphic descriptions of all the ills pregnant flesh is heir to. Morning sickness. Fluid retention. Leg cramps. Tooth decay.

Rubbish, said Kit with conviction.

She had never felt better or healthier in her life. Her hair glowed with the sheen of a Renaissance angel, her energy was unflagging and she hadn't even the slightest craving for the proverbial anomalies of ice cream and pickles—although she was getting dreadfully bored with cottage cheese.

Still, Dr. Gordon was adamant, threatening her with his most powerful weapon—disapproval—should she gain more than ten pounds in all. After the fourth examination, when the baby was kicking inside her, he told her approvingly that she was "a splendid specimen." Kit preened like a freshman who'd made honor roll. All that scare stuff in the pamphlet,

81

she concluded, was sheer self-indulgence—the traditional woman's way of making high drama out of what was, after all, a perfectly natural process. Except for the calorie charts, the only part of the pamphlet she referred to were the final two pages, listing names and their meanings.

Morning sickness was make-believe, but choosing the right name! That, both she and Michael agreed, was of prime importance. Michael's first choice was Spencer, but Kit had refused to entertain the notion. The very last thing she wanted to introduce to this young and happy household was the brooding aura of "the absent presence"—for that was still how she thought of her father. So they finally settled on Michael James Matheson III. Michael himself was a Junior, and while he didn't much care for the appellation and never used it, they both agreed that being M.J. Matheson III would carry a certain cachet. Girl's names were more of a problem.

"Suppose we name her Melanie or Amanda or something terribly fey and romantic, and she turns out to be an absolute dog?" Kit said, although she couldn't picture how any child of theirs could be a dog. "Can't you see me calling out the window—'Melanie! Melanie! Milk and cookies!' and having some little fatso trudge up?"

No, it should be something sensible and proper with a real New England ring to it. Alice or Jane or Abigail—"Abby's kind of nice"—but stopping short of Lavinia and Prudence.

They decided finally on Sarah after Kit's maternal grandmother. Sarah Abigail Matheson. Kit could already envision it entered into the freshman roll at Miss Ellery's.

The next problem to dispose of was the layette. It would probably pay to pick up some things during the July sales, but when Michael suggested it, she balked. "Don't tell me you're superstitious," he said, but to Kit's surprise she found she was. At least about this.

She knew how low the figures were for infant mortality among young, healthy middle-class whites, knew she was a "splendid specimen" getting the best prenatal advice. Yet to go out and actually purchase vests and nightshirts and bassinets struck Kit as courting disaster.

But rather than admit to nonrational impulses, she came back with the rather weak answer that they shouldn't buy anything until *it*—boy or girl—was on the scene. "Can't have Michael III in pink rosebuds. And anyhow, you can buy all the stuff in one day at Jordan's while I'm in the hospital, so what's the rush?"

There was a rush, however, to enjoy her last months of freedom.

"So are you planning to send little Michael or Sarah or whatever off to boarding school so it can turn into a proper Bostonian?" Tim asked one evening over dinner at the Mathesons' place.

Kit laughed.

"It's a little early to think about, since the poor thing hasn't even made its appearance."

"Not at all," Marian protested. "It's never too early. My mother had my name down for Miss Ellery's before I was a week old."

"Well, I can't plan that far ahead. You may as well ask me what she'll wear at her coming-out party. That is, assuming she's a she."

"She'll wear white, of course," Marian answered. "Something discreetly off the shoulder. And you'll wear something beigey and sedate, to hide your middle-age spread."

"And all the boys will wear patent-leather dancing pumps with little grosgrain bows," Tim added. They all laughed at that—all except Michael. "Oh, God," Tim continued, "my feet still ache at the memory."

"That whole thing is so antique, anyway," Kit said. "I didn't come out, although my mother would have liked it. It always struck me as a waste of time and money. And snobbish in the bargain."

"Anyhow," Tim said, intrigued by the subject, "I don't think that's a problem any of us will have to face—that coming-out crap. My bet is those cotillions will be dead as dinosaurs in a few years' time. Who cares any more? Even the debs don't give a damn. But boarding school . . . that's something else. If I had my way I'd abolish them, like Lincoln abolished slavery. By law. I'd make it illegal for any parent to send his kid to private school . . . burn 'em all to the ground tomorrow."

"But Tim," Kit protested, "you went to boarding school. And don't you honestly think you got a superior education for having gone?"

Tim contemplated his breadstick, paused for a minute.

Then "No!" He shook his head firmly. "No. I could have, mind you. I grant that it was there for the taking, but all I could think of when I was at Deerfield was girls girls girls. When I'm commissar, Kit, every child in the country will be forced to go to public school. They'll all be integrated—boys and girls, black and white, Protestants and Catholics and Jews."

"Even the universities?"

"Especially the universities. You can count on it—the day will come when girls can get into Harvard."

"And boys into Vassar," Marian asked. "You'd have liked that, wouldn't you?"

Kit changed the subject swiftly, for Tim's infidelities were causing a lot of talk in their circle.

"Still, Tim, I think you'd have to agree, boarding school kids turn out . . . nicer." It was Emily's word, but in this context true.

"Do they?" Tim retorted. "Solid upright responsible members of the community, that sort of thing?"

Both girls nodded.

"Well, that, my dears, is utter nonsense. Let me tell you a story about one of my classmates." Tim licked his lips in anticipation. "John Peabody Ewing of the North Shore Ewings."

"Peabee Ewing?" Kit squealed. "I know him. I went to school with his younger sister."

"Didn't everybody," Marian laughed.

"Oh, he was a weirdo," Kit admitted. "A real weirdo."

"Well, let me tell you the story," Tim said with relish. He turned to Michael. "Since you're the only one here who doesn't know the gent in question, a little background. Peabee's about six foot four, weighs about a hundred twenty pounds with his sneakers on—a real freak. But through those elongated veins run ten generations of Boston's bluest blood. Anyhow, a few years out of Deerfield and he turns into a screaming fag, a bit too much even for the Ewings."

"You can't condemn a whole school," Kit protested, "just because one boy becomes a homosexual."

"One boy!" Tim scoffed. "But that's not the story, Kit. Let me finish. So . . . last summer Peabee gets all togged out in his crumbiest seersucker suit, on the presumption that only the rich can afford to look that ratty, and presents himself at

Shreve Crump and Lowe. For your information, Michael, it's the Boston equivalent of Tiffany's."

"I know what Shreve Crump is," Michael said evenly.

"Yuh . . . Well, there's Peabee in his best North Shore drawl and he lets on to the salesman that he's become engaged to a nice Boston girl . . . regrettable but necessary . . . and he s'poses he should buy her a diamond or suchlike. OK, the salesman accepts this. He's seen some pretty freaky types in his day, and he begins pulling out engagement rings. Peabee looks them over"—Tim pulled a vinegar face—"but no! This one's too yellow, that one's too small. The implication is, of course, that he's marrying at least a Lodge. Well, the salesman starts rubbing his hands. I mean, he can smell this big commission coming up, so he goes back to the vaults and starts getting out the good stuff. The really heavy money diamonds—marquise cuts, emerald cuts—you girls know more about this stuff than I do. So there they are, Peabee and the salesman, with about $200,000 worth of South Africa's finest in front of them, when all of a sudden this great big greasy Mafia type bursts into the store. A real hood right out of the North End. With a gun, mind you, a gun. And it's pointed right at Peabee. Well, in about thirty seconds, he sweeps the stones off the tray and—wham bang—he disappears, leaving Peabee and the salesman limp with astonishment."

"So?" Kit was puzzled. Was that all?

"So . . ." Tim burst out laughing. "These kind of things can happen to anybody. Right?"

"Right. So how about letting us in on the joke."

"So . . ." Tim wiped a tear from his eye. "About three weeks later, the Shreve Crump guy is out at the dog track and who does he see not ten feet in front of him but Peabee and"—dramatic pause—"the Mafia type."

"Together?" Kit couldn't believe it.

"Not just together but holding hands. How 'bout that! Well, it took the Shreve man about ten seconds to figure out what the setup was and another ten seconds to call the cops. Peabee was arrested before he even left the track."

"But that's incredible," said Kit. "I mean, I never saw anything about it in the papers."

"Well, you wouldn't," Marian told her. "That family always knew how to cover its tracks."

"And what happened to Peabee?"

"I think they shipped him off to Venice on a limited allowance. He always did have a taste for Italians."

"Oh, Tim, really!"

The talk turned easily into good-natured gossip about other classmates from the "bad old days," as Tim called them. The three of them—Kit, Tim and Marian—knew dozens of people in common. Or if not the people themselves, then their brothers and cousins and fiancés and girlfriends. One name led to another. "Whatever happened to?" followed by "You'll never guess who I ran into on Charles Street last week" followed by yet another name in the chain reaction of nostalgia, till Michael, who hadn't said a word since the Peabee story, broke in coldly.

"Is this a private conversation or can anyone join in?"

The words exploded like a thunderclap.

"I'm sorry." Tim was brought up short by the implied rebuke. "How very boring for you and how very thoughtless of us."

"Us." Kit caught instantly—and knew Michael did too—the meaning of "us" in that sentence. For if "us" was Marian, Tim and Kit, then Michael surely belonged to the "thems."

"They were stupid days anyhow," she lied swiftly, "and Tim is absolutely right. Boarding schools should be outlawed. I wish I'd gone to public school like everybody else and our children are certainly going to."

As for Tim (it was the first time she'd ever seen him caught off guard), he got up from the table abruptly. "That's what I said, it's all crap. Now let's pitch in and do the dishes. OK, Mama Matheson? You're getting too big to reach the sink anyway." And so the moment was glossed over in the clatter of plates and Grandmother Sayre's rattail silver.

But later that night when the Keegans had gone, Michael returned to it, as Kit knew he would.

"Who does he think I am!" he said angrily, shoving his jacket onto a hanger. "Just who in hell does he think I am . . . patronizing me like that! 'Shreve Crump and Lowe is the Boston Tiffany's,' for Chrissakes. Where does he think I was raised . . . in a swamp?"

"I'm sure he didn't mean it that way, Michael."

"Oh, didn't he? Timothy Francis Keegan"—he spat out the name—"the flower of New England aristocracy. Well, let me tell you, my family was in Maine for generations while his were still digging for potatoes in Ireland."

Kit was shocked. It was the last thing she expected from Michael, coming as he did from potato farmers.

"I don't understand you. Potatoes are potatoes. What's the difference whether they grow in Maine or County Mayo? And if Tim's people were potato farmers, well, isn't that something you have in common? It's beneath you, Michael, it really is, to sound off like some old biddy from the D.A.R. 'We were here first' sort of stuff."

Her rebuke brought him up short. "I'm sorry, darling"—he spread his hands in penance—"it was a dumb thing to say. I guess Tim hit a nerve tonight."

"I'm sure he didn't mean—"

"But that's just it," Michael interrupted. "He didn't *mean* . . . he didn't *realize* . . . Why the hell should he? With people like him, everything comes so easily—money, status, the right friends, the right schools. All so automatic, so taken for granted. No concept at all about other people's feelings." He sat down on the bed, scruffing his toes deep into the carpet. "And not just Tim or Marian either. I'm talking about you, too, Kit," he added half to himself.

"Me!" She was incredulous. "You think that about *me?* But darling, I'm not defending deb cotillions and all that nonsense. Lordy, no. As far as I'm concerned, our kids can go to public school like everybody else, make friends at every level of society. They'd probably be better off for it."

His response was a swift pained smile. "And should they get a newspaper route and wait on tables after school? And learn their manners at the movies and their morals at the corner drugstore? Well, I've done all that, Kit, come up the hard way, and if you want my candid opinion, it stinks. I know it's fashionable to knock society and romanticize about the glories of poverty and hard work, especially when you're at the top of the heap looking down. Well, poverty isn't romantic—it's demeaning. And as for the virtues of hard work, all I can say is that hard work makes hard people. Look at my parents, Kit. They were old before they were young. They knew the bitter without ever having tasted the sweet."

"But you survived, Michael."

"Sure, I survived," he echoed bitterly, "but I hope our children do something more than just survive. If we have a girl, I want her to have soft hands and Junior League manners and a voice with music in it. Like you, Kit. And when she gets married, I want her picture in the Sunday *Times*."

"And if it's a boy . . . ?"

"Ahhh," he smiled. "The famous Michael Matheson the Third. I can see him now, looking cool and elegant in tennis whites. He'll go to Groton and fall in love with nice girls and make the Porcellian at Harvard. All the advantages. Our children will have all the advantages. They'll be fine and proud and easy and secure. Not going through life the way I did, like a boy with his nose pressed against the pastry shop window. Always on the outside looking in."

On the outside looking in. It was the first time Michael had ever voiced his insecurities, and to Kit they came as a revelation. He had always seemed to her so forceful, so stunningly sure, so intuitive in choosing the right tone for dealing with everyone from belligerent taxi-drivers to Ivy League aesthetes. Was that ease, that grace she so admired, simply "manners learned at the movies"—smiles and gestures garnered from countless matinees at a hick-town moviehouse in Maine?

She looked at the figure on the bed and found a stranger there. A stranger who shared her home, her body, her life. Another Michael—sad, vulnerable, aching from a thousand hurts, real and imagined. How extraordinary that she had known him so intimately—and yet known him so little.

He was right, of course. Kit had, by his lights, had everything, while he could look back on nothing but years of struggles and snubs and pinch-penny economies. Her heart grieved for him—this man who was surely worth a dozen Tims. And while she couldn't change the past, she could, she *would* make it all up to him in the future. What were women for if not for that?

Motherly now in shape as well as gesture, she sat beside him on the bed and stroked his hair. "But you're not on the outside anymore, darling," she comforted. "Look at yourself in a different perspective. Do ninety percent of the people go to Harvard Law? Do one percent even? One half of one percent? Well, I'm no good at math, but it's got to be the teeniest tiniest fraction that gets into Harvard Law. Gets *in*—let alone graduates! I mean if anyone's the elite in this household . . ." she could feel him relax—"why, it's you. And I think you should take all the greater pride that you didn't go to a fancy prep school like Tim and have your family grease the way. Well, if you're not proud of you, *I* am."

There! Those were precisely the kind of tactful, supportive remarks a loving wife should make; and she was pleased to see the balm take hold. The stranger was vanishing and Michael was returning. What wonderful things words were, what a long way a little flattery will go.

"You really have no idea how much my parents admire you—seeing yourself through Harvard all those years, working every summer. Why, Daddy thinks you're just terrific."

Kit swallowed. That was, perhaps, gilding the lily a bit, for Spencer had always kept his own counsel on the subject of Michael, as he did on every other subject with the possible exception of encroaching communism. Still, if that was what Michael wanted to hear, needed to hear . . .

"That's kind of you to say, Kit, but I'm sure he'd rather have had a son-in-law from the Social Register."

"The Social Register!" she scoffed. "Really, Michael, that doesn't mean a thing anymore. When you're Daddy's age, I expect your name will be in places a lot more important than the boring old Social Register. Michael Matheson"—she read from an invisible page—"Leading contributor to this month's *Harvard Law Review*. Or in *Who's Who*. No reason why you shouldn't be in *Who's Who* one of these days. I can see it now . . ." She shot him a glance. The moody stranger was thoroughly routed now and Michael—dear, handsome Michael—was stretched out dreamily on the bed, letting the honey of her words lap about him.

". . . Matheson," she continued. "Michael J. Leading civil rights attorney. Born Caribou, Maine 1931. Graduated Harvard Law 1957. Appointed chief counsel for"—she paused in her embroidery—"for the ACLU in the early sixties. Matheson's distinguished career has made him America's liberal spokesman in controversial cases before the United States Supreme Court. In . . . in 1973, Matheson was given an honorary Doctor of Law by Harvard University, where he currently holds the chair of . . . um . . . Distinguished Professor of Criminal Jurisprudence. He is married to the former . . ."

He finished her sentence with a kiss. "Married," he said, "to the most wonderful woman in the world" and, pulling her gently to him, began to make sweet, quiet love. And as she lay under his caresses, Kit could feel the baby move within her.

"Poor baby," she thought. "You'll have an awful lot to live up to."

Sarah Abigail Matheson was born in the Peter Bent Brigham Hospital a few weeks later in the predawn hours. And once again Dr. Gordon's little pamphlet had misled. For she was not "red and wrinkled" but beautiful as the sun, with fine gold hair and the requisite number of fingers and toes. Kit never tired of counting them. It was a miracle so complete, so perfect, that it banished completely the pain of stitches, the discomfort of her freshly-shaven perineum, the bleakness and sterility of the delivery room.

A golden girl. Sarah was a golden golden girl.

KATE

SOME MORNINGS KATE WOULD LOOK AT HERSELF IN THE MIRROR and see her mirror image smiling back in disbelief.

Did that striking girl in the mirror bear any conceivable relation to the Catherine Chapman who, only a year or so ago, had reached for the nearest skirt and sweater on her way out of the dorms each morning? Certainly not, the mirror image proclaimed. Gone was the unruly mop of hair, tamed into elegance by the scissors of Jean-Michel. Gone, too, the naked face once innocent of anything but lipstick; the mirror face was richer, brighter, with glowing cheeks and luminous eyes.

What the mirror proclaimed, the clothes closet confirmed. Sensible pumps had been ousted by killer stilettos. One by one the college cardigans and sensible tweeds had been shunted off to the Salvation Army, elbowed out by skinny chemises and racy Italian knitwear and the occasional line-for-line French copy.

She learned from Barry. Took lessons from the pages of *Vogue,* the windows at Bonwit's, the fashion shows at Saks. She made a point of studying women on the street—the elegant ones, the head-turners—and analyzed precisely what it was that made them click. A handbag, a hairdo, a spray of jewelry here, a splash of color there, the little touches that added up to chic.

And after a while—she noticed with pleasure—other women began to study her.

So Kate shed her Boston wardrobe. And the remnants of her timidity. And now she decided she would rid herself of that last vestige of college: her virginity.

What had passed for good form in the dormitories of Back Bay ("Don't do it. And if you do it, don't talk about it." Only Phyllis had been the exception) seemed prissy and outmoded in the more savvy atmosphere of Manhattan.

Here, virginity didn't signify a state of purity. Quite the contrary. It indicated a petty selfishness of body and spirit. Even worse, it was bad form. Like wearing galoshes to a cocktail party.

The mechanics, too, were no problem.

For while it was easier to come by a dry martini in downtown Mecca than to get a diaphragm in downtown Boston, New York doctors took a more charitable view of human error.

Thus the means were at hand. And so were the men. Kate decided to avail herself of both.

His name was Neil Edwards. He was a photographer who did occasional jobs for Marsden. He was thirty. Horny. And handsomer than anyone but a movie star had a right to be. He was also married.

Oh, what the hell, Kate thought when he asked her out for drinks on the pretext of discussing some catalogue shots. Why not a married man? He'd know his way around, for one thing. She nursed a lingering distaste for college fumblers. Besides, a married man would be less likely to gossip and, if things got sticky, easier to drop.

So she met him after work at Sherry's. They had one drink, then another, then another. Then he took her in a cab to his studio.

It was a huge downtown loft, a tangle of wires and spotlights and reflectors. She had been there before, when it was humming with business, but now, in the early evening silence, it was eerie. Erotic.

He turned on a handful of spotlights, illuminating a table

here, a couch there, leaving vast areas of the room in total darkness.

"Do you want another drink?" he asked.

She was standing in a pool of light.

"I want . . ." her voice trailed off.

"I know what you want," he answered from the darkness. "That's what we're here for."

She flushed—and hoped he attributed her color to the heat of the lamp. She'd be damned, she thought, if she'd admit to virginity—*that* had been a burden for too long. At least there'd be no blood-stained sheets to betray her secret, she thought—silently blessing the horse that had thrown her so many years ago.

"Now . . . first things first," he said. "Can you spend the night?"

"Can you?" she returned. "What about your wife?"

"I'll call and tell her I'm entertaining a client. That way we can have all night. OK?"

Kate nodded.

"Just one thing," he said before phoning. "You'll have to be out by eight in the morning. I've got a client coming at nine."

"A *real* client?" Kate countered, and, when he didn't laugh, said, "Go ahead. Call your wife."

She moved into the darkness while he spoke on the phone, fingering the buttons of her blouse uneasily. Should she undress now? Would he undress her? What was the protocol at times like these?

Before she could make up her mind, he was off the phone.

"Now, Kate," he pulled her to him. "What's it to be? Slow and easy? Hot and heavy? Missionary? Rear entry? Fellatio?"

Kate swallowed. She'd come simply to make love, and here he was offering her a smorgasbord.

"I think" she said, dry-mouthed, remembering the diaphragm in her handbag—as uninitiated as she was—"I better go take precautions before we do anything."

"Not yet," he said. "I hate the taste of jelly." And when Kate's jaw dropped in consternation, he laughed.

"You're really not very experienced, are you?"

"Not very," she admitted with relief.

"Then be a good girl and do just as I tell you. We'll take it nice and easy."

He took off her clothes with practiced ease, caressing each bit of flesh as it came into view. When there was nothing more to remove, he pulled her gently into the light. Then he undressed himself.

"You have a beautiful body, Kate." He held her at arms length.

"So have you," Kate replied truthfully.

"Now," he said, "let's see if we can do each other justice."

Moving into the darkness, he flipped off all the lights but one—a spotlight focused on an enormous butterfly chair, low slung, its suede as soft as skin.

"Now you sit here." Kate sank back into the supple suede. It welcomed her like a caress. "Just relax. Simply put your head back and relax."

Gently, slowly, he opened her thighs, spreading her legs over the rises of the chair. "And now for lesson number one."

Naked, he knelt before her on the gleaming polished floor, each hand cupping one of her breasts. Then, lowering his head like a worshipper in prayer, he buried his face in the delta of her body. She could feel his tongue licking, lapping—now tentative and fluttery, now firm and sleek as Eve's serpent. Feel his tongue like a questing traveler probing through the forest of her pubic hair, finding its way slowly to the gate of her body. Entering her now—licking, lapping. Above her she could see their bodies in the ceiling reflectors. See his hands on her breasts, his lips on hers, his dark hair against the fairness of her thighs. Within her all was wetness and heat, a fairground of sensations.

She shut her eyes and delivered herself to his tongue. In the new-found darkness, she heard the sound of fast breathing. With a shock she realized it was her own. For he still knelt there, immobile but for the hands that caressed her breasts, the invisible tongue now climbing its way high into her.

She wanted him to stop. Then she wanted him to go. To go on forever discovering her body to herself. She wanted to reach forward, to grip him to her, to force that tongue higher and deeper yet. But the hands at her breast held her pinioned while he licked and tasted and explored each hidden millimeter within—tirelessly, relentlessly, until her breathing turned into a scream of joy.

He rose and wiped his mouth. "That," he said, "was the appetizer. Now let's have the main course."

It was after three when he finally turned the lights out and fell into an exhausted sleep. Kate, too, was exhausted, replete with sex, but sleep proved an impossibility.

She had never in her life shared a bed with anyone. That, too, was a new experience—if not quite so exhilarating as those others she had discovered earlier that night.

He was, she realized, a sexual technician. Indeed, he admitted as much. In a few incredible hours he had introduced her to a vast variety of sensual experience. She should be grateful. And yet . . .

Yet never in that long night of lovemaking had he kissed her out of affection. Never once had he called her name in passion. "Baby, Baby" he had shouted in climax. But "Baby" was everyone and no one.

He was—there could be no other word for it—a lay. Kate hated the term. It was crass and vulgar. And yet it was apt. Just as she had been nothing but a lay for him.

Extraordinary, she thought, how much physical pleasure you could get from someone you didn't much care for. Well, OK . . . if that's how it is. And she should consider herself lucky that her first affair was with a virtuoso of the art.

He had fallen asleep with his arm flung across her belly, his finger resting lightly in her crotch. The position was at once too uncomfortable and too stimulating to permit her to sleep. She locked her legs around his finger. Incredible! She wanted him to make love again. Would it be the fourth or the fifth time that night? The fifth, if you counted that business with the mouth. She took his resting finger and moved it to and fro inside her to see if she could rouse him, but his sleep was so deep and unmoving that she knew nothing short of a cannon shot would get him up.

She was still wide awake when the alarm went off at seven-thirty. Wide awake and eager for more.

He removed his hand from her moistness where it had spent the night and reached over to switch off the clock. She took his hand and put it back *in situ*, but he pulled away in annoyance.

"For Chrissakes, honey, it's almost quarter to eight. We'd better get a move on. Would you settle for a cup of coffee?"

"I suppose so," she said, mildly disappointed.

"Well, you'll find the makings in the kitchenette. Brew us up a pot, that's a good girl." Kate shook her head.

If he wouldn't make love, she wouldn't make coffee. Besides, she wasn't sure she knew how.

"This is *your* studio, and I'm your guest. So if you want coffee, you better make it yourself."

He sat up suddenly with an injured air.

"It's usually the woman's job."

"Is it? Then get yourself the usual woman."

He stared at her—a long quizzical look—then grabbed for his shorts on the chair.

"Oh, what the hell," he said. "Let's go out for breakfast."

A year later she could hardly remember his name. There had been so very many since.

Nice Men. Hungry men. Considerate men. Impotent men. Imaginative men.

And almost all of them married men.

She never dated anyone she disliked; yet never seemed to meet anyone she could really care for. Nor did she see herself in any way as promiscuous. Merely free. Independent. And independence was too sweet a treasure to be surrendered.

Someday—maybe even someday soon—she'd give up the rat race and find a man who was more interesting than her work. As Emily was fond of saying, there was all the time in the world to get married; to settle down.

Her life was happy and full. The only item missing was girl friends. She had met no Jans in New York, no Helen Inces, not even a Phyllis. The structure of the office precluded socializing with the secretaries and the only friend with whom she felt she could discuss absolutely everything was the eternally sympathetic Barry.

She discovered, by accident, that she and Barry once shared the same lover—a male model with an athlete's body and a surgeon's fingers. They had a good laugh about that.

She had but one rule she followed religiously: she never slept with the men she worked for. That, she felt, might lead to gossip, messy complications. And never—not even in her own mind—would she permit it to be said that she was "sleeping her way to the top."

As for the rest, there were plenty of men for a girl who combined style with an aura of availability.

She went to their studios, their offices, their hotel rooms.

Their apartments in summer when the wives were out of town. She rarely spent the night with them and never brought them home. She wanted to keep the emotional distance.

They came into her life. They went just as quickly. And when they went, she felt no regret. Phyllis had been right in one thing. They *were* interchangeable except for physical details.

You could go to Grand Central Station any night of the week, when the tide of commuters swelled the platform, and any man in that tide was just like any other. They had wives in Westport, kids at the orthodontist and a deep-seated fear of involvement.

That suited Kate just fine.

Never look back. It became her motto.

Never look back.

KIT

"CHRIST, WHAT A DAY!"

Michael flung his briefcase in the hall closet and he went off to change.

When he returned to the living room, he was smiles, all smiles.

"Sarah's sawing wood like a lumberjack. God, she looks so cute when she's asleep, I just want to wake her up and hug her."

"You wouldn't dare."

They exchanged grins of complicity.

"Aaaah." Michael unfurled in a long luxurious motion till his legs stretched halfway across the room and looked around him, Scotch in hand, with the satisfaction of a man proclaiming: my home, my wife, my child.

It was the hour of day they both liked best.

"Were you in court today, Michael?"

"Was I ever! I had a lulu!" He took a belt of his Scotch and sighed. "Two of 'em, in fact. That machete case came up today, did I tell you?"

"No. Sounds exotic."

"Exotic! Yeah, Jaime Ortiz, a member of the Puerto Rican aristocracy!"

"You're kidding."

."Yeah, I'm kidding." Of late, sarcasm had become Michael's normal tone when he talked about his clients. The White Knight, it was clear, was getting a wee bit tarnished.

"The Ortiz case. I think it was in the papers a few months ago. Anyhow . . . these two brothers come up from the backwoods of Puerto Rico, traveling light, you know, cardboard-suitcase style. Like Jaime's got a change of socks, his Sunday go-to-meeting suit and his trusty machete. I asked him this morning—well, actually I had the interpreter ask him, 'cause Jaime doesn't speak any English—I asked him, 'Jaime, why do you bring a machete up to Boston?' He said 'I'm looking for work. I'm a cane cutter.' So I tell him 'Jaime, we don't have an awful lot of sugar cane growing here in Boston.' And he says 'But that's all I know how to do, Senor.' Go argue! So anyhow, he and his brother are rotting in some cruddy rooming house in Roxbury—no sugar cane, no jobs, no speaka da English—and one night Jaime gets out his trusty machete and zip zap wham bang, big brother's decorating a slab in the mortuary."

"So instead of cutting cane, he cut Abel."

"That's a good one," Michael laughed. "I'll have to remember it."

"But why did he do it?" Kit regretted the pun. "I mean, his own brother."

"How the hell do *I* know? Goddamn animals . . . I don't even think they know why they do it. He was swacked, I suppose. They can *always* afford booze." Michael sipped his Dewars thoughtfully. "Anyhow, little Jaime has every reason to be grateful to me and the Commonwealth of Massachusetts. I mean, nobody wanted to sit through a bilingual trial. So we did some plea bargaining and got him off with manslaughter. Jaime will be out with his little machete before the first robins of spring."

"Well, at least you had a chance to brush up on your Spanish."

"Gracias, senora, gracias por nada."

"And what was the other . . . the other lulu?"

Michael shrugged and held his empty glass up to the light. Kit got him a refill.

"The other." He looked suddenly grim. "Aaaah, you don't want to hear about the other. Believe me, it's not a case I want to defend. Everything about it is disgusting."

"You can tell me, Michael. I'm an old married woman and I don't shock that easily . . . I don't *think*."

He considered for a moment.

"Incest," he said. "Incest between father and daughter."

Involuntarily, Kit recoiled.

"See? You *are* shocked. I bet you thought this kind of thing happens only in Greek mythology. You know this isn't the first incest case I've had. There's a lot more about than you think."

"You never told me."

"Well, it's not the sort of thing I like to bring home."

"What were the circumstances?" Kit asked softly.

"The circumstances. The defendant is a waiter in a South Boston bar; he also gets welfare payments. He's got two kids—this daughter thirteen and a son about six years old. He works evenings, looks after the kids by day and as far as I can make out, he's not a drinker. So it won't be a case where I can say this guy came home plastered one evening and didn't know which bed he was falling into."

"Where's the mother all this while?"

"Gone. Scoot. Took off about four years ago and left him with both the kids. So it's just him and them in this tiny apartment. The boy's in kindergarten, the girl goes to parochial school. Anyhow, a couple of months ago one of the sharper-eyed nuns noticed that little Madge is getting plump about the middle."

"Pregnant? At thirteen?"

"This kid's a very ripe thirteen. I've seen her. So of course the Sister asked her who the lucky man was, and she finally owned up it was Daddy. The thing is, we have no idea how long this has been going on. When I ask him, all he does is cry, and the girl won't say a word. Anyhow, this morning the judge set bail and I just didn't have it in me to fight for a reduction. Let him sweat it out in jail until the case comes up."

"What kind of sentence is he likely to get?"

"What kind of sentence would *you* give a man who's knocked up his thirteen-year-old daughter? In the old days, they probably would have cut off his balls. Well, that was the old days. Nowadays, jail is the great equalizer. You know, your average Boston jailbirds—those nice respectable junkies and muggers—take a very dim view of sex-offenders. I'll spare you the gory details of what happens inside, except to say Daddy will get as good as he gave."

Kit repressed a shudder. Homosexual rape was, she knew, a commonplace in the jails. Even in the Women's House of Detention, so she'd heard.

"And what will happen to the girl?"

"She's being looked after by the Welfare Department. It's very sad. The funny thing is that she's absolutely heartbroken. Not about being pregnant . . . oh, no! About being separated from her father. She adores him—poor girl."

Poor man, too, Kit thought.

Michael's story had depressed her unutterably. She could understand—but not incest, never that!—the illimitable love of parent for child. Oddly enough, she had never thought herself particularly maternal until she became pregnant with Sarah; but now she recognized that this was the strongest tie she'd ever known.

She could never walk out on Sarah. Never. On a marriage —conceivably. After all, marriages can fail or succeed or settle down at any one of a hundred different points in between. But the one relation from which you could never divorce yourself was parenthood.

To walk away as that girl's mother had done, to forfeit your children for mere freedom—that, to Kit, was even more inexplicable than incest. After all, what was incest but a surfeit of love?

"Poor man," she said aloud, "to be so desperately sick and lonely."

"Lonely!" Michael exploded. "Are you crazy? Why, you're talking about him as if he were a human being. It's all very well to be a bleeding heart, but don't kid yourself. These people aren't human beings. They're animals. Vermin. So don't give me any of this social worker crap about poor, ignorant, misunderstood human beings. Lonely, my foot! This bum knew what he was doing. Christ, incest is the oldest taboo in the world . . . every civilized instinct rises up against it. Listen, Kit, you don't see this garbage I deal with every day—muggers, rapists, perverts, freaks. You don't see them and I hope to God you never do. And as for Daddy-O, I'd like to see him put away for the rest of his life. If not longer."

"Maybe you're in the wrong end of the business," Kit said. "Maybe you should have been a cop. Or a prosecutor."

"Maybe I should have." He put down his drink. Two Scotches were all he allowed himself. "Ah, let's drop the whole subject. It stinks. What's for dinner? Smells like chicken."

"Chicken Divan. I've never made it before."

"Mmmm," he brightened, "let's eat—and then you can tell me all about *your* day."

Her day.

What was there to say about her day? Any of her days? They fell into two categories, like Column A and Column B in a Chinese menu.

In Column A, the sun shone. Or at the very least it neither rained nor snowed. She was up at six for Sarah's early bottle, then, of course, Michael's breakfast, then her own. By eight o'clock Michael was off to work and she was alone with Sarah and the laundry. The eternal, infernal laundry. Their budget allowed them a diaper service, and the deliveryman came Tuesdays and Fridays. He would remove that great plastic pail reeking of ammonia and feces and replace it with a fresh one. One that would smell just as bad by the time the next delivery day rolled around.

If that were *all* the laundry, it would be tolerable. But it was unbelievable—simply unbelievable!—how many sheets and towels and vests and kimonos a five-month-old baby could go through. Unbelievable the sheer amount of dribbling, drooling, peeing and puking one small digestive system could originate.

So by midmorning, Kit was off—Sarah under one arm, a laundry bag on the other, down the sixty-four steps to the basement landing where the super let her keep the carriage.

Next, laundry to the Wash-o-Mat, where for another twenty-five cents they'd fold it and hold it for you. Then off to Star Supermarket for the shopping, then home by twelve for Sarah's lunch.

After lunch, it being a Column A day, there was no legitimate excuse for not bundling up the baby, getting out the carriage—again!—and making the health-restoring pilgrimage to the tiny park six blocks away. For Dr. Spock, Emily, Michael and the pediatrician all agreed that fresh air was a *must* for babies. Sarah concurred, apparently, for she would always fall asleep within minutes of Kit's settling down on her usual bench.

The James Docherty Memorial Park was the official name of this little patch of dead grass and bottom-bruising concrete benches, but it was known locally as "Mother's Rest."

On any given day, there were other women there with babies and toddlers. Women different from any Kit had ever known. Women with printed rayon headscarves covering an Everest of pink rollers, women with flesh packed firmly into toreador stretch-pants, women with voices that cut straight to the nerve ends. Their children all seemed to be named Charlene, Darlene, Tracy, Stacy, and endowed with chronic runny noses. The mothers all knew each other and usually passed the afternoon in a happy babble ranging from little Stacy's bowel movements to last night's quiz shows. Ranging that far and no farther.

Kit was unsure of protocol. Should she introduce herself to the crowd? Surely, as the newest mother in the park, formality would demand that the veterans made the overtures. She wanted their company. She didn't want their company. Felt guilty about appearing antisocial and aloof. But she could not bring herself to initiate proceedings.

Instead, she would open her book—she never went to the park without one—and read, turning the pages clumsily with gloved and frozen fingers. Bundled up like a soldier on the Russian Front, Sarah slept blissfully throughout.

"W'atcher reading?"

It was the thin blonde who formed the hub of the group who finally made the overtures and Kit, not knowing whether to be grateful or annoyed, turned the cover of her Penguin paperback outward for the intruder's inspection.

"It's Henry James," she said. "I'm reading a story called *The Jolly Corner*."

"Well, me too—I love to read. Ya always got yer nose in a book, my husband keeps telling me. Him, he don't read at all. But me? I'll read anything. Harold Robbins, Mickey Spillane . . . You like Mickey Spillane?"

"I haven't read him," Kit apologized. This was one literary discussion she was ill-equipped to enter.

"No? He wrote *I, the Jury. My Gun is Quick*. Ya haven't read any of 'em? Well, you oughtta. They're really terrif . . . give you a lot to think about." Then, sensing Kit's stony lack of response—"Yeah, well, I better be getting back to my girl friends. Nice talkin' to ya." And she was gone.

Kit breathed a sigh of relief and returned to her Henry

James. The broad avenues of Old New York had never seemed more inviting.

After that, she and blondie would nod, exchange polite smiles. No more. And Kit sat alone, unregretfully.

She would check her watch constantly. 2:45. 3:12. And then—praise God—3:30. For that was the moment, *pace* Dr. Spock, when she had done her duty. Served the legal minimum of punishing park time and could now return gratefully to pick up the laundry, go home and start dinner.

That was Column A. Nice days.

Column B was marginally better. Because on Column-B days it rained or snowed or at least promised to, thus morally absolving Kit from Ordeal by Park Bench.

On Column B days, she could stay home, watch television, sleep when Sarah slept—which she usually did. For she never seemed to get enough sleep. Yet no matter how tired she was, how deeply she slept, she was always wide awake at least one minute before Sarah. It was uncanny, this early warning system that alerted every sense in her body for the baby's first waking cry. They were bound, she and Sarah, by an umbilical cord that not even birth could sever.

She mentioned this once to Michael, but he scoffed at her. Said she'd be believing in reincarnation next. Kit didn't argue. She knew this was not the sort of thing that any man could ever understand.

But Column A or Column B, five o'clock always rolled around and this, for Kit, was the cream of her time with Sarah. Sarah, bright and lively from her afternoon nap, lighting into her dinner with gusto and great good humor. And after dinner, the ritual of the bath, the delicious sweet clean smell of baby flesh, the feel of that firm silky skin beneath Kit's fingers, the artless sensuality with which Sarah would lounge there on the bathinet and permit herself to be dried, powdered, diapered and dressed for bed.

"You sweet, good, beautiful girl," Kit would murmur. "You good girl, you lamb, you darling." And Sarah would reward her with a toothless grin, as if she understood every word. She would follow Kit with her eyes as she moved about the room, cock her ear at each new endearment.

Michael always tried to get home before Sarah went to bed and usually made it, always excepting Wednesdays when he was off at the Democratic Club. But that magic hour was the high point of *his* day too, Kit realized, and she was pleased he had turned into such a doting father.

Thus her days.

The evenings, of course, were short and fairly sweet. They rarely went out now. Kit felt nervous about leaving the baby with a teenage sitter, and those few times they had gone to the movies she had fallen asleep in the first ten minutes. Even at home, she barely lasted past the ten o'clock news on TV.

Today, however, was different, she reflected as she took the chicken out of the oven. Today there was something to tell, but whether she would tell it just yet still required deliberation.

For today, that very afternoon, she had neither gone to the park nor stolen a nap. Instead, she had visited Dr. Gordon, and he had confirmed her worst fears and suspicions.

"Diaphragms don't work unless you use them each and every time," he said crossly. "You realize your babies will be less than a year apart."

How he had lectured her, when he first fitted her out with the contraption. "Motherhood is a blessing"—she could recall his every word—"but only when it's wanted and well spaced. Otherwise it's a curse. So don't even let your husband blow you a kiss," he said, handing her the little plastic case, "without putting this firmly in place."

And here she was, just three months later, pregnant again like any ignorant washerwoman.

No, she'd spare Michael the news tonight. He'd had a rough enough day as is. Wait till the weekend when they could talk it out. It would give her time to honey him up.

"You're looking peaky, Kit," he said as she was stacking dishes in the sink.

"Just tired, I guess."

He got up. Was he going to do the dishes? "Why don't you hit the sack right now and leave the dishes in the sink? They can wait till tomorrow for once."

When she finally screwed up the courage to tell him, he took the news with amazing good grace.

"May as well get it over and done with, I suppose." They had long ago decided on just two children.

"But we'll have to move. You *do* see that, Michael. I just couldn't manage the stairs with two."

"Could you hold out at least until the lease expires? It's just another six or seven months."

But no, it was too much. The climb, the carriage, the baby, the pregnancy, the way she was feeling—not as good as last time. And three weeks later he came home and announced he'd found them a garden apartment in Brookline.

"Ground floor, three bedrooms, even a bit of a garden at the back."

"And a washing machine? Please, Michael, a washing machine?"

"Well, if you feel you can't live without it."

"Oh, Michael," she pulled him close to her and kissed him. "You're so very good to me."

"Now you be good to *me*, Kit, and this time give us a boy."

KATE

DEAR GOD, SHE WAS PREGNANT. SO MUCH FOR THE WONDERS OF
birth control.

That was her first reaction, but, on balance, Kate knew she
had no one to blame but herself. Dr. Friedman had been
categoric when he first fitted her out with the diaphragm.
"Each and every time," he'd said, handing her the little
plastic case. "It won't work unless you use it each and every
time, so don't go getting careless. After all, once is all it
takes."

Once was all it *did* take. An unforeseen "once" with a Wall
Street cowboy named Mike something-or-other, who had
little more to recommend him than raffish eyes and a neat
taste in Italian suiting. She could pinpoint the man, the date,
even the moment—but the memory brought no pleasure.

A simple lunch date, that's all it had been. A simple lunch
date to find out about mutual funds; but somewhere between
the second and third martinis, it had evolved into a different
type of mutuality. ("Have you ever seen the inside of a
brokerage, Miss Chapman?" "Call me Kate . . . and no, I
haven't. But perhaps you could show me around.")

Within the hour they were tearing at each other behind the
closed door of a brokerage conference room, while in the
corridor beyond, telephones rang and secretaries scuffled. It

had been a swift, joyless coupling; the sense of danger, the threat of imminent discovery providing the sole erotic touch.

Fifteen minutes later, she was out in the Wall Street sunshine, hailing a cab and inwardly marveling at her own audacity. She'd been worried, she now recalled, about the snail's pace of downtown traffic, about turning up late for a three o'clock meeting. And only mildly concerned that she'd taken no precautions. Besides, hadn't she read somewhere that you couldn't get pregnant if you did it standing up? Or was that just an old wives' tale?

But the old wives were wrong and Dr. Friedman depressingly right. And now she felt too much the fool to go back to him with this admission of carelessness and failure.

Not that she had any firm moral views about abortion, but it was all so . . . so *inconvenient* right now, what with the pressures building up at the office. To say nothing of the very real problem of finding an obliging doctor.

For the first time since she had moved to New York, Kate was struck with the realization that she hadn't made a single close girl friend. There was no sympathetic Jan to confide in, no worldly Phyllis to rely on for practical advice. She considered sounding out Sharon back at the office—Sharon would probably know the ropes—but this wasn't the kind of tidbit you wanted to toss into the typing pool. Might as well advertise on TV. When it came right down to it, there was only one person she really trusted. One person in all of New York.

"You mean," said Barry, "you want *me* to find you an abortionist?" He lifted an elegant eyebrow. "Really, ducks, that's hardly my line of country. If I start asking around . . . why, it could ruin my reputation in the gay bars!"

Yet, despite his chiding, Barry came through and, some ten days later, delivered her into the rubber-gloved hands of a discreet gynecologist in Queens. It was quick, clean, relatively painless and shockingly expensive. And unutterably sad.

"Don't cry, honey," Barry comforted her on the long drive back to Manhattan. "It's all over now and no harm done. Just remember the Kate Chapman motto—and never look back."

She never did, not consciously. But sometimes in her morning walk through the park, the sight of a young mother pushing a baby carriage would trigger memories of that antiseptic afternoon in Queens, set off a chain of unwanted images. Would it have been a boy? A girl? Would it have been beautiful? Clever? Normal? Healthy? Would there ever be others? . . .

Without quite knowing why, she gradually gave up walking through the park, and little by little the images faded.

"The name of the game, boys and girls, is dog food."

They were all assembled in Len's office, the half-dozen copywriters and art directors who constituted his group. Also present in a corner, hiding behind giant horn rims, was a girl Kate vaguely recognized from Research.

It must be an occasion, Kate figured, because for once Len's desk was swept clear of litter and layouts. In the center stood a solitary tin can.

"This, you'll all be happy to know, is Kennel King." Len picked up the can and twirled it around like a Tiffany salesman displaying the facets of a diamond.

"It says here"—he squinted—"that it makes dogs 'jump with joy.'"

He turned the can around to reveal the picture of an Irish setter bounding gleefully through verdant fields.

"Kennel King. The dog food of champions is composed"— he read off the fine print—"of forty-eight percent horsemeat, thirty-six percent cereal and filler and"—he frowned— "various other ingredients too disgusting to be mentioned so early in the morning.

"Kennel King accounts for slightly under eight percent of the national dog food market. So . . . although it makes dogs jump for joy, it is not making its manufacturers jump for joy. They're very, very unhappy with their present advertising agency and have invited us plus another half-dozen agencies to pitch the account. It could be a big one. Now, I'm sure you're all dying to know more about this canine caviar, so I'll turn you over to Barbara Gleeson. Barbara?"

"Thank you, Len," Miss Horn Rims picked up a bound Xerox file that looked as if it ran several hundred pages.

"As you can see, we folks down in Research have been busy correlating data on dog food consumption patterns."

She spoke with the prim didacticism of a college lecturer confronting a particularly dull freshman class.

"We think you'll find everything you need in these reports. Data on pet ownership in America, broken down into regions"—she riffled through the pages—"the FDA regulations on canine nutrition, share-of-market figures for all leading dog foods, price structures, an analysis of competitive advertising . . . the works."

She closed the file with a crisp snap, like a schoolteacher rapping for attention.

"The important thing to keep in mind," she continued, "is that, unlike cats, dogs have a *very high degree of brand loyalty.*"

In her mouth, the words became an indictment.

Kate blinked. She could see it now. The Kennel King Irish setter jumping, but not for joy—bounding down the aisles of his local A & P, an A & P that through incredible negligence had been caught short in its supply of his favorite din-din.

"What do the dogs do when the store runs out?" Kate asked. "Bite the girl at the checkout counter?"

"You may laugh," Horn Rims droned on—and Kate obliged—"but that is the key to the whole problem. As the research will show you, once a dog has become accustomed to a particular brand, he'll eat it with gusto every day of his life. And dogs are very easily satisfied." She sighed at this proof of dogged dereliction, their unwarranted stubbornness in joining the consumer revolution. "So you see, once dogs are content, there's very little motivation for them to switch brands and try out new products."

Len winked at Kate.

"Right, Barbara," he broke in. "And we should keep that in mind at all times. However—and I can't stress this too strongly—the important thing to remember is that dogs don't buy dog food. People buy dog food. And it's people we've got to convince. We have to show in some believable way that there's a real reason for them to switch from Swillies or Yummies or whatever they've been buying to"—he aped the tones of a TV huckster—"New, Wonderful, Improved Kennel King!"

"But *is* there any reason?" Barry asked. "Is there anything in Kennel King itself that we can really shout about? Some secret ingredient, maybe? The unique flavor of old shoe?"

Len shrugged.

"I guess you all know the story of the client who walks into an advertising agency with two brand-new silver dollars, absolutely identical. He plunks them down on the creative director's desk and says, 'Mine's the one on the right. You prove it's better.' Well, ours is the one on the right and we have to find some way, some gimmick, to prove that it's better. It's a tough one, but do what you can. I'll tell you this, though"—Len's face grew serious—"Kennel King is a division of ChicagoCorp, the Chicago Meat-Packing Corporation, which just happens to be one of the top forty companies in America. They make everything from soup to buttons. Now, we've been trying to get a foot in that door for the last ten years, and Gully sees this as the opening wedge. Who knows? If we land Kennel King, it could pave the way to really big business. Maybe their Soup Division. Their Processed Meat Division. I'm talking about multi-million dollar billings. You get the picture. Now Marsden's willing to spend a whole bunch of bucks on the Kennel King presentation, so let your imaginations *go*. And don't worry about coming up with something that's really far out. We can always pull our horns in later. Just remember, this is the big one. And whichever one of you guys—or gals" he nodded to Kate—"comes up with a winner, well . . . that person's going to be a hero around here for a long time to come. So for the next three weeks, I want you all to think dog food, live dog food . . ."

"Eat dog food?" Barry asked.

"Yeah!" Len rolled the can across the desk to him. "Go ahead if you think it'll help."

For two weeks solid Kate thought dog food, lived dog food, and—while she didn't go so far as to eat it (the smell of horsemeat made her want to throw up)—immersed herself totally in the world of the four-footed creatures and their two-footed owners.

She pestered Barbara in Research for every marketing paper on the subject and ransacked the shelves of her local library for everything from training manuals for breeders to Konrad Lorenz's *Man Meets Dog*. For the first time in her life she regretted never having had direct experience with dogs back in Athol. They used to make her sneeze.

They didn't now, however, and although she wasn't really nuts about them, she became as single-minded in her quest as Inspector Javert on the track of a canine Jean Valjean.

She interviewed every dog owner she knew, including Mrs. Pitkin upstairs and the liquor store owner down the block who kept Alsatians. She struck up conversations with dog-walkers on the street.

But with the exception of Mrs. Pitkin, whose dog only ate Kosher, the answers she got merely confirmed what the more formal research had already stated.

"Why should I change his food?" the owners would reply. "He's happy. He's healthy."

Somewhere there had to be a solution.

She was sitting at the bridge table that served as work space, dressing table and dining counter, picking listlessly at cottage cheese and canned peaches.

The July heat beat about her relentlessly. From the open window came the screams of kids playing at the hydrant, the jukebox from Rocky's Pizzeria, the night roar of cars and buses going down Columbus Avenue. Friday night, and everybody else was having fun. Maybe there were worse places to be, when the temperature was in the nineties, than in a furnished room in the Upper West Side. Offhand, she couldn't think of one.

Ah, the hell with The Problem, which was how she'd come to think of it. She'd eat up and go catch a movie. Or maybe kick a poodle for relief.

The two peach halves stared up at her from the plate. Stared with bland, insensitive eyes. Kate stared back. Two peach halves swimming in syrup, one the mirror image of the other.

Kate picked up her spoon and wondered. *What would tempt me to eat one peach half before the other?* For there was nothing to choose between them.

She remembered Len's analogy of the advertiser with the two silver dollars. What was it he said? Oh, yes. Mine's the one on the right. You prove it's better.

Probably one of those advertising saws that had made the rounds of every agency. And yet, if she could solve that problem, she could solve The Problem.

She visualized the silver dollars side by side there on the table. Clean. Gleaming. Identical down to the very last mill. *E pluribus unum,* they would say. *From the many, one.* How could you prove the one on the right was better? You couldn't.

Unless . . .

E pluribus unum. From many, one. She switched it around. From the one, many.

Unless the one on the right wasn't a silver dollar at all!

Kate chewed a mouthful of cottage cheese, her mind racing now.

Suppose, she thought, just suppose that instead of a silver dollar, the one on the right was a pile of change. Pennies, nickels, dimes, quarters. The same value as a silver dollar—but different. Then there really *would* be something to choose between them.

And there it was. Simple. So simple she couldn't believe no one had thought of it before. She pushed away the half-eaten cheese, gave the peaches a wink, then got out her lined yellow pad.

It was Friday—only Friday. She had the whole glorious weekend before her, and suddenly the noise didn't bother her anymore.

She got to the office earlier than usual that Monday, on the off chance that Len might have taken an early train. Sometimes he did, but not this particular Monday. Not the early train nor the next two or three.

Every ten minutes she'd pop round to his office, checking to see if he'd arrived. Nine o'clock passed. Ten o'clock. Still no Len. She began having doubts about her big idea. If it were all that obvious, how come no one else had thought of it? Or had it been thought of and discarded years ago? Finally, ten fifteen! And there he was coming out of the elevator with a plastic container of coffee.

She was at his office door before he even got there.

"Len, can I see you for a minute? It's important."

"Sure." He ushered her in. "Just let a man get his jacket off."

Jacket on the coat hook. Check the phone messages. Frowns. Check the mail in the In Box. More frowns. Initial a couple of layouts. Pull the lid off the coffee container. Then at last, *at last*, Len sat down, put his feet up on the desk and folded his hands across his belly.

"OK, Kate. What's on your mind?"

"Len, I think . . ." as she started to talk, she heard the doubt creep into her voice. "I think I may have found the solution to the dog problem."

"Yeah . . . what is it? Vivisection?"

She smiled politely. Why did every straight line in this place call for some smart-ass reply?

"Well, you see, I've been thinking . . ."—now it really

sounded stupid, even to her—"that there are city dogs and country dogs."

Len observed that such indeed was the case.

"The thing is," Kate continued," they lead totally different lives. Take your typical country dog, for instance. He's out of doors all day, running hard, chasing around. He might be a working dog or a hunting dog after birds. In any case, he leads a hell of an active life, and he's going to need a lot more calories than your city dog. Not more food, necessarily. More calories."

Len took his feet off the desk—a sure sign of interest—and nodded for her to go on.

"Now your city dog, he's a totally different case. Cooped up in an apartment all day. He gets maybe a five-minute stroll in the morning, or maybe walks his master down to the corner drugstore. No exercise. Ever noticed how city dogs run to fat? Hell, they can't even chase a pigeon down the block without panting."

She was off now—off and rolling.

She spread out her papers—notes, concepts, roughs—talking talking talking all the while. Len listened and nodded and occasionally mumbled and when she was done, leaned back and stared up at the ceiling.

Oh, God, let him like it. Dear God, please let him like it.

It struck her that God was dog spelled backward.

"Now, let me see if I've got you right, Kate. You're talking about splitting Kennel King into two, maybe three different products."

"Right."

"That's very heavy stuff, Kate. Very heavy. Do you know what it costs to formulate even *one* new product?"

"But Len,"—had he missed the point, the beauty of it?—"you wouldn't have to reformulate or add any new ingredients. Just reshuffle a little bit."

She checked her notes.

The stuff as it stands is forty-eight percent horsemeat—that's protein . . . thirty-six percent cereal—that's calories . . . and the balance is fat and . . . um . . . other ingredients. Raise the calorie content, make it fifty percent cereal, and you've got *Dinner Pail*, the high-energy food for action dogs. Cut the cereal and some of the fat and you've got *Lean 'n Mean*, the low-cal dog food for city slickers. Those are just working names, you understand."

"Yeah," Len grunted. "I don't know about that Lean 'n Mean. Have you ever been bitten by a chihuahua? And then you're talking about still another line for puppies. What was that one . . . *Puppy-Gro?*"

He reached for the intercom.

"Sharon? Get me Barry, Sid and Mario. And oh, yeah, that girl Barbara what's-her-name in Research. I want them in my office pronto!"

He hung up and grinned at Kate.

"That is one hell of an idea, Kate. One hell of an idea. What on earth made you think of it?"

E pluribus unum.

Kate smiled, but all she said was, "I studied four years of Latin in boarding school."

By three o'clock the meeting was over. The ChicagoCorp people had given the green light on two of the concepts. Dinner Pail and the now-rechristened Lean 'n Lively. They'd think about the puppy food idea; for now, it would have to wait.

Mr. Withers of ChicagoCorps made a brief, gracious speech, thanking everyone for "your wonderful effort." Len got up to say there should be special thanks for Kate Chapman, whose idea it had been from the start.

Dear, darling, wonderful, generous Len. She could have kissed him then and there.

"You must be proud of yourself," said Mr. Withers, shaking her hand with genuine warmth. "It was first-class thinking all the way. Gro-Pup." He shook his head and chuckled. "What a delightful idea! You must love dogs very much."

"Oh, I do!" Kate said fervently. And she did. At that very moment, Yes! she loved the hairy bastards.

This, she thought as she entered Gully's office, is more like it. Advertising the way it looks in Rock Hudson movies or in the pages of popular novels. Glamorous.

The room was easily thirty feet long and almost as broad, the walls white and modern, the floor carpeted a rich Wedgwood blue. Along one wall ran a complex arrangement of glass shelving, Mondrian-like in its random rectangles, and lit here and there with spotlights gleaming with George Jensen chic.

Neat, she thought. Very neat.

The great man seated behind a massive glass and chrome table was as sleek and silvery as his surroundings. Right now he was on the phone. Naturally. Everyone at Marsden was always on the phone. Barry had once told her that you could size up your position in the agency by the number of buttons on your telephone.

Kate was a two-button, Len a three. But Gulliver! From where she stood, she could count a row of five buttons, two of them lit. Plus a second phone with no buttons at all. A Wedgwood-blue phone into which he was talking, his private wire to the outside world.

Since he made no motion for her to sit down—indeed, seemed unaware of her presence—she walked over to the wall with the shelving. From what she'd heard of him, she wouldn't be surprised to find a display of scalps and shrunken heads—souvenirs he'd collected on his way to the top.

And it was, in its way, a collection of the dead and buried. A mortuary of a sort. For there on the shelves, beautifully cared for and arranged, was an array of products that had died. Corpses in tubes and boxes and tin cans. Casualties of the consumer wars. They lay there row on row, vying for attention like so many artworks in a museum.

There were bottles of Teal Shampoo. Tubes of Ipana toothpaste. Fatima cigarettes. Murads. Regent Ovals, nestling next to a matchbook that said Monogram Pictures. There was a pioneer television set, its convex screen a memento of TV's early days. There were boxes of Rinso White, bottles of Moxie. There were Chen Yu lipsticks and 3-D glasses. Bound copies of *Flair,* of *Liberty Magazine.* Item after item. Shelf after shelf. And in the place of honor—commanding its own private spotlight—the grill of an Edsel automobile.

She was so engrossed she didn't hear the click of the phone, only the smooth and cultivated voice.

"And how do you like my museum?"

He crossed the room to where she was standing. For a big man, he moved with astonishing grace. Like a shark cruising in familiar waters.

"Museum! It's more of a mausoleum, really." Kate was holding a jar of some mysterious brown cream that bore the legend Leggies. "But what on earth is this?"

"That, my dear, was well before your time. During the

war, when women couldn't get nylons, the Chesley Company brought out a product called Leggies. It was leg paint. You painted it on and"—he picked up what appeared to be an elongated eyebrow pencil—"you drew in a seam"—he traced an imaginary line up the back of his leg—"and there you were. No runs. No rips. No standing in line to buy stockings."

"Sounds terrific," said Kate. "How come it failed?"

"Well, you see . . . Chesley overlooked one little detail. If you got caught in the rain, the stuff ran like watercolor. Which, of course, is all it really was." He took the bottle from her and replaced it lovingly on the shelf. For a silent moment, they both admired the collection.

"It's fantastic," Kate marveled. "It really is. Do you mean it as a cautionary lesson?"

"Just so. I keep it here to remind myself and my clients of the ephemeral nature of our profession. But come, my dear, let's sit down."

She headed toward his desk, but he took her elbow and guided her to a beige suede sofa by the window.

"Cigarette?" he asked as they settled in, offering her the inevitable Norfolk.

"Thank you."

"I'm glad to see you don't believe all this nonsense about cigarettes causing cancer."

Kate smiled. Noncommittal.

He took her silence for agreement. "It's a worrisome thing," he said.

"Cancer?"

"No. The government. All those Cassandras in the Food and Drug Administration, acting as if the American people are too dumb to figure out what's best for them. Mark my words, the way things are going, one of these days it'll be a Federal offense to light up a Norfolk."

He suited the action to the words and lit their cigarettes. Of course, Kate realized. He's the man who wrote "Light up a Norfolk. Light up your life."

"The whole point about advertising," he said exhaling a cloud of smoke, "is that it gives people a choice. An *informed* choice. And that's the backbone of a free society."

She thought of the Russian voting booth and suppressed a smile. Was he warming up to launch a set speech? Chamber of Commerce lunch, speech number three: *Advertising: The Heart of the Free Enterprise System.*

But no. He clapped his hands jovially to indicate the
formalities were over and turned to her with a smile of
splendor and charm. He had beautiful teeth, white and even,
and the light eyes were sparkling now. She had never thought
of fat men as being sexy, but, in a silvery sort of way, he was.

"Well, well . . . Miss Kate Chapman. You know, everyone
down on the fifth has been singing your praises. It's all I hear
about from Len these days. And that Lean 'n Lively campaign"—he blew a kiss with his fingers—"brilliant. I'd be
proud to have it in my own portfolio."

From somewhere up on cloud nine, Kate mumbled her
thanks.

"And now, Kate . . . tell me something about yourself."

"There's really not much to tell." What a terrific man he
was. She was happy, so happy. "This is my first agency, you
know, and I've enjoyed every minute of it. Actually"—why
not? Why not take the plunge right now?—"Actually, I'd
been hoping to take on a bit more responsibility. I'd like to do
more television, get some general consumer experience." She
swallowed. "I'd like to have some accounts of my own."

"That can be arranged," came the soft reply. "In fact, it
already has been. It's the reason I asked to see you today."

She would have a group of her own, he told her—three
writers and two art directors. She would continue to handle
the Kennel King business; they were crazy about her at
ChicagoCorps. Plus a few other accounts—"nothing great,
but they can be built on"—and a considerable increase in
salary.

She smiled at his smiles and he moved in closer. She could
feel the weight of his leg against hers.

"Chapman . . . Chapman . . . " He furrowed his brow.
"We have some Chapmans at our country club out in Cross
Ridge. Any relation?"

That would be my uncle Harlan, she was about to answer,
when a bell went off in her mind. A little bell—courtesy of
Barry Warden—that pulled her off cloud nine and down to
earth.

*Of course. He's trying to place me. He's trying to find out if
I'm one of "us" or one of "them."* WASPS only, isn't that
what Barry had said? And suddenly, perversely, she didn't
want to give the son of a bitch the satisfaction. Didn't even
want to be one of "us."

"I'm afraid I wouldn't have any relatives at the Cross Ridge Country Club. I believe they exclude Jews from membership."

She could feel his leg muscles tighten with a tremor of surprise, but his face didn't give away a thing.

"I didn't realize you were Jewish," he said mildly. "You certainly don't look it."

From somewhere beyond, a voice spoke through Kate's mouth.

"We don't all have hooked noses, you know."

"No offense, dear." He patted her knee. Was he going to say that some of his best friends were Jewish? "It's just that I never considered Chapman a Jewish name."

"It wasn't always Chapman." What demon possessed her? She listened to herself in astonishment. "The name was Czernowitz. But when my father came to Ellis Island, the immigration officer couldn't spell it, so it was changed right on the spot. He works in a paper mill in Athol."

"Oh? What kind of work would that be?"

"He's a factory hand."

Forgive me, Spencer, for I have sinned. By now, Gully had rearranged his face into a smile.

"I admire you people, I really do. From Ellis Island to Madison Avenue in two generations. Well, you must have noticed we have a great many Jews working for Marsden in the copy department. You people really have a gift for words."

The pressure on her knee intensified ever so slightly.

"So there's no reason for you to think you can't have a good career here. You're a bright girl, and a good-looking girl, too, I might add." The smile again, the heavy knee pushing subtly at the hem of her skirt. "I want you to know there's nothing closer to my heart than seeing young talent make its way up the ladder. I'm here to help"—he moved his calf against hers—"and if there are any problems, I'd be happy to work them out with you."

I bet you would, duckie.

"Unfortunately, I don't have all the time I'd like during office hours, but perhaps we might get together one evening for a drink and a chat . . ."

Kate jumped up so precipitously she rattled the shelves, and when she found her voice it was thick with anger.

"Mr. Gulliver. I give between fifty and sixty hours a week to this office. I give my time—and that's all I'm going to give."

He stood and faced her, the florid cheeks now pale, his voice calm and icy cold.

"I take your meaning, Miss Chapman," he said. "Now I think you can see yourself out."

"Jesus H. Christ," Barry said when she told him. "You must be out of your mind. I've known a lot of Jews in this racket who tried to pass for WASPS. But this is the first time I've ever heard it the other way around."

KIT

MICHAEL MATHESON III DID NOT WANT TO BE BORN.

He made that abundantly clear within minutes of his arrival, lying there in Dr. Gordon's hands—small, wrinkled, wizened and blood-splattered. Even then he radiated an aura of aloofness, of misery and total disaffection. He did not cry. But Kit did.

"My God, it looks like a monkey!"

"It's a boy," Dr. Gordon said, holding him on end and producing the infant's first tentative wail. "A perfectly normal boy, as you'll see once we've cleaned him up a bit."

But later, when he brought the baby over for her inspection, clean and swathed now and ready to join the other newcomers in the glass-fronted nursery, Kit turned her face to the wall and wouldn't look.

It had been a rotten pregnancy. An absolutely stinking, rotten pregnancy. Twice she had thought she miscarried, and another dozen times wished that she would. Despite all of Dr. Gordon's scolding, she had gained nearly forty pounds; despite all his reassurances, had spent the last three months wracked by pains and anxieties. Her breasts had ached. Her legs had swelled up. Her tears were never more than one cross word away.

And Michael! Michael had been no help at all.

"My God, what are you complaining about, Kit? Gordon says you're fine, you don't have the stairs to cope with anymore, Sarah's the easiest baby in the world to look after—you said so yourself. So what's the problem?"

"I can't cope."

"Cope with *what*, for Chrissakes. It's just another baby. My mother had seven children by the time she was thirty—with no fancy washing machine—and she didn't bellyache all the time."

Kit had thought of his mother, lank-haired and leaden-eyed, fifty looking sixty. It was a vision that offered slender consolation.

"Well, your mother's not having this one, I am," she'd wept. "And I tell you, Michael, I cannot cope—with the housework, the cooking, the whole shebang. I want a maid."

"You want a *what?*" he'd practically screamed. You'd think she'd asked for the Kohinoor diamond.

"A maid, a housekeeper, some kind of help just for the next few months. Even if it's just for a few hours a day. My mother always had help, always—and she had only me to look after."

"Your mother," Michael had snapped," is married to a rich man. You are not."

"Oh, for God's sakes, Daddy's not rich. He doesn't own the plant, you know, he only works there."

"Rich is a relative word," he'd replied," and we are relatively poor. So you just better pull yourself together."

Which was what Gordon had kept telling her. Gordon, such a rock, such a font of sympathy and counsel when she was pregnant with Sarah, claimed he couldn't understand what her problem was. "They're normal symptoms, perfectly normal," and had refused to prescribe tranquilizers or sleeping pills. "Just get more rest and watch your weight. Everything will be all right."

All right. Perhaps not *all* all right, but right enough by the time she and the baby came home from the hospital. He was five days old and, though still no golden boy, at least he looked recognizably human.

It was Emily—in from Athol for the occasion—who gave the baby the name he would live by. Emily, all ruffles and flustered good will, who had come to help while Kit recovered. Emily, whose household skills extended no further than the preparation of canapes (Kit would rather her mother had sent Mrs. Antonelli). Yet it was Emily who had put her finger on the new baby's special quality.

"You know who he looks like?" she said on Kit's first day home. For a moment, Kit thought her mother was going to say *Spencer*.

"He looks like . . . well, I don't know if you ever saw the picture . . . *Shangri-La,* was it? No, *Lost Horizon.*"

"He looks like Ronald Colman?"

"Don't be silly, dear. He looks like"—she peered down into that little dark face—"like the old monk, the one who lives to be nine hundred years old, so wise and holy."

"It wasn't a monk, Mother. It was a lama."

But Emily was right. The baby did have a certain sage and monkish look, lying there so dour and undemanding against the crisp whiteness of the bassinet.

Kit picked him up in a surge of compassion, picked him up and cradled him for the first time. "Monk. Monk," she crooned. "My little wise old monkey."

At first, Michael objected vigorously to the sobriquet, but eventually even he succumbed. It was so apt. So undeniably apt. And anyhow, it was too confusing—two Michaels in the house.

So Monk it was.

"Well, what do you think?" Marian asked.

"Our loss is President Kennedy's gain. Congratulations."

The two women were sitting in Kit's backyard (the landlord called it a "garden") while the babies napped inside in sturdy defiance of the August heat.

"More important," Kit swatted a fly off the iced-tea pitcher, "What matters is what do *you* think?"

"Well, Tim's happy as a clam, of course. He'll be doing all civil rights work, which is just up his alley. And his father thinks it's a great opportunity. Still, I don't know. Washington's so big, and I suspect it's awfully easy for a young lawyer to get lost in the shuffle and never be heard from again."

"Well, Michael doesn't think so. He's green with envy."

That was putting it nicely, she thought, for Michael had been livid when he came home with the news that Tim had been appointed Special Counsel to the Civil Rights Commission.

"It pays when your daddy has what Tim calls 'a few connections.' Connections!" he had snarled. "The President of the United States . . . old man Keegan calls him Jack. Well, that's some connection, believe me. Jesus, *I'm* the one who does all the shitwork for the party. I do the shit and Tim gets the plum."

"Don't be petty."

"Who's being petty?" And they had argued, not for the first time that week.

Marian poured a glass of tea.

"Well, Michael shouldn't worry. From everything I hear, he's making quite a name for himself down at criminal court. Tim says he wouldn't be surprised if Mike winds up on the bench one of these days."

"A judgeship! Oh, Michael would love that." Kit gave a short laugh. "Always provided, of course, they don't abolish capital punishment. Why, he could be another Hanging Judge Jeffrys."

The moment the words were out, she could have bit her tongue off. Marian's sole response was to whistle softly.

"I didn't mean it the way it must have sounded," Kit said quickly, shocked at her inadvertent show of disloyalty. "It's just that he's so soured about his work lately. He brings it home with him in a great big cloud every night. Like Joe Btttfssplk in "Li'l Abner." The other night, he came home. He'd just won a dismissal for some client of his, I think it was a mugger, and Michael got him off on some sort of legal technicality. Instead of being pleased, you know what he said? He said 'That's not justice. That's a perversion of justice.' He said that about his own client! A couple of years ago he used to say that in his own mind, at least, he viewed all his clients as innocent. Well, now he views them all as guilty."

"He's probably right, you know. What's the proportion— ninety-five percent, isn't it? But I wouldn't worry about it. They all go through the stage when the law school idealism starts to wear off. Maybe he ought to switch to civil law. He'd probably make a fortune."

"Well, Michael's not all that interested in money. I think what he'd really like to do is go into politics."

"Without money?" Marian raised her glass in a mock toast. "Good luck to him."

"You know, Marian, you still haven't answered my question—how you feel about moving to Washington."

Marian leaned back in the deck chair and contemplated the sky.

"So-so. Only so-so. A lot of things turn me off about it. The weather . . ."

"Couldn't be worse than Bean Town on a day like this."

"And leaving old friends and . . . um . . . other things." The sky ceased to interest her. "Did you know, Kit, that Washington has the highest ratio of women to men of any city in the country? Jesus, Tim's going to go bananas down there. I suppose you heard of this business with Susannah at the office . . . ?"

Yes, Kit had heard.

"It's like a reflex action—him and women. He just can't get enough of 'em. Tell me, Kit"—Marian caught her gaze and held it. "Did Tim ever make a pass at you?"

"Me!" Kit's startled look was honest answer enough. "Good God, no, Marian . . . where did you ever get that idea?"

"Well, then you're just about the only dame in Boston he hasn't."

Kit didn't know whether to be flattered or insulted by this omission.

"He's very fond of you, you know," Marian continued. "Thinks you're absolutely terrific."

Kit felt her cheeks grow hot, hotter than even the summer sunshine warranted.

"No, he never did. Anyway, who'd want to make a pass at me . . . it seems I'm always pregnant."

"Good God, not again, are you?"

"No, not again. Or if I am I'm going to sue the makers of Enovid. I'm on the pill now."

"Yeah, well, I wish that goddam Susannah had been. Christ, what a mess *that* was!"

"Look." It was dangerous ground and Kit felt it her duty to say something mollifying. "I'm sure Tim's not the only man who plays around. You know Georgie . . . my upstairs neighbor . . . the girl with the long blond hair? Well, her husband's a terrible philanderer. She told me she even caught him with the baby sitter once. They're all the same, I guess. For all I know, even Michael . . ."

And as she said it, the unbidden image crossed her mind. Michael and somebody else . . . was it possible? It would explain an awful lot.

But Marian only snorted, as if the supposition were too preposterous to be entertained.

"Well, how would I know!" Kit went on. "I don't keep tabs on where he goes, who he sees"—she was fishing now, openly fishing. "Tonight, for instance, it's his weekly meeting at the Young Democrats Club, or so he tells me. He could be involved with some girl for all I know. I'd have no way of checking."

"Michael's not involved with any girl, I'm sure." Her friend was adamant. "Not Michael. He's too . . ."

Too what? Too loving? Too loyal? Too devoted a husband? Kit waited for the ego-boosting adjective. But all Marian said was, "He's too cautious. Not like Tim."

That rankled. It was such a put-down. But Marian's mind was clearly elsewhere. She lit a cigarette and smoked silently for awhile, and when she spoke again her voice was hoarse.

"I don't know why I stick with him. He admits he just can't change. It's like a compulsion—if it wears skirts, lay it. And Washington will be the same thing in spades.

"In spades? Not literally, I hope."

And Marian laughed. "Well, you know he's a great believer in integration."

"Then why *do* you stay? Is it because of the Church?"

"Un-unh! I wasn't brought up a Catholic, you know. I just converted to please Tim's family, so that wouldn't stop me for a minute. I stay with him because he's kind and good-hearted and funny and . . ."—she flicked her cigarette into the box hedge—"he's absolutely sensational in bed. How's that for a reason!"

Kit was stunned. Embarrassed. She couldn't think of a single thing to say when, mercifully, Monk broke the silence with a long, angry howl.

"I better go get the baby."

Sensational in bed.
The phrase popped into her mind from out of nowhere while she was watching James Meredith being interviewed on TV. She forced her mind back to the evening news. It had been a big day. The Freedom Marchers down south, live footage from the Berlin airlift, a three-car pileup on the Mass Turnpike, sports roundup (the Red Sox went down to a 3-2 defeat), the weather forecast ("Tomorrow will be another scorcher with temperatures well up in the nineties")—and all

she could think of was that lurid phrase of Marian's. *Sensational in bed*.

With a flick of annoyance, she switched off the set, watched the little white dot vanish into infinity.

Christ, it was hot. Too hot to watch television. She could feel tiny rivulets of sweat trickle down between her breasts. Too hot to read. Too hot to be confined in even the lightest of summer dresses. She slipped out of her clothes—no one could see in from the street—and stretched out on the daybed by the window, eager to catch the faintest hint of a breeze.

Sensational in bed.

She lay back and listened to the quiet. The heavy quiet of a house with sleeping children. Michael was out, of course. Out with his Dev Dems and not some bit of fluff. In spite of her coy Q & A session with Marian, Kit was sure of it. Maybe she'd go to the beach tomorrow. Maybe she'd buy some more blueberries. Maybe . . .

It was hot. Her eyes were heavy. She drifted . . .

In the dark she could feel his cool fingers—light as air, tender as silk. Cool tender fingers caressing her throat, her neck, her nipples. Soft loving fingers, now gliding on her belly, now kissing her thighs, fingers brushing her hair, stroking her breasts . . .

She awoke with a start. Tim!

But no, it was not Tim . . . only a playful breeze that had found its way in from the street. God! What had she been thinking of?

No, not of Tim. Certainly not of Tim. She had been thinking of Michael. Of course. Lying there naked as a harlot—suppose Sarah should suddenly walk in!

Yes, she must have been thinking of Michael. Better get up. Better take a nice cool bath and turn in.

Sensational in bed.

The tub was rich with the scent of Roger Gallet's Carnation, and Kit, wide awake now, admitted that the time had indeed come to think of Michael.

She had no way of knowing whether Michael was "sensational in bed." Like that old joke—"How's your wife?" "Compared to what?"—she could only answer "How is Michael?" with "Compared to whom?"

There are no yardsticks for virtuous women.

She had never discussed their sex life with anyone, nor would she. One had to maintain *some* standards of loyalty.

Yet sex sex sex was the number one topic of discussion among so many women she knew. And Georgie upstairs was the worst.

Well, Georgie *would* be, with her mania for Freud and Fromm and Wilhelm Reich—and look where Reich wound up, will you? In the funny farm. Kit just tuned out when Georgie started her pseudo-scientific jargon about vaginal versus clitoral orgasms. It made everything sound so cold and clinical.

And then Phyllis! Those remembered conversations, the endless talk about how many men she had laid that week or how many times she had "come" in a single night. Well, you could divide anything Phyllis said by five—no, by *ten*—and still have overshot the truth.

And now Marian, with this business of Tim being sensational in bed. That was different. For Marian was not prone to hyperbole.

Kit had a fleeting vision of different acts, different pleasures from those she had shared with Michael.

For the fact remained that whether or not Michael *had* been sensational in bed—and Kit faintly suspected not—he certainly was not now. He was not anything in bed.

In the past five months he had made love to her exactly four times. And the last time had not been—successful. That was almost two months ago and since then, although she had tried in her way to reassure him, he had made no overtures. None at all.

When they were first married they used to make love at least twice a week. And always, *always* on Saturday night—except, of course, when she had her period. "Shall we?" Michael would say. Simply "Shall we?" was the cue, and she would put down her book or turn off the television and they would go to bed hand in hand. She recognized that he was not particularly "experimental"—she'd read enough modern fiction to know *that*. But even if they hadn't plumbed the erotic depths, it had been pleasant and sufficiently satisfying.

But now, these last months, nothing. Why? No, she didn't think there was another woman. Marian was right—he was too cautious. So it had to be some fault in Kit. At first she thought that he feared another pregnancy, so she reassured him that she was on the pill. But all he'd said was "That's good" and changed the subject. Her appearance, perhaps?

True, she had gained a hell of a lot of weight last year, but she'd lost most of it.

She looked down at her body, lithe and glistening under the suds. No stretch marks to speak of. You couldn't call her *fat*. Certainly not fat like a Rubens Venus, and they were considered attractive. Her breasts were a little bigger than they used to be, but most men would consider that a plus. She touched them. Her skin felt smooth, sensual, her nipples suddenly taut and erect. She ran her hand down her body—the concave navel, the narrow hips, the delta of fine curly hair. And as her hand slid between her legs she felt a surge of desire, sharp physical desire so intense it made her gasp.

My God, Michael would make love to her tonight. He must! Tonight he would take her, exploit her. She would *will* him to do so. *He* would be sensational in bed.

She got out of the tub and toweled off vigorously. The abrasive touch of the terry cloth made her all the hungrier. Yes, tonight. Tonight she would seduce him, tonight they would share erotic joy. She smoothed her skin with talcum, scented herself with dabs of Sortilege in parts of her body that had never known perfume before. She would wear—what? The silk chiffon nightgown of her wedding night? The pretty ecru "baby doll" her mother had given her? No. She would wear nothing. He would come home and find her naked on the bed. Naked and scented and open and waiting—and they would make love until dawn.

It was after midnight when she heard the car drive up, the door close, the quiet footsteps in the hall. She listened motionless to the flush of the toilet, the burble of water in the sink. He came into the bedroom soft as a burglar, undressed in the familiar geography of the dark.

"Michael?"

"You still up, Kit? It's way after midnight."

He lay down on the bed spread-eagled.

She reached out to touch him; her hand found his belly.

"I was waiting for you."

"You didn't have to. Nothing much happened. Just another long goddamn boring meeting."

She moved her hand down, gently, gingerly, her fingers surprised in their progress by the waistband of his shorts. Wearing shorts on a night like this! Deftly she eased her fingers beneath the firm elastic, wove them down through the thickening hair, closed her hand lightly around his cock.

"Oh, for God's sakes, Kit!" He jerked away abruptly. "It's just too hot. Go to sleep, will you." He wriggled out from beneath her and turned his face to the wall.

She went to sleep. Eventually. And when she did, she dreamed of Tim.

Next morning he was up at the first Brrrr of the alarm clock and within seconds performing that routine of push-ups, knee bends, pedaling his invisible bicycle for yet another mile. Another mile closer to eternity. Kit watched him through half-closed eyes. His body was as slim, as beautiful, as sleekly muscled as ever. Watched him for the thousandth time. And for the first time, felt an involuntary shudder of revulsion.

They'd commandeered the entire upstairs dining room at Patsy's for Tim's farewell bash. Everyone was there: Harvard friends, office colleagues, even the great Judge Keegan himself. But tonight there would be no formidable talk of law and politics. Just lots of drinks, lots of laughs, lots of sentimental toasts.

By ten Kit was kind of high. Even Michael had gone way beyond his usual two Scotches and no one was feeling any pain. The air was full of smoke and laughter. Kit enjoyed it all and would have enjoyed it even more but for a fleeting, almost prophetic feeling that this party signified the end of an era. Through a haze of candlelight and Strega, she watched Tim socialize. Going from table to table like the father of a bride at a big society wedding. She hoped he'd come talk to her, knew he would eventually. He was probably saving his closest friends for last. Good old Tim, flushed now with wine and success, looking strangely elegant in his dinner jacket. Funny how you could see someone day after day, never give him a second thought and then suddenly find him attractive. It was weird. It truly was.

She'd known Tim for what?—three years? four years?— and had not once thought of him "that way." A real old-shoe friend, Tim was, the kind that could catch you without your lipstick on or in your rattiest Levis and you didn't care. How many hundreds of times had they traded jokes and affectionate insults, over how many hundred cups of coffee? Yet tonight she found him—exciting.

Was it the glow of success, the feeling that he was moving out of their youthful backwater into the great world at large? Was it the wine? Or was it that curious remark of Marian's?

Whatever it was, the chemistry was working. That's silly—she sipped her drink—it was probably the Strega. She'd heard somewhere that Strega was an aphrodisiac. Or was that Pernod?

From the corner of her eye, she saw him across the room talking—flirting, she suspected—with Letty Goodman. His head was close to Letty's cheek. She wished he would come and flirt with her. Sit close enough that she could feel the warmth of his body, perhaps the touch of his knee under the table. Of course it would go no further than flirting! Still . . . she didn't want to be the only woman in Boston he'd never made a pass at. She saw him move on to Anne Feeney.

And when he did come to their table, slightly drunk, arms akimbo, it was only to survey the scene—the mounds of crumbs, the broken bread sticks, the half-empty glasses of wine and Strega and cognac. It was only to say:

"My God, this looks like the Last Supper."

They all laughed, and Michael volleyed back: "The only question is which one of us guys is Jesus Christ."

"Oh, that's easy." Tim spread his arms and struck a crucifixion stance. "The real question is which one of us is Judas."

The party broke up way after two, with kisses and hugs and promises to write, phone, solemn vows to keep in touch.

"We'll miss you, Kit," said Tim, wrapping her in a sweaty bear hug.

"I'll miss you too."

He kissed her cheek.

And then they were gone. But maybe it was just as well.

Two months later, Michael joined the district attorney's office in a surprisingly high capacity for such a young man. Tim sent a congratulatory telegram from Washington.

REMEMBER. CONVICTING THE GUILTY IS EASY. IT'S CONVICT-
ING THE INNOCENT THAT TAKES SKILL.

Kit didn't think it was funny, although Michael assured her it was an old lawyer's joke. Michael was very happy in his new job, handling a lot of prosecutions. But nothing else had changed.

After Tim left, she began to fantasize.

Absurd, really crazy fantasies about affairs with movie stars, celebrities, baseball players, even historical characters.

The first time it happened she'd gone with Georgie to see a Paul Newman picture at the Cleveland Circle. It was their weekly "girls' night out"—the men stayed home and babysat.

Sweet Bird of Youth was the name of the film, and Newman had played a really rotten type. Kit was sure you were meant to hate him—a professional stud and Southern to boot, living off an aging, drug-addicted actress.

But when they left the theatre, Georgie licked her lips and said that Newman was "one gorgeous hunk of man." Kit laughed. He was OK-looking.

"Aw c'mon, Kit, 'fess up. How'd you like to find *that* in your bed when you get home tonight!"

"Well, if I did, it would surprise the bejeesus out of Michael."

And when she did get home there was only Michael in her bed, immobile and sleeping heavily. Kit got into bed beside him, taking care not to disturb, and shut her eyes.

A scene from the movie came back to her vividly. It was Geraldine Page stretched out on a hotel bed, corrupt yet seductive in a long, elegant shaft of silk. Then across the room came Paul Newman—cat-eyed, slim-hipped. Came toward the bed where the actress lay, waiting and languid and sensual.

Suddenly it was Kit—Kit there on the bed, languid and sensual. And from across the room came Paul Newman . . . The next night, she replayed the scene. Slowed it down here and there. Embroidered it. And this time the scene continued far beyond the point where the director in his discretion had cut.

For a while Paul Newman was her sole nocturnal lover. Then briefly Leonard Bernstein. Then Belmondo, Cesare Borgia, Ted Williams. She dallied on occasions with Heathcliff, Willy Brandt, Gerry Mulligan. Even submitted one long incredible night to the caresses of Dracula. Why not? The world was indeed her oyster and from it she could draw any man she wanted, living or dead or even fictional.

Gradually, however, she grew more selective. She began to

edit her fantasies, make them more realistic, force them into the straitjacket of the conceivable. She drew up new rules. She limited her candidates to the chronologically feasible, worked out logistics in painstaking detail—logistics that would result in the unlikely but nonetheless possible consummate embrace.

Cesare Borgia had to go, of course. As did Heathcliff and Scarpia and Prince André, whom she surrendered with considerable reluctance.

But that still left plenty. Plenty of powerful, handsome, successful, flesh-and-blood men who would pursue her, adore her, fulfill her.

All this, of course, called for substantial ingenuity—it could take whole nights just to figure out the strategy. After all, how would Kit ever get to *meet* Paul Newman? At an airport? A premiere? But she never went to such places. Never flew, attended no Hollywood parties, knew no one more closely connected with the glamorous world of entertainment than Hank Stratton down the street, who was the lighting engineer at the Boston Opera House.

For awhile she toyed with the idea of meeting him at a charity ball—but would Newman be interested in Boston charities? Not likely. Maybe a Democratic function of some sort or other—she believed he was active in West Coast politics. But that didn't work. It still put three thousand miles between them. Then, one lucky night, she hit upon it. Newman—she still had trouble thinking of him as "Paul"—would come to Boston for the out-of-town opening of a Broadway show. Yes, that was perfectly feasible. After all, he was a marvelous and intelligent actor—she stressed the *intelligent*—and probably was dying to work in the legitimate theater for a change of pace. A lot of them did.

So there she was. She'd been to the theater—alone, of course. She couldn't have Michael figure in her fantasies, although why he wasn't with her on this particular night was a detail she'd have to plot out later. Like baby-sitters.

Anyhow . . . she'd left the theater and was walking down Stuart Street when she realized she'd dropped one of those beautiful jade earrings her mother had given her for graduation. And as she bent down to look for it, her hair falling softly over her face in a cloud of burnished bronze, she heard his voice.

"Have you lost something?"

She stood up, flushed, but all the lovelier for it. There was no mistaking those piercing blue eyes, that firm yet sensitive mouth.

He touched her arm lightly. She was wearing her green wool crepe.

"I'll help you look."

From there on, it was easy.

Leonard Bernstein presented less of a problem. He was not just from Boston, but from Brookline itself. She expected he still had family here, probably visited them when he came to guest-conduct the Boston Symphony. The Bernstein family might even be within walking distance of Howland Terrace. There were a dozen ways in which she could meet "Lenny."

For a while she was captivated by Kingsley Amis. She'd seen his picture on the back cover of *Lucky Jim*—and what a terrific book *that* was! He was a dashing man who quite fitted her image of what a brilliant young author should look like. She devoured the biographical details. He was fifteen years older than Kit, to be sure, but that wasn't much of an age difference. And he had been to Oxford. Their affair would be marked not only by elegant English lovemaking but by marvelous literary conversations as well. He would be warm and witty and make her tea the next morning. She hoped he liked Henry James.

Amis would come to Boston on a lecture tour; Kit would be looking very smart in her Chanel-copy suit. After a talk of unparalleled brilliance, he would ask the audience if there were any questions. And Kit would say something so astute, so perceptive about his work that naturally he would want to discuss it later. He would seek her out after the lecture. "You know, you're the first person who ever recognized the symbolism of . . ."

It didn't bother her a whit that according to the book blurb Amis was already married. Married with two children. Bernstein was married. So was Paul Newman, and she suspected Joanne Woodward was formidable competition indeed. Well, Kit was married too, for that matter. So it wasn't as if she were looking for a husband.

And so she fantasized on and on, finding new lovers everywhere—in the papers, at the movies and on television talk shows, especially on the educational channel. Almost the only men she excluded from her fantasies were Tim—that was too dangerous—and Michael, for whom she now felt no sexual feelings whatever.

After a year or so, the fantasies began to vanish as they had appeared, gradually and of their own volition. One by one, her demon lovers withdrew to their proper milieu: the screen, the television, the printed page, the podium. Not, however, to be replaced by Michael. That part of their life seemed virtually over and done with.

Something had happened to Michael after Monk was born. He seemed to have lost all interest in sex. He had never, Kit realized, been particularly aggressive, and certainly never encouraged *her* to be so.

At first she blamed herself for this ebbing of their love life. Felt that motherhood had left her flabbier, less desirable. Yet her mirror reflected no radical change.

Then she wondered if the problem lay with Monk. The child was not, she knew, the golden boy that Michael had hoped for; and though her husband had struggled to conceal his disappointment, Kit felt in some subtle way that Monk's birth had dulled the edge of his desire. He never spoke now of having more children, although the children were the root of their marriage.

Or perhaps the problem was with Michael himself. Those long years of self-denial during the war, the Spartanism of his life at Harvard—perhaps they had set a pattern of lovelessness, somehow diminished his sexual drive.

She couldn't bring herself to discuss the matter openly with him—she was far too inhibited, he far too proud. She feared that were she to charge him with failure in bed, she would render him more impotent yet.

For despite all his strengths, his convictions, his outward self-assurance, she recognized that Michael's ego was a delicate creature. She loathed the thought of hurting him needlessly.

Anyhow, Kit rationalized, sex was only one part of marriage, and Michael fulfilled his commitments in all others. He was a good provider, a good father, a husband one could be proud of everywhere but in the privacy of their bedroom.

In the meantime, she had her fantasies.

She stayed on the pill mostly out of habit. Out of hope that things would one day change. And maybe, although she'd never admit it, out of the fantasy that perhaps Paul Newman really would turn up unexpectedly at 52 Howland Terrace. And as the dreams petered out, she stayed on the pill out of habit only. For Kit and her body were fast becoming strangers.

But real life events were intruding now. Events that would push everything else from her mind.

She and Georgie went to the beach a lot that summer. If the forecast was even halfway decent, they'd make box lunches the night before, fill the thermoses with iced tea and orange juice. By nine in the morning, they'd start loading the car with pails and shovels, beach chairs, towels, suntan lotion, changes of clothing for the kids. Thank God no more diapers! Add Georgie's three kids, Kit's two, and by the time they were ready to hit the road, there wasn't room for a stray mosquito in the Chevy.

Sometimes they'd drive to the municipal beaches: City Point, "L" Street or Revere. They had the virtue of proximity, but Kit didn't care for them. Too crowded, too full of raucous teenagers throwing beach balls, too many candy wrappers and Coke cans and broken bottles, too easy for Monk to wander off and get lost.

So if the traffic wasn't too bad, Kit would point the car north and head up to the more gracious beaches. North past Marblehead with its yacht clubs, past Salem with its memories of witchcraft, past Gloucester with its Portuguese fishermen. Sometimes even past Ipswich and right on out to Cape Ann.

Rich man's country, Georgie said the first time they drove to Rockport. "Think they'll run us gypsies out of town?"

But the kids loved it, and so did Kit—the great fell of rocks, the seagulls, the supple sands, the chintzy little shops that sold lavender potpourris and hand-churned ice cream. And for a few hours at least, Kit would have the illusion of a life of honeyed ease. Maybe some day she'd live in this area.

The kids would play. The women would talk a little, read a little, snooze a little, yell at the children occasionally, more for form's sake than anything else, and worry about nothing more urgent than the acquisition of a suntan.

Life should always be this way—clean and carefree.

Georgie was reasonably good company, although she did now and then get tiresome, especially when she started to relive the two years she'd already spent in analysis. To her, all life could be reduced to a predictable pattern of stimulus and

effect. There were reasons for everything, sometimes obscure, but all was capable of explication to those, like her,
seasoned with an analysand's eye. Her sentences frequently
began with "My analyst says . . ."

"My analyst says art is just a form of sublimation."

"My analyst says Harry's a very anal type."

Harry was her husband, a teacher at Boston Latin, and the
only anal thing Kit credited him with was a rather bulky rear
end.

"My analyst says . . ."

My analyst says the moon is made of green cheese.

For the most part, Kit didn't really listen, just mumbled
"oh's" and "ah's" every now and again plus the occasional
"and then what did *you* say?" Although once when Georgie'd
said, "My analyst says that if a woman didn't have a satisfactory relationship with her father as a child, she'll never be
able to have a satisfactory sexual relationship," Kit had been
brought up short.

However, even Georgie didn't believe everything she said,
and beneath all the blather had a hard core of good common
sense.

"My analyst says I may be using Geoffrey"—her oldest
boy—"as a career substitute."

They were seated on their deck chairs at Rockport while
the kids were playing nearby.

"That's funny," said Kit. "I always assumed it was the
other way around. That career women used their jobs as a
motherhood substitute."

"They're the smart ones," Georgie giggled. "If you had to
do it all over again, would you?"

"Would I what?"

"Have a family instead of a career?"

"Oh, I don't know. It's such a moot question. Once you get
bogged down, you don't even have time to think of alternatives."

"So right!"

They settled back in contented silence, letting the sun beat
down upon them. In the distance, Kit could hear Sarah
squeal. Up to something? In some sort of danger? She felt the
now-familiar rush of adrenalin. But no—there was Sarah with
Georgie's boys doing preposterous things with a pail and
shovel. And Monk? Monk played alone as always. She
watched him now, a small, dark figure following the path of a

sandpiper down the shoreline. Even in the sun, there was something wintry about him.

"Tell me something, Georgie."

"Mmmm . . . ?"

"Do you love all your children the same?"

"Aaaah," Georgie sighed and sat up. "What a question. I guess I'd have to say no."

Kit felt slightly relieved.

"I mean I love 'em all," Georgie continued, "and I love 'em all very much, but I love them in different ways. I suppose I have a particular soft spot for Geoffrey, maybe because he's the oldest, but I try not to let it show."

Kit was silent. The sandpiper had gone now, and Monk was standing by the shore stock still. Only his head moved, swiveling back and forth, in search of the vanished bird.

"What's the matter, Kit? Monk getting you down?" Kit didn't reply. "I know I talk an awful lot about myself and my problems, but that doesn't mean I'm completely imperceptive."

The lump in Kit's throat made speech painful. "You think there's something wrong with him, don't you?"

"I'm not a doctor, Kit." An astonishing admission from Georgie, who had frequently practiced psychiatry without a license. "The point is, *you* think there's something wrong with him. Maybe that's what matters."

"Sometimes," Kit turned her face to the sea and the words came painfully, "I think he's not normal."

"In what way?"

"He doesn't talk. Almost two years old and not a word. Why, when Sarah was his age, she was jabbering away like a maniac."

"Lots of kids are late talkers, Kit. And it's really not fair to compare him with Sarah. Children develop at different rates. After all, Winston Churchill didn't talk until he was—"

"I know all about Winston Churchill. That's what Michael is always saying. If it were only that. But it isn't. He's so . . . so *remote*. I just can't relate to him. Or him to me, for that matter. It's like I'm a nonperson. I walk into his room and he never looks up, never smiles, never even stops what he's doing. He keeps busy, I can't complain about that—but it's as if he's in a world of his own with a great big Do Not Enter sign for all intruders. Sometimes I think it's him, sometimes I think it's me . . . that I just don't love him the way I should.

She wiped her streaming eyes on the beach robe. Awful! Awful if the kids should come over and see her blubbering like that.

"I know what you're going to say, Georgie. You're going to say that I should take him to see a psychiatrist or maybe even see one myself."

"I was going to say no such thing."

"But it's not normal." She was more collected now. "You can't tell me it's normal. You know, I could call him right now"—she looked at Monk. He was less than ten feet away, watching a flight of seagulls wheel and plunge against the sky—"I could call him right now and he'd ignore me. Monk!"

She called. Then louder. "MONK!" Loud enough to draw the eyes of other mothers on their blankets, loud enough even for Sarah to hear. But Monk didn't move. Didn't shift his gaze from the intricate pathways of the gulls.

"You see," Kit said, "he doesn't even come when I call. Doesn't even budge. He just doesn't listen to me."

"Perhaps," said Georgie carefully, "he just doesn't *hear* you."

"Are you trying to tell me my son is deaf?" the prosecutor screamed, as if Kit was the prisoner on the stand.

Well, of course she was shocked. Too shocked to talk sense, as she had been after the last consultation. The one with Winkler.

Two weeks ago she'd taken Monk to the family pediatrician. She'd trusted him. Always had, even though she'd never troubled him with anything more serious than chest colds and three-in-one shots.

"It's possible," he told Kit after what had seemed to her a rather perfunctory examination. "Hard to say exactly. You must also consider the possibility that he's mentally retarded. That occurred to me once or twice before."

Occurred to you before? And you never said anything? You bastard. You hypocritical bastard!

She didn't say that, though. She could only manage limply, "You never gave me a hint you thought anything was wrong . . ."

"Now, Mrs. Matheson . . ." He had a way of talking down

to "his mothers," a light, jocular manner that probably came from soothing armies of children. "I wasn't sure then and I'm not sure now. Let's just say that it occurred to me."

"But it didn't occur to you to tell me. Don't I have a right to know?"

"Well, I couldn't see the point in worrying you unnecessarily." Whereupon, seeing Kit's stricken face, he added, "Of course, it could be his hearing. We'll check it out and see what's what."

He made an appointment for them at Boston Ear, Nose and Throat and patted Kit's hand as she was leaving. "Now be a good girl and don't worry."

Be a good girl indeed! You patronizing quack. I'll see you in hell before I ever step foot in this office again.

Dr. Anders at Ear, Nose and Throat was a man clearly more interested in cases than in people. Rather like Michael, she thought. He referred her to Dr. Armstrong, who referred her to Dr. Winkler.

"Franz Winkler," he said, "the best otologist in Boston. A great man."

And there she had sat in the "great man's" office—was it only yesterday afternoon?—a rambling layout on Marlborough Street with high windows, beautiful moldings, a room where perhaps a century ago Boston ladies had sipped tea and laughed and flirted.

Winkler proved to be a short, squat German with an accent so thick that Kit had to strain for every word.

"Sooo . . . we heff a little chat now, yes?" He pushed the mirrored headband back on his forehead so that at best he resembled a Cyclop, at worst a Gestapo flunky about to inflict some exquisite new torture. And what he told her was torture indeed.

There are two kinds of hearing impairments, Kit learned. There is conductive deafness, which originates in the external canal and in the middle ear and can often be cured by surgery. Then there is perceptive deafness, caused by the defective functioning of the inner ear. The inner ear—one must appreciate—is a magnificent mechanism; a labyrinth of chambers and windows, canals and galleries, of thousands upon thousands of microscopic hairs that transmit sound from the outside world to the base of the brain. It is one of the most intricate structures in the entire human body, and one of the most mysterious. The cause of inner ear malfunction is only sometimes known. The cure, never.

Monk had perceptive deafness. Deafness of the inner ear.

"Vich iss not to say he cannot learn to talk."

Ve haff vays of making you talk.

"Zat vill depend on training."

Winkler made several concrete suggestions. Since there was some slight residual hearing—total deafness is rare— speech of a sort might be achieved with intensive coaching and the help of a hearing aid. He gave her the name of two institutes and several private therapists and made a further appointment to fit Monk out with a hearing aid. He suggested as added insurance that both she and Monk be taught sign language. It would be rash to rely on speech alone.

"Ze rest iss up to you."

That was the burden of what she must now tell Michael. But as she unraveled the details, sorted out the technological terms, it struck her that it was Michael who was deaf. Deaf to her distress. To Monk's isolation.

"First you tell me he's deaf, now you tell me he's not. Make up your mind. Which is it going to be?"

"There's nothing wrong with *my* hearing, Michael. So please don't scream at me."

"I'm sorry, Kit." He blew his nose abruptly. She could see the struggle he had to keep from weeping. "I'm sorry, darling. God . . . it's just such a blow. Give me time to take it all in."

They talked about it later in the evening, and again the following day. By then Michael seemed much calmer, but hardly more disposed than before to accept the inevitable.

"Look, we can think about this two ways," Michael said, ever the optimist. "One, we can think of him as partially deaf, or two, we can think of him as partially hearing. And that's the way I'm going to think of him. Look at him watching television. He's responding. Obviously his hearing is better than your fancy Kraut specialist thinks."

Monk was glued before the set, following a Popeye cartoon.

"But . . ."

"No buts about it, Kit. I've seen him react and so have you. Now, I can't believe that if you make a concerted effort, he won't be able to talk normally. OK, a little hard of hearing maybe. Well, a lot of kids wear glasses . . . what's so awful? I'm sure if we just speak to him clearly"—Michael articulated like an elocution teacher—"he'll get the hang of it sooner or later. But sign language! Really, Kit, you amaze me. You want him to look like some kind of freak?"

"You don't understand, Michael. We've got to cover all bets. 'A little hard of hearing!' We're not even talking on the same wave length. It's not a question of a little hard of hearing. Monk is almost totally deaf."

"You keep *saying* that," Michael persisted. "You don't look on the bright side."

"I'm not sure there *is* a bright side."

"Well, I'll tell you one thing," he said evenly, his eyes narrow as a cat. "He didn't get it from *my* side of the family."

Kit couldn't believe her ears—her own very excellent ears.

"Just what do you mean by that?"

"It's not my New York grandfather who wears a hearing aid. It's not my crazy aunt Annabel who has to pull out her ear trumpet every time you ask if she takes cream or lemon."

"Are you blaming me?" Kit was fairly screaming. "Are you saying this is my fault?"

"All I'm saying," Michael repeated carefully, "is that he didn't get it from my side of the family."

Blame. Every failure, every mishap, every tragedy in life could be explained away by allocating blame. For Michael believed the world should be intrinsically clean and neat and well-ordered. Perfect. There must, therefore, be a reason for all its imperfections and that reason was people. Things didn't go wrong by accident; they went wrong by human agency. No use copping out, offering up fate or chance as your alibi. It was simply a question of correctly assigning the human culpability.

Thus: if dinner was overcooked, Kit was to blame. If Michael got caught in traffic, the Commissioner of Highways was to blame. If a half-crazed cane-cutter took a machete to his brother, he had no one but himself to blame. But blame there must be.

A sense of blame, perhaps, is what makes good prosecutors, but it does not, Kit discovered, make good husbands. She had hoped that Monk's predicament would bring them together, trigger in him some long dormant stream of compassion. But it did not. And as the days passed and the initial shock of Monk's deafness became a commonplace, she realized it never would. For Michael, too, was flawed.

The first time Monk wore his hearing aid—and a complicated gadget it was, with a fitted earpiece, trailing wires and a transistorized box that lay flat on his chest—Michael was outraged. "He looks like a goddamn Martian" was his first reaction, and later, "He's not going to wear that thing out on the street, I hope. Maybe you don't mind your son being made a laughingstock, but I sure as hell do."

"You bastard!" Kit flung back and tore out of the room, slamming the door so loud the windows rattled. So loud that perhaps even Monk in his silent world might have heard the echo.

"Michael?"

She had rehearsed her speech time and again in her mind, had waited weeks for the right moment. Tonight was the right moment, she decided, watching him linger over his after-dinner coffee. He'd had a good day in court, his mood was benign and she felt they could talk it over reasonably. Not hot words spilling out from the height of her anger, or cold words bubbling up from the depths of her depression. But calm, reasonable words.

She was willing, of course, to shoulder all the blame. That would make it so much easier for Michael to accept.

"Michael, I have something very important to say."

"About what, Kit?" He set his cup down squarely on the saucer.

"About us."

Michael looked her full in the face, but his eyes gave away nothing. Then he folded his arms and settled back.

"I know I haven't made you very happy," she began. "Perhaps I've been a disappointment to you."

Michael neither confirmed nor denied, simply sat there immobile and waiting. And suddenly Kit's beautifully reasoned arguments vanished like smoke in the wind—the words, mustered over a dozen sleepless nights and polished into a hundred imaginary dialogues, were scattered. Gone. And only tears remained.

"It's no good, Michael" she sobbed. "It's just no good. All we can do is tear at each other . . . I can't go on like this. I can't . . ."

Burying her face in her hands she surrendered to the anguish of the moment, all the fine words flown.

How long she sat there crying, she had no idea—five minutes? ten minutes? a thousand years? When the tears subsided she looked up to find him sitting there exactly as before.

He handed her his paper napkin.

"OK, now, pull yourself together and tell me what it is you want."

She blew her nose on the napkin.

"I want," she said, "a trial separation."

"A trial separation." Michael bit his lips in what was the first sign yet of emotion. But the emotion was not that of surprise. "OK, Kit. Now tell me, what do you see this trial separation consisting of?"

She started to give him her reasons, the feelings that had led her to this point . . . their arguments . . . their damaged love life . . . the increasing distance that loomed between them. But Michael showed no interest in any retrospective. *Let's cut the crap,* his expression read, *and talk turkey.*

In a way, that made it easier. Perhaps he half-accepted the rupture already.

"I thought, Michael, that if you took an apartment in Boston for a couple of months and we saw how it went . . ."

"This is my home, Kit. I'm not going to leave it."

"Or . . ." she hurried past that stumbling block, "if the kids and I found a place nearby. You could see them every weekend. After all, it would *just* be a trial."

He said nothing for one long moment. Then: "I'm sorry you want to leave, Kit. I don't want you to and I don't think there's any problem we can't smooth over. However"—Michael drew himself erect—"this is a free country and if you're determined to leave, there's no way I can keep you here against your will. But under no circumstances—repeat, *under no circumstances*—will I let you keep the children." His voice went hot with anger. "Goddamnit, Kit . . . those are *my* children! I would never in a million years let you take them away from me. Not Sarah. No, not even Monk."

Kit froze. Froze, then panicked. They were *her* children too! And children always went with the mother, everyone knew that. Michael knew that. Yet even in his anger, he sounded so sure. As if he had anticipated her every move. Oh, God . . . who ever knew what went on in that mind!

"You can't stop me," she screamed. "I'm a good mother. I'm a fit mother. You couldn't keep me from taking them away."

"You're a fit mother, Kit," he said gripping her hands with iron fingers, "but I am one hell of a smart, tough lawyer. I'd fight you in every court in the land, pull every trick in the book. I can fight pretty dirty. There's no way—*no way*—you're going to get those children unless you want to spend the rest of your life in litigation."

"You wouldn't," she wept, "you wouldn't do a thing like that." But in her heart she knew he *would*. And as she cried, he eased the grip on her hand, the victor showing mercy to the vanquished.

"It'll never come to that, Kit. We'll work it out. I promise I'll make an effort; maybe you should make an effort too. But let's never have this conversation again . . . not unless you're willing to give up custody of the children. And you don't want that, Kit." His voice was mollifying now. "And you surely don't want that for the children. That's the way it's going to be, I'm afraid. All or nothing. So just learn to live with it."

She learned to live with it.

KATE

THE WESTMINSTER KENNEL CLUB IS TO DOG BREEDERS WHAT LE
Mans is to hot-rodders and La Scala to aspiring tenors. And
among the thousands who packed the Garden that night—
breeders, fanciers, fans, sportswriters (to say nothing of the
hundred-and-two recognized breeds)—were Kate and Barry
Warden.

"Is this business or pleasure?" Barry asked when Kate
dragooned him into coming.

"Business for me, what else! But come along and maybe
it'll be more of a pleasure. You can watch me proposition a
corgi."

Because the Queen has corgis. At least that's what Doug
Withers of ChicagoCorp had told her.

"The Queen has corgis."

"That's nice," Kate had said. *Better corgis than fleas.*

"I don't think you understand, my dear. The Queen has
corgis right in her home at Buckingham Palace. What's more,
her father had corgis. The Queen Mother has corgis. It is a
royal dog."

Aaaah. Kate knew instantly what he was driving at. Corgis.
Queen. Kennel King.

"I see," she nodded. It was her sincere I'm-really-interested nod. "So you want us to do something with corgis. A commercial, maybe?"

She could see it now. This corgi romping around Buckingham Palace, maybe taking a leak up against the leg of one of the guards. Beautiful!

"What I want," Doug continued, "is to get that goddamn Irish setter off the package—nobody has setters anymore anyhow—and put on a corgi. And yeah, do a commercial with corgis. Naturally, we can't get the Queen to do endorsements . . ." *Figured that one out all by yourself, did you, Dougie? . . .* "but I'd still want the best. Champions. Maybe we could sign up the best-in-breed, you know, and somehow or other make the connection."

"The connection . . . with the Queen? With Royalty?"

"Now you're talking, Kate!"

I am? I'm talking myself right into a corner.

"You mean something like . . . 'Treat Your Dog Royally with Kennel King' "—she was thinking quickly.

"'Treat Your Dog Royally with Kennel King.' " He rolled it over on his tongue like a wine-taster. "I like that, Kate. Yes, it's one helluva good idea. What do you think?"

I think you're an asshole, but it's just crazy enough to work.

"I think it's a spendid idea, Doug. Absolutely splendid. I'll get my people right on it."

So there they were at the Garden—Kate and Barry—watching the canine Miss America contest and waiting for the corgi trials. It was not a breed with which she was familiar, and the dogs, when they finally appeared, proved a disappointment: distinctly unregal, short, squat, with an unpleasant yellowish coat. The Queen of England, Kate mused, had about as much taste in dogs as she had in hats. And the best-in-breed looked no more fetching than the also-rans. His name was Bel Gwynnyd and he was the pride and joy—Kate checked her program—of a breeder, a Mrs. Paula Aaronson of Weston, Connecticut.

They found her without difficulty in the doggy equivalent of backstage. She was a small, pale, birdlike woman, pretty in a nondescript way, but at this moment shining with the flush of victory.

Kate introduced herself and congratulated Mrs. Aaronson on her triumph.

"Oh, but it wasn't my doing," the woman said, stroking Bel

Gwynnyd under the ears. "It was Bel's. Isn't he beautiful?" Kate, who recognized a cue when she heard one, launched into a good three-minute praise of the wondrous beast, while Barry smirked darkly in the background.

". . . and of course it's because he *is* so beautiful that we *might*"—Kate stressed the word "might"; doesn't do to look too eager—"be wanting to photograph him for our product."

Mrs. Aaronson, still flustered with the thrill of victory, didn't say yes and didn't say no. And indeed, Kate told her, there was no great rush about it. They could discuss it sometime next week, perhaps? If Kate might call when things were less hectic?

"Yes, of course," said Mrs. Aaronson. "Let me give you my card."

"What are you looking so glum about, Barry?" she asked as they walked away. "I thought it all went very well."

"You'd look glum, too, Kate," Barry mumbled, "if that fucking mutt had peed on *your* Guccis!"

AARONSON: GOLDEN OAK CORGI KENNELS. Please Drive Carefully. Kate liked the "Please." Even before the house came into view, she could hear the dogs—a muffled chorus of yelps, whines and barks that she presumed greeted each new arrival.

And then the house.

It was one of the handsomest houses she'd ever seen: a center spread from *House and Garden*. Not grand, but with that special aura of having been loved and cared for by generations of New England gentry. White clapboard colonial, with black shutters, nestled protectively between a pair of giant oak trees. The Golden Oaks that gave the place its name, no doubt. At the end of the long driveway sat a battered Jeep and a new Ford station wagon fitted out with caged compartments for the transport of dogs. Along the left of the drive, a series of long, low kennels peeped out from behind a box hedge.

Kate paid the cabbie and threaded her way past the cars to the front door where Mrs. Aaronson was standing, waiting with a tentative smile of welcome.

"Did you have any trouble getting here?" A routine question, but Kate could sense tension behind it. Had the woman been waiting at the door all this time? Watching for her arrival? Maybe she was psychic.

As if in answer to her puzzlement, Mrs. Aaronson said, "I could tell the moment you arrived by the dogs. With a couple of dozen corgis living here, I don't need any doorbell to let me know company's coming. But come in . . . come in."

She ushered Kate into a long, high living room that spelled money—quiet money. From the collection of Bristol glass in the bay window to the polished grate of the Adams-style fireplace, everything in the room proclaimed a mixture of ample funds and good taste.

"Such a lovely house!" The words were inadvertent, and Kate herself was surprised at the note of envy her voice betrayed.

"Yes, isn't it!" Mrs. Aaronson flushed proudly. She was clearly eager to please, happy that her house had found favor in a stranger's eyes. "You should have seen it when we bought it . . . an absolute—how do you say?—tumbledown." Her accent became more pronounced in her enthusiasm. What was it? Kate wondered vaguely. German? Polish?

"That was ten years ago and we rebuilt completely. The floors . . . so rotten you could put your hand through them. We had to put in new ceilings, the studio, kennels. Aah . . . but I'm boring you. Here you are on business and here I am running on like a teenager."

"That's quite all right, Mrs. Aaronson."

"Call me Polly. And you're . . . ?"

"Kate."

"Kate . . . Kathe . . . That was my sister's name"—her eyes glazed over for an instant—"a name I'm very fond of. But first, you'd like to see the kennels, I suppose, so why not keep your coat on?"

The kennels were elaborate, backing on to acres of open ground for running. There was a separate shed for food preparation and equipment. Even floodlights, should some nocturnal emergency arise.

Kate made all the appropriate noises and stroked the prized and proud champion. She couldn't honestly have distinguished Bel from any of the rest, but she made what she hoped were intelligent responses to the nonstop patter of Mrs. Aaronson.

Afterward they went inside and, over coffee in the kitchen, concluded the deal with a speed and ease that surprised Kate. Yes, the money was right. No, Polly would not appear in the commercials—she said cameras made her nervous. Yes, the wording of the testimonial was satisfactory.

They arranged tentative dates with art directors, television crews, the whole army of technicians whose business it is to turn raw ideas into advertising space and time.

"And now you will stay to lunch, won't you?"

Kate had hoped to get back to the office once the preliminaries were over, but it would seem so abrupt after all the camaraderie of negotiations. And Polly was so eager to please that an outright "no" would have sounded brutal.

"I'd be delighted, Polly. Thank you."

"Wonderful!" *Vunderful* . . . yes, probably German.

"And if you make yourself at home in the living room for just a few minutes, I'll get lunch on the table."

"Can I help?"

"No, no . . . enjoy your drink and the view. Ten minutes," she said, holding up ten fingers. "OK?"

It was a room full of *things*—hundreds of them—and every object picked with care, placed with affection. On the wall above the fireplace hung a large abstract painting. It was a peculiar painting considering the nature of the room—a large angry abstract all harsh reds and blues, its strength at war with the delicacy of the other objects. It was signed with a bold black AARONSON.

Polly's? she wondered. Or was there a Mr. Aaronson? In either case, the painting was not to Kate's liking and she turned to enjoy the quieter prospect of the wintry world that lay beyond the bay window. A rock garden, and then a more formal garden waiting for spring to give it life again. And beyond that, woods, woods, woods. The dogs were hushed now. The world was momentarily frozen in time, the trees blanketed in leafless serenity.

Minutes passed . . .

"Where every prospect pleases and only man is vile." The voice was deep, tremendously deep and totally unexpected. Kate whipped around.

He was standing in the doorway, looming broad and massive like some great Russian bear. And smiling—all white teeth—at Kate's surprise. A hulk of a man in an open-throated work shirt and faded blue jeans so snug you could feel the thigh muscle straining to burst free. A look, a style of dress that would not be popular for some years to come.

"I'm sorry. I didn't mean to startle you. I'm Wolf Aaronson."

And he strode boldly across the room to Kate, arms thrust forward. For one wild moment, she fancied he was going to embrace her . . . but no. He simply reached out and grasped her hand in an unexpectedly effusive handshake. His own hand was big, rough, flecked with paint. There were tiny black hairs on the backs of his fingers.

"I'm Kate Chapman of Marsden Baker," she managed to say.

He held her hand a moment longer, then, releasing it, stepped back and drank her in.

"You make it sound like a breeding pedigree. Jack Dinmont of Ardsley Kennels, Belleweather of Sunnyside Farm . . ."

Kate gave a nervous laugh.

"I know who you are," he continued. "Polly told me all about it, and I've been commanded to bring you into lunch."

Close up, he wasn't quite as tall as he had seemed at first sight. Six foot, maybe six-one. Black wiry hair flecked with a bit of gray, high cheekbones and sharply angled brows that gave his face an almost Asiatic cast. No, he wasn't as huge as Kate had first thought. The impression was one of power rather than size. Sheer masculinity, an animal strength that made him dominate the room.

With unaccustomed meekness, she followed him into the dining room.

She was glad she'd decided to stay, for lunch was a splendid affair. Like the house, it was a mixture of the lavish and the informal. Great crusty loaves of French bread. A creamy Brie. Hungarian salami. Homemade pâté. A piping hot quiche Lorraine.

"Nothing formal. I hope you don't mind," Polly apologized.

"Mind! Good heavens, no. It's the best kind of lunch in the world, and I plan to make an absolute pig of myself."

"Please do," said Wolf, piling quiche on her plate. "I like to see a woman eat."

Kate dug in, but Polly only picked. She would glance sometimes at Kate, sometimes at Wolf—a furtive, watchful, inquiring glance to see if there was enough on their plates, if their wineglasses needed refilling.

Do I make her nervous? Kate wondered. Or does he? She sensed something odd about the household.

The talk, however, was pleasantly general. Not dogs, thank God, of which Kate had heard quite enough for one morning. But books. Theater. Restaurants. The Kennedy Administration.

Wolf dominated the dinner table as he had the living room. He had opinions—opinions about everything, opinions that paid no homage to popular wisdom. And only the scantest respect to her own. In someone else, she might have found this offensive, but she was beguiled by the insolence of his style, the beauty of his voice. Can you fall in love with a voice? Perhaps, for it was deep, soft, comforting, with just a trace of an English accent. And smooth. Smooth as a cat in cream.

They talked about Durrell's *Alexandria Quartet,* which was then sweeping through the New York intelligentsia like a hurricane through a cornfield.

"A load of homosexual wish fulfillment," Wolf said. "There's a man who knows even less about women than he does about writing."

Kate was wounded by his airy dismissal. She'd adored the books. Especially *Justine.*

Next, Jackie Kennedy, whose glossy chic Kate admired and occasionally emulated.

"The tackiest woman in America." Wolf brushed the First Lady off like a fly. "And those dreadful pillbox hats. Our cleaning woman has more panache."

After the initial shock, Kate found him amusing. *Well, if he enjoys being outraged, I'll give him something to be outraged about.*

She led the conversation around to modern art, then dropped the name of Andy Warhol, the artist whose paintings of Campbell soup cans were suddenly commanding old master prices from well-lined pockets of the *nouveau riche.* Pop art. Yes, that would be the red rag to the bull, for Warhol's work (which she perceived as patently phoney) was so utterly at odds with the angry painting she'd seen in the living room. A painting she now realized was Wolf's, not Polly's.

She leaned back in delicious expectation of a stream of invective.

"Andy? Andy's a bloody genius. The healthiest, most important influence in twentieth century art since Picasso."

"You must be kidding." It was Kate who was outraged.

"You mean you don't agree?"

"No way! I don't presume to know much about art, but—"

"But you know what you like." For some obscure reason, he seemed determined to put her on the defensive.

"I wasn't going to say that," Kate said, stung. "I was going to say, I don't know much about art, but I know when I'm being conned. Boxes of Brillo. Campbell soup cans. I'm not saying the only subjects fit to be painted are Greek goddesses in pretty dresses or windmills or sunsets. Obviously Warhol is free to paint what he likes. But I resent the fact that he's conned a bunch of foolish women into spending fortunes for that kind of rubbish."

"Why do you call it rubbish? You're in advertising. Campbell soup cans and Brillo boxes are your cup of tea, to mix a metaphor. Don't all your art directors huddle around their drawing boards trying to make a soap package as lovely as a Botticelli? Or worrying themselves sick if the color in a Kennel King ad is just the weentsiest bit off?"

"But you can't compare! We're in the business of selling products."

"So is Warhol. And as for your rich ladies blowing fortunes on soup cans, what do you think they'd be doing with the money if they weren't collecting pop art? You think they'd be endowing universities? Or handing out food parcels to starving Indonesians? The hell they would. They'd be spending it on mink-lined raincoats or hand-painted toilet paper or solid gold golf clubs."

"Oh, Wolf!" Polly had been quiet for so long, Kate had almost forgotten she was there.

"You mustn't mind my husband; he likes shocking people. Now Wolfi, admit you were teasing. You didn't believe a word of what you said."

"My wife knows me too well. I can't resist teasing pretty women, I'm afraid. No, I don't believe everything I said." He smiled, and it was like the sun breaking through the clouds. "I only believe half of it."

As a peace offering, he reached for the Beaujolais and was about to pour Kate another glass.

"No, thank you." She covered the glass with her hand. "I'd

love to stay and talk. It's been . . . well, stimulating, but I have to get back to the office. They'll be wondering what's happened to me. So perhaps if you could call me a cab, I'll take the next train back."

"The next train isn't till 3:05, and the taxis don't like to come out this far anyhow. Let's finish off the wine and I'll run you down to the station. There's plenty of time."

"OK. Thanks."

It was raining when they got into the jeep, and as Kate clambered up the high step into the passenger seat, she realized her narrow suede skirt was not quite the thing for country living. Wolf swung up easily behind the wheel and started the car with an ostentatious roar.

He drove the same way he talked. Quickly. Perversely. And recklessly, she thought, as the jeep lurched boldly over potholes, its isinglass windows an invitation to disaster. Involuntarily she braced her feet against the floor, glued her eyes to his hand on the wheel.

"I'm really a very good driver, you know." He reached over and patted her knee. She wished he'd keep both hands on the wheel. "Haven't had a fatality yet. I can tell you're not used to riding on dirt roads. Anyhow, we're almost on the highway."

"I suppose I'm just a city girl."

He shot her a side glance. "But not a New Yorker. You certainly don't sound like a New Yorker."

"How do New Yorkers sound?"

"Loud and shrill, as if they spend all their lives trying to outshout the subways. You have a very beautiful voice. Very sexy."

"Thank you . . . I guess. No, I'm not from New York. I'm from a small town in Massachusetts and grew up in Boston. You're obviously not a New Yorker either. I've been trying to figure out your accent. Almost English, but not quite."

"I'm South African. I was born in Cape Town."

"That sounds exotic."

"It's not, really. Take away the fauna and flora and Table Mountain, and South Africa is about the least exotic place in the world. A monument to nineteenth century bourgeois mentality."

"I gather you're not planning to go back then."

"Never! And even if I should entertain such a crazy desire,

I couldn't. They took away my passport years ago. They decided in their wisdom that I was a menace to society, a flaming communist menace!"

"And were you?"

"No!" He laughed, but his laughter failed to disguise the bitterness within. "My so-called communist activities were nothing more than what would be considered schoolboy idealism in any civilized country. And South Africa is not a civilized country." He snorted derisively. "No, I'd never go back. It's a prison, a prison of the mind, and I'm not very keen on prisons."

The parking lot was deserted when they pulled into the station. Not a commuter, not even a newsboy in sight. Wolf pulled up parallel to the platform.

"Do you have your ticket?"

She nodded yes and reached for the door.

"Don't go yet. It's cold on the platform. We'll wait here in the car till the train comes in."

"You're sure I'm not keeping you?" She asked.

"Very sure." Very soft.

He folded his arms over the steering wheel, then, leaning his head on the cradle of his forearms, turned to look at her. A long, unswerving, unblinking look, as if he were studying every detail of her face for a painting. Filing her away in his memory bank. His eyes were greenish, flecked with yellow, almost wolflike. And in them she discerned a wolflike flicker of desire. Yes, he was aptly named. She thought he would touch her, wanted him to touch her, wanted to touch *him*, but could not move. And so they sat there—not touching, not smiling—enveloped, paralyzed in this strange motionless silence that offered up a glimpse of eternity.

Sat and gazed at each other like children in a contest of will. Dream children in a dream contest in a world where time had stopped. Where everything had stopped except desire and the pat pat pat of rain on the window.

The train roared into the station, shattering dreams and bringing with it the old enemy time. He smiled and reached across to open her door like a master releasing a bird from a cage.

"It's been very nice meeting you, Miss . . . Kate . . . Chapman."

And when he spoke, a fragment of the dream was in his voice.

Wednesday was always panic day at the agency, the point when yesterday's planning collided with tomorrow's execution—a headlong crash of phone calls, meetings, spilled coffee, missed deadlines and generalized midweek hysteria. And this Wednesday was more chaotic than most.

By eleven o'clock it was clear to Kate that everything that could go wrong would go wrong. Some idiot in traffic had sent the *Times* ad to the *Trib* and the *Trib* ad to the *Times*. The retoucher in the Mother's Pie ad had managed to make the apples look like sheer green vomit. And Sharon!— dependable, loyal, loveable Sharon, who always brought her coffee, found lost layouts, fended off the worst of the phone calls—Sharon the indispensable was home with "the monthlies." The *monthlies,* for Chrissakes. The next secretary she got, by God, was going to be a eunuch.

For the hundredth time in two hours the phone rang, and it was all she could do to keep from growling.

"Kate Chapman speaking."

"How are you?"

That was all.

No introduction, no apologies, not even a hello—simply *how are you* in a voice as intimate as the sound of rain falling gently on an isinglass window.

She recognized it. Of course. The way a snake recognizes a mongoose. The way a Simeon Stylite up there on his column recognizes the voice of God. That voice didn't belong here amidst this Wednesday madness, and she paused long enough for him to continue.

"This is Wolf Aaronson. We met in Weston last week. Remember?"

"Yes, of course. How are things in Weston?"

She almost asked "How is Polly?" but decided not to.

"As far as I know, they're fine, but I'm not in Weston at the moment. I'm in New York . . . and I'd very much like to see you for lunch."

"Lunch." She stared down at the unruly pile of work on her desk.

"I shouldn't . . ."

"But you will."

"It'll have to be a short one."

"A long one. I'll see you in the lobby at twelve-thirty."
And he hung up, before she had a chance to contradict.

Damn damn damn, she thought, why couldn't it be dinner?
And suddenly she was glad—foolishly, idiotically glad it
wasn't, because dinner was even farther away.

*Thank God I had my hair done on Monday, thank God I'm
wearing my green Anne Klein dress.* She checked her ears for
earrings, her stockings for runs, her desk drawer for the
emergency bottle of Magie. By 12:25, she'd torn through a
raft of "can't wait" memos and told the receptionist she might
be late. She was having lunch with a client.

He was already waiting when she got out of the elevator,
just another tall man in a gray tweed suit. For a moment she
felt a twinge of disappointment. *I liked him better in faded
blue denim.* Then he came across the lobby and licked her
with his eyes and she knew she liked him best of all any which
way.

"I'm so glad you could come." He smiled and folded her
arm under his in an iron grip.

"You didn't give me a chance to say no."

"I didn't intend to. You've cut your hair. Yes, I like it very
much." He led her to the door, steered her to the street
where the jeep, looking redder and even more rural than she
remembered, was parked insouciantly between a fire hydrant
and a yellow bus line.

"We need a jeep to have lunch in Manhattan?" she said,
for she'd presumed it would be something midtown and
intimate.

"Ah, but we're not having lunch in Manhattan. We're
going out to City Island."

"That's up in the Bronx somewhere, isn't it? Oh, but I
can't," she protested. "By the time we get there, it'll be time
to turn around and go back."

"Oh, but you have to," he said, fastening her seat belt.
"I've already had them reserve the two most beautiful
lobsters in the Sound, and a pair of dry martinis for openers."

She had to laugh at his utter arrogance. "This is kidnap-
ping, you know."

"Then relax and enjoy it."

"That's what they say about rape."

He smiled, but changed the subject.

"I gather from the way you answered the phone that I
caught you on a particularly nasty day."

"You sure did." She was relaxed and enjoying it, and as the streets of upper Manhattan gradually trickled into the Bronx, she regaled him with a zesty version of all the calamities she had undergone since nine that morning.

"Mmmm . . ."

She was aware that he was watching her rather more than he was watching the road, but "Mmmm" didn't seem much of a response.

"You weren't listening to a word I said, were you?"

"Not a word," he volunteered cheerfully. "I was watching your mouth. You have a very lovely mouth—sweet and sensuous all at the same time, like a Botticelli Venus."

He stopped for a light and kissed the Botticelli mouth, until the car behind honked to signify the light had changed.

"And what do you do when you're not being bruised and braised by all those idiot photographers and clients?"

"What do I do?" she repeated stupidly.

"Yes, what do you do when you're not in the office. Your hobbies, pastimes, vices . . . In your spare time, what do you do?"

What do I do? I sleep with married men.

But that hardly seemed a suitable reply, and Kate felt herself at a loss to answer sensibly. What *did* she do?

"Well, I read and go to the movies and eat and sleep, the same as everyone else."

"That doesn't sound very exciting for a pretty girl in New York."

It didn't. Even to Kate's own ears, it had a priggish sound. *My God, he'll think I'm some boring virgin—a Rebecca-of-Sunnybrook-Farm type, a little Boston touch-me-not.*

"In my spare time I . . . manage to keep amused." She made her voice openly suggestive.

"I'm sure you do," he grinned. "I'm sure you do."

Danny's Fish Bar, when they finally got there, laid claim to a certain reverse chic in its utter lack of pretension. And if Kate had never heard of the place, other people had: mostly day fishers, by the looks of them, plus a few well-dressed Westchester matrons protecting their Kimberly knits with a vast expanse of lobster bibs. Wolf shepherded her to a corner table with a view of the water. A plain formica table set only with paper mats bearing a fishing map of Long Island Sound and a pair of dry martinis on the rocks.

"They knew we were coming," said Kate, raising the martini in a mimic toast."

"I wasn't sure if you were olive or lemon peel. My guess was lemon peel—you seem the dry rather than the fruity type."

The first martini went down so fast she could feel the cold shooting into her brain. The second round arrived accompanied by two enormous boiled lobsters, hefty bowls of drawn butter, crisp and sinful French fries—portions too large to finish, too delicious to refuse. They gorged themselves shamelessly, but it was only, Kate sensed, a preliminary to a later and rather different feast.

"And now . . ." Wolf said, as the waiter cleared away the pile of shells, the shattered carapace, "tell me all about yourself, and this time I promise to listen."

"There's not a great deal to tell, really." She censored her past to the tellable and gave him a little background about her home, her schooling, Spencer's foibles, Emily's follies, her work at the agency. Nothing out of the ordinary, but he listened intently, asked a few pertinent questions and gathered in her answers as though storing them up for future use.

"And now it's your turn," Kate said.

"Oh, you'll find me out by and by."

"That makes it sound as if you're hiding dark secrets."

"No . . . no dark secrets. People who live in rural Connecticut don't have much opportunity to pile up dark secrets."

He told her briefly about his childhood in Cape Town, where his father was headmaster of a boys' school. As a teenager he had two consuming ambitions. One was to join the army and fight in the European Theatre. "I wanted to kill Nazis more than anything else in the world. You can't imagine what it was like to be a Jewish adolescent during those years, knowing what was happening and being told you're too young to do anything."

His other desire was to paint.

"Well, you realized one of your ambitions, anyway."

"Actually, I realized both of them."

At seventeen, over parental objections, he'd gone to Rhodesia and joined the British forces there, arriving in Europe just in time for the last agonized spasms of the Third Reich. "It cured me of militancy once and for all. And after the war, I decided to come to New York and study at the Art

Students' League. Perhaps you saw some of my paintings at the house."

"Oh, I'm a ninny when it comes to abstract art. Don't embarrass me by asking me to say anything intelligent about it. Do you ever do any commercial work? Illustrations or portrait painting?"

He shook his head no.

"Can you draw?" The moment the words were out, she realized how philistine she sounded.

"Of course I can draw. That's the first thing they teach you in art school. Draftsmanship, anatomy, life classes . . . I'll draw you if you like. Just sit there!"

He fished in his jacket and retrieved a felt-tip pen; then, pushing aside the coffee cup, took a mat from the neighboring table and set it before him, blank side up.

"Oh, you needn't," Kate laughed. "I'm sure you draw like an angel."

"I needn't, but I'd like to."

He sketched quickly, surely, his eyes darting from her to the mat and back again while Kate sat there in helpless immobility. She felt insufferably juvenile.

"There!" he said after four or five minutes, and he pushed the mat over toward her with a showman's flair.

She looked at it, blinked, and looked again.

He had drawn her just as she sat there—leaning forward, elbows resting on the table. The face was hers, although considerably more beautiful, more fragile than her own image of herself, the position of the body precise in every detail but one. Except for earrings—those beautiful jade earrings her mother had given her for graduation—he had drawn her nude.

She stared at the sketch, his representation of her breasts, firm and small yet distinctly erotic—at the shadows beneath her collarbone, the curve of her rib cage, the narrowing slant toward her waist. The drawing stopped just short of her navel, ending abruptly with the hard sharp line of the tabletop.

"Would you say it's an accurate likeness?" he asked softly.

She searched her coffee cup for a suitable answer.

"Yes," she said finally, "as far as it goes."

She was afraid his roar of laughter would bring the waiter scrambling.

"As far as it goes! Oh, my darling girl."

He pulled the drawing back and posed his felt-tip above it.

"I see I shall have to complete it."

"Oh, no!" Kate was giggling helplessly. "They'll throw us out of here."

But with a few deft motions, he finished the sketch and handed it back to her. Beneath the line of the table he had drawn a slither of scales, culminating in a pert little tail. At one side of the sketch, there was a suggestion of waves and a fish gaping in open-mouthed admiration. She was no longer a Botticelli Venus but a mermaid.

Kate laughed till the tears came.

"Is that what you think goes on below the waist?"

"I had hoped you would prove otherwise."

And when her laughter stopped, he took her hand, brought her fingers to his lips and kissed them one by one.

The tide had shifted; there was an undertow now, bearing her out far beyond the familiar sands.

"Kate." She began to tremble. "Darling Kate, I have wanted you from the first moment I saw you standing there by the living room window. I almost carried you up to bed right then and there. You looked so radiant, so full of life. You were like sunshine in a room where the sun never comes.

"All week long I thought and thought of you, like a schoolboy mooning over a film star. You were in my pocket, on my breakfast table, in my studio. I drew you there a hundred times at least. Oh, Kate, the things I've drawn! I kept hoping you would go away and leave me in peace, but you refused. You kept hovering in odd corners of my mind. I must have reached for the phone a dozen times to call you, just to hear your voice. And each time I thought, 'Why should she want me? this beautiful independent young girl. Why should she want me when I'm so indisputably married?' Then I'd think, 'Well, I have every right to complicate my own life, but what right do I have to complicate hers?' All of this made perfect sense, but didn't change the fact. The fact is, I wanted you then, I want you now."

He paused, but she said nothing. He took her fingers and splayed them out as if to read a message in her palm.

"I kept remembering you sitting in the jeep at the station and I read something in your face. Did I read it correctly, Kate?"

She nodded. A faint but perceptible nod.

"Then say it. Say that you want me too."

"I want you."

"Look at me. Now say it again. Say 'I want you, Wolf.'"

"I want you, Wolf. I want you very, very much."

He released her hand but not her gaze and beckoned for the bill.

"Go call the office."

"What shall I tell them?"

"Tell them," he smiled, his face full of happiness, "that you've been taken ill very suddenly and are going straight home to bed. And absolutely not to disturb."

They rode in silence all the way back to Manhattan. She remembered little of the drive except the sense of anticipation. He didn't ask her address. He had obviously made it his business to learn where she lived. Dreamlike, disembodied, they parked in front of the building, floated past the doorman, into the elevator, entered the apartment wordlessly. And the moment the door closed behind them, fell upon each other like starvelings at a feast, swiftly, ravenously undressing each other till they were clothed in nothing but the dappled shade and sunlight that striped through the venetian blinds.

She stood before him—all light and shadow now—while his hands ran the length of her body. Great, massive, powerful hands, sculpting her breasts, stroking her thighs. Hands that seemed to liquify her flesh.

The bedroom seemed a hundred miles away—too far! too far!—for she must have him now on this white flokkati rug. She wanted no foreplay, no tender exploratory kisses, wanted nothing but that he possess her.

"Now!" she cried. "I want you now!" For an answer, he closed her to him in a single motion. They fell to the floor—mouth to mouth, belly to belly, thigh to thigh, his huge hands emcompassing her buttocks, pulling her closer ever closer to him, dwarfing her, dominating her until she was lost in his flesh.

Then, rich and strong, he entered her—moving rhythmically, powerfully, like some magnificent animal in heat. Now on top of her, now under her, always deep within her. She could no longer tell what was his, what was hers. The tangle of hair into hair, the beating of heart against heart, the mingling of sweat and tears.

Tears. For she was crying. Crying with joy. Surrendering blindly to orgasm after orgasm.

"Kate!" The roar of his voice filled the room. "Kate! . . . Love! . . . Kate!" And in one vast convulsive shudder possessed her utterly.

For minutes after, they lay there panting, locked numbly in that last great embrace. And as Kate returned from nirvana, she felt something hard and cold against her head. She opened her eyes. They had rolled across the room somehow and come to rest against the leg of the dining table. The sugar bowl had toppled, scattering its contents, mixing sugar with their sweat and semen.

Kate smiled and sighed. She hadn't even heard it drop. Hadn't heard anything but her cries and Wolf's voice calling her name.

Wolf looked too. And smiled. And kissed her bruised lips.

"What savages we are, Kate darling."

She buried her head in the hair of his chest. It tasted of sugar.

"We can't lie here forever," she said after a while, wanting to lie there forever.

"Of course not," he said after another while, then gathered her up in his arms. "Now let's go to bed and make *proper* love."

It was dark when she woke and she could hear him moving about in the kitchen. A moment later he poked his head in.

"Would you like some coffee, darling? Don't get up. I'll bring it in." A few minutes later he reappeared with two mugs on a tray and, handing her one, sat down beside her on the bed.

"Did you just move in here?"

"Into this apartment, you mean?" She was puzzled by his question.

"Mmmm."

"No, I've been here since . . . let me see, last July."

"Really! You don't have any furniture, any rugs." As if by way of emphasis he placed the tray on the bare parquet floor. "Not even a bedside table."

"Yes, I know." Actually Kate had never given it a thought until now. It was, after all, simply a place to sleep. "It's just that I'm so damn busy, I never seem to get around to it."

But of course Wolf was right. The place was as empty and

unadorned as a barracks. A bed, a few chairs, a dresser, a TV set (a professional necessity, that) plus a dining table from the Door Store. But the table was always piled high with work, leaving room only for her coffee cup and sugar bowl. To her the apartment was a place to flop, to store clothes, and an annex to her office at Marsden. But seeing it now through his eyes, it struck her as deplorably bare.

She thought of the house in Connecticut. No, not a house—a home, with all the little riches, the accumulations of much-loved and cared-for objects, the triumphant booty of a hundred country auctions. How bleak this must seem to him. She felt she owed an explanation.

"You see, I never bring anyone home."

"By anyone, you mean lovers."

She nodded.

"Then I'm the first to invade the sanctum?"

"You are. Does that please you?"

"It pleases me inordinately. And surprises me, too, I might add."

He swung his legs up on the bed and lay beside her.

"What a mysterious creature you are, Kate. How little I know you . . . and how much I have to learn."

She stroked his lips with affectionate fingers. "You know, Wolf, you're the first man I've ever slept with who said that to me."

"Said what?"

"That you hardly knew me. It's always seemed to me that once you've gone to bed with someone, they assume they know you inside out. What more is to be learned? As if making love spells the end of all curiosity."

"Ah, but it isn't the end, Kate. It's just the beginning. And perhaps you've known all the wrong men. But I promise you, I shall know you—we shall know each other before we're done. Yes, I shall know you—everything you are and think and do. I shall learn you like the good headmaster's son that I am. Shut your eyes now and don't say a word."

He placed their mugs on the floor and switched off the light.

"I shall learn you, beginning with your body."

He began touching her—not caressing, not playing—simply touching her, feeling her like a blind man reading a sculpture. With the tips of his fingers and sometimes the palms of his hands, he explored every inch of her body. Traced the little bones behind the ears, the shape of her eyelids; ran his fingers across her teeth, into her mouth, along the edge of her tongue; defined the shape of her chin, the line of her throat, the thrust of her collarbone, the curve of her breast, slowly down to her navel, her belly, the bones of her hips, the softness of her labia, her thighs, her knees, even the soles of her feet—coming back now and again to wonderful places, favorite places, until his hands had her memorized.

"Now, he said pulling her on top of him, "you learn me."

Years later, her fingertips could recall every hair on his body, her mouth remember his taste and his texture. They were memories that would come to her unbidden at unlikely times and places. More than memories. They were imprints.

The next time he came, he brought a bottle of Piper Heidseck and a porcelain box no bigger than her hand. On the box lid was an extravagantly colored hummingbird, its brilliance made more pronounced by the virgin white of the china. It was very very delicate and she knew instinctively, by the pride with which he gave it to her, that it was very expensive as well.

"Come! Look at it in the light." He went over to the window. "It's a particularly fine piece of Chelsea." He held it up to the fading daylight so she might admire its flawless translucence; pointed out the whiteness of the ground, the peculiar richness of the blue, the distinctive wine-red of the hummingbird's throat.

The more he looked, the more delighted he became, "Yes, a really lovely example of Chelsea."

"What was it meant to hold?"

"It's a patch box . . . an eighteenth-century patch box. Ladies in those days wore little patches on their cheeks to advertise their political sympathies. And kept them in boxes such as these."

A dim page from Addison's *Spectator* essays came back from an Ellery English lesson.

"Stars for the Tories, crescents for the Whigs . . . something like that?"

He was pleased she had fielded the reference. "Something like that. And what will *you* keep in it, Kate?"

She studied the tiny box, frowned for a moment, then burst out, "I've got it! My old Stevenson button, provided I can still find it. The box is just the right size."

"Perfect," he laughed, "and absolutely suitable. The great Whig ladies would certainly approve."

He took the box back from her and looked around the room.

"Now, the next question is, where shall we put it?" (The *we* was not lost upon Kate.) "You seem to suffer from a lack of surfaces. How about on top of the television set? That would make an amusing anachronism."

He positioned it in front of the rabbit ears, then stood back and laughed. "Yes! Perfect! Eighteenth-century Chelsea and twentieth-century RCA. What will the archaeologists of the future make of this, I wonder? Get some glasses, darling, and we'll have some champagne on it."

The Chelsea box set a pattern for giving, for the next week he brought her six champagne glasses of Waterford crystal. (He had not approved of drinking Piper Heidseck out of Woolworth tumblers.) The week after, it was a little Pennsylvania Dutch sewing table that he had "stumbled on" in a Second Avenue antique shop that morning.

A table, however, is more than a trinket, and when he placed it in her bedroom she realized with a shock exactly what he was doing. He was creating his own environment. Putting down, if not roots, then tendrils, furnishing a home away from home where he could look upon pretty things and feel at ease.

Kate was of two minds about these acquisitions. She liked the things in themselves, and Wolf was meticulous in instructing her about their finer points, their hidden beauties. "Object lessons," he called his little lectures, and they were always amusing. She loved the gifts doubly because they had come from *him*. Yet at the same time, she inferred from each offering a subtle condemnation of her own failure to build a nest, seek roots, make commitments. She worried, too, that his generosity was to be a device, a pretext for his taking over her apartment, her life, even her view of the world.

Kate once told him he was an arrogant bastard, and he had taken it as a compliment. In a way, she had meant it as one. She liked the nimbleness of his mind, the adventurousness of his ideas, many of which were only playful exploration. Above all, she liked the fact that they could banter about anything under the sun. Anything, that is, except his marriage.

On that subject alone, he volunteered no information. He offered no alibis, no excuses, no clarification; and though she often wandered what tales were told in Weston to explain his increasingly frequent absences, she did not press him on that point. She was sure that Wolf handled his home life with the same dexterity and bold confidence with which he handled everything else. Including her.

Thus it was with considerable surprise, when their affair was but two months old, that Kate arrived at the office one morning to find a Please Call message from Polly Aaronson.

Could Polly know? Yes, indeed she could. But if she did, would she phone Kate at the office? Phone and leave a message for Kate to call back? No. Too unlikely. It must be something else, something to do with the goddamn dogs.

Of course. The dogs. They should be shooting the TV commercial round about now. Yes, that must be it. And if so, there was nothing for it but that Kate return the call. For the first time, she felt a tiny prick of conscience. Of all her married lovers, she realized with some distaste, Wolf was the only one whose wife she had actually met. *Betrayed,* of course, would be too strong a word, for she and Polly were in no way friends.

Still . . . she decided to have Sharon place the call on the off-chance that if Wolf himself answered, he wouldn't think she was pursuing him—flushing him out in his lair.

Within seconds, Polly's piping voice was on the wire.

"You know they're shooting the dogs on Monday?" Giggle. "That sounds so terrible, shooting the dogs. Well, I was wondering if you were going to be there and . . . help out with the camera crew."

"Well, no, Polly. I hadn't planned to. You see once they start shooting . . . once the cameramen take over, it's out of my hands entirely."

A damn lie, that. Kate often went on the set and had no qualms about ordering around photographers and talking down rebellious producers. But this was one shoot, she decided weeks ago, she definitely did not want to be on.

"Well, I was wondering . . ."—there was no hiding the quaver in Polly's voice—"if you couldn't make an exception just this once. I'd really feel a lot happier about it."

"But Polly, you know we've hired one of the best camera-

men in the business." *Who the hell had they hired?* "I'm sure
he'll do the dogs justice."

"It's not that. It's just . . ."

"Yes?"

"There'll be the cameraman and, I understand, his assistant, and the producer and the art director and . . . ummm,
well, I'll be the only woman. Really, Kate, I'd feel so much
better if you were there. I mean, you know me, and you know
the dogs and you know the camera crew, and you're someone
I could trust . . ." *Trust! Oh, Polly, don't trust me!* ". . . and
you could, well . . ."

"Run interference?" Kate completed Polly's thought.

"Interference!" The relief was patent in her laughter. "Yes,
that's it exactly. Please come. I would appreciate it."

What could Kate say? She conceded with good grace.

"I'd be happy to, Polly, if you think it will make life easier.
I'll come up with the camera crew in the morning."

Polly thanked her and hung up.

The drive to Golden Oaks was as she remembered, the
STOP sign where she and Wolf had paused, the rutted dirt
roads, the dogs barking, the house—and then Polly, just as
before, waiting by the door in expectation and looking very
frail and tiny inside a floppy Peruvian poncho.

Kate had not had a chance to speak to Wolf, to warn him,
as it were, of her imminent arrival, but he must have known,
for he was nowhere to be seen. And it was clear from the
warmth of her reception that Polly had no inkling of Kate's
hidden role in her life.

So, Kate being Kate—and business being business—she
tucked her private feelings away on the spot, like a housemaid
sweeping dust under the rug. Within minutes she was plunged
—the professional now—into what proved to be an arduous
day of shooting. During the course of the day, she found
herself serving as peacemaker, mediator, interpreter and
patsy in the running conflict between Polly and the camera
crew. Polly, she discovered, had a whim of iron, was in some
ways as difficult as her dogs. But the most difficult of all those
involved in the shoot was, without doubt, Bel Gwynnyd.
Whether the kudos of the Westminster Dog Show had turned
the beast's head, Kate couldn't tell, but he acted like a spoiled
movie starlet.

Bel wanted to chase birds, fetch balls, sniff the director's crotch—do any goddamn thing but sidle up to the dish of Kennel King as the script required.

They'd been at it now for six hours solid, shot everything except that last key sequence.

"Look, Polly, we're starting to lose the light. You know the shot doesn't call for him to eat the food, just to walk up to the bowl and sniff. Is there anything you have that he's particularly fond of . . . dog candy or whatever turns them on? Maybe we could plant it in the bowl or bury it underneath and that would entice him. Isn't there some particular thing that drives him bananas?"

Polly nibbled a fingernail for a minute or two, then clapped her hands like a child.

"I know! There's an old slipper of Wolf's, my husband, you know?" Yes, Kate knew. "Bel's absolutely crazy about it. Everytime I let him into the house, he goes straight to Wolf's closet and drags it out. Really hilarious. Like catnip to a cat."

"Could you get it?"

"Of course, but it wouldn't fit in the bowl. My husband has"—she laughed—"rather large feet." An observation that called for no comment from Kate, who said simply "Perhaps we could bury it underneath. Dig a little hole . . ."

Polly shook her head. "He'd never smell it."

"What color is the slipper?"

"Maroon."

Maroon. Maroon like Kennel King.

"Well, what if we . . . um, cut it up and mix the pieces in with the dog food?"

"Cut it up?" Polly was staggered by the idea.

"Please, Polly, it would work, I know it would. And it's only an old slipper. Look . . ." She was inwardly amused at the irony of the situation. "Just let me know his shoe size and I'll see that the agency sends him a beautiful new pair from Saks. Best leather. Is it a deal?"

While Polly was getting the slipper and a pair of garden shears, Kate explained the new ploy to the crew.

"Got it, Sam? Now meanwhile, why don't you take the mutt for a walk and clear his nostrils. We want this to come as a big surprise."

It worked. Worked like a dream. And when Bel, nostrils cleared, was finally unleashed, he leaped upon the bowl with such untrammeled joy that he set the contents flying. The dog leaping, the bowl flying, the bits of food and leather scattering, the perplexity and puzzlement of Bel—it was a fabulous shot.

Polly ran to him, her darling, darling Bel. Swooped him up and held him high above her head. "You clever Bel, you clever, clever Bel"—and as she held him, the poncho fell away from her arms. There, in the fast-fading daylight, Kate saw the tattoo in the fold of Polly's elbow. She had seen tattoos like that in old newsreels. The tattooed number of the concentration camp.

"Let me tell you about Polly."

It was the Wednesday after the shoot at Weston and they were having drinks in Kate's living room.

She put down her martini, put her hands over her ears and said, "I don't want to hear."

Which was and was not true. She didn't want to hear atrocity stories, tales of woe, appeals to her compassion; dark, blood-stained histories that would blot their love, compound their guilt. *That* she didn't want to hear. But she did want to hear about Wolf's view of his marriage.

For the past three months, she had pondered constantly of how his past would affect her future. What kind of marriage could it *be*, she asked herself, that left him free to spend one, sometimes two nights a week in New York? She knew he kept a room at the Drake on the nights he stayed with her—for the look of the thing, she imagined. He always called the hotel last thing at night, first thing in the morning to see if there were any messages. From Polly.

Paula Elfriede von Brucke was the last survivor of what had been for generations one of Germany's leading Jewish families.

The first Brucke was one Chaim Baruch (the name was Germanized in the next generation). Baruch had sought refuge in Prussia from the Spain of the Inquisition where, according to family legend, Baruchs had been doctors and scholars in the Court of Granada. After more than a century of anonymity in the fledgeling German States, one Gustav Brucke emerged from the mist to establish himself as official mapmaker in the service of Frederick the Great. In 1823, Gustav's grandson (and Paula's great-great-grandfather) moved to the more permissive climate of Hamburg and founded the publishing firm of Brucke Gesellschaft in a quiet square of the old Hanseatic freeport. The firm flourished, especially in the field of textbooks, maps and scientific and technical treatises. By the middle of the century it enjoyed a unique position throughout Europe. Among university students, the family name was invoked as the final authority in many a scientific dispute. If Brucke had published such-and-such a paper, then it must be so. Their trademark—a bridge connecting the opposite shores of art and science—became the hallmark of all that was truest and finest in nineteenth century German science and philosophical thought. Paula's great-grandfather had been a personal friend of Bismarck, and it was the first Kaiser Wilhelm who awarded the Bruckes the coveted "von" in return for their efforts in mapmaking and technical publications during the Franco-Prussian War.

It was into this background of high culture and great estate that Paula was born and spent her childhood. Her earliest memories were of a great house at the edge of the city, filled with laughing brothers and a beautiful older sister; with white button-boots for daytime, black button-boots for tea; and a Scottish nanny who prepared the most beautiful puddings.

In 1939, Brucke Gesellschaft was expropriated by the Ministry of Propaganda at the personal behest of Dr. Goebbels. In 1940 the great gabled house with its avenue of oaks was taken over by the Wehrmacht for the entertainment of officers on leave. In 1941 . . .

"Please," Kate begged, "don't tell me. I don't want to hear." But Wolf continued.

Paula last saw her father and brothers being herded onto the boxcars at the station. The last she saw of her mother was in the "jewelry line" at the women's reception quarters; a tiny, mild, bespectacled woman pulling desperately at the gold wedding band she had worn for over twenty years, while Paula and her sister Kathe clung to each other like drowning children.

"You!" the guard said. "You two. Come with me." And he plucked them out of the line, pushing them, shoving them through a maze of dingy buildings until they arrived at a long and low barracks rather more substantial than the rest.

"In!" He shunted them into a tiny cubicle, unfurnished except for an iron bedstead and a chair, then left, locking the door behind him.

It was hours before they heard the footsteps and the voice in the corridor beyond.

"Very little today, Captain Gruber, mostly fat housewives and grannies. Just these two in here—sisters, I think—off the morning shipment from Hamburg."

The door opened, and through it passed the fattest man Paula had ever seen. Great layers of flesh oozed like yeast rising above the rim of a bread bowl, overflowing the high, stiff neck of his uniform; little pig eyes set in a face as broad as it was long; thick, moist lips on which a cold sore festered.

"Get up when Captain Gruber enters," the guard barked. "Up! Stand up straight." They got to their feet and stood there frozen while the captain, hands clasped behind his back, walked around them, scrutinizing them like livestock at an auction and finally coming around to settle in front of Kathe.

"*Ja, ja,*" he said, rubbing his cold sore thoughtfully. "Very good, you two . . . very attractive. Now tell me, dears, are you political or Jewish?"

"We are the von Bruckes of Hamburg." Paula was the first to find her voice. "My father is Felix von Brucke, the head of—" But Kathe cut her short and said simply, "Jewish."

"Jewish, good. I don't like the politicals, they're nothing but troublemakers. *Yiddische madele,* huh?" And his jowls shook in tempo with his laughter. "Well, you can count yourselves lucky girls, and if you're as good-natured as you are pretty"—he chucked Kathe under the chin, then ran his finger down to her breast—"you can have a very pleasant stay here. Good food, good companionship, good service to the Reich."

"Please," Kathe said, "I beg you. My sister is only fourteen."

"Only fourteen!" The jelly shook again. "Well, one's never too young to learn. Perhaps, my dear, you can show her."

He opened his trousers. "So, darlings, I think that you have never seen an uncircumcised one before."

But Paula had never seen one at all, and stared in fascination at the great red peasant sausage he presented. Like the bratwurst the maids used to eat in the servants' kitchen. And sometimes old Gretchen would let her take a taste.

Gruber put his hand atop Kathe's head and, with a wink to the guard who was standing by the door, hand on hip, gun in holster, pushed her down on her knees before him.

"Take it," he said. "You'll find it quite a change from Kosher meat."

And while Paula watched in speechless horror, Kathe took
the strange object in her mouth—and bit.

"Jewish bitch!" Gruber screamed in pain and kicked her
back against the door; a second later the gun on the guard's
hip became the gun in his hand and Kathe's brains exploded
on the floor.

"Bitch!" shouted Gruber. "Filthy Jewish bitch!" Rubbing
the pain from his cock, he swung around to the paralyzed
Paula. "You!" he screamed. "Kneel, Jew! *Kneel, kneel,
kneel!*"

And Paula knelt before him.

She knelt in that room perhaps a thousand times. Knelt for
officers, guards, favored prisoners, perverts. Knelt while the
ovens cooked in the camp beyond, while the chimneys
belched the smoke of human flesh. Knelt while six million
died. And it was in that room, kneeling like a dog on all fours,
that a sergeant from Englewood, New Jersey found her in the
spring of 1945.

Kate, too moved and distressed to speak, went into the
kitchen and lay her head down on the cool kitchen counter.
Why had he told her this horrible story? It was even worse
than she had feared. Why tell her all this? To make her feel
bad? To prepare her for his last goodbye? What possible good
could be gained by rehashing the past? And anyhow, Polly
had survived.

She poured herself a glass of water, then went in to him.

"And did you know all this when you married her?"

"I knew . . . enough. You can't imagine how touching she
was and, in her own haunted way, how lovely, how *fragile*. I
couldn't bear thinking of what she had suffered—far more
than I, far more than most men in the war. I felt that, of
course, I could never atone for what happened, but I could
protect her, make up for it in some small way. Besides," he
added, "I loved her."

And so they married. Her psychoanalyst was surprised but
ultimately approving. And Fräulein Paula von Brucke became Mrs. Polly Aaronson. They had wanted children—at
first desperately; but an ectopic pregnancy was followed by a
hysterical pregnancy, which in turn was followed by a nervous
breakdown. After that, sex became emotionally impossible
for her.

"So we had dogs instead."

"Then you no longer sleep together?"

"No, not in years. We're married and we're not married."

"How can you live like that? I don't understand."

"But Polly does, you see. That's why I'm free to come in to New York as I please, spend the odd night or two a week here."

Something jangled.

"Then I'm not the first of your Wednesday girls."

"Don't put it like that, Kate . . . it sounds so shabby. You're the first one I've ever really cared for. Kate, I love you, I'm out of my mind about you—you must believe that. My poor darling, I wish it could be otherwise. I wish we could live together, be together every night, every morning, and have children . . ." Kate started to cry. ". . . and be all in all to each other. But I couldn't do it without destroying Polly. And it would, Kate . . . it would destroy her if I left. She has lost everything she's had in the world—family, friends, honor. You couldn't in all fairness ask me to do that. You wouldn't respect me if I did."

"But what will become of us, Wolf? What can we ever hope for? Nothing more than this every Wednesday?"

"Don't cry, Kate . . . please don't cry." And as he took her in his arms and stroked her hair, his distress seemed to match her own. "Please don't cry, darling. I'll see what I can arrange. This summer, perhaps . . . we'll go to Europe this summer. Would you like that? I'm meeting my father in Italy this July, but after I see him, you could join me in Rome, in Paris, anywhere you like, and we could be together."

She cried, nodded and then cried some more.

"Then that's agreed? Good. Now go put on the sunny face that I love and we'll go out and have some dinner."

By the time she emerged from the bathroom, freshly made up, if not totally sunny, she was in full control of herself.

"One last question, Wolf, and then we'll drop the subject."

"Yes, darling?"

"What happened to the company? The . . . Brucke Gesellschaft?"

He went to the closet to get her coat, but she sensed it was a pretext to keep her from seeing his face.

"Well, that came to Polly, of course."

"Came to Polly? How?"

"In war reparations. After all, she was the sole survivor."

"Then it still exists?"

"Oh, yes. Bigger and better than ever. It's run in Germany, naturally, and Polly doesn't have anything to do with the business end of things." He held out the coat to help her on with it.

"I see. She just gets the money."

"As you say, she just gets the money." Spinning her around quickly to face him, he said quietly, "It's not what you think. The money has nothing to do with it." And by his eyes, suddenly cool and remote, she knew the subject was closed.

Over the next few weeks, she thought a great deal about what he had told her that day—about his marriage and his inability, his unwillingness, to end it. Fragile, Wolf had called Polly. But *was* she. All things considered, Polly had survived —the only one of the Bruckes to have done so. Could a fragile girl survive four years in a concentration camp brothel? No, Polly must be tough, either tough or insane, and Kate did not think she was insane.

Kate was troubled, too, by the business of the money. She believed Wolf was sincere when he told her Polly's fortune had nothing to do with it. That is, she believed that Wolf believed it.

Yet she could not be indifferent to his obsession with "things"—the lavish scale in which he lived, the incessant search for the beautiful, the sheer love and pride he took in all his acquisitions.

And she—she was his ultimate acquisition.

KIT

Afterward everyone would ask *where were you when you heard* the news?

Georgie had been at the Friday afternoon concert in Symphony Hall when the orchestra had inexplicably departed from the printed program and—after a flurry of activity—begun playing the "Funeral March" from Beethoven's *Eroica.* Michael had been in court on a particularly tiresome case when the judge unexpectedly announced an adjournment. Kit was ironing.

Ironing kitchen curtains and thinking of nothing much. That was the good thing about ironing—you could let your mind go totally blank. Ironing, half-listening to a Frank Sinatra record on the radio, not quite absorbing whatever it was the announcer had broken in with. Something about the President. Still, it couldn't be terribly important, because the disc jockey started the Sinatra record all over again. Ironing, not really listening on that November afternoon. She wasn't that much of a Sinatra fan, but occasionally they played some good jazz on this station. Aaah, that was better—Dave Brubeck. Easy loping music that made the blue-and-white checks of the gingham curtains dance along with the rhythm. If there was anything she hated, it was ironing checks and stripes, so hard on the eyes. And then the music stopped.

No. It wasn't, couldn't be true. A practical joke or maybe some publicity stunt for a new movie. You couldn't believe anything you heard on these pop music stations. After all, they were always playing commercials for storm windows at $11.99, which had to be a hype, or advertising bathroom tiling that any housewife could install by herself in half an hour. Trust them to get everything wrong.

Still . . . she flipped to WBZ. Because if anything like that had really happened, she'd only believe it when she heard it from a major network. But as the dial moved the span of the radio bands, there was no music anywhere. Only voices. Urgent voices, shocked voices, stuttering voices. Some said that Lyndon Johnson had also been shot. Some claimed the lives of two Secret Service agents and a Dallas policeman. The governor of Texas too. They said that it was the work of Klu Klux Klansmen, of an armed gang of Cuban terrorists, of a lone lunatic, of the CIA. The only consistent fact to emerge from all that muddle was that President John F. Kennedy had died of gunshot wounds at Parkland Memorial Hospital in Dallas, Texas.

Sarah was at nursery school. Monk was sleeping. Kit was ironing. And Kennedy was dead.

She couldn't take it in. It wasn't real. The blue-and-white gingham curtains were real, the half-finished cup of coffee on the kitchen table was real. But this was not real. And when the telephone rang—and rang and rang and rang— Kit had the fugitive notion that the real sound of the real telephone would shatter the vision, dispel the nightmare, bring back a world that already seemed slipping from her grasp.

"Catherine?"

She could barely make out her mother's voice, tear-choked and distorted. It was true then, but how extraordinary that Emily, who'd never had a kind word to say about the Kennedys, should be on the other end of the phone now, keening like an Irish widow at a wake.

"Yes, Mother," Kit said, crying too. "I heard the news."

"You *what?*" Emily was screaming like a banshee.

"I said I heard the news. It's terrible . . . terrible. I just heard it on the radio."

"On the radio? Catherine, why would it be on the radio?" Emily's voice was shrill, irritation mingled with the grief. "I don't know what you're talking about!"

"About Kennedy."

"Kennedy who?" For a moment Kit wondered if her mother had lost her wits. "Catherine, I'm trying to tell you . . ."—more tears, uncontrollable now—"I called to tell you your father died this morning at the factory."

And *that* was real. Indisputably real.

KATE

WHERE WERE YOU WHEN YOU HEARD THE NEWS?

Kate was under the dryer in the back room at Jean-Michel's, riffling through last month's *Vogue* and vaguely aware of the little Puerto Rican shampoo girl standing before her, gesturing, saying : . . Saying what? You couldn't hear a word above the noise of the dryer.

Kate poked a tentative finger inside one of the giant rollers. Nowhere near dry. "No, I'm not done yet." She smiled and went back to her *Vogue*.

Yet the girl remained planted there, mouth moving, face strangely contorted until Kate pushed back the cumbersome head gear. "I said," she repeated, "I'm not done yet. My hair is—"

"They shot the President."

At least that's what it sounded like. Kate turned off the dryer switch. "I'm sorry, Carmen, I didn't quite get that." But Carmen—at a loss for words in an alien language—could only shake her head.

Out in the salon, a transistor radio was blurting out absurdities. It was all so lunatic, so incomprehensible—the acrid smell of hair-dyes, the familiar trays of scissors and spray cans and pink cotton balls, the ugly nonsequiturs that burst out from the radio.

Not true, of course. Not real. Some kind of stunt, an Orson Welles radio prank, like his Martians-have-landed broadcast Kate had heard about. Any minute now, there'd be a commercial. And still the radio kept hammering.

No, not real. Nothing could be réal in this temple of makeup and make-believe, of bottled hair color and false fingernails. It would only be real if she heard it in a real place. A real place like Marsden Baker. She grabbed her coat and stumbled out into the street.

The lobby at Marsden was deserted—that was a bad sign. But in the elevator the Muzak was playing "Getting to Know You." The Melachrino Strings. That was a good sign. Surely the Muzak wouldn't be playing if something like that had really happened. She pushed the button for the seventh floor. The big conference room. They had a color TV set in there, for monitoring commercials. If it *were* real, it would be on TV.

They were all there: senior vice presidents, boys from the mailroom, secretaries, media buyers, all huddled around the all-knowing eye. For the first and perhaps the last time, democracy reigned at Marsden Baker.

Nobody spoke much. Nobody cried. It was too numbing, too totally unbelievable. A little after three the phone rang, and it was Sharon who finally picked it up. She turned to Kate. "It's for you. Your mother. She sounds terribly upset."

It wasn't until Kate was halfway to Athol that she realized the rollers were still in her hair.

SPENCER

TOWARD NOON ON THE MORNING OF NOVEMBER 22, 1963, Spencer Chapman had put down his dictaphone, got up to get a glass of water and fallen over dead of a massive coronary.

The funeral took place the following Monday. A bleak affair, followed by an even bleaker burial, for with the exception of his immediate family, the mourners' minds were far away from Athol. Were focused on a grander more somber funeral—a funeral with caissons and black-plumed horses and the sound of a distant bugler. And as her father's coffin was lowered into his grave, his daughter reflected on the cruelty of fate to have robbed him—the arch Republican, this fanatic Roosevelt-hater—yes, robbed *him*, Spencer Schuyler Chapman, of his last full moment of glory. How ironic that the grief, the honor, the mere polite attention due his death would be snatched at graveside by yet another Democratic President.

KATE

"How's your mother taking it?" Wolf asked when she got back to New York. Kate considered.

"Funny."

"Funny ha-ha?"

"No, funny peculiar. I get the impression she's relieved."

KIT

"I MUST SAY, I THINK YOUR MOTHER'S TAKING IT ALL VERY well," Michael remarked some weeks after the funeral.

"Isn't she just?" Kit agreed. There was no question that Emily had navigated the first shoals of widowhood with a minimum of tears and fuss. Self-discipline, Michael called it, and attributed it to the Spartan virtues of a proper Boston upbringing, but Kit was not so sure. Emily's calm, her unexpected competence in coping with what must surely have been the greatest bereavement of her life, seemed to Kit indicative of a certain want of feeling. Seemed almost to border upon indifference.

Naturally she didn't expect her mother to beat her breast and tear her hair, any more than she would expect her to deck out in red and go dancing. And, of course, Emily had done neither. Had steered a seemly course between excessive grief and undue callousness.

"Almost as if," Kit thought, "she were marking time."

Spencer Chapman had left trust funds for his grandchildren. Small bequests to various conservative organizations. A rather decent legacy to "that Italian woman," for once giving Mrs. Antonelli the benefit of a proper name. There was a $10,000 bequest to the Tracy Institute for Deaf Children, a bequest that moved Kit to wonder if she had not perhaps misjudged her father during his lifetime. To Kit, he left a varied portfolio of stocks and bonds, including preferred shares in Sag Pap & Pulp. The balance of the estate, including the house and all its contents, to "my beloved wife, Emily Sayre Chapman."

"What will your mother do all by herself in that big barn?" Michael said.

"Well, she has her friends and her puzzles and Mrs. Antonelli," Kit put forth doubtfully.

"That doesn't sound like much of a life." Then, in a gesture that took Kit completely by storm, he added, "She's welcome to come and live with us, of course."

But when Kit ventured the suggestion to Emily, her mother had simply fluttered vaguely and said "That's very kind of you and Michael" and declined in no uncertain terms.

Within six months, Spencer's widow had auctioned off the furniture, sold the house in Athol, donated her jigsaw collection to the Children's Museum in Boston and bought a condominium in Palm Beach.

"I've always hated those New England winters," she confided in Kit.

Kit and Michael had long discussions about what she should do with her own inheritance. "It's your money, of course, and anyhow, we don't really need it at the moment." A broker friend of Michael's had looked over the portfolio and advised her to hang on to it with minor changes. Apparently her father had invested shrewdly. He assessed the current market value at about $95,000, but it would undoubtedly appreciate as time went on.

"The best thing to do for now would be to just put it aside and forget it." She notified the broker to reinvest the dividends, took a safe-deposit box at the Shawmut Bank, locked the stocks and bonds inside it and forgot them. For the time being, anyway.

She tried with Monk. Lord knows she tried.

She drove into Boston almost daily to the speech therapists. It was costing a fortune—she had to sell some stocks—but she and Michael both felt private sessions would be better than the public clinics. At home, she devoted endless hours to supplementing the therapy. She would shape sounds over and over, placing Monk's hand on her throat so he could feel and distinguish the vibrations that differentiated "a" from "e" from "o." The results were not gratifying. Sound came to him slowly—inchoate grunts and tuts, a few misshapen vowels that hovered just this side of recognition.

The hearing-aid experiment had ended in failure—Michael was not the only one who hated the sight of the appliance. From the start, Monk waged war on the contraption, plucking it out of his ear, picking at the wire, hiding it in obscure places around the house. After nearly six months of agonized wavering, Kit packed it away. Perhaps when he was a little older, a little more mature . . .

She talked to him, of course, but when Michael wasn't around, mother and son communicated largely by gesture. Professional wisdom was varied and confusing, though Dr. Winkler was categoric that Monk should be instructed in sign language. This, naturally, would entail Kit and Michael doing the same. She was willing, Michael was not. Once again, her husband proved inflexible. Teaching Monk sign language would be "giving in," robbing the boy of all incentive to speak. Worse yet, it would consign him, condemn him, to the world of the deaf.

For another six months, Kit and Michael wrangled constantly, but Michael could not be budged. And in the end it was Kit who gave in.

It was hard to say just how much of the outer world Monk could actually hear, how much he could eventually communicate. He responded not at all to low-decibel sounds, occasionally to higher-pitched ones, but it seemed to vary almost day to day. The problem of safety was ever-present. Would he hear the whistle of a steam kettle, the growl of an angry dog, the roar of oncoming traffic? Who could tell? Kit had to adjust to the idea that he might never play freely out-of-doors. Certainly not alone.

Perhaps if his sister had been more patient, more willing to join in his games—but Sarah was either resentful or frightened, and there was little communication between the two. Sarah tolerated him as one would a tiresome household pet, and Monk, in turn, simply ignored her.

Michael, too, gradually disengaged himself from the proceedings, and when the four Mathesons went out together, it was always Michael and Sarah in the lead, laughing and chatting, while Kit trailed behind with the somber Monk.

Sometimes she felt as if she were "losing" Sarah, losing her to Michael. Certainly she was losing that intimacy that mother and daughter had shared when Sarah was a baby. Kit worried constantly that the little girl would feel short-changed, cheated of the lavish expanse of maternal time and energy that had once been exclusively her own. But there it was.

Kit might have despaired were it not that Monk often seemed to grasp much of what she said. Provided it was simple enough; provided she spoke slowly, clearly, articulately, loud and remained in full view; provided her speech was frequently supplemented by gestures. She could never be sure how much of this grasp derived from what he had actually heard, how much from the divination of her moving lips, how much from the context of her gestures.

The frustrating aspect was that while Monk could be made to understand various commands and injunctions, he could not be made to understand the reasoning that lay behind them. Thus, Kit could tell him "Don't play" and point to the iron; she could not tell him "Don't play with the iron because the iron is hot and you will burn yourself." Nor had he any sense of time, of pleasure or punishment deferred. So while she might wish to say, "Don't eat the cookies until after you've had your dinner," the message was inevitably reduced to "Don't eat" or, more frequently, "No." "No" was the word that found its way most often to her lips, a necessary word but sadly unmodified. Until finally she had but to purse her mouth into an *o* and Monk would know exactly what she meant.

The curious thing was that he was an "easy child" in many ways. Often easier than Sarah, with her endless questions and scraped knees and lost dolls and squabbles with the boys upstairs.

Quiet and for the most part undemanding, Monk seemed to live in an inner world all his own—remote and intricate, a private domain which afforded him thoughts and pleasures and miseries of which Kit had no inkling.

He loved everything that moved. On summer days he would sit in the backyard tracing the paths of insects with infinite patience, watching the play of squirrels in the trees, scanning the sky for birds.

"Perhaps if he had a pet of his own," Michael suggested. "I think every boy should have a puppy."

But Kit didn't care for dogs, and the smell of canned dog food made her want to throw up. Instead, she bought Monk a parakeet, a beautiful creature all emerald green with eyes like jet beads.

"This is Tweetie." She mouthed the word carefully again and again the day she came home encumbered with bird and cage. "Tweetie . . . Tweetie. He is Monk's bird. Monk's very own. Mommy will help you feed him and care for him, but he is Monk's bird. Tweetie. Tweetie . . ."

Monk was enchanted. "Ta-ta-ta-ta," he said, moved almost to speech by his joy in this new acquisition.

So Tweetie came to live in Howland Terrace, commandeering one corner of the living room, strewing bird seed merrily on the carpet, making the daylight hours vibrate with his raucous trilling.

The pet shop salesman had told her that he could, with patience, be taught to talk, but Kit had had quite enough in teaching Monk without concerning herself with the phonetics of avian education. Anyhow, Tweetie sang—loud, high and shrill—and Kit knew even Monk could sometimes hear him.

The boy and the bird communicated, and, on rainy days, Monk would stand before Tweetie's cage by the hour, transfixed and delighted by his new companion. Often, when the weather was too bad to go outdoors, Kit would shut the living room door and let Tweetie out of his cage to fly around. He made an awful mess, settling now here, now there, and she always made sure to clean up the droppings before Michael came home. But these flights, she knew, were the high point of Monk's day. Perhaps of his life. And it was Monk—the infinitely patient Monk—who would coax the bird back to his finger and replace him gently and tenderly on the swing of his cage once the aerial acrobatics were over.

"Ta-ta-ta-ta-ta," he would say, and Tweetie would chirp in reply.

"That was one hell of an idea, Kit," Michael congratulated her. "One hell of a good idea."

"Guess who's coming back to Boston with his tail between his legs?" Michael crowed one evening.

"Who?"

"Tim 'Lover Boy' Keegan. He's been canned. He called up this morning to ask if I know of any good apartments. Apparently our new President is having himself a field day, lowering the boom on all those old Kennedy appointees. At least the ones he can get away with. And Tim is among the expendable."

"But I heard he was doing so well . . ."

"That's politics, honey, and you can't blame a new man for wanting new blood. Take my word for it, in another six months, there won't be a single Harvard accent left in Washington. Boston Baked Beans have had it . . . from here on out it's Texas chili all the way. Of course, Tim tells it differently. According to him, he was going to quit anyway for high moral purposes. The Hanoi bombings and all that crap. But if you ask me, that's simply a face-saving device. He was canned, pure and simple."

"Don't gloat, Michael."

"Who's gloating? I'm genuinely fond of Tim. Genuinely."

In Kit's mind, the second "genuinely" cancelled out the first, in the manner of a double negative.

"So what's he going to do now . . . hang out his shingle?"

"So the man says. Remember that young Negro fellow who took his place when he went to Washington . . . Garry Winters? Well, he and Tim are setting up together, figuring they'll get some work from the ACLU and maybe some of the Negro rights organizations. Tim's very optimistic."

"Still fighting the good fight, then?"

"So it seems."

"It would be funny, wouldn't it," Kit began clearing away, "if you and Tim meet in court one day as adversaries—you prosecuting, Tim defending?"

"Nothing odd about it at all. It happens all the time and nobody takes it personally. I certainly wouldn't. After all, some of my best friends are adversaries."

"Still," Kit said, her mind far from the courtroom, "it'll be nice having him back. And Marian too, of course," she added almost as an afterthought.

"Just like old times," Marian said, settling down with the inevitable coffee. "Same old kitchen table, same old Nescafe, same old Kit."

"A few pounds fatter."

"Same old Kit."

The two women exchanged affectionate smiles.

"And how does Boston look to you after all this time?"

"Terrific. But I'm so out of touch with everyone. You've

got to fill me in on three-years gossip, and we've only got all afternoon."

It *was* like old times. They talked easily, formlessly, about mutual friends, property prices, the new topless bathing suits, the campus demonstrations at Berkeley, the quickening pace of the Vietnam War (which Marian said was the real reason Tim had quit the Washington job), about Malcolm X and *Catch 22* and why American pictures never seemed to win the Academy Awards any more, then finally zeroing in on the most infinitely fascinating subject of all—that endless source of anecdote, wonder and grievance: their husbands.

"It's probably just as well things turned out the way they did with the Johnson Administration and all," Marian said. "I don't think our marriage would have lasted another six months down there. I shouldn't put all the blame on Tim, to be fair. The women in Washington are absolutely voracious, man-eaters in the true sense of the word. And the amount of boozing that goes on . . . well, that doesn't exactly make for marital fidelity. On Tim's part, anyhow. He was like a kid in a candy store down there. Taste, suck, nibble, eat, each one guaranteed a different flavor. Only I was the one who wound up with indigestion. As far as I'm concerned, from here on out Tim is on approval, like those stamps you get from a mail-order company. One thing you can be damn sure of, I'm not just going to sit back and take it anymore. You know, I've decided to do my Ph.D."

"Political science?"

"Yup. I've already been accepted at grad school; it's just a question of settling on the subject for my dissertation."

"How about 'The Role of the Cocktail Party in American Political Life.' I gather you've already done the necessary research."

Marian laughed appreciatively. "I love it, but it would never fly, Orville. Actually, I'm specializing in post-Stalin policies in Eastern Europe. How does that hit you?"

"Whatever turns you on."

"That turns me on. I've already started to learn Russian."

"Hey, hey," Kit was impressed. "You don't make life easy for yourself, do you?"

"Let's just say that *Tim* hasn't made life easy for me, and the time has come when I feel I need options."

"Options?"

"Options, alternatives, whatever you want to call it. The

way I see it, I've been living in Tim's shadow long enough. I can't count on this marriage lasting another twenty minutes, let alone another twenty years. It may, it may not, but for once in my life I've decided I'm going to put myself first. I want a career that belongs to me alone, and who knows? the time may come when I'll need it. Maybe I'll go into the State Department, maybe teach . . . I understand you can even qualify to drive a cab in Boston once you've got your doctorate. But whatever happens, at least it will be *mine*."

"You make me feel like an intellectual dropout," Kit said, "but I feel like that pretty often these days. Like when you go to a party and someone asks what you do. All I can say is 'just a housewife' . . . with the accent on the 'just.'"

"You shouldn't feel you have to apologize, Kit. Having children is an option, too. I don't know . . . maybe if Tim and I had had a family, our marriage would have turned out differently. It certainly would have brought us closer together."

But Kit simply shook her head, sad as a rag doll. "That's a myth. Children don't bring you closer together. Not in this house, anyway."

Marian looked up sharply. "Monk?" And, when Kit nodded—"I'm sorry. If you'd rather not talk about it . . ."

"No, no," Kit interrupted. "If I can't talk about it with you, I can't talk about it with anyone. But you know, the problem isn't really Monk . . . it's Michael. In a way, I can understand it; Michael had such high hopes. From the day Monk was born—no, even before—Michael had such a perfect picture of what his son would be like. Groton. Harvard. He would row for Harvard, that was Michael's ideal. Be the golden boy. I think it would break Michael's heart to face up to the facts. So instead he cops out, simply refuses to accept Monk as he is."

"Can *you* accept it?"

Kit sighed. "Let's say I can live with it and Michael can't. He's dead set against Monk learning sign language, and now he wants him to go to kindergarten here in Brookline just as if nothing were wrong. We had the most unbelievable fight last night . . . unbelievable! Just short of throwing things. There's a special school for the deaf in Newton. They're willing to take Monk in September and I'll pay for it out of my own pocket, so that's not the problem. The doctor, the audiologist . . . everyone has recommended it. Well, last night I told Michael and he went absolutely berserk. He kept blaming me, saying that Monk was perfectly OK, that it was my fault. That I had turned Monk into a freak. Those were his very words—a freak." She began to cry noiselessly into the rough paper of the napkin.

Marian got up, "I'll make some more coffee, or would you like something stronger?" Kit shook her head, but by the time the coffee was ready she felt halfway human and better for having let go. She had always found it difficult to confide, felt it smacked of disloyalty and dreaded nothing more than joining the ranks of the "injustice collectors." Nonetheless, she was glad Marian was here, and if confession didn't lift the weight from her heart, at least it shifted it into a slightly more tolerable position.

"I ask you, Marian," she said quietly, "what kind of man is it who calls his own son a freak?"

"A perfectionist."

"Is that the word?"

"That's the word. That's the man. You know, nothing you've told me surprises me in the least. My cousin Madge always used to say about Michael—and I'm sure she was quoting, because Madge never had an original idea in her life—'There but for the grace of God goes God.'"

"Your cousin Madge?" Kit was puzzled.

"Yes, Madge Thayer. She used to be . . . she's Madge Harsanyi now. You met her. We had lunch, the three of us, years ago at the St. Charles. Long brown hair, went to Wellesley. She lisped."

Kit had a faint memory of a plain but pleasant girl with a toothy smile, a lot of well-bred small talk and a pronounced lisp.

"I didn't know she knew Michael."

"Oh, yes, they used to date a lot. It was years ago, of course. In fact, that's how Tim and I first met Michael."

"I always assumed they knew each other from law school."

"Nope . . . through my cousin Madge. She brought him over to our house the first year we were married."

"When was that?"

"Let me see . . . I was finishing my Master's . . . yes, it must have been late '56, early '57, around there. Before he met you, of course."

Kit calculated swiftly. Late '56—the Stevenson campaign— the time that Michael had dropped completely out of view.

"Was it a big romance?" And when Marian stared at her, Kit added quickly, "I'm not jealous, just curious."

"Well, we *thought* it was a big romance. They were practically engaged, or so the family assumed, and then—"

"Then Michael backed down because she lisped?"

"No," said Marian, "As I recall, Madge was the one to break it off."

"Why?"

"Why? It's funny, I can remember her exact words. She said, 'I'm afraid he'll wake up one morning and discover that I'm a mere mortal, that I have to go to the bathroom just like everybody else.' Anyhow, a couple of years later she married a Hungarian refugee and moved to the Coast. He didn't mind her lisp. With his accent, he probably didn't even know she had one. Her parents were absolutely furious, though." Marian giggled at the recollection. "They were real Old Boston diehards. Codfish for breakfast, tea with the Wigglesworths and watch out for the inferior races. Real fossils."

"Yes," Kit said thoughtfully, "Michael would have liked that."

She asked him about Madge Thayer that evening, expecting to get a rise out of him, but all he said was, "The Thweetheart of Thigma Chi?" and smiled. "She was the world's most boring girl. Nice family, though."

What she had not confided to Marion—could never confide —was the admission that Michael had become impotent.

"Why don't we make love anymore?" she'd finally asked him outright." Is there somebody else? Are you involved with some other woman?" It had taken all her courage to venture this far. "Or is it me? Do you find me . . . unattractive?"

But Michael, sitting darkly on the side of the bed, merely shook his head. His shoulders slumped in a silhouette of distress.

"No, Kit," he said slowly. "It's not you, believe me." He clenched his knuckles till the bones showed white. "It's me. I *can't!* I just can't."

He turned his face away, his body racked with shame and grief, and in that moment Kit's heart went out to him. What must it cost Michael—this proud, handsome man—to pronounce himself inferior, in this regard at least, to the commonest of thieves, the most contemptible of delinquents? What a burden for him to bear alone!

She lay her cheek against his and put her arms around him. His chest heaved with despair beneath her hands.

"Perhaps it's just some minor physical thing," she comforted. "Maybe if you saw a doctor . . ."

"I've seen a doctor. He says there's nothing wrong."

"Then maybe," she hardly dared broach the idea, "maybe if you talked to a psychiatrist."

"That's the answer to everything, isn't it?" He faced her, his eyes wet with tears. "Just lie down on the couch and tell Big Daddy. You should know me better than that, Kit. I can't do it. I can't bare my life to total strangers. Not even for this . . . not even for you. Oh, Kit"—and for once he kissed her with real warmth—"just give me time, darling. Give me time and stick with me."

"I'll stick," she murmured and held him close, for how could she refuse this appeal to her loyalty, her compassion.

Thus the subject was—for the time being—closed to discussion. But not closed from Kit's private speculation.

She thought she knew what had brought him to this state. It was Monk. It had begun with Monk's birth, and culminated with his deafness. To have seen failure, weakness, abnormality reflected in this much-hoped-for son had in some way struck Michael to the roots. Unmanned him.

KATE

POLLY'S FORTUNE WAS, IF NOT THE MAJOR SPUR, THEN SURELY AN added incentive for Wolf's marital status quo. Of that, Kate was convinced, and for a while she resented the continuing extravagance of his presents. Bought, it seemed to her, out of his wife's blood money. But eventually she came to realize that Wolf bought them as much for himself as for her. He relished the whole process from discovery to flirtation to final acquisition of each item that filled her apartment. He hated the synthetic, the second-rate, and even though he himself took little interest in the dogs, he was glad that his corgis were champions. Nothing but the best. And when Kate bought mixed nuts, he always ate up all the cashews. He was the most possessive man she had ever known, considering her home *his* home, considering Kate herself a prize possession.

Logically, the idea made her bristle. Emotionally, she reveled in it. For the first time in her life, Kate discovered she liked—no, *loved*—being possessed, being owned outright, as it sometimes seemed.

One evening she arranged a dinner at which Wolf could meet Barry, and although the dinner passed with a fair show of urbaneness and civility, she knew the two men disliked each other heartily, were each in different ways rather jealous.

In bed that night, Wolf had told Kate he suspected her friend was a "latent heterosexual." At the time it had made her laugh, but later she wondered if it did not bear some nugget of truth.

Barry was less equivocal. "It beats me, Kate," he'd chided her. "I'd just never figured you'd go for such a classic macho type."

Yes, she supposed Wolf was a "macho type." He liked to make decisions and made them with only the barest pretense of consulting her. Decisions of where they would go, what they would eat, what she would wear. He relished decking her out in positively barbaric jewelry—great chunky pieces of Mexican silver, dangling Mogul earrings, a splendid Moroccan necklace all cat's eye and coral—things far too *outré* to be worn to the office, pieces to be worn only for him. One evening he brought her a black woolen veil strung solid with Arabic coins. It was the dowry of a Yemenite bride. Kate held it up mask-like beneath her eyes. "Just like a harem girl," she said. He laughed and placed it around her neck like a scarf, but he didn't refute her. Nor had Kate said it to reprove. She liked being coddled for a change. And after the constant aggressive battles waged daily in the office, the on-the-spot decision-making each working moment required, she found relief and a certain positive pleasure in submission. He commanded. She by and large obeyed, in the knowledge that she would be rewarded for her obedience. Not with gifts, for they were but an expression of love. Love itself was the reward.

He was interested in every aspect of her life, no matter how trival. He was always sympathetic and often quite practical in helping her size up professional problems. Like Barry, he had a good insight into office politics. He would, she thought, have made a marvelous businessman.

He coddled her outrageously. On those few occasions when she was sick or overworked, he came with kindness and kisses and fruits out of season. No detail of her life escaped him.

One night, after she'd indulged in a week of heavy drinking and dining with a wave of out-of-town clients (a ritual that could not be avoided in the agency business), he had run his hand over her belly and said, "Why Kate . . . you're getting plump." Yet she had gained only two pounds. She dieted all the next week.

Ultimately he loved her because she was his, and treated her with the pride of possession.

It was only in bed that they met as equals. He was experimental, curious, constantly seeking the ways that would give her new pleasures, more pleasure. *(Do you like it better with the pillow under? Do you enjoy my finger there . . . yes or no?")* He expected her to do the same for him.

"Oh, God, how I love you!" she cried after one particularly ecstatic round of lovemaking. And later he commented, "You only say that when I've brought you to orgasm. Now if you really loved me, you'd tell me the moment I walk in the door or when I'm shaving in the morning or when I'm picking my teeth after dinner. Or something equally boring and unromantic."

He was right. She was reluctant to tell him she loved him. Wary that it might look like pressure, afraid he might see how vulnerable she was. But love him she did.

"Oh, Wolf." She ran her hand down his broad hairy chest. "I love you all the time, and you *don't* pick your teeth, as far as I've ever noticed. It's just that I love you most of all when we make love."

"I think you're mistaking love for sexual mechanics."

"What's between us isn't mechanics."

"Are you sure? Have you ever heard the expression 'Shut your eyes and think of England'?"

"No," she giggled.

"Well, that was what Victorian mamas told their daughters, the advice they gave them on their wedding nights. So you do as I say now. Shut your eyes and think of England."

She shut her eyes and tried to think of England, but could only think of Wolf's mouth on her nipple, his fingers deep inside her, his thumb manipulating her clitoris in a way he had discovered produced an almost instant climax. Within a minute her body responded, shuddered, flooded.

"Did you like that, Kate?"

She could only breathe a helpless yes.

"And did you keep your eyes shut and think of England?" He withdrew his fingers, now wet with her joy, and pressed them to her lips.

"As it happens, they were my fingers that made you come. They could have been anyone's. John Doe's or Jack the Ripper's or even a woman's. For that matter, even your own. In fact, they needn't be human fingers at all, Kate. I expect you could get a similar pleasure from one of those mail-order devices designed for the relief of old maids."

Kate sat bolt upright. "How cruel! How can you say such a thing!" she shouted. "Why should you try to spoil my pleasure!"

"I'm not trying to spoil your pleasure, darling. Don't be angry. I'm just trying to point out the difference between mechanics and love. After all, any two sexually normal people could, if they go about it intelligently, give each other infinite pleasure in bed. But that's not love. And when you tell me you love me, I want to know that it's me you love, all of me, not just my cock and my fingers."

"Oh, Wolf." His argument had upset her enormously. "If it were only that, then life would be so simple. I could kick you out and get myself a 'mechanic,' as you put it. I wouldn't spend every waking hour waiting for your phone calls, reorganizing all my time, all my freedom just to be with you an extra five minutes here and there. My God, you know that I love you more than life itself."

He pulled her to him and stroked her tenderly. He had heard what he wanted to hear.

And yet, Kate was not wholly faithful to him. The weekends were long and lonely, and sometimes, just out of sheer resentment that this was time he spent with Polly, she would take a lover for the night. It meant nothing to her one way or the other, and after awhile, she stopped. For Wolf was right. The mere mechanics were not enough.

And so it went, year after year, until she couldn't remember what life had been like without him.

MONK

BRRRRRR.

The emerald wings whirr so fast you cannot make out their shape. BRRRRRR.

Poor Tweetie is locked in his cage. The sun is shining. The sky is blue. The world is wide. But poor Tweetie is locked in his cage.

Too bad Mommy is not here to let you fly free, but Mommy is asleep.

BRRRRRR.

Now, Tweetie, do be good. If I were Mommy I would let you out of the cage so you could fly and soar and be beautiful. But I am not Mommy and Mommy is asleep.

BRRRRRR.

Don't be angry, Tweetie. Please don't be angry.

BRRRRRR.

But Tweetie *is* angry. He is angry at Monk because Tweetie cannot fly today. Did not fly yesterday. He hops on his perch and folds his wings. He is sulking.

Please let me fly, says Tweetie. I am very sad in my cage. Very sad and lonely. I am a bird and all birds fly. All but poor Tweetie. Let me out and I will play with you.

Poor Tweetie. Just this once Monk will let you fly. But you must promise not to tell. You must come when I call. You must go back to your cage like a good little Tweetie before Mommy wakes up. If you promise, I will let you fly.

Tweetie promises. Monk climbs on the sofa. The cushions are soft and he is leaving dirty footprints on the pale beige pillow. But Monk does not care. From where he stands, tall as a giant, he can just reach. Just reach the silver door of Tweetie's cage.

There! Tweetie trembles at the door. Surveys his empire. And in one glorious burst of motion flies free.

There is Tweetie, now atop the lamp, now playing hide-and-seek, now peeping out from the back of Daddy's chair, now coming to rest on Mommy's book.

Naughty Tweetie. Naughty Tweetie makes pooh on Mommy's book. Bad bad Tweetie. It is time to go back in your cage.

Monk puts out his finger for Tweetie to come. But Tweetie does not come. Flies away from Monk's finger. Perches on the windowsill by the geranium plant.

BRRRRRR.

Come, Tweetie. Please come.

Come and get me, says Tweetie. He is teasing Monk.

Monk goes to the window.

Come, says Tweetie, come closer. Monk comes, captures him. Feels the feathers beneath his fingers, soft and hot and vibrant.

I am putting you back now, Tweetie.

Slowly, slowly, walk across the room.

BRRRRRR. Tweetie is gone!

Monk looks everywhere. Under the sofa. High up on the ceiling. But Tweetie is gone. GONE. Bad bad Tweetie has gone out the window. Run away from Monk. Bad Tweetie! Will he come if Monk calls?

"Ta-ta-ta-ta-ta."

Monk leans his head out the window. "Ta-ta-ta-ta-ta." And there is Tweetie outside the window on the box hedge. His green is more brilliant, more beautiful than the green of the hedge.

Tweetie sees Monk and smiles. Grown-ups think that birds do not smile. But Monk knows they do. Monk and Tweetie have exchanged many smiles, many secrets. And now Tweetie is smiling at Monk. Smiling and saying:

Come Monk. I am waiting for you. I am waiting for you to fly with me. We will fly together into the great silent sky.

There will be no more people with their funny busy mouths, their ugly shapes. No more earphones and noises and scary machines. No more men in white coats to stick things inside your head, to search out your secrets with their cold silver toys. And you will be a bird like me, flying swift and free in the great endless silence. Come with me, Monk. I am waiting.

Monk slips out the door and onto the sidewalk, careful not to wake Mommy. It is very strange to be on the sidewalk alone without Mommy. Very strange.

But Monk is not alone, for Tweetie is waiting. Waiting as he promised on the box hedge.

Tweetie smiles at Monk. I'm glad you came. Are you ready?

Monk is ready.

Tweetie turns his head back to look at the house. He is saying goodbye to the house. To his cage, to his prison. Goodbye. And then . . .

Tweetie soars. High higher faster farther, down the street, across the road. Soars, but always looking back, calling teasing begging beckoning. He is saying, *Follow me, Monk. Follow me . . .*

Monk did not hear the roar of the car, the angry screech of brakes, the angrier still acceleration. Perhaps he did not even hear his own scream. But Kit did. And by the time she reached the street, barefoot and disheveled, it was all over.

Monk had flown away at last.

KIT

HER WORLD HAD SHRUNK. SHRUNK TO THE SIZE OF A SMALL broken body. All else lay hidden behind the cloud of her grief.

She had no memory of sirens, of police cars and howling ambulances, no memory of being gently led away by neighbors, no memory of an angry Michael shaking his fists at the sky.

Each day was a nightmare; each night a small relief holding out the promise that she might wake tomorrow and find it was all a dream.

That tomorrow would not *be* tomorrow. That it would be this time the day before yesterday, this time last week, this time last month. That she could turn back the clock and change the course of the future.

It would be that Tuesday. She would send Sarah off in the morning, give Monk his lunch. She could remember every detail of that lunch. A peanut butter sandwich on Pepperidge Farm bread. Monk loved Pepperidge Farm bread. A glass of milk and a bowl of late-summer cherries. His face was red with the cherry juice.

And after lunch, Kit would say, "Come on, Monk . . . let's take a walk." Or else they'd go shopping. Or maybe just sit around the living room watching TV. Anything . . . *anything* but "Mommy's going to take a little nap now, Monk. Play quietly."

In her dreams it was always that lunchtime.

But every morning Kit awoke to find tomorrow *always* comes, dragging reality in its wake. And so she lived on Valium and tears.

The day after the funeral, Kit took a spade and went into the backyard.

"Oh, you're gardening, Mrs. Matheson," a neighbor called over the fence. "What a good idea. It's excellent therapy."

But hollow-eyed and empty, Kit made no reply. Simply dug the spade into the dry, resistant earth. And dug. And dug. And when the hole was deep enough to hold a small body, she buried the birdcage and closed the grave with her hands.

Then lay down on the fresh-turned soil and wept.

If only guilt could be buried so simply.

KATE

"I THOUGHT WE COULD WORK THIS OUT BETTER WITH THE peasants out of the room." Gully turned to check that the door was firmly closed. "It doesn't pay to let dissension show."

He picked up the TV storyboards thoughtfully and stacked them in a neat pile between them on the conference table.

"It won't do, Kate. I won't buy it."

"You mean you won't sell it."

"I mean," he said, choosing his words with care, "that these commercials are not going beyond this conference room. Under no condition will they be shown outside this agency. Period. Exclamation point. Do I make myself clear?"

"Perfectly." Kate had anticipated his resistance and had come prepared. "Now I'd like to make myself clear, Gully. Times have changed. Herbert Hoover isn't in the White House any more. The dear old *Saturday Evening Post* has died the death. And when people these days talk about smoking, they don't mean cigarettes. Look around. Just look at your Mrs. American Housewife these days. She's not wearing Peter Pan collars or trying to look like a Doris Day retread. Not even in Pound Ridge. She's probably into jeans and tee-shirts and maybe holding down a part-time job."

"Maybe," he said doubtfully, "but that's still a long way from showing a jigaboo"—he saw Kate wince—"sorry . . . a black. That's the in word, isn't it? Showing a black girl in a psychedelic mini and an Afro hairdo out to there. And the way she's eating that hot dog . . . my God, it's obscene."

"You know, blacks eat too, Gully. They eat, they drink, they buy clothes, they spend money jus' like us white folk do. And in this particular market, they account for eighteen percent of all product sales."

"Fine, then let's take out an ad in *Ebony* just for them. But let's not put our main advertising thrust into pushing integration in prime-time television. All you're going to do is wind up alienating a lot of people."

"Bullshit!" The temperature in the conference room was heating up now. It was not the first time she and Gully had had it out. "That is sheer bullshit. People don't believe that all-white, all-WASP crap anymore. Not even your average housewife."

"And what the hell do you know about the average housewife?" Gully roared back and, with a single brutal motion, swept the offending layouts onto the floor. "When was the last time you were ever in a supermarket? Jesus, you make me sick talking as if you've got your finger on the pulse of the great unwashed. When did you ever boil an egg or iron your husband's shirts or wipe a baby's behind? What gives you the right to speak for mainstream Middle America? Miss Catherine Chapman," he spat the words out contemptuously, "of Attleboro, Massachusetts."

"*Athol*, Massachusetts."

"Asshole, Massachusetts, for all I care. What the fuck do you know about blue-collar attitudes?"

She remembered that first abortive meeting with Gully in his office. He believed it once, he'll believe it again.

"Because I come from a blue-collar family, remember?"

"You're Jewish, right?"

"Yeah . . . right."

"Sure, you're Jewish like I'm the last of the Mohicans." He smiled and stretched like a cat playing with a mouse. "You really thought I believed that crap about your father standing on the dock at Ellis Island? Or was it a pushcart on the Lower East Side?"

Kate was stunned into momentary silence.

"How long have you known?" she finally asked.

"Since the day you first came to work here. You see, I play golf with your Uncle Harlan."

His answer caught her off kilter. But she should have known. Nothing much ever escaped those pale gray eyes.

"If you knew who I was, then why did we go through that rigmarole?"

"I wanted to see if you were going to try to grease your way by pulling family connections. You didn't, and I respected that. But I never understood why you pretended to be Jewish. Why?"

"I don't know myself. Sheer perversity, I guess."

"Well, that's neither here nor there." He offered her a Norfolk, the agency peace pipe, and they lit up with the comfortable air of old antagonists.

"What is to the point is this campaign." He nodded at the layouts strewn like so much bomb-wreckage across the floor. "I am not going to show this stuff. There is no way—*no way*—the guys at ChicagoCorp are going to buy it. If we went into a presentation with a campaign like this, we'd come out looking like goddamn fools. And they'd come out looking for another agency."

"But Gully, I sincerely believe—"

"I don't give a shit what you believe, Kate. You're a bright girl, and over the years you've made yourself valuable to Marsden. Valuable—but not invaluable. So don't think you can buck the system, because it so happens that I'm the system. The answer is no and that's final."

With that, he got up to go. "And tell your group they better get together pronto and come up with new alternatives."

He walked out in complete and deliberate disdain of the layouts that paved his way. She could hear the crunch of the cardboard backing as they snapped beneath his feet.

Well, that's OK, too, she thought, regarding the broken bodies of her pet idea. *I have stats . . .*

"I've never asked you for anything before, Don."

"Except money."

Kate gave a quick, nervous giggle. "It's not money I want this time, Don. It's support. You know we did this campaign for Fabulous Franks and—"

"If it's this business between you and Gully, you know I

never interfere in creative matters, Kate. That's Gully's jurisdiction. Me, I'm just a money man. I push the figures around here and there and hope they come out black at the end of the day."

Fucking coward. They don't call him Don Fair-Weather-Friend for nothing.

"So as you see, Kate, you'll have to sort it all out with Gully. When all's said and done, he *is* the creative director."

"Creative director!" Kate snorted. "He's neither creative nor a director. He's . . . well, he's a great fixer. A marvelous salesman. He should be head of client relations, some sort of super account executive. But he should never, never in a million years be the creative director of this agency!"

"Then who should, Kate?"

"I should," she said softly.

Don formed his perfect fingers into a church steeple and regarded them with affection. "How old are you, Kate?"

"Twent—I'll be thirty next month. And younger people than I have held down big jobs in this business."

"Do you honestly think you're capable of handling $120,000,000 worth of billing?"

"Yes, I think so."

"Well, let me tell you, Kate, in the kindest possible way"—his smile was a monument to American dentistry at its finest—"About a hundred million of that business is in Gully's hip pocket. He works for this agency in a lot of places you'll never see the inside of—the locker room at Cross Ridge, the squash courts at the New York Athletic Club, the Princeton Alumni Association. He's got more connections than Ma Bell, and what he doesn't have, his wife has. So if Gully wants to be creative director or mailboy or whatever . . . if he wants to stand on the roof of this building and make like King Kong, that's the way it's going to be. I want you to go back to Gully and bow to his decision. In your own words, of course. I know he won't respect you any the less for having fought the good fight. And a few soft words will work wonders."

"You want me to apologize for having knocked myself out with the best work I've done in years. You want me to go back to my people—people I've been working round the clock—and tell them 'Sorry, gang. We've just been screwed.' I can't do it."

"We'd hate to lose you, Kate, and I mean that sincerely. Think it over."

She was thinking things over back in her office when she heard the hush fall. It was eerie. The clatter of typewriters, the chatter of the secretaries all suddenly as silent as the jungle approach of a lion. The mighty Gully himself, perhaps for the first time in Marsden history, had descended to the fifth floor, and now he stood in her doorway, pale with rage.

"You fucking cunt."

Kate rose to her feet, temporarily dumbstruck.

"You cunt," he repeated, his lips hardly moving. "You thought you could ace me out, didn't you? Who the fuck do you think you are, going over my head. You sneaky bitch. You've had it here . . . you know that, don't you?"

And suddenly her rage matched his own.

"Don't bother to fire me, Mr. Fucking Prick Gulliver, because I'm quitting right now. I'll even save you the severance pay." She slammed her briefcase down on her desk. "What's the matter, Gully, did I have you scared? You bet your ass I did, because you're past it, baby. You truly are past it."

"Get out, cunt. Get out right this minute!" You could have heard his scream three blocks away. "Over my dead body will you ever again set foot in this agency. Over my dead body."

"Save your breath, Gully," she shot back, flinging things into her briefcase. "You'll need it for sucking up to clients."

When she told Wolf what had happened on the phone that night, he said not to worry, something would turn up. Eight days later she'd signed on as copy chief for Brooking-McLeod, practically across the street on Madison Avenue. They ran a lovely story about her in *Advertising Age*, practically half a column. And from her new office on the twenty-eighth floor, she could look down on Marsden-Baker.

KIT

"You can turn inward or you can turn outward."

Of all the things that friends and family had said in the weeks that followed Monk's death, it was Marian's words that left the keenest impression.

And people, of course, had said the most remarkable things—phrases designed to comfort and destined to wound. "Above all," they said, "you mustn't blame yourself." She had heard that from her mother, her neighbors, Dr. Winkler, even from Michael. At least on this one occasion, thank God, Michael did not hold her culpable. He placed the blame squarely on that "maniac hit-and-run driver" and usually followed it up by saying he was going to "crucify the next one I get in court."

But words are not opiates, and for a long time afterwards she would play and replay the sequence of events. The cumulative cost of her failures. *If* she had made him wear his hearing aid. *If* she hadn't bought the bird. *If* she hadn't left the window open. *If* she hadn't taken a nap that afternoon. If if if if if . . .

She could brood—and for many months found it impossible not to—on the nature of her grief, mixed as it was with guilt and remorse. Sharpened by a fleeting insight so deep and dangerous that she only half-dared recognize it in herself. Yet

208

she recognized it in Michael, unspoken but unmistakable. It
was a feeling of relief.

"You can turn inward or you can turn outward."

Kit turned outward.

Haddons Landing (the apostrophe had disappeared along
with the blacksmith's forge) was incorporated in 1791, according to the black-on-white road sign at the edge of town.
Actually, the village had been settled more than a century
earlier by one Increase Haddon, and no man was more aptly
named. In 1653, he had taken his wife and thirteen children
from what he considered the rank, Godless atmosphere of
Puritan Boston to find a place where "Manne maye live in
Harmonie with his Makyr." You could still read the words on
his tombstone in the white clapboard church in Main Street.

Despite the proliferation of early Haddons, the village
grew slowly and quietly, acquiring no particular niche in the
history books. The Landing had, truth to tell, ducked the odd
witch in its early days, but more in conformity with the
dictates of prevailing fashion than out of inquisitorial
vengeance, and not on nearly so grand a scale as nearby
Salem. Nor had the Landing soaked the local countryside
with the blood of Revolutionary battles, nor deafened it with
the impassioned oratory of patriots. Remarkable neither for
low deeds nor high ideals, Haddons Landing went its own
way, and by the 1900s it was distinguished chiefly for possess-
ing some of the greenest lawns to be found in the whole North
Shore of Massachusetts.

The shops, too, were nice. Nicer than any village that size
has a right to. There was Calico Corners, which carried a
beautiful line in tweeds and cashmeres; Gourmania, where
you could buy Chivers Marmalade and fresh herbs in season;
the 1770 Shoppe with its small but discerning stock of early
Americana. If you were really desperate, the County Shopping Center was only five miles away, and it was only another
half-hour into Boston.

But on the whole, you could find anything right there in the
Landing. Anything, that is, except men. For though on
weekends the village might look and live like a thousand
others its size, during the week it was as exclusively female as
a nunnery.

Men commuted. Meanwhile women cooked and kaffee-
klatsched and cleaned house and raised children in blissful

ignorance of hippies, yippies and LSD trippies. If a stranger to Haddons Landing were to ask for the flower people, he would be directed to the Ladies' Garden Club, likely as not.

Weekends were different, though. Weekends were dinner parties, the primary source of social pleasure among the inhabitants. At first, the Mathesons worried that as newcomers, their acquaintanceships would be limited to the paid attentions of the Welcome Wagon lady. They needn't have worried, for Haddons Landing people were nothing if not gregarious. And within weeks of their arrival they were taken up—indeed, pounced upon—by what was unquestionably the Landing's "in group." Michael's reputation as perhaps the hottest young prosecutor in Boston and Kit's unexceptionable family connections combined to pave the way. They were made to feel they were not merely a welcome addition to the community but an ornament.

And why not? They were a most attractive family. Michael had made the Boston papers more than once and could take pride that his conviction rate (ninety-three percent) was the second highest in the State of Massachusetts. As for Kit, she was pleasant, aristocratic without being snobby and—little by little—turning into one hell of a hostess.

Their house was admirably suited for entertaining. Like most other buildings in the village, it was white frame with black shutters, modest in size and authentically Federal right down to the wide plank floorboards. It had a living room with a wood-burning fireplace, a dining room that visitors always called "gracious," four bedrooms, two full baths and a really modernized, wonderful kitchen. Some previous owner had added a sun room which ran the width of the house, a wall of windows designed to catch the last westerly fragments of winter light. Architectural purists might have wrung their hands in horror, but Kit wouldn't have traded it for anything in the world. It was her room.

Within six months, the Mathesons were as firmly rooted in the community as the lordly elms that lined Main Street. Michael joined the Voluntary Fire Brigade (a weekly drinking club, as it turned out, fires being even rarer in Haddons Landing than Negroes), ran successfully for Councilman and was, by popular concensus, the heart and soul of the Village Zoning Commission. Even seven-year-old Sarah joined the joiners, for Haddons Landing was made for children. In no time at all, she had flung herself full speed into the Brownies, been introduced to the local ponies, signed up for Dinny Ogden's dance classes, and made at least twenty "best friends."

Kit herself was not much of a clubwoman. After a few stabs, at Michael's insistence, with the Ladies' Historical Society and the obligatory PTA, she defected, finding the local issues ("Resolved: The STOP sign at the corner of Elm and Main Street to be replaced by a yellow blinker") somewhat less than urgent.

She made a number of friends, however, largely among the mothers of Sarah's schoolmates. It was one of them—a brisk and freckled Englishwoman named Valerie—who told her about the Wednesday Club.

"It's not a proper club, actually," (she pronounced it *akshully*) "just a very informal group of women who get together once a week to talk about . . . well, anything except property prices and local issues."

Kit had laughed appreciatively, for real estate was The A-Number-One Topic at every social function, formal or otherwise—in Haddons Landing.

"Well, come along next Wednesday and give it a go. There's nothing formal. No agenda, no membership, just talk. Talk and coffee."

Kit came the following Wednesday to find nearly a dozen women—strangers except for her hostess and Jean Pendleton, whom she knew from dinner parties and was, like Kit, married to a lawyer. The women (they refused to call themselves "the girls") were, Kit realized, the nonconformists—or at least what passed as such in the homogeneous structure of the village. Jean had spent a year in the Peace Corps, one of the first to answer Kennedy's call. There was Amy, no bigger than a whisper, who had put in ten tough years as a social worker in the slums of New York. Valerie, of course, who shared Kit's enthusiasm for Henry James. Irene, who did "little theater" in Boston. Live-wires, every last one of them.

They were mostly young, all married—some happily, some not. Their presumption, and Kit did nothing to gainsay it, was that she could be numbered among the happily married. Mostly Democrats, in a staunchly Republican town. They were all, of course, women, though nonetheless emphatic that it was not a "Women's Group" per se. Fine. Kit had had enough of *that* with Georgie and her friends. "Bitching sessions," she'd privately named them.

No. Only the great world was large enough for the women of the Wednesday Club. McLuhanism. The Black Power Movement. Consumer Legislation. The New Left. And increasingly, as time went on, the Viet Nam War.

And ultimately, almost to the exclusion of all other issues, the Viet Nam War. The War. The War. The War. There was no getting away from it. It engulfed, absorbed every other question. It encompassed every other topic: Negro rights, student riots, money for the cities, freedom of speech, the question of America's moral stance. They didn't always agree, the women, on either the origin or eventual outcome of the conflict in Southeast Asia, but they were united in their condemnation of national policy.

The meetings stimulated Kit to think, as she had not done since college, about the world beyond the confines of her home. It had been years since she had this much freedom, this much time for reading, sifting through facts. She began to take in a great many publications: *The New Republic, The Reporter, Ramparts, The Village Voice.* When Valerie's copy of *The New Statesman* arrived from England, it was handed on to Kit before anyone else.

The more Kit read the more the war appalled her. And what appalled her most of all was her helplessness, her sheer and utter impotence in the face of what she gradually came to regard as an unmitigated evil. It was all very well and good to say, as Miss Evers had said at boarding school, that moral righteousness itself effected change. But Kit had not found this to be the case.

Yes, she could argue with the women of the Wednesday Club, sometimes preach with the fervor of her abolitionist forebears. But that was preaching to the converted. And women at that.

For what did it matter what women thought? What women did? How did that change the world?

When Kit and Company went to Boston to join a Mothers' March for Peace, their efforts had provoked not anger (Kit would have welcomed that), but merely good-natured chaffing from their assembled husbands.

No, women's opinions didn't count in this world. Men's did. And for all her passion, all her carefully assembled facts,

Kit could not even come close to influencing the one man nearest to her. Michael.

"You're not starting in on that again," he would groan when confronted with the latest outrage. And once, "You're getting to be as big a bore as your crazy old Aunt Annabel."

Yet as Kit remembered, when she first told Michael she was related to the famous suffragette, he'd been enormously impressed. He had called her a "legend," spoken of her with awe and admiration. Obviously chaining yourself to lamp-posts was great stuff sixty years after the fact, but in the context of its time merely "crazy." Like opposing the Viet Nam War in 1967.

So little by little the war in Southeast Asia added fuel to their own domestic battles.

"I think they should be shot," Hank Savage said.

It was rare at Haddons Landing dinner parties—especially large formal ones such as this at the Pendletons—for guests to bring up controversial or distasteful matters. But then it had been a rare day right from the start. That very morning, hundreds of rampaging students had burned their draft cards in an auto-da-fé at Government Centre, then run wild through the streets of downtown Boston, carrying placards and upsetting trash cans. The men who were dining there that evening, most of whom worked in the State Street area, had witnessed all or part of the unrest.

"I think they should be shot down like dogs. I say, when a man refuses to serve his country in its hour of need, he's either a coward or a traitor. What do you say, counsellor?" He turned to Michael. Michael the prosecutor, Michael the voice of legitimate authority.

"Well," Michael leaned back, assuming his most avuncular courtroom manner—*He's playing the judge already,* Kit thought—"I think you're being a bit hard on the boys. You have to give them credit for a little sincerity. Some of 'em, at least. I'm willing to accept that some of these fellows—not all, mind you, just some—have sincere moral objections to the war. And they feel this is a very dramatic way to make their point."

"So you as a government prosecutor would *advise* them to burn their draft cards?" Jim Pendleton was incredulous.

"I didn't say that." He was all sweet reason now. "I merely said that if they're willing to burn their draft cards out of protest, let them. Provided . . ." He paused dramatically and took a sip of his brandy.

"Provided *what?*" Hank grumbled.

"Provided they're willing to pay the penalty for draft evasion. I make an exception of the proved conscientious objector; they don't really come into it. But for the rest, if they're that high-minded and that full of moral outrage, they should be eager to go to jail. More work for us prosecutors" —he gave an impish grin—"but that's the way it goes. At least they'd be proving their sincerity."

There was a general murmur of "hear, hear." Everyone seemed to go along with Michael's thinking except Hank Savage, who was intractable anyway. Except Hank Savage and Kit.

"I disagree," she said softly, when the murmuring died down.

"What?" Michael frowned, perhaps thinking he'd misheard.

"I said," she spoke more clearly now, "I disagree. I don't see any reason why any one of them should serve as much as one day in jail. The war isn't worth it."

"What would you do, give them medals?" This from Savage.

"What if it were your own son?" Alice Wilson interposed mildly, then sucked in her breath with the realization she had brought up such a sensitive subject. Everyone knew about Monk.

But if Kit had been wounded by the reference, she gave no sign of it.

"If it were my own son," she continued, "who came to me and said, 'Mother, I don't believe in this war, I cannot bring myself to serve in this war'—if my son came to me and said such a thing, I'd just give him the money—as much as he needed—and get him out of the country. Even if it took every last penny. Even if I had to smuggle him out myself."

"Kit doesn't mean that," Michael interjected quickly.

"I don't *what?*" Kit's voice rose an octave.

How dare he! Who was he to hush her up or interpret her for others? How dare he presume to be the arbiter of what she did or did not mean?

"I mean exactly what I say. I would do everything in my power to get him out of the country, and the hell with the law."

"But surely you'd want him to have the courage of his convictions?" Alice, the peacemaker.

"Courage? That's not courage—that's stupidity. Have him rot in jail? For what? Why should he spend God knows how many years behind bars—and I know what goes on there—when he could be learning, doing, living." She was starting to sweat. Too much wine? Too much heat? Too much passion? But nothing, not Hank's outraged splutter, not the sight of Nancy making patterns out of walnut shells, not even Michael's cold angry glare could stop the spate of words. She turned to Hank.

"Why should you call him a coward or a traitor . . . this imaginary boy who only wants to live. Dr. Spock says—"

"Spock should mind his own goddamn business," Hank burst in, "which is telling mothers when to change diapers."

"But this *is* his business, don't you see? We bring up our children, we change their diapers, see they get polio shots, worry if they're ten minutes late home from school. We straighten their teeth, make them wash behind their ears, give them lots of Vitamin C. For what? So they can go to Viet Nam and be blown to bits? So they can share some prison cell with a bunch of junkies and perverts?"

"Now Kit . . ."

"Now Kit nothing!" she exploded. "If a Jew was fortunate enough to escape from Germany in 1939, did you call him a coward or a traitor? Or maybe you believe he should have had the 'courage of his convictions' and stayed behind so he could be gassed at Auschwitz!"

The silence that followed was the silence of embarrassment. Not a word in either support or refutation.

"Am I the only one," Kit asked limply, "who thinks these boys have a right to lead their own lives? Who thinks they deserve something better than prison? Michael? Jean?"

Yes, Jean would agree. Jean must. She had voiced so many of the same sentiments at the Wednesday Club. Why just last week she was saying . . .

She looked at Jean—blunt, outspoken Jean Pendleton, who had sometimes surprised even Kit with her blue-sky talk. It amazed her that Jean should sit there quiet and noncommittal. Why? Simply because Jim Pendleton was there?

Simply?

Precisely.

"I'm asking you, Jean, what do you think?"

"I think," said Jean. "we ought to change the subject," and like a fish in water slid on to more agreeable shoals: Did everybody know there was a new play group being organized for the under-fives? And suddenly everybody was talking at once.

So there it was. For all Kit's ardor, all her fervor, she had succeeded merely in antagonizing Hank, infuriating her husband and spoiling an otherwise pleasant dinner party. She was quiet the rest of the evening.

She could feel Michael's anger, palpable as a bullwhip the moment they got in the car. He drove home in silence, paid off the baby sitter and went upstairs to bed.

Too wound up to sleep or read or even think straight, Kit kicked off her shoes in the kitchen and brewed a pot of coffee. And sitting at the kitchen table, an old chipped mug before her, relived the events of the evening.

Had she made a fool of herself? Probably. But even so, what did it matter? There were worse things in life than looking like a fool. Lying was worse. Hypocrisy was worse. Subscribing to evil simply because it was part of the social convention—that was the worst thing of all.

She was sorry. Not sorry she had spoken out, but sorry that her emotion had swayed no one, that her reasoning had not hit home. She had succeeded merely in embarrassing. Had been treated, albeit politely, as though she had done something too vulgar to acknowledge. Like picking your nose at the dinner table, or belching, or farting. She could almost smile at the memory of the averted eyes and uncomfortable shuffles when she had committed what must have been the biggest gaffe of all times at Haddons Landing.

Nearly two years in this town and she still hadn't learned that women should be seen and not heard to exchange anything more profound than a recipe for cucumber mousse. At least not when there were men around.

And Michael! Michael rushing in to explain that 'Kit didn't mean that' as though she were a half-witted child, as though the mere fact that he was her husband authorized him to speak for her. How contemptible. She got up to pour herself another cup of coffee.

"You can pour me one, too, while you're at it." He had come downstairs quietly in pajamas and slippers, and in a flash she knew what he'd been doing in the past half-hour. He had been preparing his case, readying his attack—the eternal prosecutor, whose proudest boast was that he never entered the courtroom unprepared.

"Now," he said, after scrutinizing her for several moments as if he were a scientist who'd discovered a particularly nasty specimen on his slide, "I'd like to know what—if anything— was going on in your little mind when you treated us all to that charming lesson in elocution."

She let the tick of the kitchen clock speak her answer.

"I said," he repeated, "I would like to know . . ."

"You can save the sarcasm, Michael, and the five-dollar words. You're not in the courtroom now."

"Oh, I see," he nodded with mock gravity. "We're not in the courtroom now. It appears the lady prefers the glories of the soapbox to the indignities of the witness stand."

"If you've something to say, Michael, come out with it. If not, I'm going up to bed."

Suddenly, with a viciousness that took her breath away, his foot lashed out and kicked her shoe with such force that it ricocheted off the stove and, with a resounding clang, came to rest by the sink. Her poor little silver sandal, its strap dangling like a broken limb.

"You bet your ass I have something to say. I don't mind your making a fool of yourself in the privacy of this house or among your silly women—that's your privilege. But I goddamn well do resent it when you try to make a fool of *me* in public!"

"I don't see how my speaking my mind in any way makes a fool out of *you.*"

"You don't see it." He'd calmed down sufficiently to resume his mocking tone, but she could see the vein throbbing in his neck. "The lady doesn't see it," he said, addressing the refrigerator jury. "The lady does not see that she has bored and embarrassed the pants off ten decent, innocent people who wanted nothing more than to enjoy their dinner. The lady doesn't see why she can't run off at the mouth like a middle-aged hippie, even though she is married to an officer of the court."

"I have a right to my opinion."

"Aha, the lady claims she has a right to her opinion. This is a free country, is it not? And does it not say right there in the

First Amendment of our beloved Constitution that Congress shall make no law respecting . . ."

Kit got up to leave.

"Sit down!" He hit the table so hard that the coffee quivered and slurped over. "Sit down and sit still."

For the first time in their marriage she knew physical fear. He was tough and mean and vindictive. She'd known that for a long time, but she had never seen him so white-hot with anger, never felt his potential for violence. She sat down, clutching her sides to keep her hands from shaking.

"Let me tell you, Kit"—eyes narrow as a cat—"You do *not* have the right to an opinion. You think you know it all with your little articles in your little magazines. You have tea at Schrafft's with Marian and plot the overthrow of the Republic. You go for an afternoon stroll in the Commons and call it the Mothers' March for Peace. You know zilch. Nothing. You don't have the faintest grasp of what the world is all about, or the war either, for that matter. You've never worked a day in your life, you've had everything handed to you from the day you were born. Have you ever served in the army? Held a gun? If you want to know what war's all about, ask a soldier. Don't ask the girls in your club. That's in the first place. In the second place, *I will not tolerate* your contradicting me in public. Can you imagine how it looks to other people? Or don't you care? Well, I care. The great hotshot lawyer with a big political future . . . how does it look if he can't even get his wife to keep her mouth shut? I expect loyalty from you. Not 100% loyalty, either, but *150% loyalty*. I expect that if nothing else. And God knows I've had damn little else. And in the third place"—he leaned across the table close to her—"I find it absolutely distasteful, and so did everyone else, that you should say what you'd do if you had a son. Well, you've had a son, Kit, remember? And he was quite a son. And what a fine botch you made out of *that!*"

If Kit had feared a physical blow, she feared it no longer. For Michael had rooted out her most vulnerable spot and struck in the fiercest way of all.

She would never forgive him.

After that evening, they went their separate ways as much as possible, antagonists in an uneasy truce. Formalities were observed, faces made deceptively bland on those occasions when they ventured forth as a couple. Kit now understood the wisdom of seating wives as far away from husbands as possible at social gatherings. For she had nothing to say to him. Nothing, that is, that did not threaten to release another round of acrimony.

At home, especially in front of Sarah, they managed to scrape up enough unanimity of purpose, enough small talk, to prevent—they both hoped—their daughter's stumbling into the abyss that gaped between them.

Michael spent more and more time in Boston, in a heightened round of political activity, his enterprise being rewarded with a delegate seat at the '68 Democratic convention in Chicago. As for Kit, she kept her mouth shut on those matters that had so antagonized him, more from despair than from prudence. She continued with the Wednesday Club out of sociability, although she wrote it off inwardly as hopeless. About as effective as her mother's mah-jongg afternoons in Athol. She joined a bridge club, became a den mother and began playing tennis again.

On those rare evenings when she and Michael were inescapably alone together, they assumed new patterns. If he was reading, she would watch television. If he was watching television, she would go into the sun room and read or sew. They never went upstairs to bed together. One yawn from him and she would find some excuse—a book, a movie she wanted to catch on the late show—to outstay him. And if his own hours proved nocturnal, it was Kit's turn to say, "I think I'll turn in early tonight." Theirs was an unspoken pact, no less observed for being tacit. They never touched, except in public. They never argued any more. It was easier that way.

For awhile she toyed with the idea of leaving him, like a child playing with a ball. She would toss it here, toss it there, never knowing where it would land. Go. Stay. Go. Stay. The initiative, she knew, would have to be hers, for it was abundantly clear that Michael was, if not content, at least committed to maintaining the status quo. He would never leave her, of that she was sure, no matter how sorely tempted. His picture of himself, his image to others, was so determinedly that of a substantial married man. Divorce, as he had so often pointed out, had tarnished many a brilliant political career. Stevenson, Rockefeller, men who in spite of money, caste, connections had seen their constituencies vanish in the face of domestic scandal. That vision was always before him. No. Michael would never leave her, for whatever their marriage meant to him, there was little question it meant less than his professional ambitions.

So the ball was clearly in her court. And the options, such as they were, were hers alone. But what were they—Marian's famous options? For Michael was right. She *had* never worked a day in her life. She had no skills, no job experience, no means of support other than living off her capital. Nor had she grounds for divorce. Michael had neither maltreated her nor been unfaithful. He had, it is true, denied her of her "conjugal rights," as the law so nicely put it, but that was a patently laughable charge in view of the fact that she had borne him two children. Nor could she imagine confiding her bedroom secrets even to her closest friends, let alone a judge in a divorce court. Perhaps if there had been someone else waiting in the wings . . . some man more loving than Michael. But there was not, and at a thick-waisted, bespectacled thirty-one, she could not reasonably assume there ever would be.

Lastly, of course, there was Sarah. Whatever Michael's faults—and in her own mind they were infinite—she could put forth no grievance in his treatment of Sarah. He adored her. And she adored him.

The ball was in her court, all right. And it landed inevitably on Stay.

"Foreships."

"They're not foreships," she heard Sarah titter, "they're faucets."

Kit looked in the kitchen to see what was going on.

Sarah and little Chuckie from Cannon Road had taken over the kitchen with a vengeance. The table was strewn with bodies of old broken dolls, bits and pieces from forgotten wind-up toys, a teddy bear that had lost its shoe-button eyes and a harmless collection of cutlery and pans.

"What on earth are you children doing?"

"We're playing hospital, Mommy. Look!" She held up her Raggedy Ann. "We're giving her a heart operation, right here where it says I LOVE YOU. These are the bandages"— she unrolled a length of toilet paper—"and these"—an old pair of spaghetti tongs—"are the faucets."

"Not faucets, darling. Forceps. Who's playing the doctor?"

"Oh, Chuckie is. He's the doctor and I'm his nurse."

Chuckie beamed with male authority.

"Well, OK, children, enjoy yourselves. And please try not to break anything."

An hour later, when Chuckie had gone, leaving the mess for the females to clear up, Kit said to Sarah, "Next time you play hospital, why don't you be the doctor and Chuckie could be the nurse?"

Sarah screwed up her face at the sheer absurdity of the suggestion. Obviously, Mommy was being ridiculous again. But Kit decided to press the point.

"Why not? There are lots of women doctors, you know." And when Sarah continued to look doubtful, Kit realized her daughter had never known one. Nor had she, for that matter. All their family doctors in Athol and Boston, all Monk's specialists, had always been men. The conversation had a familiar ring. Still . . .

"You know, Aunt Marian's going to be a doctor. Not a medical doctor, but a doctor of philosophy. That's a kind of doctor. You could be one too when you grow up. Or a lawyer like daddy, or a scientist, or an airline pilot. How about that? Wouldn't you like to be an airline pilot or an astronaut?"

"I've never seen a lady astronaut."

"Well, there are some, believe me . . . in Russia, anyhow. Honestly, darling," she began reeling in the toilet paper, "just think of all the things you can be when you grow up. You could be a television reporter or a big game hunter or an astronomer who discovers a new planet and gets written up in all the papers . . . or even President of the United States. Now doesn't that sound exciting? It does to me. So don't ever forget, and I'm quite serious—a woman can be anything she sets her mind to in this world."

Sarah smiled and packed her dolls away. She knew a secret.

"Then why are you just a mother?"

Ouch. Kit stopped short. "Well," she said simply, "there's nothing wrong with being a mother. I like it, especially having a nice girl like you. All I'm saying is that there are other things in the world. Look, the next time Chuckie comes over and you play hospital, why don't you be the doctor and Chuckie the nurse?"

"Oh, no," said Sarah gravely, "I couldn't."

"Why not?"

"Well, Chuckie wouldn't like that," she squeezed the last doll in the box. "He wouldn't want to play any more."

Chuckie wouldn't like that. Ye Gods, she's not even ten and already she knows the rules of the game.

KATE

"FOR A SMART GIRL, YOU CAN BE AWFULLY STUPID," BARRY USED
to chide her about Wolf. But this once the message was, "For
a dumb broad, you can be pretty smart. Congratulations."

And congratulations were in order. Some six months
earlier, she'd quit Brooking and moved to a smaller agency.
A "hot shop" in the jargon of the day, and following fast on
her arrival had come the $2,000,000 Telco account, stolen
right out from under Brooking's nose. Brooking had
screamed, of course—screamed bloody murder, accusing
Kate of unethical behavior. They'd even mumbled vaguely
about law suits. Well, let them. They had no case and she
knew it.

"Tell me one thing, Kate. Did you have the whole thing
sewed up even before you left Brookings?"

"Yup, it was in the bag. Fact is, I made Telco a private
presentation early last November."

"All by yourself?"

"All by myself."

"It must have been quite a presentation."

"Oh, it was, Barry. It was." She looked to see if anyone
was within earshot, then continued in a lower voice. "The
high spot being when I jumped out of a cake wearing nothing

but a dash of Arpege. I'm speaking metaphorically, of course."

"In other words, you slept around a bit at Telco?"

"Well, no more than necessary—but yes, I did. Emile K. Busher was the gentleman's name, executive vice president in charge of marketing. A little guy"—she raised her hand to just above the midget level—"a little guy with a toothbrush mustache, a pinky ring and the hots for big tall women."

"You surprise me, Kate. I thought you never mixed business with pleasure."

"I surprised myself," she admitted, "although you could say this was strictly business. It's funny when you come to think of it . . . the whole question of what's ethical, what's not . . . exactly where you draw the line. Like I wouldn't work on a cigarette account no matter how much bread they offered. To me, that's unethical. I've never taken a kickback from a photographer. Hell! I even return Christmas presents from reps. Yet there I was, whoring around just for a piece of new business."

"Oh, I wouldn't call it whoring, Kate. What's the difference, one body more or less. Neither of us has ever been too picky."

"OK, so I've slept around a bit, who hasn't? But I've never done it for profit. Never once in my life—well, never until last November when I went down to San Juan with this joker—have I ever slept with a client or anybody higher up in the office. Even when I wanted to. Never! I mean, I could have had a thing with Gully years ago, and I would have been in solid with Marsden. I wouldn't do it. In fact, as I recall, I went out of my way to insult him. Yet there I was down in Puerto Rico with Emile K. Busher, super-runt. And you know what?"

She had a swift vivid memory of their bodies soaked in sweat, intertwined like serpents on a caduceus, while potted palm music wafted in through the shuttered windows from the courtyard beneath their stuffy hotel room.

"You know what?" she repeated. "It was some of the most fantastic sex I've ever had. Like the song says, 'Li'l David was small, but oh, my!' Funny . . . because all the way down on the plane to San Juan, I kept wondering how I was going to explain my tan to Wolf when I got back. I could have spared myself the bother. During the four days we were down there, we never even left the hotel room."

"Does your boyfriend have any inkling?"

"Wolf?" she grimaced. "Hard to say. On the whole I suppose he must. He's incredibly sensitive . . . all antennae . . . and outside of that one weekend, I've been pretty virtuous. But anyhow, he'd never inquire. I think he realizes he's in no position to ask questions. And as far as that goes, how do I know what he's up to on his weekends in Connecticut? He might just have a little bit of nookie tucked away in the bushes somewhere."

"But you don't really think so."

"I guess not," she sighed. "I don't know what to think. And then, of course, there's his wife. According to Wolf they live like brother and sister, but I never know how much of *that* to believe, either. I'm really of two minds about the whole situation, about what I owe him, what he owes me. I'm afraid that if I really started screwing around the way I used to, he'd know. He's practically psychic. I think I'll try fidelity for a while and see if Wolf gets the message. Virtue is its own reward and all that jazz, but who knows? Maybe he'll come up with something more concrete. And Barry, you won't say anything to anyone about the Emile K. business, now that you know the whole story, more or less?"

Barry put his finger to his lips.

In fact, she had told Barry rather less than more about the outcome of her Puerto Rican weekend. For a few months after her return, when the Telco contract had been signed and delivered, the new agency expressed its appreciation with a check for $20,000. A commission, a finder's fee was the euphemism. It was common, if not textbook practice, and Kate would have had no qualms about pocketing the fee were it not for the weekend with Busher.

Finder's fees were one thing however, high-class prostitution another. The way she figured it in simple mathematics, she had earned $5,000 a night for each night spent at El Convento, which must make her one of the best-paid call girls in the world.

The more she mulled it over, the more dissatisfied she became. With herself, the situation, the money. For two weeks the check sat uncashed beneath a pile of earrings in her jewelry box. There was no conceivable way she could return it without telling why, and she had no desire to let the new agency know she had secured the business on the horizontal.

Nor could she bring herself to bank it or invest it, to treat it sensibly like ordinary money.

She'd come a long way from the great principles of Miss Ellery's, from the high ideals that she and Jan Littlemarch had shared over midnight cocoa cups, from the fervor with which she had campaigned for Adlai Stevenson. A long way. But not *that* long a way.

On April 4, 1968, Martin Luther King was assassinated on a motel balcony in Memphis, Tennessee. On April 5th, Kate strode into a Madison Avenue branch of Chase Manhattan and bought four bank checks of $5000 each. The first was made out to the Southern Christian Leadership Conference. The second to CORE. The third to the American Civil Liberties Union. And the fourth—a personal indulgence—to the Eugene-McCarthy-for-President Campaign.

When she walked out of the bank some fifteen minutes later, she felt great!

KIT

By July 4, 1968, some 26,000 Americans had been killed in Viet Nam. On that same day, Police Officer James Edward Nolan ("Sunny Jim" to his friends) lay in the Intensive Care Ward of Mass General Hospital. He had been shot in the stomach two weeks earlier during the course of a gun battle outside the Boston Five Cents Savings Bank. In his way, Officer James Nolan was also a victim of the war in Viet Nam.

Three days before the Democratic National Convention was due to open in Chicago—and it promised to be a lulu—Michael came home early from the office.

"This is a surprise," Kit said. She was in the kitchen, stringing green beans for a salad *niçoise*. Just the thing for a sultry August night. "Sarah's not even back from day camp. What's the matter . . . did they finally run out of criminals?"

"Air conditioning broke down at the office." Michael helped himself to a handful of black olives and pulled up a kitchen chair.

"Good olives," he said chewing thoughtfully, watching his wife finish up with the beans.

Let me see. That's beans, olives, tuna fish, lettuce . . . aaah, yes, mustn't forget the potatoes. They were cooling in a pan by the sink.

"Didn't you once mention that you went to school with Jan Littlemarch?"

Kit dropped the pan in confusion, for the half-forgotten name had taken her utterly by surprise.

"Yes, I did." She turned around to face him. "Why do you ask?"

"Her father was Frank Littlemarch, wasn't he? In the State Department?"

Kit, mystified, could only nod.

"It figures." Michael seemed to have found some secret source of amusement. "Well, you know the saying . . . like father, like daughter." And as Kit stood there, gaping stupidly, he said, "Tell me, honey, how well did you know her?"

"What's all this about?" She had found her voice at last. "What's happened to Jan? Is she dead . . . murdered . . . what . . . ?"

"No, no, nothing like that, I assure you. Your friend is safe and sound. Look . . . why don't you sit down?" She was trembling with apprehension. "I didn't mean to upset you. I guess I just wasn't thinking."

With unaccustomed gallantry he pulled out a chair, and Kit sat down heavily, numb with astonishment.

"Just tell me—"

"I will. But you tell me first. You were pretty friendly with her at Miss Ellery's?"

"Very," she swallowed. "We were best friends."

"She didn't come to our wedding, though, did she? I think I'd remember if she'd been invited."

"No, we'd lost touch long before then. I think she went out to Berkeley. Now, will you tell me what the hell this is all about?"

"Remember that robbery at Boston Five Cents last June? A cop was shot?"

"You know I don't follow crime news. And what's that got to do with Jan?"

"Quite simply, your friend was arrested last week in a Back Bay apartment, along with three other members of the robbery gang."

Kit shook her head in disbelief. "Oh, boy, have *you* got the wrong person. Jan Littlemarch doesn't rob banks."

"Oh, no? Well, let me tell you it wasn't a simple bank robbery. She's part of a terrorist group—the Spartacans, I think they call themselves. They'd already been involved in a raid on a gun shop. Just doing a little fund-raising for Ho Chi Minh. Anyhow, somebody finked, and when the cops got there last night, the place turned out to be an absolute arsenal—rifles, Molotov cocktails, the works. Just lucky no one was killed."

"I don't believe it."

"Well, *you* may not, but a jury will. She was caught dead to rights."

Kit buried her head in her hands, letting the ugliness sink in, while Michael went back to his olives. It was nearly fifteen years since she'd seen Jan, ages since she'd last even thought of her. She forced her mind back across the chasm of time. Recalled the savage anger, the bitterness of the tall, slim girl, arrow-straight on the archery course, pulling back to go for the bull's-eye. The memory bit hard, and Kit knew intuitively that Michael had spoken the truth. The only wonder was that, with Jan's marksman's eye, the cop hadn't been killed.

"But the cop wasn't killed," she said hollow-voiced. "And I suppose the bank will get its money back. So maybe it's not as bad as it sounds."

"Really, Kit, you amaze me. You can't seriously think that I'm talking about harmless pranksters burning up their draft cards and saying, 'Oh, what a lovely fire.' I'm talking about armed robbery, terrorism, attempted murder. You know she'd be charged with murder one if that cop had died. Premeditated. That's the law when someone is killed in the course of a felony. He was shot in the stomach, you know. Your friend can thank her lucky stars that Boston's one of the world's great medical centers. Otherwise, he'd be dead—as dead as those boys you're always weeping about in Viet Nam. This is going to be a very big case, Kit—especially once the papers cotton on to who her father was."

"Is that what you meant . . . like father, like daughter?"

"That's what everybody's going to say."

"But Frank Littlemarch was innocent!" Kit cried out. "He was the victim of a witch hunt."

"Oh, sure," Michael scoffed. "A poor innocent lamb . . . like the Rosenbergs or Alger Hiss. Come off it, Kit."

"You didn't think like this at the time, I bet."

"At the time," he answered crisply, "I was in Korea, fighting for my country."

"But you wouldn't have thought so. Why, ten years ago you would have been defending Jan, not . . ." The realization hit her like a blow in the stomach. "Are you going to be prosecuting, Michael? Is that it? Have they put you in charge of the case?"

It was the first time she had ever seen Michael look sheepish. He let his silence speak for him.

"They have, haven't they? No, you don't have to answer that."

"I'm sorry, Kit." He broke the pact and took her hand. "I'm truly sorry. I had no idea you were so fond of her."

"Oh, Michael!" The tears streamed down her face. "Isn't there some way you could get out of it? Couldn't you tell them there's a conflict of interest, that your wife is her friend? I can't bear to think of you going up against her in court."

He shook his head.

"There *is* no conflict of interst, at least as far as I'm concerned. Remember, I never even met the woman, although I may pop around and see her tomorrow. You said she didn't come to our wedding and I wouldn't know her from Adam. So where's the conflict? In any case"—he released her hand and looked moodily out the window—"I don't want to opt out of the case. I've been waiting through six years of penny-ante crime to get a forum like this. It's a hot issue, all this terrorism stuff, even without her father. If I'm lucky this case should get national coverage, and you can't in all fairness ask me to throw away a golden opportunity just for old time's sake. I'm sorry you're upset, Kit, but you've got to understand—your first loyalty is to *me*, not to her. I expect to take this case right through to jury trial. No plea-bargaining, no nothing, going all the way. With luck, this case could be the making of me."

"Like the Alger Hiss case was for Nixon."

"I should be so fortunate."

"You don't mean that!" Kit was horrified.

"Oh, Kit, Kit, Kit," he said, shaking his head in wonder at her perversity. "You've been around lawyers long enough; you must have learned a thing or two. OK, you're not crazy about Nixon. Fine, you don't have to vote for him in November. But he wouldn't be running for President today if not for the Hiss case. It made him. It made his name a household word. And what did Nixon do that was so terrible, I ask you? He did what any other good lawyer would have done. He fought his side as hard as he could, just like they tell you in law school."

"He crucified Hiss."

"Crucified! Aren't we being melodramatic? Only Christs get crucified."

"Has she got a defense lawyer yet?"

"Don't worry, Kit, she'll get one. If she doesn't have the bread, the court will appoint somebody. May have done so already."

The bread. Michael was starting to talk like his defendants. Jan wouldn't have the "bread," Kit was sure. She recalled an item in the *Globe* some half-dozen years ago. a brief obituary of Frank Littlemarch. He had been found dead in a boarding-house in downtown Washington after years of hopeless litigation. Whatever fortune he'd had must have gone to his lawyers. They're the only victors, anyhow, in law suits. Lawyers.

"Do you think the American Civil Liberties Union . . ."

"Don't nourish any illusions, Kit. It's my bet that the ACLU wouldn't come within a hundred miles of Littlemarch. You've got to realize that there's no issue of civil rights, freedom of speech and all that jazz. We're talking about major felonies—armed robbery, attempted murder."

"Could I see her? Could I visit her in jail?"

"Don't be idiotic," Michael snapped brusquely. "And anyhow, why would you want to?"

"Because she's a friend . . . because she's in trouble. Isn't that reason enough?"

"Not as far as I'm concerned." He got up smartly. "Listen. Sarah will be home any minute now, and you don't want her to find you crying into the salad. Why don't you wash up and put on some makeup? You'll feel better. I'm going to take a shower myself. Maybe we'll go to an air-conditioned movie after dinner. God," he said as he left the room. "If it's this hot here, it's going to be a furnace in Chicago. Did you do my short-sleeved shirts?"

Bail had been set at $70,000, he told her the following night. Yes, it was rather high. It was meant to be. If you set low bail in a case like this, these people just disappeared underground. No, no bail bondsman would have any part of it. No collateral. After all, they're businessmen, not bleeding-hearts.

"So let's just not talk about it anymore," he concluded. "I've got enough on my mind with the convention. Daley's got the National Guard on tap; they're really expecting action. Yes, ma'm, every Yippie in the country's in Chicago this week, with the possible exception of your pal."

But later that evening, when she was packing his suitcase for Chicago, he came upstairs and sat on the bed.

"I've been thinking about what you said. About your wanting to visit Jan."

"Yes?"

"Well, maybe it's not such a nutsy idea after all. If you like, I could arrange a meeting."

She stopped in her packing and turned to look at him with ill-disguised suspicion. He wanted something. He must, for it was unlike Michael to give quid without getting quo. But his gaze was frank and artless as a child's.

"Why this change of heart all of a sudden? Just last night you said it was idiotic."

"I said a lot of things last night that have been bothering me all day." He patted the bed beside him. It was a gesture of invitation. "Leave the packing for a while, hon, and let's talk like two intelligent adults."

She sat down warily, choosing a spot further away than he had indicated.

"I get the impression you think I'm some kind of monster, Kit . . ." She pursed her lips. "There it is, that injured look again. But what have I done that's so terrible? Have I beaten you or come home drunk or run around with other women? What have I done . . . tell me?"

"You've said awful things to me, Michael . . . awful things."

"And so have you to me. I suppose any couple who's been married for ten years will have said awful things to each other in the heat of argument. Like last night—?"

"I wasn't thinking of last night," she interrupted.

But Michael clearly was, and he pursued his own avenue of thought undeflected. "Last night, I may have made it sound like I was out to get your friend at any cost. Michael Matheson, the steamroller, falling equally upon the just and the unjust. No, don't deny it"—although she had made no move to deny it—"I know that's how you feel, and it's been troubling me all day. But this morning when I saw your Jan in court . . . well, to tell you the truth, she seemed more pathetic than dangerous. That girl's no menace, I said to myself, just mixed up. She looked so forlorn. As for the lawyer the court assigned—Jack Rosen is a real schmuck, if you'll pardon my French. Anyhow, there she was, sitting, not saying a word, just letting it all happen. Both her parents are dead, you know."

"I know."

"Well, Kit, the more I thought about it, the more I felt she probably really does need someone to talk to. Maybe if you went to visit her, you'd both feel a little better about things. Give her a chance to maybe get some of her problems off her chest."

And there it was, the quid pro quo.

"I see," said Kit coolly. "You want me to cross-examine her. Maybe she'll be a good girl and 'fess up to the old school friend."

But if Michael was offended, he gave no sign.

"Honestly, Kit, I was thinking no such thing. I was thinking primarily of you, of our relationship. I don't want to crucify her, believe me. Least of all if I feel it's going to put a wedge between us."

He pulled her gently down on the bed amid the freshly pressed shirts and folded socks and began stroking her face.

"I know I might sometimes look like the number-one rat in the rat race, but whatever I do, it's for you. For you and Sarah." The words were soothing, as soothing as his fine hands on her brow. "I wouldn't want to go off to Chicago and feel I'm leaving bad vibes behind. That's what the kids call it now, isn't it? Bad vibes? And I can guess what you're going through about your friend Jan. So see her. Talk to her. She'd probably be delighted. The poor kid could use all the friends she can get."

Poor kid. In all the years they'd been married, she had never heard Michael refer to a defendant as a poor kid. As garbage, yes. Garbage. Vermin. Subhumans. She knew his vocabulary, she knew his mind. That Michael, who always fought for the heavier sentence, the graver charge, who frequently boasted—positively crowed—about his rate of convictions, should do such a total about-face in twenty-four hours was not to be believed.

"Very well," she said. "I'll see her."

"Good!" He was pleased at this easy victory. "I knew I could depend on you. She's at the Charles Street Jail, just

opposite the courthouse. I'll call Miss Docherty from the
airport tomorrow and have her set up the visit. She'll see you
get a private cubicle. Any particular day good for you?"

"Any day next week, it really doesn't matter." Kit smiled.
"After all, Jan's not going anywhere."

Michael laughed. It was his sort of joke.

"What is it exactly that you want me to talk to her about?"

"I'm not asking you to grill her," he said, suddenly wary.
"You understand that. But if you could just get a slant on the
way she thinks, how she happened to get caught up in this
crazy business. Talk naturally, and maybe I'll find a way to
make it easier for her. You understand?"

"I understand, Michael."

"That's my kitten. Now come on and give us a kiss."

She gave him a kiss—the soft kiss of Judas—then got up to
finish the packing.

"I couldn't believe my ears when the matron told me who
was here, and now I can't believe my eyes."

Jan Littlemarch was pale, paler than Kit remembered, with
the larval whiteness of an underground grub that never sees
the light of day. She was wearing a rust-colored T-shirt and
a pair of cotton slacks that hung loose and beltless from her
hips. Had Kit run into her on Tremont Street, she would not
have known her. Fifteen years had turned Jan into a stranger
—an alien presence that had surfaced from a stratum so
bizarre, so warped and frightening, that either it or Haddons
Landing must be a dream. A subterranean depth of guns and
bombs and dirty feet and long hair. There was no world in
which these two paradoxes could coexist. There was more
than the small wooden table between them. There were
fifteen years of different worlds, opposite paths, contradic-
tory lives.

And then Jan smiled. Smiled the same stricken smile, bared
the same unassuageable anguish, revealed the same chipped
front tooth. And Kit remembered the first time she had seen
it.

"Hello, Jan." She reached her hand across the table.
Reached out for those slender, still nail-bitten fingers. For
that hand she had held in her own so often. So long ago.

And with the touch of flesh to flesh, the years fell away at a
stroke. Suddenly they were laughing, crying in each others

arms atop an emotional surge that swept the near-past into oblivion.

"Oh, Cath," Jan cried and clung to her. "You picked a helluva place for a class reunion." Then, wiping her eyes on the sleeve of her tee-shirt, she said, "If I'd known it was you I would have brought some Kleenex."

"Well, *I* did," Kit said, laughing through her tears. "You know me, Jan—always prepared."

At last they settled down, still linked by a touch, while a matron glared through the panel.

"How are they treating you? Do you get enough to eat? I was wondering if I should have brought you something."

"A cake with a file in it, maybe?" Jan shrugged. "They're treating me all right, like a lamb for the slaughter. But let's talk about something else."

They chatted a bit, shyly at first, about the old days, about the weather, about nothing. Was Cath married? Yes, married . . . had a daughter . . . lived on the North Shore. Terrific! And what about her husband?

"You've seen my husband," Kit said slowly. "He was in court last week at your arraignment." And when she'd explained swiftly and clearly who Michael was, her friend leaned back in her chair, the shipwrecked eyes suddenly hard and cold.

"I see." she said. That was all. "I see . . ."

But Kit said, "No, Jan. You don't see at all . . ."

Out again on Charles Street, the sun struck her like a glorious assault. The air smelled of honey. She breathed in great drafts of it to blow away the stench of sweat and disinfectant. It was she—Kit—who had been freed from prison.

Boston had never looked so beautiful as on that hot August morning and she was starved. Absolutely ravenous. The very first thing she'd do was go over to Brigham's and have a great big gooey, gloppy sundae—real vanilla ice cream with bits of the bean in it, drowning in hot fudge and mixed nuts. The second thing she'd do was call Tim. It was quarter to three before she finally found him in and he didn't sound particularly friendly. But there it was. "Well, Tim, I was wondering if you could squeeze in an appointment for me today."

"At the *office?*"

"Yes, it's a legal matter. Believe me, I wouldn't bother you if I felt it could wait."

"Oh, shit, honey, there's no way I could see you today. Can you tell me what it is over the phone?"

"No, I can't. And anyway I'm calling from a pay phone in Filene's. What about tonight? Could you spare me half an hour tonight?"

He sighed, clearly annoyed. "Oh, I suppose so. I should be getting out around sixish. You don't want to hang around all that time, I suppose."

"Whatever is most convenient for you, Tim, as long as it's today. What if I come by your apartment this evening?"

"Yeah . . . OK." She could tell he was in a hurry to get off the phone, could hear other phones ringing in the background.

"Okay, Kit. Come around any time after seven."

It was 7:01 exactly when she pulled up at the big apartment house on Beacon Street. She'd had time to go home, have a quick wash, change into a fresh black cotton dress, ring up the Dillmans to chat with Sarah and reconsider exactly what she was going to say to Tim.

"Don't you look nice," he said when he opened the door.

"Don't you look . . . *different*," she answered. "And very unlawyerlike."

He was wearing a white floppy shirt of Indian cotton, white unpressed bell bottoms and leather thong sandals that clicked when he walked.

"No love beads?"

"They're at the cleaners. Come on in." He ushered her into the living room. The television was on—he'd been watching the convention, the action in Grant's Park. Michael had phoned the night before to assure her he was all right. It was the first convention in history, he said, where the news was being made outside, not inside, the Hall.

Tim turned down the sound but let the picture run.

"Marian's in Nahant with her mother for a couple of days. She'll be sorry she missed you. Scotch? Wine? What's your pleasure?"

"How about a nice long gin and tonic?"

He went out to the kitchen to mix the drinks. She watched a cop swing his billy at a newsman. Live from Chicago. The greatest show on earth.

"Sorry, no lime," Tim said, handing her a drink. "The place falls apart when Marian's away."

"Here's to, Tim."

"Here's to." They clinked glasses and watched the TV in silence for a few moments.

"Now," he said, taking a chair facing her. It was going to be lawyer and client. "There's just one thing I want to say before you tell me whatever it is you're going to tell me. I don't do divorce law."

"Is that what you thought?" She gave a nervous smile. "Well, I suppose it's a reasonable assumption under the circumstances. But no, it's nothing to do with divorce. It's about . . . a criminal matter."

Tim raised his eyebrows and waited for her to continue.

"Tim, before I say anything more, I'd like you to promise me that everything I tell you will be held in absolute confidence."

"That goes without saying. After all these years, you should know a thing or two about the code of ethics."

"Well, it's just that Michael talks about his cases pretty freely. What the hell . . . everybody does. I could start a blackmail ring just from what I pick up at dinner parties. I want your word you won't talk about this. Not even to Marian."

He put down his drink and gave her a long sober look.

"You have my word."

"Starting now?"

"Starting now."

She swallowed hard twice. "I went to see Jan Littlemarch this morning. I guess you know about the case."

"Just what I read in the papers." His eyes flickered with sudden comprehension. "Of course . . . you went to school with her, didn't you? I remember Marian saying something about her being an Ellery girl."

"Yes, I went to school with her. We were . . . we were very close."

"Oh, wow! I'm sorry. It's a terrible case. Is Michael involved with it?"

"He's handling the prosecution."

"I'm doubly sorry."

"For me or for her?"

Tim shrugged equivocally. "She has a lawyer already, I presume."

"Court-appointed . . . some fellow named Jack Rosen. Michael says he's a schmuck. Do you know him?"

"More of a schnook than a schmuck, if I've got my Yiddish right way around . . . not exactly the biggest honcho in Boston. Frankly, I don't think Clarence Darrow could do much with the case, so if you're asking me to represent her, Kit . . . well, she already has a lawyer. She'd have to make the request herself."

"I wasn't going to ask you that, Tim. I'm going to ask you to represent *me*."

Tim rubbed his eyes in confusion. "I'm lost, Kit. Enlighten me."

She did. And when she had done so, all he could say was, "You're crazy."

It was as good a cue as any to mix another round of drinks, and when he came back he seated himself next to her on the sofa."

"You really have that kind of money, Kit? Seventy grand is an awful lot of bucks."

"I have it. I went to the broker this morning. He says I could have a banker's check by tomorrow." A horrible thought intruded. "The stocks were left to me out-right. I'm free to dispose of them as I want, aren't I?"

"Oh, yes, you're free to dispose of them. You're free to make a bonfire out of them if that's what you want. And that," he said thoughtfully, "is about what it will amount to. My bet is that if she gets out on bail, she'll skip, go underground. And you, my love, will be out seventy thousand dollars."

"I've considered that possibility."

"As your lawyer, I couldn't possibly advise you to do it."

"And as a human being? I know you think I'm crazy, Tim, and maybe it would sound better if I made some speech about high ideals or opposition to the war. Maybe that's part of it, I don't know. Mostly, it's Jan." She turned away from him and started to weep. "She's had her full share of suffering; she had it by the time she was sixteen. I can't bear the thought of her in prison for . . . what, twenty to twenty-five years? I can't bear the thought of her spending one night more in jail. I'm not so naive that I don't know what those places are like. What can I say, Tim? It's a friend, it's a life . . ."

He let her cry, his eyes focused on the silent image of the television screen. Police in gas masks, plunging into a maelstrom of human flesh. Policemen with guns and billies. Clubbing, dragging, seizing, trampling, staining the sidewalks of Chicago red with blood. You couldn't hear the screams of the bludgeoned, the sirens of the paddy wagons. You didn't have to. All that could be heard in the room was the low whirr of the air conditioning and the sound of a woman weeping.

"No, you're not crazy, Kit." He got up and switched off the television. "You're not crazy. *That's* crazy."

He came and took her in his arms, pressing her wet face against the rough cotton of his shirt. "If that's what you want and it sits right with your conscience, I'll help you."

They sat there unmoving while the daylight faded, then Kit pulled gently away.

"I'm OK, now . . . thank you, Tim. I'd better go and wash up."

He smiled when she returned. "That's better, but now on to some rather more pressing matters. I haven't had anything to eat since breakfast. How about you?"

"I had a sundae this noon at Brigham's."

"That's not food, sweetheart. That's fantasy. Let's go out and have a bite."

They had corned beef sandwiches at a little deli near Kenmore Square. When they emerged, a breeze had sprung off the harbor, turning the air cool and salty.

"Delicious," said Tim. "Better than corned beef. Even better than air conditioning." He tucked her arm under his. "Let's walk."

They walked down Beacon past the bars that ringed Kenmore Square, into the great avenue where purple-windowed houses bore silent testimony to a far more gracious age. Tea merchants had once lived here, clippership owners, bankers, poets, intellectuals. "I love this city." Tim was suddenly buoyant. "I wouldn't trade it for twenty Washingtons. Let's go down to the Public Gardens, shall we? Maybe we can steal a swan boat and sail away."

He guided her into the quiet park, deserted now except for the occasional walker and his dog.

"I don't think I've been here since before we were married," Kit said. "Michael and I used to come here a lot. We'd bring a few books and sandwiches and a portable chess set and spend whole days here." She pointed to a wooden bench gouged with graffiti. "That's where we sat, right there on that bench."

"Then let's pick another and sit down."

He fumbled in his pocket for a pack of cigarettes, lit up and leaned back on the bench.

"I'd like one too, please."

"I thought you'd given up smoking." He handed her his lighted cigarette.

"Only when Michael's around. He doesn't care for it, you know."

Tim lit another for himself and watched the smoke float in the breeze. "Tell me, Kit, have you thought about what's going to happen when he finds out?"

"He's never asked me for a penny so far. I'll worry about that when the time comes."

"The time will come, you know. It has to. Sooner or later he's going to ask for an accounting, and you better have a pretty good alibi."

"I'll think of something."

They smoked for a while in a silence broken only by the scrape of crickets.

She wondered what his thoughts were. She knew what her own were, painfully aware of the slim capable fingers that held the cigarette, of the scent she had breathed when he had held her close, of the ghostly shimmer of his Indian shirt in the summer darkness. She had read somewhere of a Nazi experiment. Some crazy concentration camp doctor who had submerged prisoners in icy water till they were only a hairbreadth away from dying. The first thing they did upon being revived was copulate. She could understand that. When death is close, the body hungers for the act of life. She had been near death that very morning. Not physical death, but the death of the mind, the living death of the prison. And now she, too, had a hunger—a hunger that Michael had never fulfilled.

"Why haven't you left him, Kit?"

"What?" He must have been reading her mind.

"Why haven't you ever left Michael?"

She stamped out her cigarette to hide her nervousness. "What makes you think I want to? Everyone says we're the ideal couple."

"And are you?"

She made no answer, and his expression was unreadable in the gloom.

"Kit and Mike," he said finally. "The ideal couple. No,

Kit, you've never fooled me, not even for a minute. As long as I've known you, I could never picture you and Mike as a couple, ideal or otherwise. As two separate people, yes . . . but never as a couple. I remember the first time I met you, you'd been married . . . oh, just a month or two, I guess, and Michael brought you around to that little apartment we had in Brookline Village. Remember?"

She remembered.

"And he was proud as punch . . . well, why shouldn't he have been? But you . . . I don't know. I didn't think you looked happy. Not new-bride happy. I thought you looked . . ." His voice trailed off.

"Tell me, how did you think I looked?"

Other people's insights always seemed so much sharper than her own. She wondered how much she had unconsciously given away.

"I thought you looked . . . hungry. Hungry and wary. Like someone who's been expecting steak and potatoes and only got cotton candy. I thought about you a lot those first years in Boston. I liked you enormously and, in a way, I kind of envied Mike. I used to think, 'Oh, what a magnificent girl. I want to go to bed with her.' It was always, always in the back of my mind that some day you and I would have an affair. Does that surprise you?"

"Yes. Yes, it does, very much. You never gave me the slightest intimation."

You must be the only woman in Boston he's never made a pass at, Marian had said. Would he now? Kit waited, half hoping, half afraid. It had been a day—no, a *week*—of such confusion, such emotional assaults and alarms that suddenly even this seemed no longer beyond the bounds of the conceivable. Kit and Tim. Yes, it was possible. She could go home with him tonight, go to bed with him, and no one would ever know. *He's sensational in bed.* Six years of buried fantasies came back to her in a flood of anguish and longing. Kit and Tim. Tim and Kit. Yes. They would go to his apartment, she in black, he in white. In a moment, she made the leap from the merely possible to the absolutely inevitable. It would be dark in the apartment with only the light from the streetlamps, silent except for the soft hum of the air conditioning. They would not speak. He would draw her close to him, kiss her, cup her face in his hands. He would caress her neck, slip his hand beneath the cotton of her dress, slide the fine white fingers slowly down till they touched the smooth skin of her breasts. Her nipples hardened at the image.

Yes, they would make love. There was no other way such a day could end. He would give her some sign, now, sitting here on this park bench, and they would both rise and go, silent and expectant. A sigh. The touch of a hand, the light brush of lips against her cheek. He would give her a sign and she would be his.

"No, I never did make a pass at you." The words were edged in sadness. He lit another cigarette, and there was a harshness to his voice when he spoke again. "No, I never even felt you up at a New Year's party. Not even one little pinch on the fanny. How's that for self-discipline."

This sudden unromantic turn caught her short. There was no desire, no longing in his voice now, and it was clear that he, for one, no longer considered Kit and Tim a possibility. Good God, what a fool she was . . . to have so nearly given herself away.

"Why didn't you?" She managed to screen the hurt from her words. *Why don't you now?*

"Why didn't I?" He rose and offered her his hand. It was a gentlemanly—not a loving—gesture. "Why didn't I?" They started to walk. "Oh, I guess I always knew it would never work. A question of loyalty, I suppose."

"Because of you and Michael being partners, you mean?"

"Oh, no," he laughed. "I have no loyalty to Mike. Frankly, I always thought he was a bit of a prick. I don't believe I owe him anything. We were colleagues, that's all."

"But you used to visit us so often."

"Oh, but Kit, don't you realize . . . you were the attraction. Not Mike. No. When I said it was a question of loyalty, I meant your sense of loyalty, not mine. I'm a very disloyal bastard. About sex, anyhow."

"I see," she said. "You felt I would never betray Michael."

Yet had she not done exactly that this morning? Betrayed in a far more hurtful way, perhaps, than any trifling infidelity?

"I don't know whether you would or wouldn't," Tim answered. "I rather suspected you might. No, what I meant was, you would never betray Marian."

They walked up Beacon Street in silence. Marian. Her loyalty to Marian. Kit was glad the darkness covered the rush of blood to her cheeks. And yet, she knew Tim was right. For it was Marian—always Marian—who had prevented her from making Tim the centerpiece of her sexual fantasies. One's best friend's husband. That would have been betrayal indeed. The kind of betrayal beneath contempt.

And yet she wanted him.

"This is your car isn't it, the Ford?" How quickly they'd retraced their steps. "I won't ask you up for a drink, Kit. It's been a long day, and you still have a drive ahead of you."

He took the car keys from her and opened the door. There was going to be no love affair—not tonight, not ever. The moment had passed. She slid in and rolled down the window, and still he stood there, reluctant to leave. Just stood there clutching the keys. What was he waiting for? Surely he knew, too, that the moment had vanished forever.

"You have my keys, Tim."

He leaned toward her at the open window with an expression she had never seen before.

"I think I should tell you." The words were so soft she strained to hear them. "I should tell you why I was so brusque when you called me at the office. She would have told you in a day or two anyway. Marian is leaving me."

"Oh, Tim!" Even in the lamplight, she could see his face was contorted with pain, stricken as Jan's had been that very morning. "Do you want to come in the car and talk about it?"

He bit his lips and tried to salvage a smile, but what emerged was a grimace.

"No, there's nothing to tell. I guess I went to the well once too often."

"A girl?" But of course. What else would it have been. He nodded. "It was stupid. Ugly and stupid. I didn't even care for her. A waitress in Schrafft's—would you believe it? But she had a sweet Irish accent and lovely hair. Hair like yours, Kit."

"Maybe Marian will reconsider . . . ?"

"No. This time she won't. I'm . . . it's all over and that's that. I'm moving out the end of next week. I was out looking at apartments today. Funny, now that the coast is clear, so to speak, it's like I've lost all desire to screw around. The ultimate antiaphrodisiac. Tim Keegan, the greatest cocksman on the Boston-Washington circuit, and I couldn't get it up even for you. Enough said." He handed her the keys. "On that other matter, get in touch with me when the money is ready. I'll handle the rest. And for God's sakes, be careful what you say around Michael. I don't like to think what would happen if he found out. About the Littlemarch business, I mean."

"I'll watch it. And Tim . . . I'm sorry."

"So am I, Kit." He leaned through the window and kissed her. "Drive carefully."

Michael was livid when he discovered that his bird had flown the coop.

"Jesus, Kit, you saw her just two days before she jumped. What did you two talk about when you went there? She must have said *something*."

Kit's face was as innocent as her answer. "If you really want to know, we talked about old times."

"Old times?" Michael was incredulous.

"Old times," she repeated. "After all, Jan knew perfectly well who I was. You could hardly expect her to treat me as a confidante."

Her husband's sigh mingled disgust in equal part with contempt. "Well, some asshole is out seventy grand. I suppose they'll catch up with her sooner or later."

They never did. That Christmas, Kit received a postcard depicting the souks of Algiers. It was inscribed simply: "Having a wonderful time. Wish you were here!" There was no signature.

And once in '75, Kit thought she recognized her—certainly someone who looked like her—in a TV documentary on Arab terrorism. The film was made in a PLO training camp in Iraq, and Kit had a momentary glimpse of a slim woman in army fatigues thrusting a bayonet into a sawdust dummy. Perhaps it was Jan, perhaps not.

On the whole, Kit preferred not to know.

She had robbed Michael. Robbed him of his greatest moment as surely as he had robbed her of love. In one magnificent gesture, she had shot her bolt, shot her fortune, redressed the balance of injury.

It made her like him more, this secret triumph. Made him less an object of fear than one of pity. And as their life returned to normal rhythms, she accepted that it wasn't so bad. Wasn't so good.

It was just tolerable.

KATE

"MARRY ME."

"This is so sudden."

"I love you. Marry me."

"Really, darling, I don't know what's got into you." Wolf poured them both another Hennessy. "Bad day at the office, is that it? Anyhow, I thought it was the man who's supposed to propose."

"I'm perfectly serious. I want you to leave Polly and marry me."

"Oh, Kate," he sighed. "Please don't make life difficult." *He* was the one who was making life difficult, no not difficult—*impossible*. She'd had it up to here with this once-a-week crap, plus the annual two weeks in Europe for good behavior. Had it up to here with the absent Polly. Polly the Martyr. Polly the Crucified. She-Who-Must-Not-Be-Hurt.

A few weeks earlier, he'd left his address book in her apartment, and she thumbed through it to see if it contained her number. It did, and under C. The entry read "Clarendon Picture Frames." When he'd phoned that evening with his "How are you, darling?" opener, she'd answered, "You must have the wrong number. This is Clarendon Picture Frames." He hadn't been abashed; he'd been furious. But when she saw him next, she twitted him again about it. "Well, what do you expect, Kate? You want me to rub Polly's nose in it?"

Not that Wolf mentioned Polly very often. He didn't have to. Polly's presence was implicit, the third party who got into bed with them each time they made love, a ghostly voyeur who refused to be exorcized. It had been over five years since she'd last seen Polly, the day they shot the corgi commercial out in Weston. But nothing had changed except Kate herself. She was thirty-one now, the best years of her life were slipping away. True, she'd never really thought of herself as a domestic person, but since she'd quit Marsden, advertising had lost some of its glamor. She'd done that bit—proved herself. Right now she was earning more money than most men her age and had a vice-presidency into the bargain. Naturally, she wouldn't give it up without some reluctance. She would give it up only for Wolf.

Anyway you looked at it, it would be a richer life, more satisfying—each day beginning and ending with someone she loved.

They loved each other and it couldn't be the money that was holding him back, at least not anymore, for Wolf was beginning to enjoy considerable success as an artist. At that show at the Gimpel Gallery last year, he'd sold practically everything. And next month he'd have a show in San Francisco. OK, maybe she'd fly out for that one, and they could spend a weekend eating lobster on Fisherman's Wharf. But the New York show had really pissed her off. Wolf had told her tactfully, but in no uncertain terms, that she was not to come to the opening. Obviously. For Polly would be there, making one of her rare forays into Manhattan.

It always came back to Polly. *Polly couldn't survive if I left her*. The hell she couldn't. She'd survived four years in a concentration camp. She could damn well survive without Wolf. Especially with all that lovely money. She'd find somebody else to soothe her wounds quickly enough.

Kate had lately begun to suspect that marriage to Polly was not quite the bed of nails Wolf had first implied. Every now and then he'd drop an innocent remark about a dinner party or a houseguest or some other local entertainment. Apparently the Aaronsons knew a lot of people in that part of Connecticut, so life wasn't all tears and torment.

By now Kate was firmly convinced that Polly had no real clue to her husband's other attachment. Oh sure, she must have figured he screwed around some in New York, but that was all. Nothing serious, no great entanglement. Like Kate herself, Wolf managed to keep the parts of his life in mutually exclusive boxes.

So there it was. Polly owned Wolf. Wolf owned Kate. And Kate owned . . . nothing.

KIT

AND WHEN HER HUSBAND DIED, HER HAIR TURNED quite gold with grief.

The Oscar Wilde epigram was the second thing that flashed through Kit's mind as Emily picked her way through the crowd at West Palm Beach Airport.

Kit's very first thought had been "My God. That's not my mother." True, Emily had boasted, "My dear, you wouldn't know me," when they'd talked on the phone the week before, but Kit had no idea that the old cliché would take such a literal turn. Gone was the large, soft, vague woman who had shepherded her through childhood, and in her place stood a trim blonde stranger in a Lily sundress as flamboyantly colored as a postcard sunset.

"Catherine." Dry, scented cheek pressed against travel-grimed cheek.

"Mother."

"And Sarah!" The blonde apparition swooped down on the unsuspecting child with a pair of kisses worthy of a French general.

"Hello, Grandma Chapman."

"Grandma Chapman indeed! Call me Emily. Everybody does. After all, darling, you're not in Boston now."

Expect nothing and you'll never be surprised, the wags say. But Kit had expected someone who was recognizably her mother. Had anticipated an environment that contained some recollection, however faint, of the home where she had spent her childhood.

The apartment was unrelentingly modern, with an expansive view of the ocean. Soft creamy beiges with hot orange accents, the walls vibrant with abstract graphics. A large chrome-framed lithograph full of thrusting reds and fierce yellows caught her eye. It was by some artist Kit had never heard of—a Wolf Aaronson—and she didn't much care for it. But if the apartment smacked of the professional decorator, Kit had to admit the total effect was stunning. For that matter, so was Emily. In Boston, women her age had blue hair; here they had blond. OK. When in Palm Beach . . .

But it was more than that. Walking behind her, one might have added up the figure, the clothes, the jangling enamel bracelets and taken her for a woman half her age. Yet close up, the differences between this woman and her Massachusetts mother were even more astonishing. There was something about her face—leaner, tighter, tougher—that not even the Florida sun could be held accountable for. Kit tried to recall the last time she'd seen her in Boston three years ago. Surely there had been a certain puffiness under the eyes, the start of soft turkey wattles under the chin.

They were gone now. And the realization—when it came—almost made Kit cry out in horror. Of course. Her mother had had a face-lift. She had traded in her past at the plastic surgeon's. Kit was shocked. Shocked, too, at the unexpected depth of her revulsion.

After all, there was no logical reason why Emily should not spend her money as she wished, in the pursuit of beauty and youth and happiness. And Emily seemed quite happy indeed, certainly far gayer than she had seemed in Athol.

Kit had come to Palm Beach ostensibly for a filial visit, but actually to see if she might find some refuge there for herself and Sarah—some exit from her futile marriage. Had come, in fact, to woo and win her mother. Back in Haddons Landing it had seemed so clear. Emily was rich, unencumbered, and above all—Emily was her mother. She would take them in, comfort them, give Kit the breathing space she needed in which to shape another life.

But the new Emily was a personage she had in no way been prepared for. At sixty she had suddenly achieved an enviable social niche. Her days were a round of poolside entertainments and outings, her nights an unbroken stream of dinner parties. She had even managed to snag herself a "boyfriend" from the small supply of eligible males—a retired insurance man from Trenton who treated her with a gallantry that belied his years. And after two weeks of watching Emily make the Palm Beach rounds, Kit realized there was no room for her and Sarah in her mother's blithe regime. It would take all Kit's courage merely to broach the subject of her own distress with this strangely blond and frivolous butterfly. But broach it she must, and the night before she was due back home, she decided it was then or never. Kit would seek her out in her lair. Not a confrontation, she hoped, but a plea, woman-to-woman, daughter-to-mother. She opened her bedroom door. The light was on in Emily's room.

Now. Before she goes to sleep.

She knocked on Emily's door and entered without waiting for an answer.

Her mother was seated in front of her dressing table, a marvelous arrangement of mirrors and light bulbs and a collection of jars that would have done credit to a movie star's dressing room.

And so, indeed, would Emily: her face a molten mask of scented cream, the blond hair firmly tucked beneath a plastic mob cap.

"Hello, darling, you see me at my worst. Sit down and I'll be with you in a sec."

Kit sat on the satin bed coverlet and watched the woman in the mirror wipe her face tenderly with a succession of pastel cotton balls. Even with the golden hair now pushed out of sight, the face was still that of an alien.

"Just let me get this muck off and we'll have a nice chat. Just like old times." Emily smiled and Kit smiled back. It was not, she could see, a routine that might be hurried.

"It's Estée Lauder's Renutriv," Emily informed her. "And then I follow it up with Lancome Night Cream."

"I didn't come here to exchange beauty tips, Mother."

"No," Emily resigned herself. "I don't suppose you did. What is it, dear . . . some trouble with Michael?"

If Kit had had a set speech it failed her now, and the words that came out sounded stilted even to her own ear, like a script in an afternoon soap opera.

"Yes, Mother. It's Michael. I'm thinking of leaving him. The marriage hasn't worked out. It wasn't quite what I expected."

"Marriages never are," Emily smiled wisely. "But that doesn't mean they don't work out. Has Michael been running around with someone? Is that the problem?"

"No."

"And have you?" Emily's voice was suddenly sharp.

"Absolutely not, Mother. No, it's nothing like that."

There was no conceivable way she could ever bring herself to discuss the intimate side of her marriage, least of all with her mother.

"Then what is it, Catherine?" Emily probed. And when Kit didn't answer, she continued. "You've come all this way to talk to me. That was clear from the outset, and I suppose I've been a bit of a coward putting it off. I know I've never been much of a one for mother-daughter powwows; it's the way I was brought up. Still, that doesn't mean we can't start now. You can talk to me, dear, and maybe I can be helpful. Try me. Tell me what Michael has done."

"Oh, Mother." Kit twisted her hands. "It's not anything he's done. If it were only that simple. He doesn't drink or chase after women. He always behaves properly in public. If I were in court and had to build a case against him, I wouldn't know where to begin . . ."

"But you're not in court," Emily reminded her.

"Well, that's how he makes me feel when I'm with him. As if I'm on trial. I don't know how to explain it. He . . . he stifles me."

Emily's round eyes conceded nothing, and Kit inwardly admitted having made a weak indictment. "I guess that's hard to understand . . ." she trailed off limply. But once again her mother surprised her.

"Oh, no, dear. That's something I understand very well. Very well indeed, believe me. And I sympathize completely. But Catherine, you must realize that's the nature of marriage."

"That men should stifle women?" Kit burst out indignantly. "I can't believe it and I can't believe you do, either. Perhaps we're talking about different things."

"Perhaps. You tell me what *you* mean by being stifled."

Kit struggled to put the emotions into words, to conjure up a comprehensive list of injustices done her, of love denied, of identity spurned. Yet even as she spoke, she knew she was offering up a vague and paltry list of grievances.

"It's that"—she hated herself for the inadequacy of her rhetoric—"he has some mental picture of me, of what I am or what I ought to be that I just can't recognize as myself. He sees somebody who's terribly sedate, terribly genteel, like a female mirror of himself. I mean, Michael's always saying how glad he is that I'm intelligent, that I've had a good education . . . but the moment I think anything through for myself, all hell breaks loose. Especially"—the words tumbled out rapidly now—"if it differs from the way he thinks. And it usually does. God forbid that I should venture an opinion on anything—books, politics, anything! No, I'm always expected to be floating in the background, some meek, bland, dumb-bunny wife, and limit my conversation to 'Oh, Michael, you're so wonderful. Oh, Michael, you're so smart.' That's my husband's idea of meaningful dialogue. I have to censor everything I say, at least when we're in public. And if any part of me intrudes, if I talk too loud or laugh too loud . . . even if I wear anything he thinks is too loud . . ." She gave a short derisive laugh. "Miniskirts! The whole world is wearing miniskirts. Even you are. Not me. If Mrs. Michael Matheson should show an inch of leg above her knees, he'd have me arrested for indecent exposure. You know what he gave me for Christmas? A cable-knit cardigan. OK, it cost a lot of money, but it was a disgusting old-lady lavender, the kind of color I've never seen on a woman under ninety. And two sizes too large into the bargain."

"Well, what did you expect . . . a silk negligee?"

Kit thought that an oddly insensitive remark coming from a woman who seemed to have developed quite a penchant for expensive lingerie. She studied Emily's yellow crepe peignoir. It was a decidedly provocative garment.

"Why not a silk negligee! My God, mother, I'm only thirty-two and already I see myself turning into some sexless, colorless nothing. I look at you and I look at me and I think . . . Wow! I'm older and dowdier than my mother."

The comparison made Emily fidget with discomfort, and Kit scrambled gracelessly to divert the drift of her talk. "I know I'm not making an awful lot of sense and a cardigan sweater's hardly grounds for divorce. It's just a symbol, really."

"Of what?"

"Of the way he keeps trying to mold me into something I'm not, never was and don't want to wind up being. If I'm so unsatisfactory, why did he marry me in the first place?"

"What your father could never figure out," said Emily, "is why you ever married *him*. Spencer was not happy about it, you know."

If Emily had turned into the frog prince, Kit could not have been more surprised.

"I had no idea. He never said a word."

"And if he had . . . would it have made any difference? You were so determined to get married, and, after all, you were of age."

"But why?" Kit was goggle-eyed. "What was it Daddy didn't like about Michael?"

Emily was embarrassed. Clearly, she had no wish to add further fuel to her daughter's fire. But Kit persisted. "Now that you've brought it up, you may as well tell me. Not that it would make any difference."

"Well," Emily dragged out reluctantly, "your father thought he was a social climber."

"Daddy always was a terrible snob."

"It's funny you should say that," Emily returned, "because he thought Michael was the snob."

"Michael!" To her own amazement, Kit flew to her husband's defense. "Whatever his faults, Michael never made any pretenses about coming from anything but a poor family. As I recall, he went out of his way to mention it to Daddy the first time they met."

"Exactly. And that's what Spencer thought was so snobbish. He used to call it Michael's 'I am poor but I am honest' act. Personally, I didn't agree with him. As far as I can see, Michael's always behaved very well, and I must say, Catherine, when your father died, he was the perfect gentleman. Whatever your complaints about him, you must admit he always wants to do the right thing."

"Getting back to cases . . ."

"Getting back to cases." Emily was suddenly and uncharacteristically forceful. "This separation idea is yours, I presume." Kit nodded. "Now, before you do anything rash, there are several things you have to consider. First of all, there's Sarah. Do you really think it's fair to break up your marriage simply because you're bored?"

"More than bored, Mother." Kit's anger was rising.

"Bored, stifled, suppressed . . . whatever you want to call it, Catherine. Almost everything you've said about your marriage I could have said about mine. It's what every woman says with minor modifications. Spencer and I . . . well, I loved him, naturally, but we didn't always see eye to eye. He wasn't an easy man to live with, but then I suppose none of them are. And when I got married, you can be sure I felt just the way you did when you married Michael. Full of expectations. Your father was very handsome, you know." Her face was suddenly illuminated with a smidgin of memory, and for a moment she looked young again. Not Estée Lauder young, but truly young. "Very handsome and full of beans. He never should have taken the job at Sag Pap & Pulp. He hated Athol, really hated it. He felt from the first that it was some kind of Siberia. I think you were the only bright spot in his life. You know why he named you Catherine, don't you?"

"After his grandmother." Kit was puzzled.

"That's what he wanted his father to think. Actually, he named you Catherine after the girl in that book . . ." She frowned. Literary references were not her strong point. "You know, Catherine and Heathcliff?"

"*Wuthering Heights!*" Kit could hardly believe it. That sour, dour man dreaming of romance on the moors while scowling behind the *Wall Street Journal?*

"Poor Spencer," his widow sighed. "He was such a romantic. But, you know, romantics have a hard time of it in this world. They get bitter. I think the saddest day in his life was the day President Roosevelt passed away."

"But Mother!" Kit protested. "Daddy *hated* Roosevelt."

"Well, of course he did," Emily answered reasonably. "But what you don't understand is how much your father *loved* to hate him. When FDR died, it was his life's labor gone. Very sad. But that's neither here nor there. The point is, your father went his way and I pretty much went mine. He had his work and his golf and the Republican Club, and I had . . ."

"Jigsaw puzzles."

"Yes." Emily's tone was suddenly defensive. "I had my puzzles and my bridge ladies. And you, too, may I add. Life was perfectly tolerable."

"Tolerable, yes." Two weeks of accumulated injuries suddenly brimmed over. "So the minute Daddy died, you ran away from it all as far as you could. I don't see you doing any jigsaw puzzles *these* days." It was an accusation.

"You should be ashamed of yourself, Catherine." It was the admonition of a parent to a naughty, willful child. "Do you think widows should be thrown into the grave along with their husbands? What do the Indians call it . . . ?"

"Suttee."

"Suttee . . . yes. They burn the women alive, don't they? Is that what you think should have happened to me?" The blue eyes were icy with anger. "Well, let me tell you something. I had been a good and loyal wife for thirty years. But your father is dead, you know, and I'm not quite ready for the boneyard. I could smell your disapproval from the moment you stepped off the plane, from the moment you saw the way I live. I don't really owe you an explanation, Catherine, but you seem to feel I do. Very well, then. I gave your father thirty years of my life. I ran his house exactly the way he wanted, I made him comfortable and I was completely faithful. He never had cause to complain, nor do you. Because I gave to you, too. I gave you life, I gave you time, I gave you my youth. When you were small I was always there when you needed me. For twenty years, I did my share of worrying and fretting and bringing up, just as I know you do with Sarah. Well, maybe I didn't do the best job in the world, but I did the best I knew how. All my life, I've lived for other people—for my parents, for your father, for you. I think I'm entitled to live for myself now. Next year I'm going to take a trip around the world. Why shouldn't I? It's just possible I'll have fifteen or twenty terrific years ahead of me before I pack it in. As I see it, they're coming to me. I've done my duty to you and to your father. I don't owe any more. I'm sorry, dear, that I can't be of more help to you, but you're a big girl now. Surely you wouldn't want to come home to mother after all these years."

No. Kit did not. Not any longer.

"And as for you and Michael, that's something you'll have to decide for yourself. I want you to know"—it was the closest Emily could come to comfort, but perhaps it was merely indifference—"that whatever you do will be all right with me. I can't advise either way. But really, dear, you should consider yourself lucky."

"Lucky? How?"

"Well, you're financially independent. If you decide you want to break it up, you have a nice cushion. You'll have plenty of time to figure out what you really want to do with your life. You have options, so to speak."

In spite of herself, Kit had to smile at the irony. How shocked Emily would have been if she'd told her about Jan. How foolish she herself was to think her mother could ever offer her anything other than words. They had never been close. No. There had only been the illusion of closeness.

"I think I'll turn in now, Mother. We have a long day tomorrow." She kissed the oiled and aging cheek. "I'll think about what you've said."

"Good night, dear."

"Good night, Mother."

Kit closed the door behind her. Closed it firmly on what she had seen as her last real hope for independence. Options! There were no options. There was no place to go but home.

Michael was waiting at Logan Airport when they got back, with a large bunch of roses and the most welcoming of smiles. And if there was to be nothing so formal as a "reconciliation," he made it clear from his amiable chatter all the way home about friends and neighbors and household matters that he was very glad to have her back.

And in her way, she was glad to be back. To be home. For better or worse, Haddons Landing was the only home she had. And *this* was the only family she had.

KATE

LIKE SCROOGE, KATE HATED CHRISTMAS. NOT THAT SHE was crazy about Easter and Thanksgiving and New Year's Eve—but Christmas was decidedly the worst. Everything around her proclaimed the joys of family, from the nativity scenes in department store windows to the sudden hominess of the fashion magazines. At the local movie houses Disney reigned supreme; even the run-of-the-mill TV crime shows had departed from their gut-crunching format to accommodate tales that featured winsome tykes and the proverbial crook with a heart of gold.

Usually Kate did the sensible thing and visited Emily in Florida, thus combining filial duties with the acquisition of a good tan. This year, however, her mother was off on a round-the-world cruise (was there no limit as to how that woman spent money?), So Kate was sticking it out alone in New York.

Alone: that was no understatement. In fact, she suspected she was the last living soul in the city. Everyone she knew had gone off somewhere to do the family bit. Even Barry, looking unusually straight in a dark suit and striped tie, had taken off for his home town in Michigan.

Wolf was in Weston. Naturally. Where else would a

married man spend Christmas Eve? Worse yet, he wouldn't be back in New York until after New Year's. His whole week, apparently, would be taken up by the social obligations of suburban Christmas. She understood, didn't she? She understood, but it pissed her off nonetheless. It's not even as if the Aaronsons were Christians!

The first Christmas of their love affair, Kate had given him a fisherman's sweater. Even now she could recall the almost sensual pleasure she'd had in buying it—in describing his height, the width of his shoulders, the breadth of his chest to the salesman at Abercrombie & Fitch. Lovely to the touch, it was hand-knit and signed by a crofter on some remote Irish island. Kate had a vision of Wolf tramping through the cold, damp woods of Connecticut, wearing her gift like a talisman. It would be like those scarves which a lady in the Age of Chivalry presented to a favored knight-in-armor. Something to be worn next to the heart, a charm that would invoke soft memories when milord was off in battle.

She had given Wolf the sweater a few days before Christmas, and he had been delighted. But before he left to catch the train to the country, he placed it in "his" drawer in her bedroom dresser.

"But aren't you going to take it, Wolf?"

"I thought I'd leave it here," he'd smiled. "Be rather convenient having it in New York."

"But it's not a city sweater, darling. It's for the country."

"I think," he said softly, "it would be more convenient to leave it here."

Kate hadn't pursued the issue. Obviously, he had no intention of returning home with a bulky and unexplained Irish sweater, especially if he already owned one rather like it. Which seemed probable, since he and Polly seemed to own at least one of everything. And while Polly may not have known the content of his Wednesdays in New York, she undoubtedly knew the contents of his wardrobe.

Kate never again gave him anything more personal than art books. But the incident rankled.

Just as it rankled now, this Christmas Eve, that she was alone in a Manhattan apartment with no livelier prospects than watching a rerun movie on television.

She fished a frozen dinner out of the refrigerator. Swanson's Chicken Pie. Yuk. Well, maybe it wouldn't be so bad

washed down with a decent Sauterne. She put it in the oven
and settled down in front of the TV set.

London Films presents
A CHRISTMAS CAROL
Starring Alistair Sim   Hermione Baddely. . . . . . .

Bah, humbug!

KIT

THE TREE WAS PERFECT. NEARLY EIGHT FEET OF PUNGENT SCOTCH pine rising proud and resplendent above a rainbow-colored clutter of presents. A page out of *House Beautiful,* Kit thought wryly, gathering up the last bits of tinsel rain. Sarah would be thrilled.

Then, as she had done every Christmas since childhood, Kit poked through the pile of presents, singling out those with her name on the gift tag, trying to puzzle out the contents from the package shape and size. That little flat one was from Michael's parents—she recognized the wrapping paper from the year before. A scarf, she imagined; they always sent a scarf. The shiny job in psychedelic paper had come from Emily, arriving air express from Cannes. A year's supply of Estée Lauder face cream? Kit mentally kicked herself for being so snide. In fact, Emily always came through with knockout presents. And why not? There was a woman who had turned shopping into an art form.

Now what was this from Michael? she mused, pondering a large square carton at the back. Too big to be a clothes box. Heavy, too. Something for the house was her bet. She pushed the wrapping flat against the package and could just make out the words THIS END UP. A portable TV set? Some new appliance? Maybe it was the Kitchen-Master she'd been thinking of getting—that jumbo gadget that sliced, diced, chopped, blended, did practically everything but digest the stuff for you. Could be. In any event, it was definitely something for the house. Funny how Michael thought that a present for the house was a present for her. As if she and the house were one and the same.

She'd done well by Michael this year, buying him a gorgeous fisherman's sweater she'd seen advertised in The *New Yorker*. One of a kind, the ad had promised, hand-knit on a remote Irish croft—"The ideal gift for the active suburbanite." Yes, Michael should be pleased with his present. And Sarah with hers.

Sarah had been promised her first full-sized bike this Christmas, and Michael had told her he'd pick it out himself. His choice proved to be a sleek British Raleigh with half a dozen gears and all the extras; God alone knew how much it had cost. Oh, Sarah would be in heaven tomorrow morning.

Still, Christmas comes but once a year, as the cliché ran, and Kit had to admit she loved every moment of it. It was the woman's season, she thought. The once-a-year break when she, not Michael, set the tone. The law work was slow, the courts quiescent, and even the politicians left off politicking. It was Kit's season: time to cook, to plan, to entertain, to go to parties, to wear long dresses, to try out new perfume, to be the dominant spirit in the household.

She looked around her living room with quiet satisfaction— the glittering tree, the handsome furniture, the glow of old silver in the breakfront. Perhaps the Romans were right in worshipping the gods of domesticity. Perhaps Michael, too, was right when, in the sole reference he ever made to her abortive Palm Beach flight last summer, he attributed it to an attack of "cabin fever." Even Emily was right, in a way.

Kit didn't have an awful lot to complain about, she told herself, and probably less than most other women. She had friends, security, a beautiful home, a marvelous daughter. True, on the debit side there was Michael. All right. So Michael hadn't proved to be the shining knight she'd thought him at twenty. But the fault was hers for having misread him with twenty-year-old eyes. Michael was what he was, she conceded—what he had always been. He would never change.

But she had changed. There would be, she knew, no more grand gestures or sudden flights to Florida or dreams of

improbable glory. Like Voltaire's Candide, she would culti-
vate her garden and forgo visions of "the best of all possible
worlds."

Life was perfectly tolerable once you accepted that. Once
you settled down, settled in. Besides . . . what other options
did she have?

KATE

ON THEIR LAST DAY IN FLORENCE, THEY TOOK A TAXI UP TO WHAT Wolf had promised her was "a church such as you've never seen before." Well, Kate didn't know about that! Over the past seven summers, she and Wolf must have visited every major church in Europe—and a not inconsiderable number of minor ones. They'd climbed the perilous stone steps of the bell tower at Chartres. Gone down to Nelson's Crypt in the bowels of Saint Paul's. Argued about the futuristic façade of the Sagrada Familia in Barcelona ("Sheer Disney," Wolf had called it). Lingered before the Pietá in Saint Peter's.

Each trip was the same, yet different. He would meet Kate at an airport—Rome, London, Paris, Vienna—for a holiday that would be theirs alone. It was then that they became, in deference to hotel desk clerks, "Mr. and Mrs. Wolf Aaronson."

Kate lived year round for those two weeks, when they would live in that splendid isolation which no phone could interrupt, where no Polly could cast her invisible shadow. She had long ago stopped wondering how it was that Wolf could drop from sight, be incommunicado for such a considerable stretch of time from a wife so dependent upon him. Not that that was Kate's concern. And anyhow, Polly wasn't all alone back in Weston. She had the kennelman, the housekeeper

263

and nearly two dozen dogs to keep her company. So, for those two weeks at least, Polly didn't exist.

But each trip was an infinite treasure chest, a source of retrievable happiness from which she could pick and draw over the next fifty weeks. It was only, inevitably, the last day or two before departure, when the reality of New York loomed so close, that Kate would become cross and unhappy. They almost always argued before the flight home. Little petty foolish arguments that elicited in Kate an anger all out of proportion. For she knew, as did Wolf, that whatever the apparent cause, it was only a screen for the real and interminable argument between them.

Why won't you leave Polly and marry me? answered by *Why won't you accept things as they are?*

But this time, as the taxi wound its way up into the Florentine hills, Kate was determined to do nothing, *nothing*, that would destroy the delicate balance of this last day.

Inside, the church was cool and blissful, a richly-hued oasis from the burning sun. The waddling sacristan—all flab and effusion—showed them around the Michelozzo Chapel, extolled the beauties of the Gaddi altarpiece, claimed a kinship of sorts with the two Americans on the basis of an uncle in Cincinnati *(Chinchinnati* he pronounced it) until finally, tip delivered and received with numerous *grazias,* he abandoned them to the treasures of the church and the crypts.

They emerged into the blinding sunlight, poked about the little souvenir shop, refreshed themselves with clammy bottles of orangeade.

"One more thing I want you to see, darling." He led her through a gate around the side. "It's the cemetery."

"Not more dead," she wailed.

"Ah, but *this,* you must admit, would be one helluva place to wait for the resurrection."

And Kate had to agree. A cemetery, yes—but gloriously beautiful, a bizarre and miniature city of souls. It was ringed with great family vaults, immaculate and imposing, making Kate wonder if in certain parts of Italy the dead didn't live better than the living. Landscaped avenues of tombstones; some officiously lording their status with heroic marble, some modest and discreet, some downright lachrymose.

"Come over here, darling," Wolf called out. "This has to be seen to be believed." She picked her way through the avenues of the dead to come to where he was standing.

"Have you ever . . . ?" he asked.

"No, I never."

Facing them was a life-size sculpture of a man and a woman. They were dancing the fox trot by the look of it, her arm resting lightly on his shoulder, his hand encircling her waist. It was a scene from a highschool yearbook. The dashing young man was wearing a World War II uniform, each ribbon sculpted in loving detail. And the girl, her hair elaborate in a 1940s pompadour, was decked out in what had to be her best strapless evening gown. It was the marble counterpart of a *Saturday Evening Post* cover, created by a Norman Rockwell of the chisel.

"That's certainly a change from angels and trumpets." Kate was delighted. "What does the inscription say, darling? My Italian leaves a bit to be desired."

Wolf peered over the rim of his sunglasses and chuckled. "As far as I can make out, the *Signor* was an officer who married on leave and was killed in action a few months later. And his wife, the *Signora* . . ."

"Let me guess. She died of grief."

In spite of herself, Kate was touched.

"Is that how you'd like us to be immortalized?" she asked as they threaded their way out of the cemetery.

"Doing the fox trot? Good Lord, no. You should know as well as anybody what a joke I am on the dance floor. No, with you I think I'd choose a position a bit more deliciously obscene. I'd certainly find a better place for my hand than around your waist."

"You're incorrigible," Kate laughed.

"I'd get us kicked out of all the best cemeteries. But in any event," he continued, "should I die, I can't quite see you expiring out of grief. You'd find yourself some nice young man, a bank manager, maybe, or some Brooks Brothers account executive, and live happily for another fifty years."

"No, Wolf. I don't think I could ever love anyone again."

But Wolf, who was usually flattered by Kate's avowals, seemed suddenly irritated. He turned away from her eyes and scanned the path ahead. "It's too nice a day to sit around and wait for the bus back. Let's walk down to Florence, shall we?"

Kate was disturbed by this sudden shift of mood, and in the long silent descent through the hills, she thought back to something that had happened in Rome the week before.

They had been checking into the Hassler, standing at the reception desk, heads close together—"Signor and Signora Aaronson"—amidst a very matrimonial pile of luggage and packages, when a hearty American voice called out, "For Chrissakes, Wolf Aaronson. What are you doing here?"

Wolf about-faced, and from the corner of her eye Kate caught a glimpse of a middle-aged crew cut of a man, Bermuda-shorted, plaid-jacketed, decked out with the inevitable tourist camera.

"Hello, Jerry. This is a surprise."

"Anette!" she heard the stranger shout across the lobby. "Anette, will you look who's here, for Chrissake?" While Kate was figuring out how best to disentangle herself from Wolf's side, the desk clerk returned and, with typical Italian flourish, handed her the key to their room. "*La chiave*, Signora Aaronson, the key to your room. I hope you and the Signor will enjoy your stay." A loudspeaker would have done the job as well.

"Aren't you going to introduce me to your friend, Wolf?" No point in playing invisible now; it was plain from Jerry's voice, with its overtones of American Legion conventions, that he had sized up the situation exactly and was licking his chops over Wolf's discomfiture.

"Kate." Wolf tapped her on the shoulder and she turned around, foolishly clutching the outsize room key. "I'd like you to meet Jerry Welker, a neighbor of mine from Connecticut." They shook hands. "And this," Wolf said, acknowledging the advent of a small plump woman with harlequin glasses and too-pink lipstick, "is Anette."

"Wolf, darling, how are you.... and what a surprise!" She gave him the classic suburban greeting, a brush of lips on either cheek. "And what are you doing in Rome?" she burbled, her eyes remaining fixedly on Kate. "Polly told me you'd gone off to Hamburg."

"I was in Hamburg," Wolf said evenly, "and now I'm in Rome." He mollified his tone rather too quickly. "I just thought it would be a good chance to do the galleries."

Anette's thin, knowing smile indicated that that wasn't all Wolf was doing. She turned to Kate. "I'm sorry," she said sweetly, "I didn't catch your name."

"Kate."

"Just Kate?"

"Kate . . . Marsden." It was the first name that popped to her mind.

"Oh, I see . . . the same name as that advertising agency in New York." Kate smiled wanly.

Later, up in their room, Kate had asked Wolf if he'd been upset by the incident.

"Not upset, Kate. Just annoyed."

"Jesus, I didn't know what to say when she asked me my name. I just said the first one that came to mind. I'm sorry."

"Kate," Wolf interrupted angrily, "I said I am *not* upset, so will you please not go on about it?"

But yes, he had been upset then. And he was now, she concluded as she watched him walking well in front of her down the path that led back to Florence. She seemed to read in the angle of his head, the set of his shoulders, a portent of unhappiness.

"Wolf!" she shouted as he disappeared around a bend. "Wolf! Wait for me." She ran to join him, to put her arm through his elbow, to dispel the American shadows that were looming in the Italian sunshine.

Halfway down the hill, they stopped to catch their breath at the Piazzale Michelangelo.

"It's beautiful, isn't it?" Wolf said, and Kate, knowing how little given he was to clichés, could only nod. It was beautiful. The city below, its domes and tiled roofs a glowing rose in the late afternoon sun, the sinuous curve of the Arno, and on the far hills, a distant glimpse of white and pink villas, punctuated by the deep sombre green of the cypress trees.

In unspoken agreement, they sat down on a bench to gaze, to capture the beauty of the hour for later memories. Life had never been so beautiful, so perfect.

"Let's not go back," Kate said dreamily.

He smiled. "Park benches make for pretty cold sleeping."

She turned to look at him and against the delicacy of the day's tender colors, his profile seemed stronger, more massive than ever. Impassable. Had he misunderstood her meaning or had he merely tried to deflect her?

"I mean, Wolf . . . let's not go back to America."

"Oh?" Just an uninflected "Oh?"

"I'm serious, darling." She leaned her head on his shoulder, rubbed her cheek against the denim of his shirt. "Why should we? What is there waiting back there for either of us?"

The hills beckoned in the distance, each villa rich with its promise of joy. "We could get a little villa in the hills over there. I can't imagine they're all that expensive. You could paint. My God, I should think you could paint here. Everybody else has."

"And what would you do, Kate?" His eyes were fixed on the hills. "Tell me, what would you do?"

"For money? Oh, I don't know. I suppose I could get some kind of job teaching English. Or maybe hustling tourists."

"That isn't what I meant. I meant . . . what would you do for *me?*"

She sat up and stared at him, but his face was expressionless.

"Would we dine on prosciutto and melon? Or would you be the little Italian housewife and cook and clean and mend my shirts?"

"Why, does Polly cook for you?"

He faced her and his eyes were cool. "Of course she does . . . Polly is a superb cook."

Kate was surprised. Surprised that even after all these years together, she had so feeble a picture of his home life.

"I could too if I had to . . . if you wanted me to."

"Could you, now?" The cold eyes narrowed, and Kate became suddenly aware that despite the warmth of the afternoon, she was on very thin ice indeed.

"You never have, Kate. You know, it's funny. Not once in the seven years we've been together have you ever cooked me a proper meal, made me a dinner with your own two hands. And I don't count sending out for Chinese food as home-cooking, or throwing a steak under the grill."

She was stunned by the abruptness of this unforeseen assault, at the depth of rancor his voice conveyed.

"My God, I didn't know it meant that much to you, or I would have. You know how hard I work."

"Not once in seven years," he repeated. "You have no sense of what it is to make a home, Kate. I don't think you ever will have."

"That's unfair," she cried out. "I've never had the chance. You've never given it to me. Seeing you once a week in New York . . . should I give up those precious hours to spend time in the kitchen chopping onions?"

"It never occurred to you . . . admit it, Kate."

"That's not so," she protested. "I've thought of it time and time again, what our life would be like if we were married."

"Is this a proposal?"

"Yes," she sighed. "It's a proposal. You know how long this has been on my mind. It's not the first time I've mentioned it."

"No, it's not." He rubbed his eyes wearily, and put on his sunglasses. *The better not to see you, my dear.*

"And even," Kate hurried on, "even if we weren't married, even if Polly wouldn't give you a divorce, we could at least live together openly. I mean . . ."—the words spilled out in her haste—"every time we meet there's such a compulsion just to eat, drink and make love . . . quick quick quick, because the hours aren't long enough for anything more. We even begrudge time for sleeping. I would like . . . I would truly like for you to come to me on a Wednesday night and maybe we wouldn't make love. We wouldn't have to. We could just go to bed and watch the late show, or read, because we knew we could make love on a Thursday or any old time. I'd like to get up on a Sunday morning and have bagels with you and then go back to bed to read the *Times* and maybe make love before lunch. Yes, I'd like us to make love on a Sunday morning."

"I don't know if they have the *New York Times* in Florence, but I'm certain they don't have bagels."

"Don't be sarcastic with me, Wolf." She began crying. "It could be here, in New York, in the suburbs, anywhere . . . so long as we're together all the time. I just can't go on like this, not forever. It's not enough."

"Would you like to break it off, then? Is that what you're trying to tell me?"

"No." The thought so alarmed her she could feel the adrenalin pouring through her body. "No. Just the opposite. I want more, not less. Don't you understand?"

"I understand this, Kate. That every time we get ready to go back to the States, you get very moody, very testy. You think because we've had a marvelous couple of weeks, that that's what being married would be like. Well, Kate, you couldn't be more wrong. What we have here is a kind of euphoria . . . no cares, no responsibilites, nobody trying to get us on the phone. It's not real, you have to recognize that. And I don't know if you could tolerate me, if we could tolerate each other, on a round-the-clock basis, under any sort of pressure. You're not like the girl in the statue at San Miniato, living for one man only, devouring him with uncritical eyes. Don't let's be carried off by the romance of the spot, Kate. Anyhow," he rose abruptly, "it's time to go back to the hotel and start packing."

"You'll think about what I said, won't you?" Kate dried her eyes. He promised he would and they began walking back.

"Remind me," he said as they crossed the bridge into Florence, "to pick up some prosciutto at that place we had lunch yesterday. The waiter said he'd pack it up for the plane." He pecked her lightly on the cheek. "That'll be a nice memory of the good times we've had. The *good* times."

They parted at Kennedy. He'd left his MG (the jeep had long since died) at the long-term parking, but she sensed he was anxious to get back to Connecticut and offered to go home alone in a cab.

"You're sure you don't mind?" he said, visibly relieved. She shook her head no, and they kissed.

"I'll call you tomorrow, darling, or at the office on Monday. Get a good night's sleep."

New York. As always, the first sight of the Manhattan skyline overpowered her, pushed everything else into unreality. A villa in Florence!—what a crazy dream. Wolf had been so right to pooh-pooh it. As the cab inched across the 59th Street Bridge and floundered in the slow-moving stream up First Avenue, Kate opened the window and drew in a deep breath of that gritty, sultry, sewery, filthy New York air with the grateful gasp of a rescued swimmer. Past Friday's, past Maxwell's Plum, swinging harder than ever with Saturday night action even in this steam bath of an evening, then across 66th Street and home.

"Evening, Max."

"Good evening, Miss Chapman." The doorman sprang to the luggage.

"Anything happen while I was away? Any burglaries, rapes, misdemeanors?"

"Nope. Everything was quiet while you were gone. But hot! You could fry eggs on the sidewalk."

"It was hot where I was, too, Max. Thanks."

In true New York style, Kate's first reaction on entering the apartment was one of relief. No, she hadn't been burglarized.

Not *this* time. Her second was to switch on the air conditioner.

Tired tired tired. Too tired to unpack. Just better put the prosciutto away before it spoils. She took out the package wrapped in a mummy mix of waxed paper, tin foil and bits of colored string. She sniffed it gingerly. No, it didn't seem to have turned. What a funny, foolish, impractical thing for Wolf to buy. She thought uneasily of their conversation at the Piazzale, when she'd actually believed for a moment he would leave her. But no. No man ever gave a woman a prosciutto ham for a farewell present. Too tired to think about it. Kate trailed into the bedroom. Too tired to wash. *I'll just take off my shoes and lie down.*

The phone kept ringing, ringing . . . tearing through the texture of her dream like an electric drill through cotton wool. It was 11:27 by the bedside clock. Go away, she muttered, but the ringing would not go away. Groggy with sleep, she picked it up.

"Kate." At first she didn't recognize the voice, so twisted and muffled. "Kate, Kate."

"Is that you, Wolf?"—wide awake now. "Where are you? Are you all right? Did you have an accident?"

"No accident. No, it was no accident. I'm home. I want you to come now."

She could barely discern the words through the stertorous breathing, the quick gasping intakes of breath.

"Wolf, Wolf," she begged. "Please . . . just tell me what happened."

"Come now," came the strangled answer. "Just get here. I can't talk. Just come."

Polly was dead. What else could it be? Polly had committed suicide. It was no accident.

"I'm on my way, darling. I'm coming."

Forty-five minutes later, she was bowling down the turnpike in a rented Hertz. Her mind was half on the road, busy even at this unlikely hour with the cars of returning theatregoers and Saturday night dinner party guests, and half on the image of Polly. Dead. She had to be. Those fucking people in the hotel in Rome, they'd blown the whistle. They couldn't wait to get back—she had seen it in their eyes—couldn't wait to lay this extra portion of misery at Polly's door.

It had been seven years since she had last driven down this road. But the moment she came to the junction, she recognized the secondary road, as clear and unmistakable as a childhood room revisited. Just here at this junction, she'd once said she was a "city girl." Just here on this rutted road, Wolf had touched her for the first time. And now, so many thousands of embraces later, the house loomed again before her. It was brilliant, every room ablaze with light like a ballroom awaiting a great party.

This time, there was no Polly standing at the door to greet her, all nervous and giggling; no Polly framed there, house-proud and husband-proud, to welcome her in.

Kathe. That was my sister's name.

Kate parked the rented Ford alongside Wolf's MG, got out and walked toward the beckoning house. Only the crunch of her footsteps on the gravel broke the silence. Only that and the whirr of crickets on a summer night.

The door was unlocked, his luggage stacked just inside it, still freshly tagged and stickered from the flight. MIL-JFK. Bright cardboard labels against the Mark Cross leather.

She turned into the room where first she'd met him. But now, despite its multiple treasures, the great living room yawned bleak and silent. He was seated dead center in the room on a little tapestry chair. Hands folded. Eyes glazed and vacant as a blind man.

No police, thank God. He hadn't called them yet. He had called her first.

"Oh, Wolf!" She ran across the room to him, her arms stretched out in love. She wanted to cradle him, absorb him, hold him fast and tight; the construction of the narrow armless chair did not permit it. Made even the simplest act of physical comfort awkward and graceless. Leaning over, she drew his head to her breast, felt the wiry hair scratch against her chin. Stayed there motionless for God knows how long, till her back ached, her muscles tensed with pain. Shock. Warmth was good for shock, she knew. Should she free him from her grip and get him—what? A blanket? A brandy? She could feel his hot, sweaty flesh against the silk of her blouse, his tears soaking through to her breast.

How long they stayed there, she could not tell, but finally he pulled himself free and buried his face in his hands.

"Shall I get you some brandy, darling . . . should I call you a doctor?"

He didn't answer. Even the crickets were hushed now. Never had she known a silence so intense.

The silence.

It was the silence that was wrong. Not the house ablaze with light, not the absence of Polly at the door. It was the silence that was out of kilter.

"Wolf," she said softly, "where are the dogs?"

He raised his head.

"Go find them."

They were the first words he had uttered since her arrival. "The dogs are in the kennel. Go see."

She didn't want to leave his side, not now, not under any circumstances, but when he repeated his words they were not a request. They were an order. "Go see the dogs."

It was moonless on the path, the sole source of light provided by the overspill from the house. Farther down the path she could just make out the separation in the hedge that led to the kennels. Beyond the hedge, it was black as pitch. For a moment she hesitated, deciding whether to go back to the house for a flashlight, then she remembered Polly had installed lights in the out-buildings. *So I can see my babies at night,* she had said. Kate continued down the passage, the hedges plucking at her skirt. Her foot hit something. A tin can. It clanged and echoed angrily through the silence. As her eyes adjusted to the darkness, she could make out the long low shape of the buildings. She groped her way to the side of the food shed. Was it here, along this wooden wall? With one hand she held her nose against the stench, with the other she traced a path down the wall—groping, feeling, embedding splinters in her palms and the softness of her fingertips till she encountered the smooth plastic of the switchplate. She turned on the light.

It was Dachau.

A Dachau lit up in merciless brilliance for the benefit of the invading army. A death camp of contorted bodies, of drying saliva, of vomit, of greenish excrement, of corpses lying in every imaginable posture of agony. Teeth bared, mouths distended, jaws locked in the grimace of death. Legs twisted into surrealistic angles, bodies angled in the paroxysm of the death throe. She shut her eyes but the vision remained, imprinted on the inside of her lids. There in the far corner of the kennel, a body still twitched. She came close. But no—it was not the twitch of life, only the resettling of a black cloud of flies that the sudden light had startled into motion. The stink was unbelievable.

In the glare, she walked toward the second kennel, not looking for dogs now, but for something else. She counted the bodies, twelve . . . thirteen. Her gaze was transfixed for a moment by the sight of a gaping stomach wound where maggots feasted greedily. Had the dog rent its own flesh in the final spasm? Or had the soft belly been savaged by another, a sibling perhaps, made mad by pain? It was only a puppy. She continued down the length of the kennels. Sixteen . . . seventeen . . . There they lay—the children, the grandchildren of Bel Gwynnyd, sacrificed to a memory of blood and death. A tin can clattered. She looked down. She did not have to pick it up to recognize the label with its bounding corgi chasing through the fields. Kennel King. Polly's ultimate joke.

Blind, stumbling, swallowing on her vomit, Kate retraced her steps toward the house.

She had seen all that there was to see, but not all that she'd expected. The holocaust was not complete.

"Where's Polly, Wolf? Where's your wife?"

"Not here."

She came to him and peeled his hands from his face.

"Tell me, where's Polly? She's alive, isn't she? . . . *isn't she?*" Kate fairly screamed.

"She's alive." Wolf rose heavily from the chair and went to the sideboard. With trembling hands, he poured out two brandies. "She's at the Hardesty Clinic. It's a private psychiatric hospital. She'd been there before."

Kate shuddered with relief, and then again with anger. She saw it all now. Like Medea of legend, Polly had slaughtered her children and spared herself. And Kate had never hated Polly so intensely as in that instant of revelation. It wasn't suicide that Polly had chosen. It was revenge.

"She didn't try suicide, then . . . did she? *Did she, Wolf?*"

Little by little, Wolf began to talk. No, she had not. Had stopped with the dogs. And Wolf had found her upstairs before the easel in his studio, sitting still as a corpse, eyes unseeing, ears unhearing, locked tight in the stranglehold of memory. He still didn't know everything that had happened, not all the details. She had dismissed the housekeeper two days before. The kennelman never came weekends. No, she never used to give the dogs Kennel King, nor indeed any commercial dog food. She had always ordered her own special blend from a wholesale butcher in Stamford. No, he had not called the police. It wasn't as if it were attempted suicide. It was a private matter. Private among the three of them.

Kate made coffee, poured them both more brandy. They talked in short inchoate bursts until at last the horror, the shock, the sheer physical exhaustion of the day and night overpowered her.

They went upstairs to a bedroom—his? Polly's? She didn't know, didn't care, all she craved was a dreamless sleep.

The pale summer dawn crept through the eyelet curtains, bringing in its wake a dull muffled sound. Kate dragged herself from sleep, suddenly disorientated at this awakening in an unknown room. Yes, it was Wolf's room. Now, after seven years of kisses and caresses and every kind of lovemaking, she was in Wolf's room at last. On Wolf's bed. The dream of years achieved. He was not there. She shut her eyes again in search of sleep, but the gentle thud thud beneath the window persisted. She knew that sound now. It was the sound of digging.

From the window she could see that he had already gouged a great hole in the grassy patch that lay beyond the rock garden. She watched him from behind the white cotton curtains, watched the massive arms plunging the spade relentlessly deep into the ground. He worked in a slow, unbroken rhythm. At the far end of the lawn, like an ugly blot, were piled black plastic bags of the kind that suburbanites use for storing the raked leaves of autumn when summer has come to its end. But these bags were bulging with a different freight.

She watched him in silence for perhaps an hour, then went downstairs and let herself out through the kitchen back door.

"Wolf," she called across the gaping trench. "Wolf, let it rest. Don't do that."

For a moment he stopped and rested his foot on the spade.

"Go home, Kate," he said softly. "Go back to New York."

Four days later she came home from the office to find Wolf in her bedroom, packing clothes into a suitcase. The same suitcase they had shared on so many trips abroad. His eyes were bloodshot and red-rimmed, but whether from sleeplessness or crying she could not tell.

For one long, uncomprehending moment she stared at the open suitcase, her brain refusing to accept the testimony of her eyes.

"I've come to say goodbye, Kate."

"Nooooo . . ." The howl that escaped was more animal than human. She shut her eyes to block out the sight. "No no no no no"—until he came and led her gently out of the room. As if her bedroom had become perilous ground. Handed her onto the living room sofa.

"I'll get you a drink. No, maybe coffee would be better. Just sit there."

He came back minutes later with a coffee tray and a wet washcloth. "Here," he said, handing her the cloth. "Wipe your face and try to pull yourself together a little."

She did as she was told.

"Now have some coffee. You'll feel better."

But her hands were shaking so, she dared not lift the cup. "No. Please, just a cigarette."

He lit one for her, one for himself, then sat in the easy chair opposite, not leaning back, not looking at her.

"You must have known this would happen some day, darling. It's no good anymore. Not good for me . . . not good for you."

"Not good for Polly, isn't that what you mean?" Suddenly anger triumphed over tears. "My God, Wolf, don't you see you're being blackmailed . . . blackmailed into this in the nastiest possible way. If Polly had really wanted to kill herself, she would have. She would have done it long ago instead of staging"—she swallowed and sought the words—"that obscene Grand Guignol with the dogs. Don't let her do that to you. *To us!*"

"Oh, Kate." He sunk his face into his hands, his shoulders leaden with despair, and when he lifted his head again she saw the wetness in his eyes. Yes, he was crying, but for her or for himself she could not tell. "Don't think this is easy for me, Kate, and please don't make it any harder. It's not what happened the other night. At any rate, not just that. I tried to tell you when we were sitting at that square in Florence, tried to prepare you. This isn't a sudden decision, you know. It's something I've been considering for a long time."

"How long?" The steel edged into her voice.

"A long time." He would be no more specific than that. "But this had to end, you've said it yourself. We couldn't go on forever like this. I've loved you very much, Kate. I still love you . . ."

"You've *used* me," she burst in.

He started to shake his head in denial, then considered.

"Perhaps I have," he said slowly. "Although I never set out to. But if that's true, Kate, to be honest, you've used me too."

"I've *what?*" she shrieked. "How can you say I ever used you? What did I ever get out of this relationship? How have I exploited you? Tell me! Because you gave me a few pretty things . . . did I ever ask you for them? What am I . . . some cheap gold-digger . . . is that what you think? Well, this is what you can do with your fucking gifts." She grabbed the nearest thing at hand, the little Chelsea patchbox, and flung it across the room. It exploded against the wall like the crack of a bullet and shattered into a hundred tiny knives. The explosion sobered both of them. And when he spoke again, he was dry-eyed, his voice even and low.

"That is not what I mean, Kate, and you should know better."

"Then what did you mean? What did I ever ask you for?"

"It's what you didn't ask, Kate, at least not until a couple of years ago. You knew I was married when we met. You once told me you had gone with other married men. You used me, Kate . . . oh, yes you did, as an excuse for staying single all these years."

She sucked in her breath, but he continued.

"You wanted love *and* you wanted independence. It was the perfect relationship. For you, anyway. You never had to make any real commitment. I never threatened your career, your way of life, never made any great emotional demands on you. You had love on a part-time basis with no obligations, and it suited you right down to the ground."

"Not true," she sobbed.

"True, Kate. True. When we first started seeing each other—and my God, I was absolutely besotted with you—I asked if you would give me a child. Remember?"

"Yes, I remember, but that was so absurd, Wolf. You asked me if I would have a baby—a bastard, let's face it—without any promise from you that you would marry me."

"I would have if you'd become pregnant."

"So you say now, but you didn't say it then. That was asking me to take a hell of a chance."

"And you weren't about to take any chances, were you? Yes, I would have married you then. Those first couple of years, Kate, you could have done anything you wanted with me. I was just waiting for you to ask. Waiting for some sign of real commitment from you. It's probably as well in the long run, for much as I've loved you, Kate—and I still do—I can never picture you as a wife and mother."

"What *am* I," she cried, "some kind of subhuman monster? Don't I have the same instincts as other women?"

"You're just not the marrying kind."

"How would you know? You never asked me."

"If you really wanted to get married, have children, make a home, you would have done it long before now. I never asked you for fidelity. You were free. If marriage meant all that much to you, you were perfectly free to find someone eligible, single—someone closer to your own age and style. You could have booted me out overnight, and I'd have had no grounds to complain. Please, Kate," he said, getting up, "let's not part on such an angry note. It would just spoil all those good years we've had."

He went into the bedroom to finish packing and, for the first time, the reality of what was happening bore down on Kate. He was really leaving. Leaving her. Leaving forever. Anger bowed down before grief, a grief that was suddenly not to be borne.

"Wolf!" She ran into the bedroom and flung herself at his feet, clinging, hanging on to his legs with such force that he had to prise her up bodily. "Please, Wolf." She clung, refused to be plucked off. "Please, Wolf, don't go. Let's make love. Let's make love just one more time. I'll do whatever you want, anything, only please don't leave me. I need you. I need you as much as Polly does."

But he was already at the door.

"Kate," he said softly, "you've never needed anyone in your whole life." And he was gone.

She ran to the door, but he was nowhere in the hall. Yes, he had fled. Fled like an outlaw before the sheriff. Gone. She shut the door against the emptiness without, felt the crunch of tiny china slivers beneath her feet. The Chelsea box. She stooped down, gathered the fragments, piling them into the palm of her hands. Then closed her fist and squeezed, squeezed until the blood ran freely, till it dripped the red of death onto the white of the rug.

The seven fat years were over.

She spent the next two months alternately working and crying. Work was the glue that kept her together, but the moment she was alone or even with Barry, nothing could stem the tide of tears, soften the sense of loss. Almost anything would set her off. A line of poetry. The taste of prosciutto. Even a bedroom scene from a James Bond movie triggered a spate of weeping so copious that Barry had had to lead her out of the theatre, like a guide-dog leading the blind.

"For Chrissakes, Kate, it's a comedy," he said as they got into the taxi.

"Nothing's a comedy," she snuffled.

He took her back to his place and gave her tea and Valium.

"You've got to pull yourself out of this," he spoke like a reproving parent. "Nothing's going to change the past. And anyhow, no one man is the end of the world. Believe me, I should know. Good God, Kate, you're what . . . thirty-one, thirty-two?"

"Almost thirty-three." She continued weeping.

"And you're acting like a love-struck schoolgirl." He took her hand. "Now listen to daddy. You're a fantastic and fascinating woman, one of the snappiest broads in New York. Believe me, there isn't a man between here and Timbuktu who wouldn't be happy to get between the sheets with you."

"Is that a proposition, Barry?" She smiled through her tears.

"Well, if I were ever so inclined to swing that way, believe me, honey, you'd be the first beneficiary."

"For this relief, much thanks."

"Seriously, Kate, you ought to look on all this as a great chance to change your life. Buy some new clothes. Change your job. Get yourself some new lovers."

"It's just that I can't stop thinking about him."

"All the more reason. Let's face it, Kate. You can't fuck and think at the same time."

"You think sex is the answer to everything, don't you?"

"It's the best hangover remedy there is."

"You're probably right."

"You'll know I'm right if you really think about it."

She thought about it and decided he was right. She was ripe for a change. She heralded her new life by changing jobs and hiring on at a new agency that had hotted up from zilch to zowie in less than three years.

"You'll be working mostly on California Jeans," Steve Redman had told her at the interview.

"Well, I don't know if that's my line of country," she replied. "I've never worked on fashion before."

"Jeans aren't fashion, honey. They're a basic human commodity. Like food or shelter."

"Or sex?"

"Very definitely like sex. And if you keep in mind that you're not selling clothes, you're selling aphrodisiacs, you can't miss."

"I'll keep that in mind," she said, smoothing out the gentle pleats of her new Halston skirt.

The campaign she devised was all the aphrodisiac market could ask for, and certainly all the censors would permit. It was a series of TV spots, featuring tight-assed, blue-jeaned kids gyrating in discos, sashaying down Sunset Strip, swiveling their hips in Rollerdromes—all against a background of acid rock. Each commercial ended with the same visual: a girl's thumb resting sensuously on the pull of her zipper. Freeze frame. Kate had originally wanted to place the girl's thumb on the pull of the boy's zipper, but the networks had howled. The commercials were all to be filmed and sound-recorded in California, using L.A. locations and studio facilities. She'd be going out to the Coast every two weeks.

California is a great place, Fred Allen once said, if you happen to be an orange. California, said Kate Chapman, is a great place period. It really blew the mind . . . and everything else you had to be blown. There was something in the air that you could even sense when the plane dipped down through the yellow smog that blanketed the city. No, not "something" in the air. It was sex. Sex in the air. Pure sex in more flavors than Baskin-Robbins had ice cream. An uninhibited wildness she'd never known in New York. Just the word California made her go moist inside, with a reflex as sure as Pavlov's dog salivating to the bell.

California, where you went to Californicate. For what Aimee Semple MacPherson had been to the California of the Twenties, sex was to the California of the Seventies: the new religion, practiced with the intensity and whole-hearted enthusiasm for which the state is noted.

Kate arranged·her schedule so that the shootings took place on a Thursday or Friday. That way, she told the office, she had the weekend to rest up. "The pause that refreshes," she liked to call it.

She could feel the excitement rising when her cab pulled into Kennedy. Just the sight of the planes on the runway turned her on. How beautiful they were—great silver cocks, powerful and hard, waiting to transport her to the land of the ultimate lay. She'd case the first-class waiting room for possibilities, although she generally steered clear of New Yorkers. Too close to home. She liked to keep her California life in a separate compartment, divorced completely from her workaday world. One trip out, she'd sat next to Paul Newman. She quite liked him, found him intelligent for an actor, a breed she generally held in low esteem. They'd chatted pleasantly about this and that, but he'd fallen asleep right after lunch. Oh, well. You can't win 'em all. But for the most part, she'd sit alone, luxuriating in the low humming throb of the airplane, surrendering to the subtle vibration that seemed to her as sweet and long as foreplay, recalling pleasures of weekends past, anticipating new variations on the theme. By the time the plane was banking over Los Angeles airport, her insides had turned to cream.

California, here I come.

An hour later she'd be in her room at the Beverly Hilton, peeling off the layers of her smart New York clothes. She preferred the Hilton to the Wiltshire or Beverly Hills. It was more impersonal, more anonymous. And she liked that. Then a drink, then a shower, then it was time to slip into California gear. You needed to wear so little most of the year. She began going barelegged and braless, something she never did in New York. She enjoyed the feel of cloth rubbing up against her nipples, the sensuousness of silk, the sexy abrasiveness of linen. And within the hour, she'd emerge as from a chrysalis, mothlike. Ready to spread her wings and fly.

She usually spotted what she wanted in the first day's business—on the set or at the casting session. The supply, as Barry had foreseen, was infinite. Who needed singles bars when you could find your candidates right on the job: photographers, sound-recorders, directors, producers and an unending procession of slim-hipped male models with total tans. She'd scan the field, size up the talent and, often within the very first hour on the job, she had her weekend set up. The signals were simple. By New York standards, crude. A lick of the lips, a brush of the breast, an absent-minded sucking of the thumb. But in the sex-charged atmosphere of L.A., the signals were received with instant recognition by any man worth his balls. Or any work-hungry model with an avid eye on a contract for the next round of commercials.

By the year's end, her little California phone book had become a private directory of erotica. Everything from specialists to general practitioners. Whatever you were in the mood for, the men were here. And so was the technology. Waterbeds. Vibrators. Saunas. Jacuzzis. The place was a fucking Cape Canaveral, and the pilots knew their stuff. There was Larry, a film-cutter with a library of porn so you could watch and perform simultaneously. Swing along with the bouncing balls, so to speak. And Steve—a set-dresser who'd liberated a gynecologist's couch from some Kildare soundstage and brought it home complete with straps and stirrups. Nils. The first time she went over to Nils's place, he'd taken out his electric razor. "I'm not much of a one for candy and flowers," she'd told him, "you don't have to shave for me." "I'm not going to shave for *you*, sweetheart," he'd replied. "You're going to shave for me." It was fun, but she'd itched for three weeks afterward.

Then there was Chris.

"Let my fingers do the walking," he had said, and proceeded to trip her to paradise. If they gave Nobel Prizes for fucking, he would have been on the next flight to Stockholm. But the morning after, as Kate lay dreamy and limp from a nonstop night of sensation, he remarked: "You know, one of the commonest female fantasies is being balled by a lion."

"Is it?" she asked lazily. She wasn't interested in his research.

"Yup," he continued, "it's in half a dozen textbooks. But you're the first woman I ever met who thought she was being fucked by a wolf."

Kate sat bolt upright.

"What do you mean."

"Well, last night, baby, every time you came you kept hollering Wolf! Wolf! like a nut case. And I wasn't even up on all fours. Crazy Kate Chapman," he laughed mildly, "the girl who cries wolf!"

Two hours later she was on the plane to New York. Two days later, she quit her job. "Those trips to California were killing me," she said by way of explanation.

KIT

In 1937, Benito Mussolini was at the height of his power, undisputed master of all Italy. Having pacified the Libyan nomads by such traditional methods as starvation and internment camps, having bombed the Abyssinians into submission, this latter-day Caesar could, with some justification, proclaim a Second Roman Empire.

Only one small cloud darkened the blue sky of his realm. And though Il Duce could now claim the allegiance of Turin autoworkers and Abruzzi peasants alike, although his word was law from the shores of Lake Como to the dirt streets of Addis Ababa, victory eluded him, for within his realm there remained one unconquered fiefdom: Sicily. From time immemorial the simple farmers and fishermen who inhabited the island had seen foreign invaders come and go. For generations they had pretended to be governed by Crusaders, Moors, Venetians, Frenchmen and now this newcomer, Mussolini. But then as now, every true Sicilian knew in his heart that there was only one real source of power, only one ruler that had preceded and would survive all the rest.

And so, Mussolini declared war on the Mafia.

By the early forties, the jails of Palermo and Agrigento were bulging with imprisoned Mafiosi. Within their pungent confines, Mafia sharks and minnows shared prison meals and cells with Communists, Socialists, Jews, anti-Fascists, with the whole range of Il Duce's political enemies.

When the Allies landed in Sicily in July of '43, one of their first acts was to open the prisons. Whether this was done in the erroneous belief that all the inmates were dedicated Freedom Fighters, or whether (as has been subsequently claimed), the move was engineered by Lucky Luciano, the fact remains that within a matter of days, the Americans freed the entire Sicilian Mafia intact. Among the newly liberated was a young man named Luigi Zametti.

The astonished Zametti, in a heartfelt expression of gratitude to his benefactors, promptly emigrated to the United States, settling down in Boston where an uncle ran a small chickpea business. Zametti loved America—as, indeed, why should he not? By his reasoning, any country naive enough to mistake him for an innocent victim of Fascism was a country where a clever man could surely make a fortune. Within a year of his arrival, he married Luisa Scaccione, a North End girl of Neapolitan descent. Among the "family," it was considered an unconventional union, brides of Sicilian origin being deemed preferable. But though, traditionally, there is no love lost between Sicilians and the more urbane Neapolitans, the marriage was by all counts a happy one. Luisa was sweet and loving, with passionate brown eyes and all that could be desired in a wife. Between her daily visits to Our Lady of the Flowers (she was a fixture at early morning mass), she found time to bear and bring up seven children. Indeed, Luigi Zametti prospered in everything. By 1970, he was the second largest importer of chickpeas into the United States. And the fourth largest importer of heroin.

Everyone knew it. The FBI knew it. As did the Treasury Department, the Internal Revenue, the immigration authorities, the Justice Department, the cops who patroled the streets of Boston. But knowing it and proving it were two different things. Year after year, law suits were brought at great expense, trials mounted with cunning and care, case after case meticulously prepared, only to founder in the courts of law. Key witnesses had an annoying habit of dying, disappearing, or simply playing dumb. Fear, loyalty and the Sicilian pledge of silence, *omertá*, all conspired to make it impossible for Luigi to be convicted of any charge more serious than double-parking.

On Michael's first day as Chief U.S. Attorney, Massachusetts Federal Circuit, his assistant presented him with a file comprising over two thousand pages. "There's lots more in the basement," he said. "Go ahead, Matheson, eat your heart out." Michael's predecessor had done just that.

The case became a hobby with Michael, if not an obsession, and it was a rare weekend that he didn't come home to Haddons Landing with some tag end or other of the Zametti file stuffed into his briefcase.

"Zametti again!" Kit would groan at the sight of yet another overstuffed file, and Michael would nod and disappear into his study. For over a year, he occupied himself with every detail of Luigi Zametti's life, concerned himself with the financial minutiae of Zametti Chickpea Importers. Like an accountant, he would pore over each little entry of the impounded ledgers looking for the fatal flaw, the faintest clue. But Zametti paid his taxes with an assiduity that would have done credit to a scoutmaster, and each item in the books could be offset by some legitimate expense in the world of chickpea imports.

One figure puzzled Michael, however. On the first day of each month, a sum of six hundred dollars—no more, no less—was remitted to a small farm near Agrigento. Zametti dealt with many local farmers, but this figure was different. So constant, so free of fluctuation, so impervious to the ups and downs of the Sicilian chickpea crop.

"Why would he remit six hundred bucks exactly each and every month?" he muttered over dinner one evening.

"I don't know," Kit remarked. "Maybe he's supporting an aged mother. The Italians are very big on family." Michael knew Zametti's mother had been dead for over twenty years, but the offhand comment gave him a hunch.

On a fine day in early April, Luisa Zametti was brought to his office for what was labeled a "routine interview." There she sat, plump and sullen on an old leather chair, while Michael offered her coffee and *canoli*. Mrs. Zametti ate the *canoli* and licked her fingers cautiously. Then, folding her arms across her ample bosom, she waited for the questioning to commence. She knew them, these fast-talking vermin, trying to sweeten her with pastries. But instead of questions, Michael pulled out a small yellow file.

"Do you read Italian, Miss Sciaccone?" he asked as he handed it over.

"Hey, fella. The name is Zametti."

Michael smiled and opened the file for her, handing out the papers one by one. Some were stats, some were handwritten depositions scribbled by semiliterate fingers. The last paper was the clincher. It had been secured three weeks earlier by an energetic T-Man sent down from Naples. A dogged sort, this Treasury guy. He'd begun with the Cathedral in Palermo and gradually worked his way through every church register in Western Sicily until finally, in the tiny village of Caltabellotta, he struck pay dirt. The handwriting in the document was spindly but clear—clear enough for anyone with even the most casual knowledge of Italian to get the message. The message was that on December 4, 1937, in the village church, a marriage had taken place between one Luigi Ercolo Zametti and Carla Guiseppina Santini. The same Carla who, with her two grown sons, now ran a small farm near Agrigento and supplemented her earnings with a monthly check of $600 U.S.

"So you see, Miss Sciaccone, not only are you not married to Mr. Zametti in law or in the eyes of the Church, but your children . . ." he sighed. "Well, perhaps you'd better discuss that with your priest."

For the first twenty minutes, the putative Mrs. Zametti cursed with a vigor nowhere contained in Michael's crash course in Italian. For the next twenty-five minutes, she wept and beat her generous breast. Then she crossed herself—twice, in fact.

And then she sang. Sang every aria in the Italian repertoire and a few Michael had never thought of. No, the U.S. Attorney was unaware that Zametti owned a house of prostitution in Belmont. That he had put the fix in the recent dog-racing scandal. Come the indictment, these little items would be frosting on the cake.

So Luisa sang. And Michael smiled. And the United States Government had found its unimpeachable witness.

There was hardly a front page in America that didn't give prominent display to the photo of Zametti emerging from court. He'd broken away from his escort just long enough to clap his left hand over his right arm and raise his right fist toward the sky—a gesture Bostonians had not enjoyed since the palmy days when Ted Williams cursed antagonists in Fenway Park.

Whether Zametti's imprecation was aimed at the fickle Luisa or the tenacious prosecuting attorney, who could say?

But there wasn't a picture editor in the country who could pass up such a splendid shot. And in most of the New England newspapers, plus a number of the national magazines, one might also find an accompanying shot of a handsome man with a radiant smile, jacket slung debonairly over one shoulder, tripping gaily down the courthouse steps. "Boston Mafia-Buster Mike Matheson," read the caption in *Time* magazine. He looked delicious.

Michael was radiantly happy with the outcome of U.S. vs. Zametti and its attendant publicity. ("Better than Littlemarch," he was fond of saying to his wife.) And when Michael was happy, Kit—though perhaps not equally euphoric—was at least less unhappy. For one thing, her husband was almost never home now, his new-found fame paying off in political—if not cash—dividends. True, the cash would have come in handy, for they were living up to every penny of Michael's income, while other lawyers his age were making a fortune in private practice. But if adulation were the coin of the realm, then Michael was very rich indeed. Hardly a week passed without a speaking engagement somewhere in the area; hardly a night in which the phone didn't ring a dozen times requesting his sympathy, his expertise and sometimes his presence.

He had oratory for every occasion, his primary themes being *A Return to Law and Order* with its closing paragraphs pleading for a revival of capital punishment: *Only You Can Stop the Mafia* ("Every time you place a bet, you're betting on *them!*"); and for more sophisticated audiences, *Crime Without Punishment*, an effective argument for the complete overhaul of the American judiciary. Everybody loved Michael. The women of Hadassah applauded his unflinching support for the State of Israel. He always made a point of referring to "the Judaeo-Christian traditions upon which this country was founded." The Sons of Hibernia clutched Michael to its collective bosom for his advocacy of legislation that would permit the flow of Federal funds to parochial schools. And in spite of—or perhaps because of—the Zametti case, he was the darling of the Knights of Columbus. And though he made no reappearances in *Time* magazine, his speaking engagements usually generated publicity in such news media as the *North Shore Courier* and the American Legion newsletters.

One afternoon, a few weeks after Zametti, a pretty little features editor from a local paper came around to interview Kit for the women's page. "What's it like," she asked, "being married to the second most attractive man in Massachusetts?" The first, presumably, was Ted Kennedy. Kit had smiled and reddened and mumbled something about its being "kind of hectic." The girl from the paper had smiled knowingly and then had asked Kit for her favorite dinner party recipes. When the interviewer had gone, no doubt carrying with her an image of a busy and beloved housewife, Kit asked herself the same question. *What's it like being married to Michael Matheson?* She imagined the shock on the girl's little chipmunk face had she answered, "We haven't slept together in six years." Of course, Kit would never have said such a thing, and even in her own mind dwelt upon "that part" of marriage as little as possible. She suspected it was overrated. Yet how could one *not* think about it from time to time, when the images were everywhere—the new explicitness in books, in movies, even in TV commercials for blue jeans. She was struck by the greater frankness with which women talked these days, including quite nice women—women of her own generation. She was no longer so naive as to assume that their marriage, even in its earlier, happier days, had been sexually varied or fulfilling. In tacit agreement both she and her husband stepped back from the quagmire that any discussion of their sex life would entail. She sometimes wondered if it were some quality in her, some deep-rooted frigidity, that was the cause of Michael's impotence; or whether it was the other way around. Occasionally she'd see other couples go home from dinner parties, long-married couples, too; and there would be about them a certain glow, a sense of intimacy so sharp you could almost smell it; the distinctive look of two people who could hardly wait to get in bed with each other. She envied them. She felt cheated. And yet the thought of Michael making love to her filled her with revulsion.

Her world was the world of women—women friends, women's organizations, her daughter, her daughter's girl friends. Even Moses, their cat, was female.

Curiously, Michael was fond of flirting at dinner parties in a generalized and (to Kit) patently insincere manner, particularly if he'd had a few drinks. Teenage daughters, visiting aunts, wives of long-term colleagues—all were beneficiaries of Michael's sometimes extravagant flattery. But Kit knew, even if the recipients didn't, that the sweet words and the glowing smiles were simply "buttering up" rather than any serious sexual overture. She'd seen him work the same trick at women's organization meetings, be they Hadassah or D.A.R.

To Kit, the wonder of it was that nobody saw through Michael. Like the last Duchess in Browning's poem, he had "a heart . . . too soon made glad." His smiles were indiscriminate; his flattery, though always tailored to the woman or the occasion, skimmed the surface of the surface. And while he demonstrated a certain aptitude, a quickness to recognize the button of special interest and push it accordingly, Michael struck Kit as basically insensitive. Two-dimensional. A machine programmed to make appropriate responses. Certainly, he had no insights where Kit was concerned, no inkling of her deepest thoughts and feelings. He had, she recognized, neither curiosity nor comprehension about her own inner life.

He still brought his cases home from the office, discussed them freely with her. She knew he valued her opinion in many areas, welcomed her occasional insights. "I should give you a medal for Zametti," he'd said, although he'd given her flowers instead, acknowledging that her offhand remark about Italian family feeling had led to the break in the case.

But though he frequently plumbed her mind—she didn't care, she quite enjoyed it—he never tried to plumb her emotions. Never asked her if the hurt of Monk had healed. Never recalled her abortive flight to Florida. Their marriage was full of darknesses, of treacherous quicksands. One false step and the whole elaborate structure would sink without a trace. Sex . . . Monk . . . love . . . loneliness: they were the "no go" areas of their relationship, near which neither of them dared to venture.

More than once Kit was struck by the resemblance between their marriage and that of her parents. A sense of history repeating itself.

Like Emily, Kit knew her husband perfectly.

For years, she had studied him in detail—his tastes, his prejudices, his weaknesses—studied him the way a prisoner might study his jailer, upon whose whims and good will he was dependent. She neither invited his confidences, nor discouraged them when they were volunteered; and though Michael never conferred with her on the making of those decisions that he viewed as his alone, he frequently used her as a sounding board.

So it was with some surprise, when the 1972 primaries were moving into gear, that he told her that he had decided not to run for Congress from their district. In fact, he had never bothered to inform her that the place on the Democratic ticket had been offered. Never asked her to advise and consent.

"But I always assumed you wanted to go to Washington," she said after her initial astonishment.

"Oh, I do. I surely do, and that's precisely why I turned it down. All you have to do is look at the records and you'd know this district hasn't elected a Democrat since '36. And they sure as hell ain't gonna this year. Take it from me . . . it's going to be a Nixon landslide, and the only place I could go on McGovern's coattails is down the toilet. Well, I can't see us spending fifty, sixty thousand bucks for *that* privilege."

"Us?" Kit said.

"*Us.* You and me."

"But doesn't the party pay the cost of campaigning? Doesn't it come out of public funds?"

Michael snorted. "The bare minimum, that's all you get from the party. The bare minimum. Believe me, hon, it costs more than a train ticket to get a man to Washington. Look at Ted Kennedy, for Chrissakes. You don't see an awful lot of paupers on Capitol Hill. No," he mused, "before I spend that kind of money on an election campaign, I want to be pretty goddamn sure I'll be coming up roses."

That kind of money. They had less then $3000 in their joint account. Kit felt a tremor of unease.

"I'm sure you made the right decision, Michael," she said. "And anyhow, I don't think I'd much like living in Washington."

KATE

THE PLANE WOULD BE LATE COMING OUT OF NEW YORK, they told her when she checked in at Kennedy. Fogged in at the other end. Kate strode furiously into the first-class lounge. Why do they always pull that? Tell you on the phone they're going to leave on time so you race out to the airport when the goddamn plane hasn't even come in yet and you could've slept another couple of hours. If she ever had a crack at an airline account, she knew what the ads would be. "Welcome to No-Shit Airways." *Don't call us. We'll call you. Tell you when the planes are running late. And that's no shit.*

She got a Campari from the bar and looked around to see if there were any interesting pickings in what Barry called "the male companionship line." As usual, she was the only woman in the first-class lounge, and as usual the men ran to beautifully barbered corporate types. DuPont zombies, Wall Street robots—you can't tell the players without a score card. Neat men in neat suits with neat attaché cases, leaving behind neat wives in Old Greenwich and Pound Ridge. Four of them had commandeered the largest table and covered it with neat charts, neat graphs. *Can't start the business day too early, buddies, can you?*

She took another look around and then she spotted him,

sitting alone by the window, munching Cheezits in an absent-minded fashion. Late forties, Kate thought, maybe more, maybe less. In need of a haircut. But she liked his looks, almost scruffy in a worn tweed jacket of a peculiar mustard shade. The seat next to him was unoccupied except for an enormous old-fashioned briefcase. OK, not exactly an ad for Tailor and Cutter, but better than the DuPont zombies. English, probably. Only the English managed to look so tacky with such blithe unconcern.

"Is someone sitting here?"

"Oh, sorry." He hardly looked up. "Let me get this out of the way." He removed the offending briefcase, then returned to his examination of the empty runways.

She sipped her drink for a minute in silence. Not exactly the friendly type, but what the hell . . . she'd give him one more opening.

"Do you know how late the London flight's going to be?"

This time he turned and gave her his full attention. He had frank blue eyes, very bright, and a wide generous mouth full of humor.

"They never tell you," he said, shaking his head gravely. "They are sworn not to tell you. They have special schools where they train people in the art of not telling you."

"I see," Kate said. "Torture will get you nowhere. Pull my nails. Tickle my instep. I vill not talk, *mein Kommandant*. Like that?"

He laughed. "Exactly." He pushed the bowl of Cheezits toward her. "Compliments of TWA. Is this your first trip to London?"

"I've been there a couple of times over the last few years on holiday, as you British say. But this time I'm going there to work."

"Nonsense. Nobody works in London." He glanced over at the zombies. "At least not like you Yanks. You'll find London is the Xanadu of the twentieth century. Do you know anyone there?"

"A few business acquaintances, and I imagine I'll be meeting people through the office."

"Yes, the natives are very friendly—especially to pretty women."

He was amusing. She liked him. And she was pleased that when their flight was finally called, he asked if they might sit together. "Unless you're planning to do very efficient things with charts like your fellow countrymen." He nodded to the zombie table, where a furious reassembly of graphs was going on.

"Absolutely not."

By the time they boarded, her anger at TWA's tardiness had fully vanished, and she was quite looking forward to the next six hours.

He did, she gathered, something mathematical at Cambridge, and was just coming back from a seminar at the Courant Institute at NYU. Kate told him a bit about her work in advertising and her plans for the London office.

"Sounds very interesting," he said in a tone that led her to doubt he found it in any way interesting.

He told her he had a son studying chemistry at UCLA, a married daughter in Edinburgh and a sister who lived near Albert Hall and illustrated children's books. There was no mention of a wife—living, divorced, or dead—and Kate felt it would be gross to ask the question. They discovered they shared a passion for the novels of Henry James and an aversion to Neil Simon comedies. Lunch came and, in the manner of Eastbound flights, dinner followed with hardly a break. The intercom announcement that they were approaching Heathrow took Kate by surprise.

"I'll be taking a taxi into the city. Can I give you a lift somewhere?"

"That's very kind of you, but I have a student waiting for me at the airport and he's going to run me straight back to Cambridge."

She hoped her voice masked her disappointment. "Your students must be very fond of you."

"Very fond of me, or very much afraid of me. And I sometimes suspect the latter. However, I do get into London every now and again, and perhaps next time I come you'll let me take you to dinner."

She hesitated for a moment and he misread her pause.

"I'm a perfectly respectable widower, by the way."

"Oh, it's not that." There was relief in her laughter. "It's just that you never told me your name."

"It's Hetherington. Richard Hetherington."

Kate gave him her name and her office phone number, which he jotted down in a little leather diary. They separated in the terminal, Richard to a line labeled U.K. AND COM-

MONWEALTH ONLY, she to a longer line that welcomed ALL OTHERS.

It was after midnight when the taxi pulled up at a red-brick service building in South Kensington. The flat the company had found for her was handsome in a turn-of-the-century way. High-ceilinged, wide-windowed, with a large bedroom and a larger living room furnished right down to the color television set. There was an old-fashioned bathroom, dowdy but comfortable, with an absolutely enormous tub. No shower. Damn. The kitchen was just adequate, but Kate wasn't planning to spend much time in it, anyway. She noticed that someone had stocked it with bread and instant coffee. She made herself a Nescafé and took it into the living room. Or would it be a sitting room? She must start thinking English. And start thinking J.S. Atherton Advertising.

She unpacked her briefcase—her clothes could wait—and began leafing through the material Ron Maxwell had given her. From that very first interview in New York, he'd been highly cautionary.

"Before we go any further, I think you should know exactly what you're getting into. Frankly, it's the most fucked-up foreign branch we have. Beats me why. We pay top money. We have lots of talent, but nothing ever comes out right. They've lost over two million pounds of billings in the last few months, and that's a lot for a London agency. Believe me, its with reluctance that we decided to import someone from New York, bring in an outsider. The locals aren't going to like it very much.

"I imagine not."

"So if you take the job, don't go expecting roses."

"If I wanted to win popularity contests, I'd try out for Miss America. Who would I report to?"

"Directly back to me."

"Not to the London manager?" Kate arched her eyebrows. It must be some cute setup if she could bypass the man ostensibly in charge. She liked that. "And I'd be free to hire and fire."

"Yup."

Kate understood. Completely. They were looking for a hatchet man to send to London. An outside avenger, free of old associations and niggling sentimental qualms, of pints of beer shared, of family visits exchanged; an outsider empowered to cleanse, scourge and even execute when necessary, while the higher-ups looked on in mock horror and protested their innocence of all this nasty New York-style bloodshed. Hatchet-man! Hit-man was more like it, but Kate had never numbered herself among the squeamish. "As long as I'm free."

"Of course," Ron had said, "you'd have to work out the personnel problems with Derek Taylor." Up shot the eyebrow again, but Ron was reassuring. "Don't worry about Derek. He's the accounts supervisor, been there for dogs' years, very popular with the staff. They tell me he's very good."

"If he's all that good, how'd he let the agency get in such rotten shape?"

"That would be for you to find out. Are you interested?"

Interested? That was hardly the word. Desperate was more like it, for change had now become a necessity. She wanted nothing so passionately, so urgently, as to pull up her life by its roots and start all over. As though these last years had never happened.

London. It would put three thousand miles between her and the ghost of Wolf's love.

"Yes," she said, giving a slight involuntary shudder. "I'm interested."

Over half a dozen successive meetings they sorted out the details. Money. Housing arrangements. Best way to beat the tax men of both continents. The works. And so here she was, four weeks later, sitting in a furnished flat in South Kensington looking at her watch. It was two in the morning. Tomorrow was Sunday. She'd sleep all day and be fresh and ready Monday at nine o'clock.

Briefcased and bushy-tailed, Kate arrived at Atherton's at quarter past nine. Give 'em a chance to catch their breath. For some reason, the door was locked. She knocked, rang, wondered if she'd come to the right address, banged on the door for another several minutes. Finally a commissionaire, his chest full of World War II ribbons, opened up. He blinked at her like Rip Van Winkle waking from a twenty-year snooze.

"I'm Miss Chapman, the new creative director from New York."

"I wouldn't know, miss."

"This *is* Atherton's, isn't it?" she inquired crisply. "The advertising agency?"

He nodded yes.

"And nobody's in yet? Not even the switchboard operator? The receptionist?" Kate couldn't believe it.

"The receptionist gets in at nine-thirty, miss."

"And what about the rest of the cast? Don't tell me." She swept past him into the building. "I'll find out for myself."

Inside it looked like a normal advertising agency. Ground floor: reception desk, waiting room, file rooms, research library. Up the stairs: creative department here, she could see, with the usual heaving mess of layouts and storyboards, the acrid smell of Magic Markers, the nude promotion calendars on the walls. It looked pretty much like any other art department except for one small detail—no moving bodies.

She found a door with her name on it, hung up her coat, sat down on the swivel chair and waited. And waited. It was twenty to ten before she heard the first sounds of motion in the corridor. She opened the door and peered out. A gaggle of secretaries had arrived, like a swarm of heavy-footed gnats, each bearing a plastic container of coffee.

"I'm Kate Chapman. Which one of you is mine?"

A short pudgy girl detached herself from the swarm and clomped over in a noisy trot. Bursting blue jeans stuffed into cowboy boots. Kate winced.

"Good morning, Miss Chapman. We weren't expecting you so early. My name is Joyce, and I'm your secretary."

"Very good. I'd like you to get me some coffee—black, no sugar—then come into my office. What time does the rest of the gang get here?"

"The rest of the gang?"

"The other employees, Joyce." Kate enunciated each syllable. "The lowly folk who empty ashtrays and answer phones. The people who presumably inhabit these offices during working hours and feed from the company trough. The writers. The art directors. The account people. Mr. Taylor. Savvy?"

"Oh, they start coming in about ten. A little later on Monday."

"Why later on Monday?"

"Because of the weekend, Miss Chapman."

"The weekend. Where I come from, the weekend stops at midnight on Sunday. I thought we Americans shared the same calendar as well as the same language. Now, Joyce, I'd like you to prepare a memo. You *do* take shorthand, don't you?" Joyce scurried out and returned with her pad. "Fine." Kate sipped away. "Now I'll tell you what I want to say and you can work out the wording. I want every creative person in this agency to pull their best work together and make up a portfolio that they think will do them justice. I also want them to include their five most recent ads, whether or not they think them fair samples. They are to treat this—and you are to make this abundantly clear—as if they were being interviewed for a new job. Then I want you to make appointments with them to see me . . . I think we can allow a half-hour per person. How many people are we talking about, Joyce? Twenty? Thirty?"

"About thirty, Miss Chapman."

"Fine, I'll give them all this week to get it together and I'll start interviewing next Monday morning. Beginning at nine o'clock sharp. Got it? OK. That memo is to be distributed to all copywriters, art directors, layout men, supervisors, TV producers—all of them without exception."

"Including senior people?"

"Without exception, Joyce." Kate finished her coffee and reached for her briefcase. "That's it for now. Let me know when Derek Taylor arrives."

Joyce got up, folded her pad and hesitated by the door.

"Yes, what is it, Joyce?"

"Well, Miss Chapman . . ." The girl was visibly mustering her courage. "It's just that some of the people you're asking for interviews have been here for years and years . . ."

"And if they're worth their salt, they have nothing to worry about."

What was it that Englishman had said on the plane about London being Xanadu? He knew whereof he spoke, obviously, and Kate wondered mildly if she would ever hear from him again.

Richard came down to London a couple of weekends later, and after that almost every weekend, arriving Friday night and going back Sunday evening. Kate knew it was only to see her. The better she knew him, the better she liked him, and the easy affability which had struck her on the flight seemed a constant of his disposition. He was a man of broad, if not comprehensive, culture, with a casual interest in sports, a keen interest in politics and a knowledge of literature that quite amazed Kate in both its range and its complexity. But his ruling passion—outside of the inevitable mathematics—was music. Their weekends were usually structured around an evening at Covent Garden, or piano recitals on the South Bank, or chamber music wherever it could be found. He knew the Beethoven quartets the way a schoolboy knows his five-times table, and once admitted to a childhood fancy for a career as a violinist.

Because she liked him, she made a conscious effort to adapt herself to his particular interests. What she didn't know, she could learn. It was this characteristic, after all, that had formed the basis of her success in advertising: an ability, a flexibility, to interest herself profoundly in whatever matter was on hand, be it dog food, color-printing processes or—her current business problems—the chemistry of perfume and the physiology of scent.

She bought herself a Grundig stereo and, under Richard's tutelage, gradually acquired a knowledge and abiding love of the chamber-music repertoire. The one area of his life from which she was barred was the nature of his work. What exactly did Richard *do* all week long in Cambridge? It puzzled her. She knew it was something vastly more complex than shuffling figures around on a blackboard (he did the theoretical work *only,* he told her). Mathematics, even on its crudest level, had always been a sore point with her. She recalled her inability to cope with simple algebra back in her days at boarding school. With aversion, she remembered that loathsome Farmer Brown bringing his x amount of apples and his y amount of pears to the market; even now it was all she could do to balance her bank statement within a hundred dollars here or there. As a rule she rounded off to the nearest zero and called it a day.

Yet she knew Richard's work was the backbone of his life. She worried that her relationship to him would never be quite whole, never be sufficient in *his* eyes until she had a grasp, however minimal, of the texture of his days. She asked him time and again, but he usually put her off with a good-natured "it's awfully technical," or "it would bore you terrifically." Finally, one Friday evening over coffee at Quaglino's she cornered him. "Just tell me, for instance, what you were working on this morning."

"This morning," he replied, "I was working on negative numbers."

"Negative numbers?"

"Well, the lay term is imaginary numbers."

"Imaginary!" Kate looked at him sharply.

Richard laughed. "Of course, that's long been a point of contention. Leibnitz called them 'a flight of God's spirit.' What were his exact words? Oh, yes . . . 'Imaginary numbers are an amphibian between being and not being.' Let me put it to you simply."

He did. Simply for him, that is, and she listened in a growing tide of incomprehension. He might as well have been reading the telephone book in Swahili.

"Well, *that*, of course," he concluded at the end of five minutes, "is putting it in layman's terms. The actual work is a deal more complicated."

"You know, I didn't understand a word you said," she sighed, thoroughly disgusted with herself.

"Of course you didn't," Richard said, patting her hand. "Most of my students don't. Sometimes even *I* don't."

"But what's the practical application?" she asked.

"There isn't any," he said cheerfully. "Not in your sense of the word. Occasionally applied scientists find a functional application for theoretical work, very often they don't. Either way, it has nothing to do with me."

"Now I understand even less."

"Kate, that's the difference between applied and pure mathematics. Art for art's sake and all that. There are lots of clever people, women in particular, who have no gift for theoretical concepts."

"I don't believe that for a minute," she said, although she'd heard it before.

"Whether you believe it or not doesn't alter the fact. Women are physiologically different from men. Their brains are different. Their bodies are different." He took her hand and kissed her fingertips. "And I, for one, am very glad of it."

"Vive la différence?" she smiled.
"Vive la différence."

They remained friends and became lovers. Kate was pleasurably surprised with his performance in bed. Perhaps not quite on the scale of passion she had known with Wolf, but he was tender, imaginative and, above all, considerate.

He also had a delicious sense of the absurd.

They had gone one evening to the austere National Theatre to see one of the weightier Norwegian dramas.

On stage, tragedy piled upon starkest tragedy: sickness . . . incest . . . poverty . . . torment. No human depth remained unplumbed. And when it seemed that the gamut of agony must now surely be exhausted, a lugubrious voice intoned: "Father, they have come to take away the furniture."

Kate heard a muffled snort and turning, discovered Richard in paroxysms of suppressed laughter. She answered with a giggle. He responded with a guffaw. And within minutes the two of them were being unceremoniously escorted from the theatre amid a sea of shhhs and outraged eyes. By the time they reached the door, they were howling like zanies. "What I love about you," she said as he flagged down a cab, "is your absolutely crazy sense of humor."

"What I love about you," he kissed her into the taxi, "is everything."

"In that case, let's go home and go to bed."

She was, she realized, more sexually knowledgeable than he, at least in the varieties of her experience. It didn't bother her in the least, for he gave her great joy; yet she was wary lest some aspect of her lovemaking would unwittingly reveal a sexual sophistication that bordered on the lurid.

One Friday he'd come down to London in a state of near-exhaustion. Apparently not even a Cambridge life was free of stress.

And though he'd dutifully taken her out to dinner, she could see his eyes were heavy with fatigue.

"What I'd like if you don't mind, Kate, is just to go back to your flat and lie down." She didn't mind, she assured him, and no sooner had they come home when he sprawled out on the bed fully clothed.

Gently Kate took off his shoes, his socks; unbuttoned his shirt; slithered off his pants and shorts. Then kissed him lightly on the lips.

"Not tonight, darling," he made his apologies. "Right now I'm too tired to make love."

"You don't have to," she said. "I will make love to you."

She washed and undressed and when she reentered the room, Richard was all but asleep. She kissed his closed eyelids. Then, crouching over him like a cat on all fours, she began running her breasts over his thighs, teasing his hairs with her nipples, caressing his cock with vaselined fingers. She could feel him stir, grow hard beneath her hands.

"Now just keep your eyes shut, my love, and I will make you happy."

With that she slid her smooth fingers between his buttocks and gently massaged the opening of his anus. He was trembling with pleasure, she noted delightedly. Why not? Men had pleasured *her* that way. Then, running her tongue up the length of his cock, she placed him little by little into her mouth. Her lips kept rhythm with her fingers, her tongue darting over the tip of his penis. Slowly, soundlessly, she worked him deep into her mouth, worked her fingers deep into his body, until at last he came with a great shout of ecstasy. Reared up. And as suddenly fell back.

"My God, darling," he said to her afterwards. "Where did you ever learn to give such pleasure."

"I learned it," she lied softly, "from you."

After awhile, she stopped thinking of it as fucking or balling or screwing. She began to think of it as making love, something she hadn't done in a long time. Increasingly, she looked forward to their weekends with happy anticipation, a break that seemed more than ever necessary from the rigors of the office. For things were not going well there. Not well at all.

Within a matter of weeks, Kate had sorted out the thirty-one odd bodies who constituted the creative staff of Atherton's, and having mentally winnowed the hotshots from the hopeless, proceeded to lay her plans for what would eventually be known as the Great Atherton Blood Bath. Not that all of them were losers; Kate had found a lot of talent lurking behind the typewriters and drawing boards. Straightaway, she pegged five employees for handsome pay raises. There was one girl in particular, a carrot-top from Glasgow named Jeannie with an accent thick as haggis, who wrote like an angel. Only twenty-two, but the kid had the stuff.

The problems, Kate discerned, lay largely with the higher-ups, old employees whose berths were so secure they'd come to think of the agency as a rest home. Coasting. In Madison Avenue, they would have been out on the street years ago, but the English, Kate discovered, were a softer race. Nobody pushed. Nobody competed. Nobody let advertising interfere with their tea breaks. The usual response to all hell breaking loose was "Not to worry."

But Kate worried, and she didn't plan to worry alone. Shape up or ship out—that was going to be her message. She finally drew up her "death list." The only person she'd have to take into her confidence was Derek Taylor.

As she'd been told in New York, everybody liked Derek. Kate liked him, too—a tall, lanky Etonian with old-fashioned manners, the kind of man who stands up when a woman comes into the room. So having completed her strategy, she invited him to lunch. Roast beef and trimmings at Simpson's; that should make him mellow.

"I suppose you're wondering why I've asked you here today." Her smile was as sweet as the dessert.

"I've got a pretty good idea. How bad is it?"

No point in horsing around, she could see, so she handed over the death list. It was numbered in order of preference for firing. He scanned it, then handed it back to her.

"That's not trimming the flab, Kate. That's mass murder. You're talking about firing one in three."

Kate sighed her this-hurts-me-more-than-this-hurts-you sigh. "Derek, don't think I'm enjoying this, but Atherton's either reshapes drastically or it goes down the drain, with you and me as the primary casualties. Let's discuss the names one by one and see if we can't reach some kind of accommodation."

"OK." He took the list back. "Let's start with your number-one victim. John Howarth. You can't really be serious about firing old John. OK, I appreciate that he's a little old-hat. Maybe you can shift him around a little bit. The man's only four years away from his pension and he'll never find another job. Never. So can't you hang on a few years and leave the man with some dignity?"

They haggled about Howarth for a good half-hour, and Kate wound up using him for a negotiating counter. OK, Howarth could stay (for now was her mental proviso), but only if Kate had a free hand with the rest. The lunch concluded on a dissonant note, and Kate realized her ultimate problem would not be diddling John Howarth. It would be Derek himself.

A few weeks later, Derek Taylor stormed into her office. "That was a rotten thing you did to John Howarth. Absolutely rotten."

"What?" Kate was all innocence. "You asked me not to fire him, and I didn't."

"To make a fifty-six-year-old man report to a twenty-two-year-old girl. By my reckoning, that's rotten."

"Oh, come on. Jeannie is terrific. She might even be able to teach him a thing or two. What is it you don't like about the situation . . . the idea of a man reporting to a woman? Does that put you off?"

"That's not what bothers me, Kate. The fact is, I never think of you as a woman." He gave her a chilly smile. "You've got balls."

She returned his smile with an even colder one.

And I'm going to have yours one of these days.

Richard was always after her to come up to Cambridge. "Come beard me in my den," he'd say. But though he'd put it gaily, she suspected some more serious intent. Suspected that he was auditioning her for a more serious role in his life, trying to place her in his own perspective, to set her off against his own patterns of friendship to see if she fitted or floundered.

I'm on approval, she thought on the train from King's Cross, like a packet of mail-order postage stamps. But Richard was on approval, too, and she was openly curious about how he would appear in his own environment. She wondered what his house would be like? A half-timbered relic? Something rustic and folksy? Or would it be mathematically modern? How little she knew—only that he lived alone and dined most evenings at the High Table.

He was waiting with an umbrella at the platform, and any lingering apprehensions vanished in the warmth of his welcome. "You look marvelous, darling," he said, bundling her into the Rover. "A treat for tired eyes." And Kate gave a small inner amen of relief.

His house, however, was not a treat for tired eyes. An

unattractive pile of Victorian red brick set squarely in an
untended garden, it looked formidable rather than imposing.

"Welcome to Castle Dracula." He had sensed her disappointment. "It's not as bad inside as outside."

Well, not quite. He had for the occasion laid on a crackling
fire in the sitting room, and it was definitely a room one could
live in. A pleasant chaos of books, books and more books,
sofas and easy chairs verging on the shabby, odd bits of china,
an ivory screen and an oriental rug that took her breath away.

"Shall I show you around?"

"Please."

There were nine or ten rooms in all, but only three showed
signs of his occupation. The sitting room, and leading off it a
long rectangular study with one wall of French windows and
the remaining three walls of floor-to-ceiling bookshelves. She
looked at what must have been thousands of books—in
English, French, Russian, German. The titles dealt almost
exclusively with mathematics. She opened one at random, a
handsome maroon-leather volume. It bore the imprint of
Brucke Gesellschaft. She snapped the book shut.

"I had no idea the literature was so enormous."

And then his bedroom upstairs. Books here, too. On the
shelves. On the dresser. Lying open on the night table. *The
Waning of the Middle Ages*—Huizinga. Well, everybody's
entitled to a little light reading. She noticed that the bed was
made up for two, pillows side by side, the sheets already
turned back.

She was pleased. At least he didn't have qualms about
offending the locals; she knew there was a Mrs. Plumm who
came in to "do."

All the other rooms were dead and silent: the somber
formal dining room; the bedrooms nursing memories of
another woman's mortality, of children long grown up and
flown away.

They ate before the open fire while he told her what he'd
planned for the weekend. Tomorrow morning they'd make a
tour of the Colleges; a dinner party in the evening; Sunday a
picnic in the fens or, if the weather was bad, they could lunch
at a country pub.

It all sounded pleasant, and Kate was smiling as she
climbed into bed. But not smiling once she got between the
sheets. "Cold" would have been too cosy a term for it—the

sheets were glacial, Arctic, icy, polar, Siberian; the word
hadn't been invented to encapsulate their chill. "My God,
Richard," she cried in anguish.

"Oh, is it cold?" He climbed in beside her cheerfully.
"Don't worry darling. I'll keep you warm."

Later she lay in the crook of Richard's arm—warm now,
and contented, watching fondly as his chest rose and fell in
sleep.

She could go farther and do worse, she thought. But no,
she failed to do him justice. No question, Richard was good.
Good *to* her. Good *for* her. He softened the hard edges of her
life; he was her refuge. And perhaps she in her way was good
for him, bringing him an excitement he had never known
before. He thought her funny, charming, glamorous; she
lifted his spirits from the rigor of work.

And yet it was strange lying here in this bed where he had
lain so many years with his wife. Where he had loved and
fathered children. Led a life so different from her own.
Momentarily she felt like an intruder in his house. For what
could she and Richard ever be to each other except the lovers
they already were? It was so much easier to share a body than
a life, so much easier to walk away unscathed.

Yet she loved him. Not quite the way she once had loved
Wolf, for you could never love the same way twice.

Her mind darted back to that instant in the library when
she picked up the Brucke Gesellschaft book. Wolf. Polly.
What a nightmare that had been. And what a nightmare it
had led to. Suddenly the burden of her past seemed intolera-
ble. She burrowed deeper into Richard's arms and shut her
eyes against yesterday's images.

As for Richard, she would wait and see.

The next day he showed her his rooms at Trinity ("founded
before Chaucer wrote the *Canterbury Tales*"); had the porter
unlock the Cavendish Lab ("this is where Chadwick discovered the neutron"); elucidated on the fan-vaulted ceilings of
King's College Chapel; fed her tea and "squashy" cakes at
the Copper Kettle; even tried his hand at punting on the
Cam. He was proud of Cambridge and eager to have her
share in its beauty and traditions. But in all the Cambridge
complex, what struck Kate most was Richard's place in it.
Students held doors open, porters sprang to, even fellow dons
went out of their way to be agreeable. Richard took it all as
his due.

No doubt about it, Richard Hetherington was what they used to call in Boston "the campus catch."

"Where do you hide your televison set?" she asked a few weeks later.

"My television set?" Richard frowned. "I don't think I have one."

"Oh?"

"I think I used to," he recalled, "but it broke down a few years ago, and I never got around to replacing it. Something you wanted to watch?"

"Actually, I have a beer commercial running on *Upstairs, Downstairs,* but no matter. I can catch it some other time."

When next she came to Cambridge, he had a little Sony color set installed in the bedroom. They watched an old Bela Lugosi film in bed that Saturday night, and nibbled on cheese and Huntley & Palmer biscuits. It was quite pleasant. Richard was sweetening the pot.

London was always a letdown after their weekends. For while the parry and thrust of office politics engaged her days, the evenings were long and lonely. She missed Barry, with his tart gossip and good-natured bitchiness, but in the current climate at Atherton's it seemed unlikely she would find another such intimate among her colleagues. After office hours, they avoided her like Typhoid Mary.

Occasionally she'd go alone to the theater or take in a concert by some violinist whom Richard had talked about so she could call him and tell him about it. Their phone calls were the highlight of her week.

For the most part she spent her evenings in the flat, wishing away the hours till bedtime. She'd read. Watch television. Pick at odd bits of leftover work. Sometimes even kill an hour or two playing solitaire.

KIT

THERE ARE OVER TWO DOZEN DIFFERENT KINDS OF SOLITAIRE. Most are played with one pack of cards, some require two, and there are several varieties that call for picture cards only. The names are as diverse as the rules: Kings, Castles in Spain, Monte Carlo, The Lady of Sark's Delight. There are certain variations that simply refuse to be won, that defy all the mathematical odds. And after a while, Kit ruled those out. She preferred the kind that, though they offer a challenge, nonetheless hold at least the promise of occasional victory.

She never cheated. Not even when she flipped a card face-up inadvertently. What would be the point if you cheated? She scorned cheap victories; they would have merely spoiled the pleasure of her all-too-rare honest triumphs.

You wouldn't think solitaire could be so fascinating. Kit certainly hadn't—at least not up until about a year ago. About the time that Sarah went off to boarding school, and Marian moved to upstate New York for a teaching job at Vassar.

At first, Kit had felt sinful about her sessions with the cards, but there's just a limit to how much you can read, how clean you can get the house. And she drew the line at watching daytime TV. Summers she didn't play much: she had her gardening then, her days at the beach. Sarah was often about somewhere, too, although the days when Sarah looked to her mother for her main source of companionship were long gone.

But winters—winters were something else. New England winters were harder than they used to be, Kit thought, and she hated the whole idea of plowing out, putting chains on the tires, skidding on the ice that lined the lake road. For what? So she could sit around at some stupid club meeting, listening to the same old yatter from the same old women? Even shopping in winter had become a trial. She hardly ever went into Boston.

On the whole, Kit preferred the comfort of her sun room, the companionship of Moses the cat and the challenge of the "fifty-two men," whose variety was infinite. You could deal the same deck of cards five thousand times running and never once come up with the same combination. How many people could you say that about? And when you were playing, time just sped by.

Nonetheless, solitaire remained a secret vice. Like solitary drinking, it was the sort of closet practice you wouldn't dream of owning up to, not even to a friend. And when she played, she always kept an ear out for the doorbell, for the sound of a car pulling up in the drive, lest someone discover her at her shameful indulgence. At the first signal of approaching callers, she would break off the game, shoving the cards together—some face-up, some face-down—and jam them in the drawer of the sewing table.

She should go out more, she told herself quite often. And Michael was always after her to accompany him at one or another of his speaking engagements. It looked good, he said; but she loathed the whole process. She felt lumpish and exposed sitting up there behind him on the platform, afraid to cross her legs in case she revealed too much thigh, trying to look interested and adoring when she only felt glazed. And the business of smiling and smiling at people she didn't know, didn't want to know. "How much can it cost you to sit there and smile?" Michael would say. To appease him, she'd go now and then. But each time was with increasing reluctance; thus each invitation constituted the basis of an argument, with Michael viewing himself as the aggrieved party.

At least she had the days to herself, free of commitments and bickering. Free for herself and her solitaire. To make it more interesting, she'd devise little contests, pretending each card won or lost was a dollar. You could make fortunes that way or lose the shirt off your back, and sometimes when the run of cards was poor, she'd get depressed.

But you could also use the cards to help with minor decisions; even pretend they shaped the outcome of events. If I get more than ten cards up this hand, I'll make *quiche Lorraine* for dinner. If I win the next three out of five, that means Sarah will make the honor roll.

And so she spent the long afternoons playing solitaire.

Solitaire.

The English name for it is "Patience."

KATE

SHE'D GO UP TO CAMBRIDGE ABOUT ONCE A MONTH, SOMEtimes because Richard was too busy to come down, sometimes simply to show that she, too, was willing to make concessions. The weekends fell into a pattern, lazy to the point of domesticity.

His colleagues were friendly and unfailingly kind, but she was realist enough to know their kindness was not because Kate was Kate, but because Richard was Richard. She teased him about it once, saying that they were the prince and the showgirl and suspected that his denial, though commendably prompt, was not heartfelt.

Most of all, she treasured their hours alone.

And so it was that on a spring afternoon, the windows open to the thick smell of lilacs, they sat over Scrabble and coffee. Like an old married couple, she thought.

"Zed, ee, em, ee." Richard placed the tiles down triumphantly. "Zeme. That's nineteen points."

"I never heard of a zeme. You made it up."

"I did not."

"You promised not to use technical words."

"It is not a technical word." Richard looked injured. "It's a seagull . . . no, wait, it's not a seagull. It's . . ." He fished around in his capacious mind for a moment.

"It zemes to me . . . ?" Kate offered.

"Ah, now I remember. It's a magic spirit, rather like a banshee. I believe it haunts in the Caribbean."

"In which case it's a proper noun and doesn't count."

"It's not a proper noun any more than a banshee is."

"Come on, Richard. Confess you made it up."

"You just don't like to admit when you're beaten, Kate. Why don't you challenge me?" The phone rang. "You look it up in Oxford while I get the phone."

She was halfway through the Z's when she heard him on the hall phone sounding for all the world like a dustman who's just won the sweepstakes.

"Werner! How absolutely marvelous!"

There it was: *zeme:* a West Indian fetish or guardian spirit. And lower case into the bargain.

"Well, what are you doing at Heathrow?" It must have been a rotten connection, Richard was shouting. "No, no, don't dream of spending the night in London. Get in a cab to King's Cross and take . . . there's a four-forty something to Cambridge. I'll meet you at the station. No, no, don't worry about it. I'll drive you out to the airport in the morning. Look—I'll even strap you in." Pause. "Bloody marvelous! See you about sixish then."

He sprang back into the room light, bouyant as a dancer. "That was an old student of mine, Werner Heschelbach. Used to be a Senior Wrangler . . . marvelous lad . . . first-class mind. He's on his way to Boston to take up a post at MIT. That's your territory, isn't it?" Richard was burbling in his excitement. "He's working on . . . well, it gets a bit abstruse, but anyhow, some problems related to mine, so I invited him to stay the night. I hope you don't mind, darling. It'll be a bit of a bore for you, but it's really the only chance I'll get to talk to him."

"I don't mind, darling. I can always occupy myself."

"Splendid! Let's forget the Scrabble, shall we?"

He walked over to the table and began piling letters into a heap.

"You were right about zeme, Richard. It *is* a West Indian spirit."

But Richard was smiling, fishing through the letters, arranging them into some new pattern.

"Do you know," he said musing over his handiwork, "that there are fourteen points in I LOVE YOU?"

Werner's first-class mind was not enclosed in a first-class body, and if Kate had been expecting a blonde, Aryan dreamboat, she discovered otherwise. Small, sallow, with the face of a weasel, he reminded Kate of photos she'd seen of Dr. Goebbels.

"Werner, I'd like you to meet a particular friend of mine, Miss Kate Chapman. Kate, this is Werner Heschelbach."

"Aaaach," he bowed over her hand, "iss a great pleasure to meet you." He punctuated each silibant with a fine spray of spit. "You are a massematician also?"

Kate shook her head no, and that was the last notice either man paid to her over the ensuing six hours. When she got to the car, she took the back seat.

They dined at a charming country inn some twenty miles from Cambridge, a first-class restaurant suitable for a first-class mind. Richard had taken her there once before on the occasion of her thirty-fifth birthday. Obviously, tonight was another special occasion. *For them if not for me,* she thought as she picked at her duck *Montmorency.* For however great the charms of the table, or indeed of Kate, they ran a nonexistent second to the men's delight in their reunion.

At first she tried to follow the conversation, but it was unrelievedly technical. For one bright moment, there was a hint of scandal which promised to bring the talk down to a more or less recognizably human plane. Someone named Oerdecker seemed to have run off with the wife of someone named Helffer, thereby scandalizing the academia of Basle. Kate perked up instantly, hoping the conversation might now pursue a livelier course—perhaps the sexual peccadilloes of Nobel Prize winners. But her hope was short-lived, and after a few exchanged titters re the lubricious Frau Helffer, the talk turned again to mathematics.

About how somebody named Groucho was doing something boring at MIT. And somebody named Harpo was doing something equally boring at UCLA. And somebody named Chico was doing something supremely boring at the Physics Institute in Copenhagen. And how a group of boring people were doing excruciatingly boring things at the boring Planck Institute in boring Berlin.

She looked at Richard, but he didn't look at her. He was

listening to Werner with that same rapt expression he had
when he was listening to the Beethoven quartets. And when
he talked, his eyes danced, his mouth seemed more beautiful
and mobile than ever. She toyed with the idea of kissing him
on the mouth. She didn't. And still they talked. She fantasized that she might slide her hand under the table, unzip his
fly and stroke his cock. She didn't. And still they talked.

She ate and smoked and excused herself and went to the
bar to get more cigarettes and came back to the table knowing
she hadn't even been missed. And still they talked. She
counted the bottles lined up on the bar. Forty-three different
kinds if you didn't count duplicates; if you did, the total was
sixty-five. Gilbey's Gin was in the lead with six; Glenlivet's
and Bell's were tied for second place with three each. And
imagine! Two different brands of curacoa. She hadn't even
known there *were* two different brands of curacoa. She ate
her trifle. She ate Richard's trifle. She contemplated Werner's
untouched *mousse chocolat,* but suspected he might have
showered it with spit. She thanked God when the maitre d'
started lowering the lights to remind them that they were the
last diners left.

They got back to Grange Road at midnight. Kate served
coffee and brandy. The men sipped and drank and smoked
and still they talked. At about one, Kate leapt into a pause in
the conversation to announce she was going to bed.

When Richard did come up after three in the morning, he
made ardent, powerful love; as though the stimulus of
intellectual exchange had fired him to new erotic heights.
Kate wanted to go on all night. But no, Richard said they'd
have to be leaving the house before eight in the morning to
get Werner to the airport on time.

After dropping Werner at Heathrow, he took Kate to lunch
at the Connaught—a lunch so expensive she knew he was
offering it as a penance. But not penance enough for those
hours of exclusion.

"You're very broody today," Richard remarked and waved
for the bill. "Come, I'll take you back to your flat."

They drove home in silence and it wasn't until they were in
her sitting room, *her* environment, that she finally cut loose.

"I find it very odd, to say the least, that when I come up to
see you, I can damn well take the train back. But when
Werner comes—oh ho ho—then it's chauffeur service all the

way. I'm surprised you didn't get on the plane and strap him into his seat belt."

"Why, Kate! I do believe you're jealous."

And when she didn't answer, he continued. "In the first place, I haven't seen Werner in three years. Yes, I wanted a chance to talk to him. Is that a crime? In the second place . . . My God, I drive into London three or four times a month to see you, Kate—at a considerable inconvenience to myself, I might add, and to my work. I spend almost every spare moment I have either thinking of you or trying to be with you. I don't know why you should begrudge me a few hours with a colleague. It's very petty. Now be a good girl and make us some coffee."

When she came back from the kitchen, he was sprawled out on the sofa, reading the *Times*, smoking and dribbling ash down his shirt front. *Richard is sweet and I am a shit.* She sat on the floor in front of him, leaning her head back onto his lap.

"I saw you on television Tuesday," he said, tangling her hair with casual fingers.

"Did you?"

She had been on a BBC forum entitled *Advertising: Take It or Leave It.* It was one of those worthy discussion shows that popped up frequently on public service television, and Kate was that part of the panel chosen to represent the advertising community. She feared it would be an onslaught from the encroaching forces of consumerism—her adversary had been introduced as the Ralph Nader of Britain. He proved, in the event, to be a mild young man with a speech impediment and so faint a grasp of business realities that Kate's carefully marshaled arguments rolled out like honey from a spoon. And landed with the impact of a bomb in the Blitz.

"Well, what did you think, Richard?"

"I thought you looked smashing in purple. You ought to wear if oftener."

"I mean about the program. About what I said."

"I think you talked a good deal of rubbish,' was his comment.

"You mean you agreed with that whole-food crank?' Kate was outraged.

"Oh, he talked a good deal of rubbish, too, and he was nowhere near as pretty as you."

"Thank you very much." She slid out from under his hand

and turned to face him. "You think what I do is just so much junk. What you do is elegant, of course. That's the word you scientists are always using, isn't it? Elegant? But what I do is so much shit." For once, she didn't watch her language with him.

Richard sat up. "Well, Kate, if you really want to know what I think—yes. I think it's a waste of time and talent. Harmless, but a waste. However if it makes you happy, just carry on advertising."

"Don't patronize me, Richard, and don't treat me like an idiot child. I've just about had it with your intellectual snobbery."

"Oh, for God's sakes, Kate. There's just no talking to you today, you're so damn prickly. It's hot and I'm tired. I'm going to take a bath and go home."

He left the room abruptly.

I have blown it. I have finally blown it, just like I did with Wolf.

London was lonely enough without the consolation of Richard, and if he walked out of her life—just vanished as Wolf had once done—the loneliness would be unbearable. Worse yet, she recognized the justice of what Richard had said. She *was* jealous . . . jealous of the exclusivity he shared with Werner. Jealous of his work. Jealous of that unknown and unknowable life that was spent apart from her. Richard had always treated her well; you couldn't ask for a more affectionate man. Loving. He was truly loving and she loved him for it, basking like a cat before a fire. He never entered a room without going over to her; without acknowledging her presence with a touch of her hand, a brush of her hair; without underlining in some small way the deeper bonds that held them together. It was clear he missed the casual contact of marriage, the everyday ease of intimacy.

She poured herself a coffee, drank it, poured another and took it in to him.

"I'm sorry I was so rude, Richard, and I'm glad you like me in purple. I'll wear it again for you."

"Yes—please."

"What did your first wife do, darling?"

First wife. Now why had she said that? Emma had been Richard's only wife. "First wife" made it sound as if she were already scheming to be his second.

"Emma was a crystallographer."

"Is that like a mineralogist?"

"In a way." He seemed cheerful now. "It's a completely separate discipline from mine. And you know something else?" He soaped his chest languidly. "We were married twenty years, we had two children, we were reasonably happy. And we almost never talked shop."

He reached out a sudsy paw and unzipped her dress.

"Richard, you're getting my clothes all wet."

"Then take them off and come in with me. There's plenty of room."

It was so lovely and warm lying there on top of him, feeling his soapy hands running over her body, into her body. "Now," he said entering her. "Isn't this better than arguing?"

By the time they got out, the water was cool. He picked up the bath sheet and wrapped her to him.

"I bet you never made love in a bathtub before."

"No," she lied. "I never did."

A couple of months later, Richard was awarded the C.B.E. at the Queen's Birthday Honours.

"Commander of the British Empire. Well, I don't know if that impresses the Queen, but it sure as hell impresses me."

"Oh," he demurred, "they give it to anybody who can make one and one add up to two."

"Even an imaginary one and one?"

They both laughed.

"I was reading a biography of J.B.S. Haldane the other day."

"Were you, Kate? I didn't know you were interested in science."

"I'm interested in scientists. And you know what Haldane says?" she continued. "He says no one can study math for more than five hours a day and remain sane. Do you agree?"

"Absolutely," he put down his book. "Let's go to bed."

She was becoming addicted to Richard. It worried her. On the nights he spent away from her in Cambridge, sleep came hard. She missed the curve of his body, the shelter of his arms, that closeness of nestled spoons in a silver tray. She missed him again in the mornings, for their mornings were always born in love—his hands, his cock arousing her even before they awakened her.

"Ah," she thought, "the joy of love before breakfast."

When he was away too long she masturbated, but it brought her neither true pleasure nor sleep.

"Move in with me, Richard," she asked him once.

"I can't, darling. You move in with me."

But it wouldn't be the same in Cambridge, of course. He'd have work. She'd have none. All those long empty hours in between, she thought. *That* would be sacrificing the days for the nights.

They were in her bed after an evening of Mozart, wine and lovemaking, and Richard had set the alarm for seven-thirty.

"Half-past seven on a Sunday morning?" Kate was appalled. For the past three months he'd been involved in some particularly important new project—important to him, that is—and she had sensed his restlessness all evening long.

"I thought I'd catch the nine o'clock," he said, switching off the lamp. Then, as if it were the most logical of *sequiturs*— "Kate, let's get married."

"Before or after you catch the nine o'clock train?"

"Anytime. I'm serious, darling. All this running back and forth to London is wearing me down. Why don't you chuck your job Monday morning and move up to Cambridge? We could be married next week if you like."

Much to her surprise, she was annoyed. Annoyed and depressed. It was hardly the most romantic of proposals, more like an exercise in logistics. Kate + Richard = marriage. A problem in simple mathematics. She said nothing, merely pulled the blankets up around her.

"Really, Kate, you act as if I were making you an indecent proposition. You must have thought about our getting married one time or another. After all, we've been together over two years."

"Of course I've thought about it," she dragged out reluctantly. "More or less. I just haven't thought what I'd say if you did propose."

"Why not say yes?" He switched on the light. "Look at me, Kate. Don't turn away and try to duck the issue."

He looked so stern, so worried, she had to smile.

"That's better. Now give me one good reason why not. It

can't be your job that's keeping you on in London. You do nothing but complain about it."

"No, it's not the job." She kissed him lightly on the cheek. "Not entirely. You know I've stayed on in England mostly for you."

"Well, then—if England, then why not Cambridge? It's not the end of the world. You could move in tomorrow. The house is liveable, and we could even put in central heating." The supreme sacrifice was yet to come. "All right, if you think the house is too big to handle, we could look around for something else."

"In Cambridge?"

"In or near. I wouldn't want to be more than twenty minutes to work, you know."

"Couldn't you work in London, or maybe just go up to Cambridge on the days you're needed?"

"Don't be absurd."

"I'm sorry, Richard. It's just that I don't have the foggiest notion what I'd do with myself up there." The words came out in an anxious flood. "You have your work, fine. And your students and dining at the High Table . . . sixty, seventy hours a week all accounted for. Well, what am I supposed to be doing while you work? What in God's name would I do with my time?"

"Do?" He looked puzzled. "You'd do what other women do, and I don't mean scrub floors and wash dishes. You can do anything you want in Cambridge. You could garden, read, go to lectures. You could take up the Indian nose flute if you choose to. Perhaps you could find some kind of advertising job up there."

Kate laughed outright. Advertising in Cambridge. That was like expecting Carl Yasztremski to play Little League Baseball!

"Well, maybe you could write a book. Isn't that supposed to be the secret dream of all advertising people. Yes, why don't you write a book?"

"About what?"

"About anything you like, Kate. You know, you make it sound as if I'm offering you a prison sentence. Cambridge isn't Reading Jail, after all. There's plenty of social life, cultural life—enough to keep you going round the clock."

"I'm well aware of that, Richard. But believe me, everything you've said about gardening, lectures, what have you . . . that would be my life apart from you. It's what we'd have together I wonder about. It's not as if I could share in your work."

"We've been over that a dozen times, Kate. No, you couldn't and I wouldn't expect you to. But that's not all there is to life."

"It may not be *all* there is," she snapped, "but it's all that really matters to you."

"That's not fair, darling. You matter. You matter more than anyone else."

"But not more than any*thing* else. Not more than quadratic equations or Niemann's geometry . . ."

"Riemann's geometry," he corrected.

"Riemann's . . . Niemann's—whatever it is that you and your disciples are up to in the big back room of yours."

He recoiled as if struck.

"You are being most unjust, Kate. You're talking about apples and oranges."

"No. I'm talking about *quid pro quo*. You ask me to give up my career, my independence, my whole way of life without your making one single major concession."

"Such as . . . ?"

"Such as moving to London. Or getting a consultancy in New York. Or anyplace where I can continue to be somebody in my own right—not just 'the wife of the eminent mathematician.'"

"Someone in your own right! What rubbish you're talking. How can you compare your work with mine." The more he thought of it, the angrier he got. "In fact, how *dare* you compare your work with mine!"

In an effort to control his rage, he went out of the room to get cigarettes. When he returned he seemed marginally calmer. He lit up for both of them, handed her one, and sat down on the side of the bed.

"You're a mystery to me, Kate. I simply can't understand why you think what you do is so important. Peddling deodorants to spotty shop assistants? Pumping more beer into the stomachs of football hooligans?"

"You're a snob, Richard."

"And so are you. You don't give a tinker's dam about your shop assistants with their unwashed armpits. What is it, then? Is it the money? I fancy you earn rather more than I do."

Kate didn't fancy. She was certain—but that was beside the point.

"No, it's not the money. Money's never mattered much to me."

"Not the money," he repeated. "What is it, then? Is it the wheeling and dealing you're so keen on?" His cigarette traced a convoluted pattern in the air. "All those little Machiavellian ins and outs of office politics? Is it having your own secretary? Hiring and firing? The fun of putting the fear of God into employees? Is that it, Kate? Is it the *power?*"

"It's a great many things. Advertising has been very good to me."

"Very good indeed," he concurred. "It put you on a first-class flight to London and ordained that we would meet. I'm grateful for that aspect of it, but now it's served its function."

"And tell me, what is the function of your mathematics? At least my shop clerks, for whom you have so much contempt, feel better and *smell* better for what I give them. That's practical. But what is the use of what you do? What conceivable connection does it have with real life?"

"What is the use of what I do?" He leaned back on the pillows and studied the ceiling. "What do you think the use should be? Should I devote myself to the laws of probability so that I can break the bank at Monte Carlo? Is that your idea of use?"

"Don't be trivial."

"Ah, that's trivial. We want something grander. Very well, I shall go to Houston and work on the space project. Sending men to the moon or wherever. That marvelous technology that has benefited mankind by giving the world the Teflon frypan. What could be more useful than that?"

Dreamily he stubbed out his cigarette.

"Useful. You tell me, Kate, what is the use of a painting by Turner? Or a poem by Keats? What is the use of a Beethoven quartet . . . and what could be more real?"

"You compare your work with Beethoven's?" She was aghast.

"Don't think me pompous, but yes, I do. There are certain aspects in common."

"You see it as an art form, in other words."

"More than that, Kate. Even more." A note of reverence crept into his voice. "I see it as an act of creation."

An act of creation.

There was no reply possible to such an assertion. How very odd Richard was. On the surface so free of cheap vanity with his rumpled shirts and his National Health glasses. And beneath it, all the arrogance of a Nietzschean superman. Yet she suspected his comparison to Beethoven was a valid one. They shared, if not the same problems, certainly the same blinkered selfishness of the artist. A kind of undoubting purity that brooks no compromise, that admits of no competition. At heart she knew he had correctly appraised the respective values of his work and hers. No, she thought sadly, she wasn't jealous of Richard. She was envious.

"Let me think about it, Richard. Your proposal, I mean." It had somehow fallen out of the conversation. "Give me a few weeks to think it over—that is, if the offer's still good."

"Oh, it's still good, Kate. And it will stay good—but only on my terms."

Early next morning, she saw him off at King's Cross. He was pathetically eager to get back to work, good old Richard van Beethoven. It was too fine a day to sit around the flat and brood, she decided. May as well brood out-of-doors. She took a taxi to Marble Arch, getting off at Speakers' Corner. The soap boxes were out, the crowds were milling, the hecklers were heckling, and the orators—as usual—were solving the insoluble, pondering the imponderable. *Is there a God? White Man—Out of Rhodesia.* And on the next stand *Black Man—Out of England.* Was this the real world Richard was so fond of referring to?

She headed into the park, arriving finally at the Round Pond. Suddenly weary, she took a bench facing the water. She watched the boats. Followed the kites. And thought about Richard's proposal.

And then about Richard.

And then about Wolf.

How is it, she wondered, that out of all her lovers—all her hundred-odd lovers—she had cared deeply for only two men. And that both these men had each, in his own way, placed themselves beyond her reach. With Wolf it had been Polly—tortured, twisted Polly. But with Richard it was far more elusive. After all, Polly might die, or leave, or go crazy once and for all. And then the situation would be different. Well, perhaps not different for Wolf and Kate—that dream had been poisoned in the kennels of Weston. Maybe for Wolf and some other woman.

But Richard. His true love would never desert him; never die; never grow old or wrinkled or tiresome. Marriage to Richard would be a *ménage à trois*. Kate and Richard and theoretical mathematics, with Kate taking the back seat of the car. Know the enemy and he is yours . . . wasn't that the saying? But she could never know this enemy. So what did that leave her? The odd bits and pieces of Richard's life, the leftovers from his private intellectual feast.

She peered all around the problem, tried to solve it as though it were an advertising premise subject to rational solution. Perhaps if she could keep her job and come up to Cambridge weekends . . . It would suit *her,* but she knew Richard would find it unacceptable. Really no different from what they already had. And he had made it clear that if marriage there was, it would be on his terms only.

It was almost five when she reached the flat, and she could hear the phone ringing furiously inside. Richard. She scrambled to unlock the door. Yes, it would be Richard calling to compromise.

"Is this Miss Kate Chapman?" The thin voice of the overseas operator. "Hold on please for Donald Farebrother."

Farebrother! What in Christ's name would get the President of Marsden-Baker to the phone on a Sunday at—she looked at her watch—not yet noon New York time? He should be having cocktails at the country club, like any self-respecting agency head.

"Hello, Kate." He couldn't have sounded friendlier if he were soliciting the chairman of General Motors.

"Hello, Donald. This is a surprise."

"How are you? How's London? How's the weather?"

"The weather's fine, Donald. In the midseventies, although the forecast is for scattered showers. If you want a complete report, I'll turn you over to the meteorological bureau."

She heard his short nervous laugh and then a crackling on the line.

"And how's London treating my favorite advertising gal?"

"London's treating me just fine, Donald. The natives are very friendly." *Cut the crap and get to the point.*

"I was wondering if you were happy there."

"Reasonably happy." She knew instantly what the point was going to be. "Reasonably happy."

"We've missed you here, Kate . . . really missed you. I was wondering if you've ever considered coming back to Marsden."

You were wondering that on a Sunday afternoon? "In what capacity, Donald?"

"As creative director, naturally."

"What about Gully?"

Pause. Then, "Gully died last Friday."

"Well, well, well. What did he die of? Martini poisoning at the New York Athletic Club?"

"That's unkind of you, Kate. Actually he died of lung cancer."

Lung cancer. She should have guessed it. All those years of unswerving fidelity to Norfolk Cigarettes . . . it almost made you believe there was a God.

"I don't quite follow you, Don. If he died of cancer, then you must have known for some time that he was sick. Why did you wait until today to call?"

"Well, he worked almost up to the end."

"Yeah, but he didn't work right up to last Friday and then take time off to die."

Donald sounded a trifle sheepish. "I realize you and Gully didn't always get along . . ."

"I see," she interrupted. "So you waited until after he was gone to make me an offer. You wanted him to die happy . . . is that it?"

"Something like that."

"That's very sweet of you, Donald. Now what kind of money are we talking about?"

He named a figure. She named another. They haggled for a bit and finally settled. It wasn't the legendary hundred thou, but it was close enough.

"And a seat on the board?"

"That comes with the job, Kate. You know that."

"I just wanted to hear it from you. What about stock?"

"We'll give you options up to thirty percent of your annual salary. I know this is very sudden, Kate, and I'm sure you'll want a few days to think it over . . ."

"Donald, I've been thinking it over all afternoon."

"You're kidding. You must be psychic."

"Must be. When do you want me to start?"

"Would a month's notice be sufficient for you?"

"I can be there two weeks from tomorrow."

"It's a deal, then?"

"It's a deal . . . and oh, Donald. When I get there, I want to find Gully's office just the way he left it. I plan to do the redecorating myself." She started to laugh.

"What's so funny, Kate?"

"You know what Gully's last words were when I left Marsden? He said if I ever came back it would be over his dead body."

"He must have been psychic too."

Richard was stunned when she broke the news. Stunned, hurt and angry.

"Why are you such a coward, Kate? What the hell are you afraid of? Why do you run from every emotional commitment?"

"I'm *not* a coward," she protested tearfully. Yet "coward" had been the first word that came to mind the moment she'd hung up on Farebrother. She could shout down a client, do battle with colleagues, stake her whole professional life on a campaign. Yet the prospect of marriage scared her shitless.

She was running and she knew it. In some crazy way it was easier for her to change jobs, change continents, than to commit herself to the unknowns of marriage.

And though work wasn't *all* she knew, it was what she knew best. It was her identity. Her passport to prestige.

As Kate Chapman, her voice was listened to, her decisions respected on all sides. She was somebody. As Mrs. Hetherington, she would be nobody—merely the reflection of someone else's achievements.

She could never cut Richard out of her life, nor would she ever want to. But in the meantime she needed time. Time and space.

"Try to understand," she pleaded with him. "This is the job I've been waiting for all my life."

"I had hoped," his voice was ringed with sadness, "that you'd been waiting all your life for me."

She reasoned, he argued; she cried, he comforted. She promised. "It's not as if we wouldn't see each other, darling. I'll come to England as often as I can. We could still have some weekends, take our holidays together . . ."

In the end, he agreed to give it a try.

She would go—but keep her options open.

She was full of plans on the flight to New York. London suddenly seemed distant and unreal.

The first thing she was going to do was buy herself a condominium. Something big and really homey for a change. Park or Fifth, say, in the Upper Sixties. And she was going to furnish it decently for once. She'd entertain, have dinner parties, get herself a housekeeper who could cook. Then she'd get a cat. A Siamese, maybe. No more of this living like a gypsy.

Next, she'd buy herself a fur coat. Leopard. Leopard would be great, but what with these goddamn Friends of the Earth crazies raising such a stink, she'd probably be stoned to death the first time she wore it. OK, settle for mink. A nice dark natural ranch, but sporty. Maybe cut polo-coat style. She wondered if that fellow was still at *Women's Wear Daily*, the one who said he could get her a deal at Jacques Kaplan. Wondered if Mr. Alex was still at Michel Kazan. He was the only one who really understood her hair.

Oh, it was good to be going home. Going home to Marsden. After nearly eighteen years, she had come full circle. Well, she always had a special feeling for that crazy place. First jobs. They were like first lovers. The sentiment struck her as both suitable and profound.

Who the hell was her first lover, anyway? Oh, yeah . . . that photographer freak down in the village. Couldn't even remember his name. First job—first lover? No, that couldn't be right. Guess it would be more accurate to say that first jobs are like first *love*. First love—who could that be? The Brewster kid back in Athol? No, that was a childhood crush, and what the hell . . . she was only eleven. Nope, it would have to be that Michael guy in her senior year in college. Michael Matheson . . . yeah, good-looking, but Jesus! what a prick. Could you imagine if she'd actually *married* him? The thought made Kate laugh aloud.

No, he wasn't her first love, wasn't even close. And suddenly she knew who her first love really was. It was Marsden.

Marvelous crazy rat-racy, snake-pitty, ulcer-making Marsden. She could hardly wait to get back. And when she did, the

very first thing she was going to do would be to rip out the
Russian voting machines . . .

With a suitable expression of deep mourning, Miss
Dempsey ushered her into Gully's office. Yes, it was almost
exactly as she remembered it. The museum of failure. A few
new trophies now graced the shelves. The final issues of *Life,
Look,* the *Saturday Evening Post.* A chlorophyll flea collar.
Aerosol cans of flavored vaginal spray: vanilla, strawberry
and champagne. More ghosts for the graveyard.

"Do you know if this collection is the property of Mrs.
Gulliver, by any chance."

"No, Miss Chapman. Mr. Gulliver willed it to the agency."

"How very generous, Miss Dempsey. Very generous. Now
I'd like you to catalog every item on these shelves, and don't
forget the Edsel grill."

"Yes, Miss Chapman."

"Because Marsden-Baker Advertising is about to make a
magnificent gesture. We're going to donate it all, lock, stock
and Moxie, to the Museum of Modern Art. That's where it
belongs, along with their Man Ray toilets. And when you've
got this stuff out of here, I want you to get the decorator who
did Bill Eastland's office at ChicagoCorp and have him come
round to see me. I'm going to redo this joint from top to
bottom."

"Yes, Miss Chapman."

"Because from here on out, nothing—but *nothing*—comes
out of this office except success success success."

KIT

SUCCESS SUCCESS SUCCESS—IT HAD COME MICHAEL'S WAY AT
last. All through '75, he worked hard for the party; all
through '76, for Jimmy Carter. And when the Georgian
governor squeezed into the White House, Michael was
absolutely jubilant.

To Kit, it appeared that Michael belonged to every organization known to man, with the possible exception of the Girl
Scouts. He rarely dined at home, and the only occasions on
which they went out together were when Michael pressed her
into service at those party functions where the presence of a
wife was deemed desirable.

So she didn't know whether to be pleased or wary when, on
a Friday in early October, Michael suggested they make a
night of it. "What do you say we get togged out, go into
Boston and really do it up? Jimmy's Harborside, or maybe
Locke Ober. Just the two of us . . . just like the old days."

"In the old days we used to go to the Canton Palace," Kit
remarked. "But Jimmy's Harborside will be fine."

"The Canton Palace!" Michael laughed at the memory.
"What a mole-hole that was! You know, it burnt down a few
years ago. I think there was a fat fire in the kitchen."

"You are going to marry Michael Matheson," her fortune

cookie had read. It was the only fortune-cookie prophecy that
had ever come true. Most of the usual messages were frauds.
*You are going to take a long journey. You will be successful in
your new venture. Romance is right around the corner.* Still,
what could you expect for the buck twenty-five combination
platter—an accurate vision of the future? No, Kit didn't
regret the fiery demise of the Canton Palace. Over the years
she'd come to think of it as "the scene of the crime."

Jimmy's Harborside was definitely better. They started the
evening with whiskey sours and Boston clam chowder, then
Michael insisted on gigantic boiled lobsters. And when Kit
asked for salad instead of French fries, he'd said "Go ahead,
have the potatoes," even though he was usually after her to
take off some weight. "Come on," he coaxed. "Just this
once . . . a few more calories can't hurt you."

He was putting himself out to be nice and Kit, under the
mild glow of alcohol, felt flattered and happy. Who could
have thought dinner with Michael could be such a treat!

They chatted about old friends, old times as they hadn't
done in ages. Michael asked after Marian, with whom Kit
kept in weekly touch and who was doing very well indeed at
Vassar. And, of course, they talked about Sarah. After a
bumpy senior year at Miss Ellery's, she'd settled in very well
at Oberlin. Kit would have wished her daughter had chosen a
college closer to home, but apparently Oberlin had awfully
good biology courses, so Oberlin it was. "It's not the end of
the world, honey," Michael comforted. "And anyhow, she'll
be coming home for Thanksgiving. Let's have a big one."

No question—he was being very nice, very tender, very
considerate. Hard to remember that this was the same man
who'd forgotten her fortieth birthday just a few months back.
He ordered them coffee and strega.

"Now," he smiled, pouring lavish dollops of cream in her
coffee, "which do you want first—the good news or the bad?"

Kit's face lit up. "You've been offered a judgeship." It was
what she'd wanted for years: prestige, good money, an end to
all this hassling. Superior Court of Massachusetts, Judge
Michael J. Matheson presiding.

"Nope," Michael said. "Better than that. I've decided to
run for governor."

"Governor of Massachusetts?" She was incredulous.

"No, governor of the Fiji Islands," Michael snapped.

"Really, Kit, you amaze me. Of course governor of Massachusetts. Why do you think I've been knocking myself out the last couple of years?"

"But Michael," she protested, "the election isn't till November '78 . . . My God, that's over a year away. Have they offered you the nomination already?"

"Let's just say I'm reasonably sure I can get it. And once that's in the bag . . . well, honey, you're looking at the next governor of the Bay State. Which brings me to the bad news."

Without warning, Kit's stomach churned violently.

"Kit, darling," he took her hand. "I've never asked you for anything before. I've always given to you, given to you without stint. But this one time in my life, I'm going to ask you. You know political office doesn't come cheap—at least not the first time around. You just don't go around to town meetings with a bullhorn anymore. You need a PR firm, an advertising agency, there are printing costs, air-time . . . Hell, Nelson Rockefeller spent thousands of dollars just for free shopping bags when he was running for governor of New York."

"But we're not Rockefellers." Her hand was trembling and he squeezed it.

"No, and this isn't New York. Obviously it wouldn't be on that kind of scale. But you know, with the new legislation, there's a legal limit on private and corporate donations. No one can kick in more than a thousand bucks for any one candidate . . ."

"No one, you mean, except the candidate's wife."

"Well, the money's got to come from somewhere," he said reasonably.

Kit felt nauseous. All that cholesterol, all those whiskey sours and now . . . Maybe, just maybe, he could be talked around.

"Are you really sure you *want* to be governor? I must say, I don't care for the idea of being the governor's wife. I'd always thought you'd be happier in a judgeship. Or what about running for national office?"—that would get her off the hook until 1980. "You always used to talk about something in Washington. It would seem to me that once you get bogged down in State office, you can only go so far."

"The facts are otherwise." Michael had obviously given this much thought. "What was Carter except governor of Georgia? FDR was governor of New York. Look at Earl

Warren—from governor of California to Supreme Court
Chief Justice. What is it, Kit?" he eyed her suspiciously. "Do
you begrudge me the money?"

Argument was fruitless; his mind was made up. And when
she didn't answer, he began to bear down. "Let's face it,
honey. You've had a free ride for nearly twenty years. You've
never had to work; you've never gone without. You live in
one of the best towns in New England. Every meal you've
had, every stitch you've got on has been bought with my
hard-earned money. You owe me something, too, you
know."

"How much?" She was having trouble keeping her food
down. "Do you think you could ask the waiter for more ice
water?"

Michael grabbed a pitcher from the adjoining table and
poured her a tumblerfull. "Frankly, I don't know. I'm a
pretty good fundraiser, I'd try to keep your contribution
down as much as possible, although I'm not going to skimp on
essentials. Could be $50,000 . . . could be $150,000. I won't
know till the campaign is under way."

"But I don't have that kind of money, Michael."

"Oh, come off it, Kit." He shook his head at her perversity. "I always knew you were lousy at math, but my God . . .
this beats everything. I figure your stocks should be close to a
quarter of a million now. I mean, Sag Pap & Pulp alone—it's
gone wild. You got a three-to-one split on that merger back in
'71.

Sag Pap & Pulp. The sole beneficiary of Kit's Sag Pap &
Pulp holdings was, likely as not, now training terrorists in
Iraq. Subconsciously, her first choice of stocks to sell for the
liberation of Jan Littlemarch had been stocks in her father's
own company. And while Kit's math was bad, it was not so
bad that she didn't know her total worth was now in the
neighborhood of $18,000. Including dividends.

"Didn't we sell some Sag Pap when Monk was going to the
speech therapist?"

"No, You sold Pepsi-Cola. Anyhow, we'll sort it all out on
Monday. I'll have the broker work out the current market
value. The dividend account is at the brokerage, too, isn't
it?"

Kit nodded mutely.

"OK. Monday, we'll go down to the safe deposit box and
get out the stocks."

"You mean I have to go to Boston with you?"

Michael shrugged. "Well, the box *is* in your name. However, if you want me to save you the trip, I'll make you out a power-of-attorney form so I won't have to bother you at all. Is that all right with you?"

"All right." She managed a thin smile. "You know you're welcome to whatever I have."

Victory gained, Michael beamed fulsomely.

"That's my little kitten," he said.

KATE

It was crisp for early October. There wouldn't be too many country weekends left.

As usual on a Friday, Kate was meeting Barry at the Plaza. They always had a drink or two before setting out. Six months ago, he'd talked her into sharing a rented farmhouse in Dutchess county, just a few miles north of Poughkeepsie. A great big barn of a house it was—nothing fancy, but beautiful countryside. Some twenty acres of apple orchards stood between it and the nearest McDonald's.

They'd started going up in spring when the countryside was all blossoms, but now it was the end of the apple season and the trees had lost most of their leaves. Barry had said something about picking windfalls, making pies, putting up jellies. Good old Barry. He had everything it took to make an ideal wife. Oh, what the hell . . . who was she to be choosy.

He hadn't arrived when she got to the Plaza, so she took a table in the corner of the Oak Room and ordered. Margarita for him, martini for her. For once the place wasn't crowded, but then she was early. It was hardly five o'clock. She looked around. No familiar faces. Just a few out-of-towners here and there, and, at a table across the room, a large party of suburban women, resting up from the rigors of an afternoon's shopping. Kate dug into her *Wall Street Journal.*

"Excuse me. Didn't you used to be Catherine Chapman?"

Kate looked up. One of the suburban women had detached herself from the group and was now standing over Kate's table. She was little and plump, with beautiful skin and she looked ever so faintly familiar.

"I still am. And you're . . . ?"

"Phyllis. Phyllis Asgard from college."

"For God's sakes!" Kate put down her paper. "Phyllis. Phyllis Asgard. It must be twenty years since I've seen you. Sit down and have a drink with me."

"You're not busy?"

"Just waiting for someone. Sit down, sit down . . ."

Phyllis sat, and the two women passed a swift silent moment sizing each other up. Assessing the damages and triumphs of twenty years. Putting invisible price tags on dresses, fur coats, handbags, jewelry. Well, Phyllis had it all over Kate in the jewelry department. That diamond ring must be a good three carats.

"You look marvelous, Catherine."

"And so do you. So tell me, Phyllis, what have you been doing with yourself the past twenty years?"

Kate signaled the waiter for another round of drinks. Phyllis ordered a whiskey sour.

"Well, I'm married, of course."

Of course.

"I'm Mrs. Campbell Syme now."

"Any children?"

"Boy, do I have children. Four of them. My oldest just started Barnard last month. You should see her . . . she's a beauty. Head of the drama society in high school."

"Congratulations." She was afraid Phyllis would be trotting out the pictures next.

"And how about you, Cath? You know, I used to think of you pretty often. I kept looking for your name on the bestseller list, or maybe something in the magazines. You sure were ambitious."

"I sure was. But no, I never did go into journalism. I've been in advertising all these years."

"Advertising." Phyllis sounded mildly disappointed. "Oh well . . . I suppose it's fun."

Fun! Don't you know, you dodo, that you're talking with one of the great people of advertising? That I am executive vice president of Marsden-Baker? That I probably earn twice as much as your precious Campbell? That only two months ago I was named Advertising Woman of the Year and presented with a gold plaque? No, of course you don't. And if you did, what would it mean? "Well, I don't know about it's being fun," Kate admitted. "But it's a living."

"And you never got married?"

"Never ever. Not even once."

"Really." Phyllis seemed to find that extraordinarily peculiar. "I always assumed you were married. In fact, I thought you were going to marry Mike what's-his-name, that lawyer from Harvard. He was such a good-looking guy."

"Michael Matheson." Kate said. "But did you ever meet him? I can't recall."

"Well . . ." Phyllis edged in closer, having checked around to make sure her friends were out of earshot. Her voice became very confidential. "Well, you weren't supposed to know, Catherine, but after all these years . . . what can it matter?"

"What can *what* matter?"

"Mike and me . . . we had a little thing going. More of a roll in the hay than an affair."

Well, I'll be dipped, you rascal, you. And I always thought you told me everything.

"You and Michael? Tell me more."

"You're not angry?"

"Angry? After all these years . . . all those martinis under the bridge?" Kate laughed. "No. Just fascinated. It's funny, I could have sworn you two never met. Details . . . details. Give!"

"Well, he came up to the dorm one day looking for you and you were out somewhere and I was in . . . and umm, the next thing I knew, he was in, too."

"When was all this . . . do you remember?"

"Let me think. About Christmastime in our senior year. That's right. I remember he'd come to bring you your Christmas present."

"That's really weird. You know, we went together for almost a year, and he never once made a serious pass."

"I guess that's because he was thinking of marrying you."

"Male logic." Kate let out a whoop of laughter. "By the way, how was he?"

"How was he?" Phyllis repeated.

"In bed. On a scale of one to ten, with say ten at the top. How'd you rate him?"

Phyllis giggled. "What a memory you have. Well, on a scale of one to ten"—she shut her eyes in an effort to recall that long-ago roll—"he was practically off the scale."

"That good?"

"That bad." Suddenly her face became very grave. "Of course, I stopped doing that sort of thing as soon as I got married. You mustn't even think such a thing."

Kate pulled her face about into her the-client-is-oh-so-right sincere expression. "Of course not, Phyllis."

"Anyhow, I've got to be getting back to the girls." From the corner of her eye, Kate saw Barry come in. "But listen, Catherine, I'll give you my number and maybe we can get in touch, have lunch some day." Phyllis fished in her bag for pencil and paper. An elegant little black bag, sweet and feminine, just like the underwear Phyllis used to snitch from Crawford Hollidge. Well, Kate presumed she had given up shoplifting these days. Along with one-shot screwing.

And there was Barry.

"Barry, I'd like you to meet an old friend of mine. Barry Warden, Phyllis . . . umm Syme."

They exchanged murmurs. Phyllis gave Kate her phone number and moved off in a cloud of Nina Ricci perfume.

"You won't believe this," she told Barry when the suburbanites had safely departed, "but that was my roommate from college. I haven't seen her in twenty years."

"That is a very sexy dame."

"You think so?" Kate furrowed her brow. "I could never see it myself. But every living male in Boston saw it. They not only saw it . . . they had it. You know," Kate sipped her drink thoughtfully, "she just couldn't get over the fact that I wasn't married. And then, to top it all off, you turned up. I bet I know what she's thinking right this very minute. That after all these years, the best Catherine Chapman can do is a screaming faggot."

"Not screaming, Kate. Don't be nasty."

"I'm sorry dear," she patted his cheek. "I didn't mean to be bitchy. It's just that the whole thing took me by surprise. Let's talk about something else."

They planned the weekend. Kate's Triumph was in the garage for repairs, so they'd take Barry's Jag for a change . . .

"You know we hired Chris Feathers?"

"The kid who did the Sprinkles campaign?"

"The same."

The kitchen was redolent with the tartness of cinnamon and sliced apples, the sweet fragrance of melted butter. It was baking hour in Dutchess County and Kate was vigorously kneading dough while Barry struggled with the complexities of the antique oven.

"Jesus, Kate." He cast a disapproving eye across at her handiwork. "It's only dough. Gentle, living, breathing dough. You don't have to punish it, you know."

"Come on . . . what do I know about cooking? That's your territory, not mine."

"Why don't you just roll it up in a ball and let it rest a bit?" He sighed and handed her a mixing bowl. "How much did you have to pay him . . . Feathers?"

"Would you believe forty?"

Barry whistled, and Kate continued. "Yup, forty thousand bucks *plus* stock *plus* a vice-presidency *plus* I had to go down on my hands and knees and beg him. How's *them* apples!"

"Not bad for a kid in his twenties. Is he worth it?"

"Yes . . . yes and no. He's all kinds of bright, that's for sure, but . . ." she picked up the paring knife and plunged it into the dough with a swift vicious stab. "Christ, Barry, everything that fucker does rubs me the wrong way. He wears an earring—one teentsy weentsy gold earring in the shape of a swastika. Cute, huh? And the other day he turned up in my office wearing a bush jacket and jeans."

"So what? Everybody wears jeans these days."

"Yeah, but not with the words 'Kiss My Ass' embroidered across the backside. When I saw that, I blew my stack. I told him, 'Chris, you are not going to the client like that . . . no way.' Well, he told me to keep my hair on, baby . . . they'd love it." She contemplated the knife in the dough. "And you know what? They loved it. Jesus, I wonder why I even bother to put on lipstick in the morning."

She wiped her hands and lit a cigarette.

"It's a new generation, Kate. A new generation."

"It sure as hell is, and I just don't understand them. It's like there's some kind of competition going on to see who can be the more outrageous. You don't woo your customers any more . . . you assault them. Bang! Shock! Zowie! I keep having to remind my group that 'Fuck You' is not an advertising headline.''

"No? I always thought it was a pretty good one. Short. Direct. Attention-getting. Remember that ad we once did for Mrs. Cooper's Cake Mix? 'Mothers' . . . ?''

Kate let out a peal of laughter.

Years ago, she and Barry had worked on an ad for a layer-cake mix to run in the Negro press. The headline had been simply MOTHERS! set in giant seventy-two point type. How were they to know in those innocent years that "mothers" was a shortcut for the ultimate obscenity once you got north of 96th Street? The mail response had been an eye-opener.

"My God, Barry . . . that must have been fifteen years ago.''

"At least. The point is, love, that we're both still around to laugh at it. Let's face it, a lot of bodies have fallen by the wayside since then. A lot of bodies.''

"Yeah, I know. It's just that I'm starting to feel . . . kind of crowded down at the bottom. All those little piranhas nibbling away at my feet. All so artsy, so goddamn creative. Creative!'' She spat the word out. "I've always loved the way agencies bandy that term. He's the guy who wrote 'Stop Itch'—very creative. Or somebody was the first person to put a transvestite into a brassiere commercial. Creative! I can see it now on my tombstone, set in Caslon Bold. Here lies the girl who invented Lean 'n Lively Dog Food, Miss Catherine Creative. R.I.P. With luck I'll be buried next to the dame who wrote 'Modess Because.' Now there's an epitaph for the ages. It'll be the creative corner of the cemetery, like the poet's corner of Westminister Abbey. Only more creative.''

"Why the diatribe? It's just a word, Kate.''

"Well, in the context we use it, it's nonsense.''

"So what's creative . . . having babies?''

"Why not? Anyhow, lots of things are creative. Music's creative. Sculpture. Painting. Mathematics is creative . . .''

"Math!'' Barry laughed. "Well, who knows . . . you may be right. Like I have this accountant at Birns Brothers. You wouldn't believe the things he can do with figures. My last year's tax return ran more pages than *War and Peace*. Even the revenuers were impressed. Yeah, I guess you could say math's creative, if you look at it that way."

Kate slumped into a kitchen chair and stared out over the orchards.

"That wasn't what I meant," she said softly. The sun was setting behind the apple trees, so she must be facing West. England was three thousand miles the other way.

"You still hear from your English professor?"

Oh, Barry, you fucking mind-reader. "We keep in touch. He writes, I call him every couple of weeks. I saw him over Easter, you know. We went to Corfu. I don't know," Kate said, turning from the window. "Looking back on it, I just don't know if I did the right thing."

"I thought your motto was 'Never look back.'"

"When you're forty, where else can you look?"

She got up and shook off the mood the way a dog sheds water. "Come on, Barry. Let's be creative and make apple pies."

She saw the light through the crack in his door, knocked and let herself in. Barry was sitting up in bed reading a lurid-covered paperback and wearing—ah ha! she'd never seen them before—tortoise-framed glasses. Kate herself had avoided the inevitable four-eyes look by wearing contacts for the past ten years.

"I couldn't sleep so I thought I'd come and . . ." she peered at the book. "Jesus, Carlos Castaneda. How can you read that crap?"

"I can't when other people are talking," Barry answered, and peering at her over the top of his glasses, folded the book on his knees.

"You look cold, kid." He pulled out a pillow from under his head and placed it alongside him. "Crawl in."

"You might at least have given me the warm side of the bed," Kate grumbled, climbing in beside him. "Cold beds have been the story of my life."

"Of everyone's." They sat in silent felicity for a while and listened to the night sounds of the country.

"You may as well tell me what's on your mind," Barry finally said, "or I'll go back to my Castaneda."

"Go right ahead."

"Naaah, you're right. That stuff is shit." And when Kate

didn't reply, he asked, "You want anything? A drink? A Valium? Some apple pie?"

"I'll settle for a cigarette."

"I thought you were going to give up smoking," he said, passing across the Marlboros.

"I gave up sex instead. It's easier."

They lit up, and Barry settled an ashtray across his knees. "I'd Walk a Mile for a Camel," it read. Wow! That one goes back.

"Barry, do you ever wonder what it all comes down to . . . I mean, bottom line?"

"Oh, Christ, Kate. Don't go all epic on me. Just because you met an old classmate in the Oak Room."

"It wasn't that."

"Anyhow, I didn't *really* think she was sexy. Too dumpy. You, you're as skinny as the day I met you."

"That's what comes of not eating potatoes for fifteen years. Fifteen fucking years without a single French fry. Do I get the Purple Heart or don't I? No, it wasn't meeting Phyllis that got me down . . . or only partly. It's just . . . this seems to be my week for seeing ghosts. You know who I ran into coming out of the Biltmore on Monday? Wolf Aaronson."

"Well, you were bound to run into him sooner or later."

"We went back to the bar, had a couple of drinks for old time's sake . . . and you know what? He's *married!*"

"He always *was* married, Kate. I thought that was the whole hang-up."

"He's married, but not to Polly. *Not to Polly!* He married some young girl, they have two kids, expecting a third . . . they live on a farm somewhere in Bucks County. Can you believe it?"

"It just doesn't figure. What happened to Polly?"

"It seems she fell in love with some dog-breeder and moved off to Manitoba. Like all of a sudden she didn't need Wolf anymore. Ain't that something?"

"When did all this happen?"

"About a year after we split. While I was out in L. A. competing in the '72 sex olympics, he just picked himself out some nice young girl. Two kids and a third on the way."

"It looks like he got himself a breeder, too."

"It could have been *me,* Barry. It *should* have been me!"

She was weeping unashamedly now, wiping her streaming eyes and nose on the rough terry of her robe.

"Ah, Kate, Kate." Barry put his arm around her bony shoulder. "Don't let it eat at you. You and Wolf . . . it was never in the cards."

"Never in the cards, huh? Well, fuck the cards. I want a whole new deck." She fished blindly in the pocket of her robe for something to blow her nose on, but like taxicabs on a rainy night, tissues are never there when you need them.

"Fucking house! You can't even find a Kleenex when you need it." She stormed out of the room, returning a couple of minutes later clutching a box of man-sized tissues.

"That looks like you're planning to do some serious crying," Barry said.

"No," she dabbed her nose and got back into bed. "Just a temporary lapse. And anyhow, you were right. It never was in the cards. It's . . . oh, Barry I don't know. Here we are, we've been grinding our guts out for the last twenty years, and will you tell me what we have to show for it?"

"Well, I don't know about you, Kate, but I've got a townhouse on 85th Street, an E-Type Jag . . . and sufficient male companionship. Which, by the way, I still don't have to pay for."

"Well, I may have to before too long. I mean, who is there for me? Men who've already been married and couldn't make it work? Losers. Married men? I did that number already. Fifty-year-old bachelors with prostate trouble? Now there's something that boggles the mind. And even *those* guys are into young girls. I really have to scrape just to get someone presentable enough to take to an industry dinner. Another few years and I'll be renting 'em from an escort service."

"Have you ever thought of trying the gay bit?"

"Barry, I've tried everything once, including girl meets girl. I guess I was never really interested in women. I don't have any close women friends. In fact, I don't have any friends at all except for you. And as for family! Jesus, you should see my mother. She's so busy playing the merry widow down in Florida, she couldn't care less. I could walk right into her on Madison Avenue and not even know her. She's about twenty years younger than I am. A real Shirley Temple. Well, good for her, she's happy. And being married to my father all those years was no picnic. It's just that right now, I have absolutely no picture of my future . . . there's nothing in it for me."

"There's work."

"The original four-letter word. Work! I make more money and do less work than ever before in my life. I don't work any more, Barry. I supervise. I delegate. I make decisions about other people's work. I attend meetings. I get bored in the board room. But I don't actually work."

"So why don't you . . . quit?"

"Quit and do what? Sit around in a little Mexican beach house with a little Mexican beach boy? Get buried alive in some art colony in the Costa del Sol where I can pretend to swap fishing yarns with the natives? Maybe I should have gotten married. It's about the only thing I haven't tried."

"Well, Kate, you and I aren't the marrying kind."

"Speak for yourself, Barry." She lit another cigarette and smoked dreamily. "In all my life, I've only had two proposals of marriage."

"All it takes is one."

"Only two proposals. Funny when you think of it. All those men—hundreds would be my guess—and only two wanted to make an honest woman of me. The first was this guy back in Boston. I was crazy about him when I was in college. And then Richard, of course. Well, that's still open."

"What about Wolf?"

"Wolf!" She snorted. "I proposed to him a lot, on an average of once a week, but I don't recall his ever proposing to me. So here I am, all alone and lonely. All the men I've known, and still it all comes down to either business or sex. Well, I'm tired of it. I'm tired of sleeping around and I'm tired of sleeping alone. How's that for a snappy headline?"

"Terrific. I'll set it in a nice *Bodoni* typeface."

She got out of bed and pulled her robe tight. "You can go back to your Castaneda now, Barry. I've bored you enough for one night."

"Why not sleep here with me, if it's any comfort."

She patted his hand. "You're a good, dear friend, Barry, and thanks for the offer. But I'm looking for something more than comfort."

Over Sunday lunch, she told him she'd decided to stay on a few days and think things out. They'd never miss her back at the office. "So if it's OK with you, Barry, I'll drive you to the station and bring the car in later this week."

"Well, it's OK with me, but it *is* a brand new Jag . . ."

"Just show me the wind-up key and don't worry."

KIT

She put the casserole in the oven and sat down to wait in her favorite corner of the sun room, sunless now in the deepening October twilight. Kit's Corner, Sarah always called it; only Moses the cat was bold enough to compete for possession of the tapestry wing chair where Kit had passed so many empty hours.

Poor Moses. The dear old puss was getting fat—fat and faded. The bright ginger fur had long lost its sheen. Perhaps it had been a mistake to get Moses fixed; still, who wanted to be bothered with litters? And as they say, you can't miss what you've never known.

Come on, Moses, move over. That happens to be my chair, you know. Moses shambled out of the way, only to resettle a minute later even more comfortably in Kit's lap. Kit reached for her old familiar Bicycle deck. May as well pass the time with a few games of solitaire.

She should, of course, be spending the time profitably, preparing the grounds for her defense. She should marshal arguments, think up lies, plot comebacks, plan lines of retreat, explore options. But instead, she dealt out the cards and waited.

Waited. As she had waited all her life for some grand event to shape itself on the horizon. As she had waited in boarding

school for the greater arena of college. Waited the years in
college for graduation. Waited that long impatient summer of
her engagement for the fulfillment of marriage. Waited to
have children, to have children grow out of diapers. Waited to
buy a home, to furnish it. Waited for Sarah to grow up and
grow away.

She had waited for glory and fame and love and revelation.
Waited for the relentless tide that would come and sweep her
off to who knows what stormy waters, what superb and
uncharted seas. Waited for the flood tide of life, for a
tomorrow that every day retreated farther and farther from
her grasp. But life had flowed by her, ebbed past her, each
year the shoreline had receded.

And now she sat waiting for her husband to come home,
like any other housewife in any suburb on any ordinary
Monday evening.

No. Not ordinary. For by now Michael would know, and
the long wait was nearly ended. And suppose, just suppose,
that this could somehow be patched up, tidied over, tucked
away in some secret corner of embarrassments like an unwanted wedding present? Even supposing *that,* what more
could there be to wait for?

Emily had waited just so. Waited in *her* sun room, marking
off the years of marriage in jigsaw pieces, the way a prisoner
marks off a sentence by gouging scratches in the wall. But
Emily had outwaited, had outlasted her jailer. Blonde, silly,
foolish Emily, with her bangle bracelets and her expensive
Palm Beach tan. A delayed victory—still, victory it was.

But Kit! Kit had wanted something more for herself, had
dreamt of being bold and noble. Where had it gone—all that
promise, that brightness? Where was that sense of having
lived life to the full? She thought of girls she'd gone to school
with. Girls like herself with talents, spirit, with "all the
advantages," as Michael was so fond of saying.

Helen Ince, who'd published a book on Eliot and now was
a staff reviewer for the *New York Times*. Madge Berger, who
was directing off-Broadway plays. Phyllis, too, must have had
something of a career, even though it was probably a career
of men. As for Jan Littlemarch . . . Well, that was sad.
Tragic, really, but you couldn't say Jan's life hadn't been
lived, lived to the hilt! How much they'd had in common up to
a point: the departure point of marriage and children.

Kit sometimes wondered what would have happened

if . . . but that was pointless. Sheer speculation. There was no *if*, there was only Kit, here at forty, waiting in the sun room of a house at Haddons Landing with half her life already behind her. More than half, for the Chapmans had never been a particularly long-lived clan. Here she sat, playing solitaire, with the best years of her life—the phrase made her smile—as dead as last year's diary. What had she to look back on except decades of nothingness? PTA meetings and recipes for pot roast and deciding whether to do the living room in toile or green velvet. Forty years of nothing. Of waiting. Of role-playing. Of being Spencer's daughter, Michael's wife, Sarah's mother, Monk's chief mourner. She had played every role but that of Catherine: Catherine in her own right. What would she have been if she had brought forth the full flower of her gifts? Something more, perhaps, than a plumpish, bespectacled housewife, laying a red eight on a black nine and waiting for her husband to come home from the office? Her life had been mortgaged from birth, mortgaged to other people, and now there was nothing more to wait for. Except Michael's death. And her own.

She heard the car pull into the driveway, the scrape of his key in the door. Heard him calling from the hall, "Kit, where are you?"

Every instinct cried out for her to break up the cards, to hide her shameful pasttime from his eyes. No. This time she would play the game out, even if he caught her in the act. Was it a crime to be found playing solitaire? Did it figure in his penal code somewhere? She had apologized enough for one lifetime. Black three on red four; six of hearts on seven of hearts; move the king over to fill the empty column. Ah, it was turning out beautifully. For there beneath the king lay the long-coveted ace, liberated at last from the pile. She was going to win—no question about it. If she played her cards right, she would win.

"I'm in the sun room, Michael," she called out.

Let him come.

But he went upstairs first, and she could hear him moving about, showering, changing his clothes. Then she heard him in the kitchen, pouring his drink. What a creature of habit he was. He only came into the sun room with the last of the daylight.

"Why do you sit in the dark, Kit?" He switched on the floor

lamp and sat down opposite her, placing a coaster at the edge of the card table. For a long while he sipped his Scotch in silence. He was very pale.

Then: "I spent a very curious morning at the safe-deposit vault." She made no reply. "Do you have another safe deposit box somewhere else?" She shook her head.

"Very curious," he repeated. "I saw that the last time you signed for that box was in 1968. They keep a record of access, you know."

"Do they?"

"They do. And do you know what I found in that box?" he said slowly. "I found ten shares of First Boston, six miserable shares of Bendix . . . ."

"I know what's in the box."

He leaned back on two legs of his chair and studied her carefully. "Where is it, Kit? Where's the Sag Pap & Pulp, the AT&T, the Xerox? . . . what have you done with the rest of the stocks?" She could glean the hatred from his low, controlled tones.

"I sold them."

"I see." He sat forward with a clatter and gripped her chin in his hands. "Are you on drugs?" He was scrutinizing her pupils. "Have you been supporting a drug habit behind my back all these years?"

"Don't be ridiculous."

He released her and folded his arms. She could still feel the pinch of his fingers on her chin.

"I'm waiting."

"I told you, Michael . . . I sold them."

"I can see that you sold them." Each word was clipped and biting. "I am waiting for you to tell me why."

Kit looked down at the supine Moses in her lap. Happy cat—ignorant, innocent, never having to explain or expiate.

"I sold them for Jan," she whispered.

"Who?" Michael frowned.

"Jan." Funny, he must have forgotten all about Jan. Probably even forgotten her name. What was she, anyhow . . . one of the thousands of cases that had come across his desk? Just another name in his fifteen-year string of prosecutions. Why, the Massachusetts prisons were bursting with Michael's trophies—rapists, muggers, thieves, swindlers, murderers, Mafiosi. Men and women who would remember

Michael Matheson's name for far longer than he would remember theirs. So what was one name more or less? She raised her voice.

"I sold them to raise bail for Jan Littlemarch."

He froze for an instant, then sprang to his feet with a vehemence that sent the cards skittering. Sent poor Moses running for cover.

"Don't joke with me, Kit. And don't try to lie!"

She stared at the bleached whiteness of the knuckles clenched before her on the table.

"I'm not lying to you, Michael. It was my money. She was my friend."

"What the fuck are you raving about?" he screamed. "You honestly expect me to believe that . . . that you threw away a fortune for somebody you hadn't seen in years? I want to know why and I want to know *now!*"

She raised her eyes from the white knuckles to the still whiter lips, to the hard cold eyes. There was no pity, no compassion in those eyes, but then there never had been. All she had ever seen in those eyes was a reflection of her own dreams and hopes.

"We were lovers, Jan and I."

The eyes blinked, flickered with confusion.

"I don't understand."

"What is there not to understand, Michael? You with your vast experience of the world. The imperfect world. Jan and I were lovers at boarding school."

"Don't give me that!" he shouted.

"Why? Do you find it so hard to believe?" Christ, he was stupid. Blind, hateful and stupid. "We were lovers in the physical sense of the word. And let me tell you this, Michael." She drew herself erect. "Jan gave me more pleasure in a few short weeks than you have given me in twenty years."

"You fucking dyke."

With his first punch, he shattered her glasses. And then he was on top of her, pummeling her, hitting her, the white knuckles slamming against the bone of her jaw. The wing chair sheered over under the force of his assault and sent them both crashing onto the cold vinyl of the floor. The cry that started in her throat was stifled by an acrid column of blood and regurgitated food.

"You fucking whore! You cunt!" Louder, louder even than the pounding of the blood in her ears, was the stertorous heaving of his breath. She struggled to break free from his grasp, but he had flung himself on top of her, like some mad parody of love. His thumbs flew to her throat, pressing firmly, relentlessly against the soft pulsating flab of her esophagus.

She could feel his cock grow big and hard against her thigh. Oh, God, no! She would rather he killed her, but he was so unbelievably strong. He was iron and she was flab. He released her throat and forced her jaws apart. "I'll give you what you like, you fucking pervert . . ." and suddenly her elbows were pinioned hard beneath his legs.

"You bitch! You cunt! You fucking whore . . ." She wanted to scream, scream out in agony. But when the scream came, it wasn't hers, it was *his*. *His* scream. *His* agony. For Moses had sprung from God knows where and raked her claws deep into Michael's cheek. "Get off!" Michael screamed. Let loose a stream of vicious cuts at his assailant. But Moses clung, held fast. Clawing, ripping now at Michael's shirt, now at his face, with the tenacity of a jungle cat; till Michael jumped up, his arms an angry windmill, and tearing the beast from him, flung it bodily out of the room.

He was standing in the doorway now, panting hard, rubbing the flesh of his cheek. He stood there unmoving until his breath came back, looking down at Kit on the floor where she lay in a pool of vomit.

"Get up." He walked over to her and kicked her lightly with his toe. She vomited again and groaned.

"I could have killed you." He looked down and rubbed his cheek again. "I should have killed you. In France it would have been considered a *crime passionel*. They would have given me the Legion of Honor, you bitch. But no, you can be grateful, I'm not going to kill you."

Kit turned her head and spat out a tooth. She wanted to get up, get away, but it was too painful. So much easier just lying here in her blood and vomit.

Michael pulled up a chair and finished the remains of his Scotch.

"How many people know about you and Littlemarch?" His voice was as cool as a Federal courtroom. She tried to shake her head, but it hurt too much to move. He understood her minimal gesture.

"No one knows. No one but you and me . . . right? And that's the way it's going to stay." He placed his empty glass beside her on the floor. "I'm going to wash now and have my dinner. You can clean up here and we'll talk in the morning."

He left the room without looking back.

KATE

FIRST THING MONDAY MORNING, SHE RANG THE OFFICE TO TELL them she'd be taking a few days off. For the rest of the morning she puttered about the farmhouse, eating leftover apple pie, washing it down with innumerable cups of Nescafé. She napped a bit in the afternoon, and then got up and had another meal of apple pie and coffee. Barry was right—all that kneading did make the pie dough kind of leathery, but it tasted good. And more calories than she'd had in ages. She should probably get out the car and go down for cigarettes, but it had suddenly turned so cold. If she didn't know better, she'd say that was a snow sky; but it never snowed this early in October.

She turned in around midnight, but sleep was elusive. Never should have drunk all that coffee. She sat and smoked butts from the ashtray. And then the butts of the butts and then there were no more leavings to smoke.

What time would it be in England now? Ten in the morning? Eleven? She couldn't recollect if the Brits were still on summer time. She went downstairs to look for her phone book, and a forgotten pack of Marlboros tumbled out of her bag. *There is a special providence in the fall of a sparrow.* She smiled. No phone book, though. Must have left it at the office.

"Long distance operator please. No, honey, that's Cambridge, England, not Cambridge, Massachusetts. Person to person . . . Dr. Richard Hetherington. There should be a listing on Grange Road. And if he's not there, try Trinity College, and then the Cavendish Lab . . . Yes, I'll wait."

And while the girl placed the call, she lit a cigarette gratefully. This was going to be the toughest selling job she'd ever done. She waited, checked her watch again. It was almost five o'clock in the morning now. Not even light yet.

KIT

Five o'clock in the morning. Not even light yet. She could sense, rather than see, Michael standing over her. He must have dragged her up to bed, because she had no memory of how she got there. No memory of anything at all except the hard cold floor of the sun room. Her mouth was ablaze with pain, her throat too sore for speech. Every bone, every muscle in her body ached and throbbed in its own separate rhythm.

"I'm leaving for Springfield in half an hour. I have a breakfast meeting there."

She forced her eyes open. He was fully dressed, holding his gloves in his hand. There was a heavy layer of talcum over the claw marks.

"Now I will tell you how things are going to be."

She shut her eyes and let the pain wash over her.

"Last night never happened. Littlemarch never happened. As far as anyone else knows, none of this ever happened. This is my home and I have no intention of giving it up. You can leave if you want to. It's a free country. But if you do, you can be damn sure Sarah will never want to see you again. If you leave, I will make it abundantly clear to her that you have been an unfit wife and an unfit mother; and as you know, I can be very persuasive. Think it over. But if you stay, there is going to be no more of your high and mighty act, is that clear? We can get along as we've done before, although I'll be expecting a marked improvement in your behavior. Things are going to be *my* way, for a change. You will accompany me everywhere I specify—every political meeting, every boring dinner, every time I go out fundraising. And thanks to you, there's going to be a hell of a lot more fundraising than I anticipated.

"When we appear together you will demonstrate your complete loyalty and regard for me. When I speak, your smile will be the warmest, your admiration everywhere in evidence. You will be active in such organizations as I tell you. You will never contradict me, either in public or in private. You will entertain such people as I instruct. I will be the envy of every politician for having such a devoted, hard-working wife. As far as our sexual relationship goes, it will be as it's been all these years—nonexistent. Frankly, you were never any good in bed. We will, however, continue to share sleeping arrangements. Anything else would look bad.

"I'm leaving the house now to drive to Springfield. I will be back tomorrow night around seven. I expect dinner to be waiting."

She lay quietly till she heard the car drive off, then dragged herself into the bathroom. The tooth that was broken was a lower back one; you'd only be able to see it when she smiled. Well, she didn't have an awful lot to smile about. That split lip didn't look too good, either. She cleared her throat, tried speech, but all she could manage was a hoarse whisper. And God, she stank of vomit. No open cuts, though, outside of the lip, although the bruises were just now starting to blossom.

After the initial shock, the hot tub felt wonderful. Soothing. Maybe she'd just lie here all day, letting the suds dimple around her, watching the water trickle through her fingers. She saw the gray dawn slither up the window and thought of what Michael had said. His closing statement. That was the term they used in court at the end of the trial, and Michael always prided himself on his closing statements. If it hadn't hurt so much she would have smiled.

What a fool he was! To think seriously that she would spend another night in this house with the man who had nearly killed her. She could never, never erase the memory of his words, his rage, his hatred. Maybe Michael could live with someone he loathed, but she couldn't. Not anymore.

What was the point of living like that?

What was the point of living at all? Through the steam of the bathroom, she could make out the elegant bone-handled razors resting in their box on the corner cabinet. Michael had given them up only recently; life was too busy for ritualized shaving. But he kept them sharp—sharp and gleaming as surgical knives. Beautiful things, they were.

Why not? A few small quick slits on the inside of both wrists, then pop back in the bath. Relax and let the warm blood mix with the warm water. It couldn't be too painful. Certainly not as painful as living. Probably not even as painful as her broken tooth.

Kit shut her eyes. She could picture Michael's return on Wednesday night; he'd be expecting dinner. Pictured him calling out, going upstairs, walking into a bathroom drenched with blood and death. Oh, he would be furious. *Furious!* The ultimate scandal. As bad as Chappaquiddick. Worse if she left a note.

She could see him now, standing over her body, screaming, shaking his fists at her corpse: *"How could you do this to me!"*

Oh yes, she *could* do it to him. With pleasure. She could do it to herself with no regrets. Trouble was, she couldn't do it to Sarah. Funny how personal loyalties always kept you from doing what you wanted, from acting on your instincts. Anyhow, just because marriage was over didn't mean life was over. It wasn't too late to reshape the future. Other women had. She would. But not here . . . not in Boston, where twenty years of her submission had been witnessed. She lay there for a long time, soaking, till she realized she was hungry. Goddamnit, she was hungry! What a crazy world . . . a half hour ago she was thinking of killing herself, and now all she could think about was food. Nothing hot—her mouth still hurt too much—but she could probably manage some bread and butter.

She dressed in old clothes and went down to the kitchen; last night's beef bourguignon was resting on top of the stove. She had a spoonful of gravy; it was cold and gelatinous, but not bad. Not bad at all. The nice thing about beef bourguignon was that it always tasted better next day. She noticed the cat's plate was licked clean and overturned.

"Moses?" It was hard raising her voice above a whisper, but Moses must have been psychic, because a moment later she came lumbering in. There was a new wariness in her eyes.

Cream for you, Moses . . . cream for your breakfast. You saved my life, you silly old tabby.

By seven-thirty she and Moses were in the Volkswagen headed for New York. Too bad Michael had taken the Buick; the Volks was really only a station car. But what the hell . . . you can't win 'em all. She had about seventy dollars in cash, a few hundred more in her checkbook and a wallet with half a dozen credit cards. That should tide her over. Of course, once Michael knew she was gone, he'd cancel the credit cards. He could do that. They all read Mrs. Michael Matheson. That would be Thursday morning at the earliest.

Three quarters of the way to New York now. Why New York? She hadn't even been thinking, had no idea what she was going to do once she got there. Well, the first thing, when she got her voice back, would be to call up Sarah in Oberlin. Call up and explain what happened, without going into too many details. She remembered Michael's threat: "I'll tell her you're an unfit mother." Christ, Michael was such an idiot. He thought the whole world shared his blinkered view of what was permissible sexual morality. He really believed that a bright, sophisticated eighteen-year-old girl would be struck dumb with horror because her mother had once had an adolescent lapse. Michael was the one who would be struck dumb if he ever cottoned to the fact that Sarah was living openly with a boy in Ohio. Why the hell did he think she went out to Oberlin in the first place? Sarah didn't worry her . . . Sarah would understand.

Toward noon she stopped for gas at a station outside of Westport. New York was less than an easy hour's drive away. New York! Funny how people of her generation always instinctively headed for New York, the way kids now head for San Francisco and Katmandu. *Dreamsville*—that's what they used to call it when she was in college. The place where small-town girls went to become big-time writers and artists and actresses. The Apple for all aspiring Eves.

OK . . . New York. And *then* what? Kit wasn't a fresh-out-of-college kid anymore, and New York had managed quite nicely without her all these years, thank you very much. Besides, she hardly knew a soul in the city. Oh, a few relatives maybe, but no close friends.

Trouble was, everyone she knew lived around Boston. Everyone except . . . of course. Marian! That was it— Marian. She'd call her up at Vassar right away. Amazing she

hadn't thought of it before. Good kind wonderful capable
sensible Marian. Kit could trust her, tell her everything, and
Marian would know what to do. Even now, she could picture
Marian's bright smile, the warmth of her welcome, her
comfort, her compassion.

Kit paid for the gas and went into the phone booth. There
was no answer at Marian's house; she was probably still at
school. No matter. Kit bought a container of milk for Moses
and asked the attendant for directions to Poughkeepsie.

KATE

After she'd spoken to Richard, she crawled back into bed. Jesus God, it was starting to snow. Well, sleet, anyway. Freaky weather for this early in October. According to Richard they were having an unusually mild autumn in England.

She'd find out for herself soon enough.

A mild autumn, he'd said. He'd said a lot of things during the course of that forty-minute phone call.

Shit or get off the pot. That's what he'd said. Of course, those hadn't been his words exactly, but that's what it all came down to, bottom line. Three years of long-distance loving had taken its toll, worn down the edge of his good humor. "I want a commitment, Kate. Yes or no. In or out." And she could tell he wasn't kidding. So there it was. Take it or leave it. If you can't beat 'em, join 'em. So what could she do?

Still, it was hard to believe that by this time next week, she'd be Mrs. Richard Anthony Hetherington of The Beeches, Grange Road, Cambridge.

Well, right now she could do with a few hours' sleep. OK. Sleep till noon, leave the farm around one, be back at East 71st Street by three. Pick up her passport, pack a few things.

Be at Kennedy by seven tonight. The plane didn't leave till after eight. Plenty of time.

What to take? White didn't seem suitable for a bride her age. In fact, considering the implications, it was laughable. Maybe that new Ralph Lauren with the blouson top. He'd never seen it before; besides, Richard liked her in purple. And oh . . . don't forget to pack warm pajamas.

Pajamas. She laughed. No, she wouldn't need pajamas . . . for tomorrow night and every night thereafter she would be clothed in Richard's arms.

Suddenly her body ached for him—his warmth, his touch, his passion. She hugged herself close in the remembrance of love—in the anticipation of love to come.

With a surge of emotion, she realized that she was surrendering nothing—nothing that she really treasured. Prove herself? She'd done it a thousand times already. Had proved herself smart, shrewd, successful. Not that she was knocking it. It had been fun in its day, but now that day was past. She could come to Richard now not out of defeat, but in triumph—the triumph of discovering she no longer needed the trappings of power.

She needed love. She needed warmth. She needed *Richard*.

During all that hectic noisy time apart, she had waited for some sign, some augury, like a mystic waiting for the word of God. But there were no revelations except those of the heart—if you could only drown out the din long enough to hear them.

KIT

EAT, THE RED NEON SIGN COMMANDED. MY GOD, HERE IT WAS almost two o'clock and Kit realized she was ravenous. Absolutely ravenous. Her jaw still ached, her face looked as though she'd gone ten rounds with Muhammad Ali, but all her stomach could think of was food. She'd been behind the wheel for almost six hours now, and the rain was making the driving difficult. May as well take a break now, she thought, if she wanted to get to Poughkeepsie in one piece.

Inside the Blue Moon Diner, the smell of fried potatoes and steaming coffee gave an unaccountable lift to her spirits. It had been ages since she'd eaten in a greasy spoon. "Ptomaine Palaces," Michael always called them, and placed them off-limits for the family. But Michael wasn't here to say no . . .

She ordered ham and eggs and a double portion of French fries, then coffee and apple pie. Everything tasted indescribably delicious.

"Hey, hey!" said the kid behind the counter. "That's some shiner you got there."

Kit managed the first smile of the day.

"You should've seen the other guy."

By the time she got back in the Volks, the rain had turned to freezing sleet.

KATE

SHE OVERSLEPT, AND BY THE TIME SHE HIT THE ROAD IT WAS quarter to two and sleeting steadily. For the first time in years she felt nervous about driving. Jesus . . . Barry's car had more gadgets and dials and buttons than a spaceship and about a million different gears. Damned if she could even find reverse, though it must be in here somewhere.

Beyond Poughkeepsie the sleet was coming down harder, great, cold, glutinous dollops that clung to the windshield and froze on contact. Where the hell was the heater in this car? Where the fuck was the defroster? She pushed a likely button, and the eight-track stereo burst out in Elton John all around her. Sorry, wrong number. She stopped the car along a deserted stretch of road and poked around in the glove compartment. Maybe the driver's manual was still inside. Or at least an ice-scraper. Christ, if she didn't do something about the visibility, she'd have to creep all the way back to New York City.

KIT

Kit didn't see the woman till she was almost halfway around the bend. *My God!* This woman—standing in the middle of the road, scraping ice off the windshield of a Jag. It was so sudden . . . so startling. Almost like an apparition. And Kit had lurched, swerved, spun. Had nearly gone off the road herself and into the Hudson in a rush of adrenalin. Had—God only knew how!—come within inches of taking a life. Perhaps the other woman's. Perhaps her own.

With a screech of brakes, she pulled the car over to the shoulder, heart pounding, and switched off the engine. The silence was complete, awesome. Then from down the road she heard the roar of the sports car starting up. Turned her head in time to see the taillights disappearing in the direction of New York. Thank God, no harm done. But now that it was over, she began to tremble. Tremble uncontrollably out of sheer relief. Even Moses was trembling—the claws sunk deep in the upholstery, the fur bristling as though he had seen a ghost.

KATE

Jesus H. Christ! They don't care who they give a driving license to these days. That goddamn woman had damn near killed her.

At least Kate thought it was a woman; she couldn't be sure. The whole thing happened so fast. She could see the Volkswagen pulling over farther up the road. Really, Kate had a good mind to march right up there and give the driver hell. Maybe even report the incident to the police. Except that would take all afternoon, and she didn't have all afternoon. Not if she wanted to catch her plane.

Oh, what the hell, no harm done. The anger slipped away as suddenly as it had come. *And let's be honest,* an inner voice commanded, *it was your own damn fault, standing out there in the road as if you owned it.* True. The odd thing was that she hadn't heard the other car approaching.

With a shrug, Kate got back in the Jag and drove off.

KIT

SHE WOULD SIT HERE FOR A BIT, PULL HERSELF TOGETHER. Maybe wait for the weather to let up. It was still sleeting needles and Kit felt in no condition to drive right now. Fatigue, anxiety, the cumulative stress of the last few days had drained her of everything but the desire to sleep. "Let's you and I take a catnap, Moses." She settled the animal on her lap. But sleep was elusive, and in her mind's eye—vivid as an instant replay on television—she kept reliving that moment on the highway when death had seemed so close. She could see it so clearly. The bend in the road. The sports car. The woman.

The extraordinary thing was, the woman looked so familiar. Weird. Weird almost to the point of uncanny, because outside of Marian, Kit didn't know a soul in this part of the country. Yet something about that woman had clicked. Even now, the image refused to be banished, remained frozen on her retina. The image of a tall woman—about Kit's height, in fact—slender and elegant in a mink polo coat. Maybe it was the hair—the same exuberant color Kit's hair used to be before it started getting gray. Too bad she hadn't seen the woman's face. But it was undoubtedly the face of a stranger.

And yet . . . there *was* something about her that nagged at

363

Kit. An aura that was almost tangible. But an aura of what? Of success? Or money? No, of something more than that.

Of independence! Yes, that was it. That woman had simply radiated strength and independence—Kit was sure of it. Call it fatuous, if you will, this conjuring up of a whole set of attributes from one split-second image; yet portrait painters did it all the time, illuminating a whole and complex personality from a single characteristic stance. So that one quick look told you everything.

Kit was sure now that she had never met this woman, yet that she *knew* her in some wordless, intuitive way. Knew her, and rather envied her, to tell the truth. Oh, to be like that! Free . . . unencumbered . . . independent. To be on the road. On her own. Accountable to no one but herself. God, what bliss . . .

She shut her eyes and listened as the tack tack of the sleet turned to rain.

"You OK, lady?"

He was rapping at the glass in a fast staccato: a county cop in a rain-streaked slicker. Kit rubbed her eyes and rolled down the window.

"Yes, I'm fine. Really quite all right, thank you." Good lord, it was dark out already.

"You sure now?" His voice was edged with concern. "I saw you parked here the last couple of hours and wondered if you were maybe in some kind of trouble."

"No," Kit assured him. "No trouble, officer. I just pulled over to rest my eyes and guess I must have fallen asleep. Be on my way in a moment."

"Well," he shrugged, "OK if you say so. But take it slow and drive carefully. Tell you one thing . . . a day like this, I wouldn't want *my* wife out on the road alone."

Watching him drive off, Kit had to smile. He wouldn't want *his* wife . . . She knew that tone of voice from way back. Well, she wasn't his wife. Wasn't really anybody's wife any more. She was simply a woman alone on the road—the image of that afternoon flashed before her—just like that woman in the mink.

Just like her! It struck Kit with the force of revelation. Just like that woman she had envied. Because Kit, too, was free now—freer than she'd ever been before. For once in her life she didn't have to be home by dinnertime, didn't have to be anywhere. No more small children to feed and tend and tie her down. No more Michael to placate with a thousand little lies. She was free—accountable to no one in the world but herself.

Free to eat crackers in bed or paint her toenails purple or thumb her nose at the whole world. Free to laugh when she felt like laughing, bitch when she felt like bitching. Free to make up her mind or to shoot off her mouth without fear of incurring disapproval. For who was there now to disapprove?

And no one, absolutely no one, knew where she was: she found the idea absurdly exhilarating. Right now, this very moment, she could go anywhere. Try anything. She had choices. A chance to carve a new life.

Years and years ago her college counselor had told her: *A girl like you can be anything*. She remembered that long-forgotten interview; remembered, too, that she had accepted Michael's proposal that very same day. Had exercised an option of sorts. But there were always others.

OK. So she wasn't a girl of twenty anymore. She was a woman of forty—so much the better!—with a different set of choices before her. Twenty years older. Twenty years smarter. And whatever might be said about her marriage, it had taught her something. Taught her, at least, what to avoid. And if she were going to make mistakes in the future, they'd be different mistakes.

So . . . The first order of business would be getting a job, achieving some kind of financial independence. That, she could see, might be tough. With a wry smile, she pictured herself turning up at The *New York Times* and asking if they had any openings for a forty-year-old cub reporter.

But who knows? She was a fairly decent writer. Had done a great job over the years of editing the North Shore Women's Club newsletter. And Michael always used to pick her brain when he was working on a speech. Even *he* admitted she had a knack for turning phrases. Maybe she could, after all, get some kind of job with a small-town paper, doing articles for the woman's page or reporting on local politics. And if not some kind of writing job, maybe proofreading. Or selling advertising space.

Or what about cooking? She was, by common knowledge, "the best damn cook in Haddons Landing," and the competition there was pretty keen. Maybe she could get some kind of chef's job in a good restaurant. Better yet, maybe do some catering on her own—dinner parties, business lunches. She could prepare the food, buy the wines, maybe get a discount from the wine merchants . . . not a half-bad idea. Shouldn't cost too much to set up, and she still had some money of her own.

Or working with the deaf. Now there was a thought. She'd certainly had valuable experience along those lines.

Or real estate! That was a natural. You couldn't spend all those years in the suburbs without becoming an expert on real estate: property prices, acreage, the comparative merits of swimming pools. Wasn't there some kind of course you could take that qualified you for a realtor's license? She'd look into it.

Or market research. Interviewing. Now there was something that might be fun. And they were always looking for well-spoken women.

Or . . .

The possibilities were, if not endless, at least considerable, and she hadn't even scratched the surface of her abilities. Joyously, Kit felt a surge of confidence, of power, felt a new buoyance that penetrated every inch of her body. She could do it. Any of it . . . all of it. In her heart she knew she could do it! Could make it work, this new life that stretched before her. And if it proved to be tough . . . well, it couldn't be any tougher than the "easy life" she was leaving behind.

In another minute or so, she would start the car, drive off into another life. For she knew now she could go anywhere she chose. Anywhere except back.

Not that she could wipe out twenty years of marriage. She didn't want to. They hadn't been wasted. Besides, it wasn't as if marriage was to blame. She had gone into it expecting too much and had wound up accepting too little. OK. Perhaps she had been cheated in her marriage. Perhaps in a way she had cheated herself—pretending to a blandness, an acquiescence that she had never really felt because it was what her husband had wanted.

But all men weren't Michael, thank God! That was *one* mistake she wouldn't make twice. Maybe she'd have love affairs now; the thought intrigued her. And maybe someday, when she'd pulled herself together, she'd meet someone she could care for with her eyes wide open. Someone who'd take her as she was. Add a richness to her life she'd never known.

Maybe. Maybe not. It wasn't something she was going to

count on. But one thing she knew; as long as she lived she would never again mold herself to suit someone else's image.

The rain had stopped now and, in the night sky, a harvest moon had elbowed its way through the clouds. And if the road ahead promised a few more twists . . . at least from where she sat the way was clear.

Kit squared her shoulders and drove off.

KATE

She tapped her feet to the Muzak in the first-class lounge and ordered a Campari on the rocks. Yup. The gal at check-in said they'd be leaving right on the button; apparently that upstate storm never hit down here. Good old TWA. She gave the bartender a five-dollar bill and a smile.

Out of habit, she scanned the joint. Yes, it was there, right there at that table that she'd first spotted Richard. Picked him up, if you wanted to put it bluntly. Dear Richard. The seat was now occupied by another lone male traveler. Ouch! Good-looking. Really chewy. Tall and beautifully dressed with the lean snap of the Wall Street gunslinger. He was smiling at her. She turned away. Felt absolutely no desire to chat him up.

How surprised Barry had been when she called to tell him where she'd left the car. That and all the rest of it.

"Married! You?" he exclaimed.

"I told you I'd try anything once. Well, Bar, aren't you going to give the bride some fantastic wedding night advice? Or at least wish me luck . . . ?"

"Well, my advice is . . . don't let the poor bastard come within a mile of your pie crust. It's grounds for divorce. And as far as luck goes . . ."

"Yes?"

"Luck you don't need, baby. You're one of life's winners."

Good old Barry. Always so supportive, so sure she'd land right side up. On the basis of what . . . an impulse? A predawn phone call? "The Snap Decision That Changed My Life." She could see it as a *Reader's Digest* article, one of those inspirational numbers they wedged between "My Most Unforgettable Character" and "This Month's Condensed Book."

But it was true: you pick up a phone and your whole life changes direction. So instead of being the next president of Marsden-Baker Advertising, you're the next Mrs. Richard Hetherington, waiting for the night flight to London. This time tomorrow, she'd probably be sitting in Grange Road, pouring tea for Richard out of a little Wedgwood pot with pale yellow roses. . . .

From the recesses of memory came the unbidden image of another pot of tea . . . a pot of tea spilling over a beige silk dress in the corner booth of a Chinese restaurant. The memory teased her. A pot of tea. What if she hadn't spilled it? Would she be sitting here now, waiting for her flight to be called, sipping Campari? As likely as not, she'd still be in Boston, married to that lawyer, kids certainly, active in politics maybe. Would it have been an interesting life, she wondered?

Not that she was one for iffy propositions. But if, for instance, she hadn't spilled that tea, where would she be right now? At a country club, chances were, doing the suburban bit, drinking cocktails with the other wives.

Curious, all the lives she might have led. She might have become a sex junkie out in California—almost did, for that matter. Or be working in Washington as a lobbyist for the Pet Food Association—one of the odder job offers that had come her way over the years. She might have gone to São Paulo to set up the Brazilian branch of Marsden. She might have borne Wolf's children. She might have . . . Really, the possibilities were infinite.

You were always choosing, whether you wanted to or not. Which was as it should be, except that every time you said yes to something, you were saying no to something else. Every time you opened a door to one way of life, you were shutting a door to another. Wouldn't it be fantastic if you could lead all those different lives simultaneously? Like reincarnation, only better, because you'd explore every potential. Would you be the same person at the end of it? Or would a dozen different lives transform you into a dozen different people? The idea intrigued her. She wondered if there weren't a book in there somewhere. *Imaginary Lives* . . . like Richard's imaginary numbers.

Yes, she was sure there was a book in there somewhere. Probably take her a year to write it, but for once in her life she had time.

No, she wouldn't call it *Imaginary Lives*. Sounded too arty. Something short. A nice zippy title. *Choices, Options, If* . . . Something that would look good on a movie marquee. Maybe Jane Fonda playing all the different roles. Or if not Fonda, maybe Diane Keaton. She'd keep them in mind when she was writing it.

Out of habit, Kate began scribbling notes on the cocktail napkin. Did Richard have a decent typewriter stashed away in his library? She couldn't remember. If not, she'd buy one. One of those new IBM Selectrics. Her wedding present to herself.

She could pick it up on the way home from the airport tomorrow.

Home! She laughed to herself as she folded the cocktail napkin and put it in her bag. She was already thinking of that place on Grange Road as home. Well, the first thing she'd do—after buying the typewriter, of course—would be to rip out all those stone-age electric radiators and put in central heating. Then she'd clear the junk in the attic, build some kind of desk—a bookcase arrangement where she could work in peace. Then she'd . . .

TWA announces the boarding of Flight 102 to London Heathrow.

Kate Chapman was first up the ramp.